DREAMS OF ECSTASY

"Is this what your dreams are like, Susanna?" he murmured against her open mouth.

"I don't know," she gasped. "I don't know." Court touched her breast then, feeling the wild beating of her heart beneath his fingers.

"Don't." She tried to pull away from him, but he used his weight to bear her down on the blankets where she had lain before, and he covered her mouth with his, stilling her protests, as he continued to stroke her, so gently, as if she were a wild young animal he sought to hold in captivity, and she submitted to that gentleness, to that touch that sent pulses of invading heat through her body.

WANTON ANGEL

Elizabeth Chadwick

LEISURE BOOKS ■ NEW YORK CITY

A LEISURE BOOK

July 1989

Published by

Dorchester Publishing Co., Inc.
276 Fifth Avenue
New York, NY 10001

Printed in the United States of America.

I
The Fire

1

From the highest point in the pass that breached the mountains to the east, Aaron Court reined in his horse and stared down into the darkening valley, watching yet another proof of his grimly held conviction that good times were always balanced by bad times—if not overbalanced. He had been away from the town for two days—in Denver on business and then in an adjacent valley bargaining for a horse that had caught his fancy before the winter snows had set in. The business had been concluded, the horse purchased, and thus he found himself in the pass as nightfall erased the mountains around him but not the town below, where a satanic glare seemed to be turning the structures into eerie, angry transparencies in the dusk. Court sighed as he shook out his reins and guided the new horse onto the down-turning road. Amnonville was once again aflame, and he wondered how many of his assets were turning to hot ash and rubble before his eyes: his office certainly was gone, along with most of the north end of the town. What other losses he had suffered he would know soon enough.

A half hour later Court had again halted his horse, this time in the middle of Copper Street. As he leaned forward to pat the trembling muscles of the animal's shoulder, he stared at the remains of the building that had housed his office. The sign "Aaron Court, Attorney at Law" lay in the street, blackened, half devoured by the flames; the building was a skewed shell with a few tongues of fire licking indifferently at what remained of the frame; in the center among the ashes was his safe, glowing red with a life of its own, blackening the papers inside, no doubt. Court made no move toward the legal records of his clients. Time enough tomorrow to see to that, and in the interim there was little likelihood that anyone would try to haul off or break into that uninviting piece of incandescent metal.

All around him his fellow citizens milled frantically; they called out commiserations to one another and to him; they threw futile buckets of water at doomed structures; they sweated and cursed and scrubbed ineffectively at soot-blackened faces. But Court rested calmly in his saddle, an island of cold philosophical acceptance in the midst of frantic emotion. He gentled his nervous horse with one hand and unbuttoned his sheepskin jacket with the other, for the air on Copper Street rippled with heat, although the night was chill. Once he had calculated what it would cost him to rebuild the structure devoured by the fire, Court nodded absently to several people who had spoken to him, and then he turned his horse toward the sound of dynamite. He presumed that someone was attempting to create a firebreak and save the southern end of the town before the icy spring wind drove the fire on. Two blocks down he spotted the town's one Silsby fire engine spraying water on a hardware store whose stock had been bought with Court's money. He added the hardware inventory to his losses since that battle, though still being fought, was hopeless.

To his left on the next block he could see that the Fallen Angel was in flames. He remembered well enough the arrival in Amnonville of Lilith Moran some years back, not so many months after he had followed a gold strike there from Denver himself. She had built the first Fallen Angel and announced that although she preferred to be paid in gold, a man who wished to avail himself of the pleasures of her establishment could also pay in real property, and she had named the place accordingly. "Moran's Land, Cattle, Claim and Fallen Angel Company" could be seen still in ornate gold script across the burning exterior, and many a male resident of Amnonville, temporarily out of funds, had left a valuable title in her safe in exchange for the ministrations of her "fallen angels." Although Court owned no stock in her "company," he mourned its loss, for Lilith Moran was a beautiful woman—a madam with a head for business, some strange preferences in bed, and a lively sense of humor when she chose to give it rein, and her Fallen Angel Company was the town's most elegant saloon, dance hall, gambling parlor and whorehouse. Its demise would be an incalculable loss to the social life of Amnonville, at least that portion which Court found worth pursuing—not that Lilith wouldn't open up in a tent as she had after previous fires, but a tent, especially with winter still lingering into spring, would not, could not provide the same atmosphere and comfort that—

Court reined his horse sharply as he drew even with the whorehouse. The first floor was completely aflame inside and out, and fire was climbing the white columns and leaping into the balcony where the prostitutes had displayed themselves and their finery on sunny days. In the middle of this balcony appeared one slender girl, wearing a long white nightgown—her hand covering her mouth, her eyes wide with terror, and her long black hair flowing around her. She stood transfixed about six steps from the railing with the fire a menacing backdrop.

Court jammed his black hat over the new horse's eyes, dragged the animal's head toward the building, and applied his spurs. "Jump!" he called out sharply to the girl. She stared at him, but she did not move. "Come on," he commanded again as he maneuvered the terrified horse toward the balcony. She edged closer to the railing, staring fearfully down at him with huge blue eyes. The flames behind her and to the sides of her framed her in a pulsing red glow, making her hair gleam and seem to flicker. Except for the small fingertips peeking from beneath lace ruffles at her wrists, the bare toes beneath the embroidered hem, and the lovely frightened face above the high lace at the neck, her gown covered her completely in modest white. Then a sudden gust of wind molded the fabric to her body. Court caught his breath in surprised admiration as he looked up at her; she was the most beautiful girl Lilith had ever brought to the brothel, more beautiful than Lilith herself.

"You have to jump," he called to her. "The balcony won't hold much longer."

The girl glanced fearfully to either side and saw the flame fingers edging closer, reaching out for her. Again she moved a few steps and touched the railing, measuring the distance of the fall. "I'll catch you," Court assured her, but she seemed not to believe it possible. Instead of jumping she climbed over the rail, planting her toes carefully between the spindles and clinging with one hand as she clutched the skirt of her nightgown around her legs at knee level. "For God's sake, girl, hurry," he shouted urgently. The fire to her left was now eating along the railing toward her. The young woman let go of her skirt and lowered herself hesitantly with both hands, releasing her foothold just as the flames curled into the lace at her wrist. The sudden pain brought a scream, and she let go abruptly and plummeted into his arms.

Because Court had seen that she was afire, he whirled his frightened horse and dumped the girl within seconds into the water trough in front of the blazing building. That instant reaction effectively put out the flames that seared her arm, but her screams had been cut off a second before when her head hit the hard wooden edge of the trough. Cursing, he dismounted and lifted her from the shallow water; then kneeling in the street with her wet body limp in his arms, he leaned close to her face and felt her warm breath on his cheek. She was unconscious; her arm was burned, how badly he could not tell; but she was alive. Court struggled up, managing to lift her with him into the saddle, and headed toward the doctor's office, which, when he finally worked his way through the milling, panic-stricken crowds of people and animals in the street, proved to have suffered the same devastation as his own office and the whorehouse.

"Where's the doctor?" he shouted to a man standing at his stirrup, staring at the flaming collapse of Amnonville's one medical facility.

The man looked up, first at Court, then at the girl. "Been doing a little looting over in Crib Alley?" he asked, grinning.

Court ignored the implication that he had abducted a whore for himself while the city was burning down. "The doctor?" he again demanded.

"Dead most likely," replied the man who, having lost interest in Court and his unexplained, bedraggled female companion, had turned back to the fire.

"It's a hell of a time for him to pick to die," Court muttered.

"Building collapsed on him when he went back in after a patient," said the man.

Court turned his horse around and headed toward his own house, which was just beyond the town on the south side and, therefore, presumably still standing. The girl's wet body was growing cold in his arms despite the heat all around them, and in fact his own clothing, where it was damp from contact with her, was uncomfortably cold. He decided to do what he could for her himself and then to come back to town to find help if she seemed to need it, although where help could be found with the town's one doctor dead—Court snapped his fingers. All he had to do was find Lilith; the girl was her responsibility, after all. In fact, Lilith would owe him a favor for saving such an obviously valuable business asset.

He spotted a friend in a water bucket line and shouted to him, "Henry, have you seen Lilith Moran?"

The man had just filled his bucket from a cistern sunk in the street for fire-fighting purposes. When he heard Court, he passed the bucket to the next man and stepped out of line, pausing to wipe sweat and ash from his forehead and clap his hat back on his head. "By God, Aaron, you're a cool one," he remarked. "Here the whole damned town's burning down, both cisterns are running low, the river's too far from the fire to do much good, and you're out looking for a woman. Ain't one enough for you?" He gestured to the girl that Court was holding across his saddle.

Court frowned. "That's not—"

"Won't do you no good anyway. Lil's out of business—at least for tonight. Her place was burning down last I—"

"I know that."

"And I ain't seen her."

Where Court's hand rested on the girl's ribs, she felt icy, and he was afraid to waste any more time looking for Lilith, so he turned his horse south again and rode into the undamaged section of town and finally into the outskirts where he owned a substantial log house in which he lived when he was in Amnonville. The outside of the house was dimly lit by the lurid red glow of the fire, but the inside was dark, and Court had to tread carefully in the central hall and through the door to his bedroom, where he laid the unconscious girl gently on his bed. After spreading a blanket over her, he hurried back out to stable his horse. Finally he returned, lit lamps in the house, and frowned thoughtfully at the girl as he stripped off his damp clothes and put on a heavy woolen shirt and a pair of trousers that would be more comfortable and more serviceable than a black suit for fighting fires, tending the injured, or escaping to the mountains—whatever the night had in store for him.

The girl was still unconscious when he went over to inspect her injuries, and she failed to stir as he moved his fingers carefully through her tumbled black hair until he located the swelling on the side of her head where she had hit the water trough with a jarring impact. Next Court removed the cover and carefully cut the white, wet nightgown away from her body with his knife, taking special care when he was removing the remains of the sleeve from her burned arm. The gown, he noticed with interest, was of fine linen, intricately embroidered and edged with delicate lace at wrist and throat. It was a very modest and expensive piece of clothing for a whore to be wearing, especially since Lilith's fallen angels never bothered with nightgowns—at least when entertaining customers. Court's eyes twinkled as he reminded himself that Lilith was an innovative madam and perhaps had decided that this girl might bring in more money and intrigue her customers more in her virginal white gown than in the revealing and gaudy clothing usually worn by her colleagues. Lilith was probably right. The girl was special—not only because of her great beauty, but because she had a fresh unused look about her face and body.

He turned his attention to the arm, which had a nasty burn from the wrist upward. She was lucky at that; her hand was almost untouched, and the flame had only moved six inches up the arm before he had dropped her into the water. Had her hair caught fire—he shook his head and went to a medicine chest where he had a burn salve that had been given to him by a Mexican friend who ran sheep in the mountains. Court covered the burn with a thick coating of the salve and wrapped the arm in clean linen handkerchiefs. Then he put the girl, naked, under the covers of the bed and went into the dining room to get himself a drink. He had no smelling salts with which to revive her, if that was possible, and was not sure that he would be doing her a service if he could revive her. Both the burn and the head injury were likely to be painful. In fact, he had no idea how serious the head injury might be. For all he knew, she might never regain consciousness. Again he wished that he had been able to find Lilith, and he considered leaving the girl to go back into town to—his thoughts were interrupted by a trace of sound from his bedroom. Court took his drink down the hall and found her stirring, her eyelids opening slightly and then falling closed again, the lashes a black smudge on pale cheeks.

He drew a chair up to the bed and sat there for perhaps five minutes, drinking, watching her, and speaking to her occasionally until at last she opened her eyes fully and seemed to be at least marginally aware of his presence, but even then she did not respond when he asked her name. "Do you remember what happened to you?" he persisted.

"No." Her voice was a soundless whisper, and she accompanied the answer with a shake of the head that caused her eyes to open wide and fill with tears.

"Better not move your head again," Court advised. "I pulled you off the balcony at Lilith's, and because you were afire, I dropped you in the horse trough. You hit your head." The girl did not seem to understand. "Does your arm hurt?"

"Yes," she whispered.

"What's your name?"

Again she gave no answer. The tears were slipping down her cheeks, and she began to toss fitfully, rolling her head on the pillow and whimpering unintelligibly to herself. She paid no attention when he told her to hold still. Not knowing what else to do,

Court sat down on the bed beside her and held her shoulders down. Still her head rolled restlessly, so he transferred his left hand from her shoulder to her hair and held her head still in that fashion. Immobilized, the girl then looked up at him with vague, tear-filled eyes as if he were her tormentor, the cause of her pain, and Court stared back at her, disturbed and resentful. He could not see himself spending the night holding a weeping prostitute pinned to his bed, not for humanitarian purposes at any rate. Consequently, he decided that the decent and practical thing to do was to give the girl a good dose of opium, which would relieve her pain and probably put her to sleep as well so that he could go back to town and get Lilith to take her away.

He released her and went to the medicine chest for the bottle and then into the next room for a spoon, and all the time he was gone, the girl tossed and whimpered. But then his plan, designed to save himself as much trouble as possible, proved to be difficult to execute, for he had the very devil of a time getting the bitter dose into her, and when that was accomplished he had to hold her down again until the drug took effect. To avoid observing her pain, he stared at the wall and listed in his mind the properties he would need to check when he finally got back to town. That inventory could be accomplished while he searched for Lilith.

The soft skin and fragile bones of the girl's left shoulder under his hand were distracting, and the silky tangle of hair in his fingers, the fluttering pulse in her temple under his thumb, made him look at her from time to time. "We'll have to get together some night," he murmured to her. "What's your price?" The girl looked back, uncomprehending, but her restlessness was subsiding as the opium soothed her, and she gave him a dreaming smile. Court smiled back, and releasing her hair, he stroked her cheek and neck. "I reckon you're going to be just about the most popular girl in town," he told her. "You might just bring in enough to build the new Fallen Angel all by yourself." The girl's lashes drooped and rested on her cheeks, a last tear forced from underneath the lids; then she was asleep. Within five minutes Court left for town, locking the door behind him.

2

Three hours later the lawyer was back in his own house; he was sweat-soaked, covered with ash, dirt and soot, and his mood was close to rage. He had lost four buildings before the fire had been controlled, that control being effected only because the wind had died, and nowhere had he been able to find Lilith Moran. Everyone he asked had assured him that Lilith had saved her girls and a good many other business assets from the ashes of the Fallen Angel, and several people had seen a heavy wagon in the streets loaded with whores, petticoats, gambling equipment and other items that had survived the fire, but no one knew where they had gone. Before giving up the search in anger after midnight, Court had taken a surfeit of good-natured and admiring jokes about his single-minded pursuit of women in the face of general and personal disaster. He could not even find a woman to take care of the girl because no other madam would take in one of Lilith's whores, and no respectable woman would take in anyone's whore.

Admitting at last that he was stuck with her, at least for the time being, Court rode home and stamped angrily into his house. She was still peacefully asleep in his bed, looking cool, clean, unpained, uninjured, and very beautiful, while he, having spent a dirty and exhausting three hours in her behalf, still had to strip off his filthy clothes and wash himself with icy water in a cold room before he could go to bed.

Once Court had cleaned the worst of the dirt and sweat from his body, he stalked over to his bed and threw back the covers. His expression softened, for the girl was a charming sight, small with softly rounded curves. She had a perfect body—soft skin the color of rich cream, a tiny waist, full pointed breasts, a gently rounded belly, and sweet curves from thigh to knee, knee to ankle. Silently forgiving Lilith for disappearing and leaving the girl to him, he sat down on the bed and rubbed his thumb gently over her nipple as he studied her face. Her eyelids fluttered and opened over deep blue eyes, wide and vague.

"Are you in pain?" he asked, continuing to caress her. "Does your arm hurt?" He glanced at the handkerchiefs which were still in place on her wrist and forearm.

"No." She stirred under his touch, her nipple hardening.

He was pleased that she responded, that she was not one of those whores who were basically indifferent, who faked their interest, if they bothered to show any.

"And your head—does it hurt?"

"Sleepy," she murmured.

He nodded. "In a while. In a while you can go

back to sleep.'' He stretched out beside her and pulled the covers over them. The lamp on the table was still lit, casting a dim light in the room.

''You're very beautiful,'' he murmured to her.

''Thank you. You're very kind,'' she replied.

To Court her response seemed incongruous under the circumstances, more proper to a drawing room than a bed. He covered her mouth with his, using his tongue to part her lips. She was good; her responses were like those of a young girl, sweet and hesitant. He wondered if it was the opium or well-coached talent. ''Where did Lilith find you?'' he asked as he kissed the soft joining of her neck and shoulder.

''Lilith?'' The girl was trembling as he moved his mouth from her neck to the small rosy tip of her breast.

Court gave up talking to her. The opium or the fall had obviously befuddled her mind, although not her body. She arched her back when he began to stroke lightly, then insistently, between her thighs. When she was damp and trembling under his caresses, he rolled his body over hers and began to enter her. Only then did she offer resistance. He nodded admiringly at her technique, reflecting that Lilith had taught her well, but he murmured to her, ''Relax, little one. You don't have to play those games with me.'' Then he moved forcefully into her, and she gasped, but Court kissed her into silence as he rested inside her for a moment. She was warm and tight, and she excited him more than any woman he had been with in a long time—even Lilith, who could be extremely innovative when she chose, on rare occasions, to take a customer, although playing the innocent was never Lilith's way.

Court began to thrust with mounting excitement,

but the girl had stopped responding; she lay still beneath him, bemused, as if surprised at what was happening. Her eyes were not closed; they were still wide and vague. Disappointed, wanting to evoke again that sweet response that had made her seem special and different, he slipped a hand beneath her and raised her hips, moving more gently, more deeply into her. Then at last she trembled, her eyes closed, and she moved with him, hesitantly, with ever so slight an awkwardness, but picking up the rhythm, lifting in tiny satisfying circles, and they took each other into an intensifying spiral of sensation and aching pleasure until they reached an almost unbearable and perfect summit and fell back together from the pulsing aftermath into clinging, drowsy lassitude. Finally, Court shifted away from her but enclosed her again in his arms. "You're lovely," he whispered. "What's your name?"

She made no reply, just slipped silently, opium-dazed, into sleep. For a moment he watched her. She looked like a chaste young girl, and he was touched, felt as if he too had regained some measure of innocence and wonder long gone from his life. Then he shook the fancy away, smiling rather grimly at the idea of anyone, especially Aaron Court, developing an attachment to one of Lilith's soiled doves. Exhausted from his trip and the night's events, determined to avoid any ill-advised entanglements, he turned reluctantly away from her and dropped into heavy sleep.

3

The next morning when Court awoke, the girl was moaning softly in her sleep and hard to rouse. He gave her a second dose of opium to dull the pain and told her that he was going into town to look for Lilith. Without answering or seeming to comprehend, she turned onto her side and curled up, instantly asleep, still clinging to his hand. So appealing did he find her that he was tempted to stay, to awaken her, when the drug had eased her pain, and make love to her again, but he reminded himself that there would be time, that he could always find her again at Lilith's when he wanted her. He disengaged his hand, dressed, and left to saddle his horse.

As he rode back into town, a haze of smoke still hung over the valley obscuring the forests that rose steeply on all sides, and the acrid air stung his throat and burned his eyes. Everywhere devastation lined the streets, and dazed, disheartened people wandered about. Court shrugged it off. The town had burned before and rebuilt; it would probably burn again. Those who could were making the most of the disaster. One respectable woman whose house was intact was cooking breakfast for homeless survivors—and charging them disaster prices. Court ate an expensive plate of flapjacks and ham at her table and sipped hot, strong coffee as he made discreet inquiries after Lilith Moran.

No woman in the room, of course, acknowledged Lilith's existence, much less her present whereabouts, but the men all knew and were eager to tell her story, as long as their wives were not listening. It seemed that Lilith, in order to begin recouping her losses, had simply piled those girls and properties that had been salvaged into two large wagons and gone out to visit neighboring mining camps. Various estimates—all high—were given as to how much money her girls had made circuit riding while the town was burning. There was some resentment among citizens who surmised that the miners might

have come in to help fight the fire had they not been
tempted by livelier entertainment, but for the most
part Lilith's business acumen was retold with
laughter and admiration. All the tale tellers agreed
that Lilith herself was back at the hotel, having left
both girls and gamblers behind and more than
welcome in the miner's quarters at the rich Forbes
No. 5 Mine. It was said that she had found herself
missing a girl and had come back to look for her.

"Must be a pretty special girl," suggested one
cattleman, who had heard of the fire and come in
from his ranch to view the disaster and to see what
money could be made from the misery of the unfortunate townspeople. "Never heard of Lilith leaving
a bonanza to look out for one whore. They say she's
even got the gambling running out there, and Forbes
is fit to be tied 'cause his men don't want to go into
the mine. In fact, between the liquor and the
altitude, half of them are crazy drunk, and Forbes
wouldn't let them in the mine if they'd go."

Court nodded and drank off the last of his coffee.
Rather than waste time looking Lilith up first, he
went out to get the girl so that he and Lilith could
both return to business; at least four breakfasters
had asked for appointments with their lawyer for
that day. Not caring to bring a naked female into
town across his saddle, he bought a dress from a
woman on the street who was selling her belongings
one by one to the highest bidder. Then he rode home
and managed with some difficulty to persuade the
groggy young woman to don the garment. He would
have put it on her himself, but that idea seemed to
suit her no better than the dress, which was several
sizes too large and unfashionable to boot.

On the way into town with the girl asleep in his

arms, clad in her new dress and a blanket, Court experienced an inexplicable desire to take her straight back to the cabin and keep her for himself, particularly to keep her away from Lilith and the Fallen Angel. He almost wished she were not one of Lilith's girls. To overcome this unsettling and uncharacteristic possessiveness, he speculated with wry cynicism on who owed what to whom. Having rescued the girl from probable death on the balcony or at the least broken bones from a fall to the street, perhaps he was entitled to a free night in her company. In fact, since he had provided not only rescue but room, board, and medical services, perhaps he was entitled to reimbursement. Court grinned, but humorlessly. With no precontractual agreements having been made, the whole matter would rest on the value that each party placed on his or her services. The girl at the moment seemed hardly interested in bargaining. In fact, he found it disturbing to think of her taking money for her favors, a reaction which was obviously ridiculous on his part, and he also found it impossible to imagine her haggling over her fee. Lilith, on the other hand, he knew to be a sharp horse trader. She would doubtless—he reined up in front of the hotel, breaking off his speculations as he swung out of the saddle and slid the girl off with him. She still felt damnably good against his body, and his arms tightened compulsively around her.

Lilith, looking very worried for a woman who had probably turned the best profit made during the fire, was conveniently situated on the porch talking to several men as he carried the girl up the stairs. He lowered her reluctantly onto a soot-coated wicker settee that had been set out on the hotel veranda to herald the arrival of spring, if and when it made an appearance. Then he called out grimly, "I think I have something that belongs to you, Lilith."

The owner of the Fallen Angel turned from her agitated conversation and, glancing at his companion, rushed toward them. Much to Court's astonishment, she knelt and threw her arms around the girl, crying, "Susanna, I've been looking everywhere for you."

The girl opened her eyes and stared at Lilith with no initial recognition. Finally she asked tentatively, "Leah?"

"Lilith," came the quick correction. "I've been so worried, Susanna. I'm sorry I—" Lilith broke off, for the girl had fallen asleep again, her head resting on Lilith's shoulder.

Court had watched this scene with wonder and growing uneasiness. Lilith treated her girls well enough, but he had never seen her express affection to any of them. They were a commodity to be trained, used, and then sent on when their popularity waned or when she wanted new faces, and they were sent on more valuable than when they came, but they were also dispatched without regret on Lilith's part. Consequently, her treatment of this girl was very unusual, cause for wonder, and his creeping unease also stemmed from the fact that, although there was an obvious difference in age, there was also a resemblance between the two, recognizable now that he saw them together.

"Where did you find her?" Lilith demanded of him. "I've been looking everywhere."

"She was at my place," Court replied.

"And maybe you'd like to tell me what she was doing there." Lilith was grimly angry and suspicious, for whatever reason.

"Well, I plucked her off the balcony at the Fallen Angel before it collapsed." Lilith turned white under his sharp gaze. "She was on fire, and then she hit her head when I put the fire out in the horse trough. After that," continued Court dryly, "since she was soaked, burned, and unconscious and since I couldn't find you or a doctor, I took her home and did what I could for her. Bandaged her up, gave her some opium for the pain."

Lilith drew her breath in sharply at the mention of opium. Some of her girls used it, but Lilith disapproved and generally moved those girls on faster than she might have otherwise. "And what else happened while you had her at your house?" she demanded. "Why didn't you bring her back in here?"

"Where were you if you were so worried about her?" Court retorted just as sharply. "I came back in about midnight to look for you, and no one had a clue as to where you were. Out at the Forbes No. 5, weren't you?"

Lilith's face colored slightly, and she glanced at the girl, who was still asleep and missing the discussion entirely. She ran her hands distractedly through her hair and confessed, "I forgot about her. I mean I thought I'd got everybody out and into the wagons, and I didn't miss her till we got to the mine." Lilith shook her head. "I'm just not used to having her here. I suppose I shouldn't have jumped on you, Court. At least you got her out of there."

"Think nothing of it," he replied. "Your concern is touching, even if you did forget her. In fact, I've never seen you so—"

"She's my sister," snapped Lilith. "Of course I'm concerned."

Court had to revise his estimate of the situation very quickly. "She didn't tell me her name. She took a hard knock on the head and then the opium—"

Lilith was again glaring suspiciously at him. "Why is she wearing this dress? This rag isn't hers, and she has no shoes and—"

"She was wearing a nightgown when I got her off the balcony, Lilith. Did you want me to leave her all night in a wet nightgown, half burned off, and bring her back to town in it while I was waiting for you to get back from your business at the mine?"

The proprietress of the Fallen Angel suppressed a sharp response and stared at her sister. "Is she badly hurt?"

"Christ, I don't know. There's no doctor, and—"

"No doctor?"

"He's dead."

"Well, that's the last straw," snapped Lilith angrily. "How am I supposed to get health certificates for my girls when the doctor's dead? The sheriff probably killed him himself so he can fine me for every single girl—"

"Do you want me to represent you?" asked Court, who was delighted to avoid discussing the sister.

"Don't change the subject. I want to hear about Susanna's injuries."

"You want a diagnosis?" asked Court sarcastically. "I may be able to get the sheriff off your back, but I don't know a damned thing about head injuries or burns either. I did the best I could."

"I didn't say you didn't."

"Who was I supposed to get to look at her? Red Lucy? Or maybe I should have asked Judge Galt's wife for help. I'm sure she would have been delighted to take in your sister.'' Court disliked the situation more every minute since he did not know what Lilith wanted to hear or what her relationship to her sister was.

"All right, Aaron. All right. I'm sorry I snapped at you. I'm tired."

"So am I," Court replied sharply.

"And I appreciate your saving her life. Thanks. Now I think I'd better get her into the hotel."

"Do that," he replied and, mounting, turned his horse away without offering further assistance.

Aaron made his way impatiently through the congested town and rapidly thereafter to his house where he planned to sleep until noon and then return to keep appointments with clients. His bed was rumpled where he and the girl had made love and slept the night before, and he threw back the covers thinking of her. Then he swore. Her blood was on his sheets, which meant that she must have been a virgin, not feigning reluctance, not holding him off as a game. How could he have failed to realize? For that matter, had he known, could he have passed up such an appealing young woman? "Pray God Lilith planned to take her into the business anyway," he muttered, then realized uneasily that he didn't want that at all.

Either way Lilith was going to be a very angry woman when she found out what had happened beyond the chivalrous rescue and the medical treatment. But what a delight the girl had been, especially for a novice. He almost regretted that he had not made love to her in the morning, since he might never have the opportunity again.

In Court's opinion, respectable girls, if a man allowed himself to get mixed up with them, were invariably more trouble than they were worth. They wanted marriage, an institution that Court knew to be a disaster for everyone involved. And yet young Susanna was a terrible, and possibly respectable, temptation that he hated to pass up. Plagued by his own ambivalence, he cursed the perverse fate that had thrown Lilith Moran's sister into his path.

II
Amnonville

4

Lilith's first priority was to provide for her sister. Therefore, she installed Susanna in the hotel room that she had taken for herself, and she then hired, with some difficulty, a nurse, a poor woman who had lost everything including her husband in the fire.

Initially the woman had balked at working for such an infamous employer. Lilith overcame those objections with a generous salary. Then the woman made it clear that she would never, under any circumstances, work at Lilith's place of business. Smiling ironically, Lilith agreed; it was obvious to her, if not to Clara, that the customers at the Fallen Angel might like to look at Susanna, who was not for sale, but they would hardly be enchanted with plain-faced, barrel-bodied Clara Schmidt, no matter how low the price. Finally the woman had sniffed suspiciously when she entered the hotel room, suspecting that its strong odor was an indication that the previous tenant had died there of smallpox and thus forced the hotel to fumigate. Had half the town died of smallpox in the room, Lilith would have used it; there were no other rooms in town that night. However, she assured Clara Schmidt that had anyone died of smallpox anywhere within fifty miles, the news would have come to Lilith at the

Fallen Angel. Clara believed that; it seemed reasonable that bad news would circulate first in bad places, while virtuous women like herself went ignorant of imminent danger. Then Lilith explained the odor as carbolic acid and soap used to rid the room of bugs left by some visiting cowboy or miner. Clara believed that too, since her late husband had been neither a cowboy, a miner, nor a man infested with bugs, and she had therefore never been forced to use such a concoction in her house. She accepted the job and the lodgings as if she were doing Lilith a favor.

Having taken care of Susanna for the time being and feeling sure that once Susanna awakened, she would herself provide the answers Court had evaded, Lilith began immediately to look to her own future. First she made a careful tour of the section of town that remained intact and chose the structure that would serve as a temporary home for the Moran Land, Cattle, Claim and Fallen Angel Company. The visits to the mines had been profitable, but the presence of her girls there was infuriating the mine owners, who, as it turned out, never allowed liquor in the miners' dormitories, much less women and gambling, and Lilith did not want to lose the good will and the business of the owners, for although a wealthy man might not spend more on women and drink than a poorer one, he could and did spend more at the gambling tables. Moreover, Lilith reasoned that the disaster in town would send desperate men flocking to her doors for distraction, if she had doors to open to them, and the miners, as always, would come to her also.

She viewed the house she had chosen with qualified satisfaction. It was large enough. It was also in a respectable neighborhood and owned by a respectable family, an obvious drawback, but Lilith did not plan to offend the respectable neighborhood any longer than absolutely necessary, and as for the respectable inhabitants of the house, they were the wife and children of Grant Harwell Penvennon, a man who loved money more than anything else in the world, and Lilith planned to offer him an irresistible amount of money for the temporary use of his house. She did, and he did not resist. By nightfall his wife, in a state of shock, fury, and moral indignation, was moving her children and furniture out to make room for the most notorious woman in town.

Having subverted Grant Penvennon, Lilith then looked up the owner of a smaller house that adjoined the Penvennon property and asked him bluntly if he really wanted his wife to spend several months living beside a whorehouse. This owner, who under ordinary circumstances would not have spoken to Lilith, much less done business with her, took her money and his wife and household furnishings and fled from the imminent contamination of the Fallen Angel Company. Only later did he discover that it was not actually the Penvennon house that was to be converted into a brothel; it was his own. The Penvennon house accommodated the saloon, dance hall and gambling rooms. By then, however, it was too late; he had signed the lease and received his money. Lilith was moderately pleased with her arrangements and went off to begin acquiring men and material for the construction of a new, a bigger, a more luxurious Moran Land, Cattle, Claim and Fallen Angel Company.

5

While Lilith was corrupting respectable residents and residential areas of Amnonville, Aaron Court had risen at noon from his bed, disposed of the incriminating sheets and the girl's nightgown—what had Lilith said the girl's name was?—and ridden into town to have lunch at a saloon and hear the news. As he helped himself to the pickled beets and fish, the hard-boiled eggs, the potato salad, and the sourdough bread piled with boiled ham and salami, to which the purchase of two beers entitled him, he listened to many tales of woe, among which one interested him particularly. He heard this tale from a mining friend to whom he had provided a grubstake several months earlier so that the prospector could give up his winter job at the smelter and take to the mountains again. Actually Grassback Holbein had three matters of interest to report. The first, an item of personal interest, was a bad case of frostbite in his left foot, gained when he had ignored oncoming snow to pursue a promising claim. He had come into town to consult the doctor about his foot, only to find that the doctor had selfishly got himself killed in the fire. The second, an item of business interest, was the new claim, which looked fair-to-fabulous and in which Court was a partner as a result of the grubstake; having failed to find the doctor, Holbein had filed the claim and had a copy of the papers for Court. The third item was one of general interest and, if anything, Holbein seemed to enjoy its telling more than the first two. With good-humored relish Court's new partner informed him that Lilith Moran had herself "one hell of an embarrassing problem" that was causing merriment at her expense all over

town, or had been until necessity forced the townsfolk to turn to weeping and poking through the
ashes of their homes and businesses. Aaron sym-
pathized over the foot and was glad to hear that a
promising-to-fabulous amount of gold was to be
added to his fortune, but he was more interested to
hear of Lilith's embarrassing problem, which he
silently but fervently hoped had nothing at all to do
with him. He soon found out that it did involve
him—peripherally at least.

"You might not believe this, Aaron," said the
prospector, "but Lilith, she comes from a fancy St.
Louis family, and she's got herself a li'l sister, purty
as a picture she is, named Susanna, who musta been
brought up in a closet or sumpthin, 'cause that girl,
she don't know nothin'. She been writin' to Lil fer
years, ever since Lil got fed up with her high-toned
family an run off—an she thinks Lil is jus the
sweetest sister that ever lived, so when her parents
gets killed in a buggy accident, what does she do but
set right off on the train—now that's a story in itself. Seems they got stuck for nine days at the Corley
Station what with snow on the tracks and more
falling, an when this here lil girl gits off the train, she
walks up to these two fellers she sees standin agin the
wall—" Holbein doubled up with laughter for which
an impatient Court could see no reason "—an she
says, 'Pardon me, sir—' " Again Holbein became
helpless with laughter.

"Am I missing something?" asked Court dryly as
he watched his partner, choking, gurgling, and
wiping the tears from his eyes.

"Just that—" Holbein fell to laughing again, and
Court ordered himself another beer and took
another helping of salami and sourdough to tide him

over what looked to be a long story. "Jus that them two fellers wasn't fellers; they was corpses." By this time numbers of men up and down the bar were listening and joining in the laughter.

"Corpses," agreed another luncheon guest of the saloon.

"Frozen solid," added a third drinker with a shout of laughter.

"That's it," said Holbein. "That lil girl was tryin to git information from two corpses Corley had dug outa a snow slide an set up agin the wall to thaw come spring. When Miz Corley tole the girl, poor lil thing, she fainted plum down an had to be hauled off to the railroad dormitory by the engineer an the fireman.

"Anyways—" resumed Holbein, after drinking off his beer and wiping his eyes one last time "—anyways once they got the track cleared, she climbs back on the train to come out here an live with her sweet sister Lil—Leah, she calls her—an hep her with her business—which she don't know nuthin about. She thinks the Fallen Angel's a restaurant with singin an dancin an such—why, that girl, she wouldn't know what a whore was—much less a frozen corpse—if you mentioned one to her." The man slapped the table and laughed in great guffaws, and Court, to be companionable, joined in with a few grim chuckles. "Wouldn't know a whore if she saw one," repeated the prospector with glee. "An Lilith, she ain't tellin her neither, an the word is out that anybody who wants to stay on the right side of Lilith, which is everybody in pants from here to Denver, ain't gonna tell this girl Susanna nuthin neither. Well, I'll tell ya, Aaron, if that ain't sompthin. Here's this lil girl—she's been here three, four

days—trippin around, chattin with the customers—
an believe me, she's so purty ain't a customer don't
want to grab her, but ya cain't a course, cause
Lilith's right there glarin—so here's this lil girl
runnin around, askin folks if they's enjoyin their
drinks, an don't they think they shouldn't gamble so
much cause it ain't moral an they probably got wives
an little ones at home what needs the money fer
shoes an blankets an such, an she's mendin curtains,
an offerin to teach the whores tattin so's they can
cover their tits with lace, an just generally surprisin
the hell outa everone. Why, Aaron, if'n that girl din
go to bed at eight o'clock, poor Lilith wouldn't
know what to do. I'll tell ya, Miss Susanna wouldn't
know one end of a man from the other, and here
she's livin right there, innocent as a babe, in the
town's finest cathouse."

"Um-m-m," said Court, reflecting with gloom
that his friend's news was now out of date, that
Sister Susanna was no longer "innocent as a babe."

"Yep. Lilith's got a real problem on her hands."

"Um-m-m," Court agreed, hoping that Lilith had
not yet discovered and would not discover the
additional nature of her problem. Maybe the girl
would keep her mouth shut.

6

It was after nightfall when Lilith returned to the
hotel room to find that her sister had been awake
and coherent for a short time that afternoon and
that the nurse had managed to feed the girl a half
bowl of soup before she dropped off again.

Lilith was pleased and thanked the woman, and
Clara Schmidt replied, her mouth set in lines of

self-righteous disapproval, "I wouldn't work for you, Miss Moran, if I could help it."

"You're not working for me; you're working for Susanna, so you don't have to worry about being morally contaminated," remarked Lilith dryly. "Do you think she's going to be all right? I wish I could get a doctor."

"He's dead," said Clara. "Even all your ill-got money won't buy you a doctor in this town tonight."

"But it very likely will buy me a nurse with better manners," Lilith snapped. "I asked you if she's going to be all right."

"Far as I can tell," Clara admitted grudgingly. "She can't get up; she's dizzy, but she seems to know what's going on, and the burn looks like it's gonna heal. Someone put some real potent salve on it."

"Good. I want to talk to her. Why don't you go downstairs and have dinner." Lilith handed the woman some money. "And I'll want you to stay with her tonight. I have things to do."

Clara sniffed, took the money, and left. She thought she knew what Lilith Moran had in mind to do that would keep her from seeing to her own poor sister.

Lilith sat down beside the bed as soon as the nurse had gone and looked thoughtfully at Susanna, who was curled on her side with one hand beneath her cheek, sleeping like a child—Susanna who, ten years ago, had been the only member of the family to regret Lilith's flight, who had cried in the dark as they had whispered together for the last time, the grown sister and the young child; Susanna who, although she had done nothing else that was underhanded or secretive in her life, had managed to write

Lilith every week and to receive letters from her for all that ten years without her parents being the wiser; Susanna who had paid for Lilith's rebellion by leading a completely isolated and protected life for the same ten years; Susanna who now expected to be a help and a companion in a business the nature of which she could not even begin to understand; her sister Susanna, the one problem for which Lilith had no solution. Lilith sighed and awakened the girl, knowing that her sister would not know how to lie to her about what had happened on the night of the fire, the night Susanna had spent with that scoundrel Aaron Court.

"Are you hungry, Susanna?" Lilith asked, putting off the more serious topic.

"No, Leah. Lilith, I mean. Was Lilith in the Bible? I can't quite remember the story."

Lilith did not care to tell her sister why she had chosen to rename herself, so she ignored the question. "Maybe you'd like some more soup. There's some here."

"No. I think I might throw up. My head still hurts a lot and my arm, and I think I might throw up. Maybe you should go out of the room, Lea—Lilith. I know you don't like throwing up. I remember when I ate all the grapes on the trellis vine and I threw up, and then you threw up too, and Mama—"

Lilith did not want to remember the beating Susanna had been given, nor the fact that their mother had beaten an innocent Lilith as well. "I have a stronger stomach these days, Susanna, and I want to talk to you. Do you remember what happened to you?"

Susanna frowned and was silent for some time. Finally she said, "Yes, I guess so. When I woke up, the room was full of smoke, and there were flames at the end of the hall coming from the staircase when I tried to go down." She stopped and swallowed convulsively. "Then—then—"

"The staircase was burning. Then what?" Lilith prompted.

"Then I had to go the other way—to the balcony, you know." Susanna put both hands to her head. "Can't we talk about it some other time, Lilith? I—"

"Do you feel worse?"

"It was so frightening. It makes my head ache just to remember it."

Lilith was all the more determined to hear the whole story because Susanna seemed so reluctant to tell it. "What happened then?"

Susanna stared miserably at the wall, her eyes haunted, but she dutifully continued, "I got out on the balcony, and I didn't know what to do. I didn't cough so much there, but I could see the fire, and all the other buildings were on fire, and I couldn't call to anyone in the street because I realized that I only had on my nightgown, and I was embarrassed."

"For God's sake, Susanna," Lilith cried, but then she cut herself off. "What happened when you were on the balcony?"

"Then—then a man rode up on a horse. And he called out to me and told me to jump, but I was afraid. I was afraid he couldn't catch me, or that my nightgown would fly up and show my legs. And it was very hard to climb over the railing. I had to hold my nightgown around my knees with one hand. But the fire kept coming closer, and he kept telling me to jump." Susanna stopped, picturing the scene in her mind. "He wore a black hat,' she resumed, "and black clothes with a woolly coat over his suit. He was very handsome," she explained solemnly. "Like a prince in a storybook."

Lilith's lips thinned. Aaron Court was undoubtedly handsome, but he was certainly no storybook prince. "What happened then?" she prompted.

"Why, he rescued me," her sister replied simply.

"I know that. But what happened later?"

Susanna's eyes were wide and surprised. "I don't know, Lilith. I dropped off the porch and—and I opened my eyes—and there you were."

"But you were gone all night."

"I didn't know that."

"You don't remember?" asked Lilith suspiciously.

"No." Susanna rubbed her eyes. "I guess he took good care of me. But I don't know his name."

"I do," said Lilith ominously.

Susanna drifted back into sleep, and Lilith moved to a more comfortable chair to await the return of the nurse. She planned to pay Aaron Court a visit that evening; in fact, he could provide her with a bed for the night, and he would also provide her with a more detailed account of the kind of "good care" he had given her sister.

7

One of the more colorful, if less admirable, institutions of Amnonville and the surrounding territory was the Packard Gang, led by the family patriarch Job Packard and comprised of various Packard sons, nephews, cousins, friends, and hangers-on. The Packards would steal anything: they stole from banks, stores, houses, hotels, trains, stagecoaches, travelers on horseback and on foot; they stole money, merchandise, mine shipments, cattle, horses, and occasionally even women. Even less occasionally, when there was absolutely nothing else of value to steal, the Packards had been known to rustle sheep—lesser members of the clan, that is; Job Packard would have nothing to do with either woman-stealing or sheep-stealing, saying that the first was too dangerous and the second too degrading. The Packards also murdered people, but not as their vocation. Murder was definitely a secondary activity at that time with the Packards, although they were not averse to bloody feuds when the family honor needed avenging.

When the gang in their mountain retreat heard of the most recent fire in Amnonville, they immediately scented a great opportunity for wholesale thievery. An expedition, headed by Job's eldest son and second-in-command, Isaiah, was mounted the very night after the fire. Job, who in his mid-sixties no longer cared to venture out on chilly nights, gave the raiding party his blessing and the benefit of his advice. For instance, he warned them to stay away from the property of the more touchy citizens who might be expected to defend their possessions and even come into the mountains after thieves, people like Aaron Court and Benny Ripon, a part-time gunfighter and part-time jeweler, and people who might take revenge in other ways, people like Al Bleiberg, the butcher, who might refuse to sell their stolen cattle, or Sheriff Maxie, who might alter his laissez-faire attitude toward Packard activities, or Lilith Moran, who might bar them from the delights of gambling, drinking, and whoring at the Fallen Angel. The Packard Gang took all this patriarchal advice to heart and rode off laughing and joking among themselves.

They reached Amnonville around ten in the evening, and having decided to concentrate on horses, because they were feeling high-spirited and reckless, they began to round up every animal in town whose owner was not actually standing beside it with a cocked gun. In all they had collected between thirty-five and forty good horses by eleven when Elias Packard said to his older brother, "Isaiah, I seen somethin I jus gotta have. How about me and Hogshead here jus pickin it up an meetin you in about fifteen minutes outsida town?"

"Suit yourself, Elias. We got one more stable to hit. Jus see you don't make no noise. This here raid is goin real smooth, what with all the suckers bein all wore out an in bed early."

The something Elias Packard just had to have was the contents of a safe he had seen lying amid the ruins of a building on Copper Street. He reasoned that anyone who had a safe had a lot of good things to put in it. Secondly, he reasoned that since the safe was still there unopened, the owner was dead and unlikely to be around to protect his valuables. Consequently, Elias Packard and his closest friend, Hogshead Bates, were standing in the middle of the ashes of Aaron Court's law offices, kicking his safe and discussing in whispers how to get into it, when Aaron himself visited the site for the fourth time since the fire to see if the safe was cool enough to be opened. He arrived just as Packard and Bates had discovered, much to their disgust, that the safe could not be opened with a crowbar.

"Think we could shoot it open?" asked Elias.

"Reckon we could," replied Hogshead, "but we

ain't supposed to make no noise. If'n we couldn't shoot it open, we could sure blow it with dynamite or even gunpowder."

"That'd be just as loud as shootin it open," said Elias with contempt.

"Well, what are we gonna do? Why don't we see if we kin find some more horses instead."

"No sir, I want the safe. I'll bet if we dragged it into the mountains an dropped it off a cliff, it'd bust right open."

"Give it up, Elias," said Court quietly. "All you'd get would be papers flying everywhere."

Elias whirled, drawing his gun, and Court shot him in the gunhand and then through the right shoulder. Hogshead did not stay to see the outcome. After the first shots, he jumped on his horse and spurred toward the edge of town. Court sent one bullet after him and then another toward Elias, who was cursing viciously and attempting to pick up his gun with his left hand. The third shot caught Elias in the upper thigh and took the fight out of him, although not the fury.

"You're sure as hell hard to kill, Elias," Court snapped as he relieved him of his weapons and hauled him up onto the new horse.

"You'd better git me to a doctor," Elias groaned, "if you know what's good fer you."

"I'm getting you to the sheriff. If he wants to get you a doctor, that's his business. If it were my say so, I wouldn't give you a rag to stop the blood, you thieving son of a bitch."

"Won't do you no good to put me in jail. Pa, he'll get me out anyways. An then he'll take care of you. An there ain't nobody gonna prosecute me, and ain't no judge nor jury gonna try me."

Court shrugged as if it were all one to him. There was some truth in what Elias was saying. Most people were afraid of the Packards, who looked after their own and were not squeamish about how they did it. "Sheriff," he bellowed as they came abreast of the jail, which had lost two cells to the fire. "Sheriff, you better get out here. There's Packards in town."

The sheriff appeared at the door, clad in a nightshirt and pulling on his trousers. "Packards?"

"Twenny, thirty Packards," added Elias. "They'll be along fer me. You better jus let me go."

"You better get a posse. They've probably taken everything in town by now," added Court.

The sheriff cursed and began to clang his alarm bell, rousing men all over town, whose first assumption was that, phoenixlike, the fire had sprung up again from its own ashes.

With so few horses left in Amnonville, the assembling of a mounted posse proved to be very difficult. However, Court, the sheriff, Benny Ripon, and several of Lilith's men led by Carlos Mondragon all had horses, thanks to Job's preraid lecture to his family, and these men all headed promptly in the direction in which Hogshead Bates had been seen to flee.

In the meantime the shots had been heard by the Packards, who were assembling their stolen horses on the edge of town, and they headed precipitously back into the mountains. Because the small posse was close behind them, they lost some men and a good many of the horses, and they also failed to notice the absence of Elias until they were all the way home.

Isaiah swore fluently when he discovered what

had happened to his brother, and he knocked
Hogshead Bates three feet into the wall of a family
stable for failing to defend Elias; then he stamped in
to his father and explained the situation, finishing
by saying, "I reckon we'd best go back after him,
Pa. Folks get mad when you take their horses—
wors'n if you jus shoot down their friends. They
might hang him or somethin'."

Job glowered at his eldest son. "Elias disobeyed
me. I told him to stay clear of Aaron Court. If he
ain't gonna honor his father the way the Bible says,
he gotta expect to git shot. We'll jus leave him in
there a while."

"But Pa, what if they kill him?"

"If'n he's already dead, it won't do no good to go
git him," said Job reasonably, "an if'n he ain't
dead, they ain't gonna kill him cause they know
we'll git em if they do, so we might as well let em
doctor him till he's better, and then we kin git him.
They ain't gonna hang him neither. They know
better'n that. They know us Packards don't put up
with no hangin of our kinfolks. How many horses
did ya git?"

"Had about twenny-five left when we got home.
Lost two men sides Elias."

"Anyone good?"

"Nah. Jus Elias."

"I'm goin ta bed." Job stamped back to his
room.

8

Aaron Court returned to his house around midnight
and found Lilith in his parlor drinking his bourbon
and reading one of his books. He was not quite sure
why she was there. A natural assumption would

have been that her sister had described the night spent at Court's house after the fire and that Lilith had come to talk to him, to shout at him, possibly even to shoot him—she had been known to shoot people, although she usually left such activities to her second-in-command, a hard-faced Mexican named Carlos. On the other hand, Lilith was wearing a sheer lace and silk gown, one that he had seen before and associated with warmer sports than gunplay—unless she planned to shoot him in his bed. Rather than give himself away by jumping to any dangerous conclusions, he fixed himself a drink and welcomed her hospitably.

Lilith nodded. "I knew you wouldn't mind putting me up," she murmured. "One does have to depend on old friends in times of trouble."

"By all means," Court agreed, glad that he had got rid of the sheets her sister had slept on.

"It shouldn't be more than tonight, possibly tomorrow night, until I can open up again."

"That's fast. Where are you taking the Fallen Angel? Back to the tent?"

Lilith smiled demurely. "I rented Grant Penvennon's house."

Court roared with laughter. "I'm sure your new neighbors are looking forward to your arrival. Will you be having open house for the neighborhood ladies?"

"Well, certainly if they want to visit, my doors are always open." Lilith put down her drink and rose gracefully. "I've been waiting several hours for you, Aaron. What kept you so late?"

"If I'd known you were here, Lilith, I assure you that I'd have shot Elias Packard and taken him off to jail twice as fast," replied Court gallantly. "I wouldn't even have volunteered to ride posse."

"Damn! Are they in town again? Was there much shooting?" She preceded him toward the bedroom.

"Some," he replied.

Lilith frowned and murmured, "I'll have to get a guard for Susanna—at least till Job gets Elias out of jail."

"Does that assumption indicate a lack of faith in local justice?" he asked. "Or do you doubt the truth of the charges I filed against Elias?" He put his arm around Lilith's waist from behind.

"You never did finish telling me about Susanna." Lilith had no interest in local justice and changed the subject abruptly.

"What else is there to tell?" he countered. He now knew why Lilith was paying this unaccustomed call on him—she was either checking out her sister's story or fishing for information from him. He tightened his arm around her waist.

"Did she sleep in this bed?" asked Lilith.

"Of course she slept in this bed. Did you think I'd make her sleep on the floor?" Court deliberately sharpened his tone. "Anything else you'd like to know, Lilith?"

"Where did you sleep?"

"I was out looking for you, or have you forgotten?"

"All night?" Lilith was becoming impatient.

"If you think there was something funny going on, maybe you should ask your sister, Lilith. You know what kind of girl she is."

Lilith flushed and whirled on him. "She's a good girl."

"I haven't said she isn't," replied Court. "You're the one who's implying otherwise."

Lilith eyed him narrowly; his face showed

nothing. "She doesn't remember what happened after you got her off the balcony," Lilith admitted.

"There's not that much to remember," said Court, wondering if the girl could really remember nothing. He decided that the conversation had gone as far as he wanted it to go, that a distraction was in order. Therefore he crushed Lilith's body against his own and bruised her mouth in a hard kiss.

When he lifted his head, Lilith drew away and murmured coolly, "Perhaps you could take off your gun. I'm sure it impresses the Packards much more than it does me."

What a cold bitch she was, Court thought.

"Of course, the fee is the usual," she added with a slight smile. "And you won't be too long about it will you, Aaron? I've had a tiring day."

Court smiled back at her. Susanna's face had drifted through his mind's eye, wiping out any interest he might have had in her sister. "Evidently you mistook my intentions, Lilith," he murmured. "I was offering you a bed and a friendly goodnight. I wasn't offering to share the bed with you."

Lilith flushed and gave him a hard, questioning look.

"Nothing personal, you understand," he continued softly. "It's just that I'm familiar with your sexual preferences, and I've had enough violence for one night." Court made her a polite half bow and left the room. He had always disliked the perverse desire in Lilith that drove her to arouse passion and cruelty in her partner while remaining unmoved herself. When she did respond, and that was only to pleasure well leavened with pain, she disguised the pleasure. In the past, he had found her interesting, provocative, but now she inspired only distaste, although he knew that by leaving her, he might well be making an enemy. Lilith relished the passion she inspired if not the customer in whom she inspired it.

9

Time drifted for Susanna. She was unaware of the Packard raid on the city, slept through the shooting. People came and went from her room—Clara, who was there most of the time and who was kind to her in a gruff way; her sister, who visited several times a day but seemed to live somewhere else (Susanna had a hard time remembering from one visit to the next where Lilith was and what she said she was doing); waiters who brought food; a funny bearded, grizzled man with big guns on his hips who stuck his head in the door and spoke to Clara from time to time; and even a young doctor who, unknown to Susanna, had been imported by her sister to circumvent the greedy sheriff. (Before the ashes of the fire had cooled, Sheriff Maxie had tried to collect fines from Lilith on two girls whose health certificates had expired that day at noon.) The new doctor examined Susanna and said she should stay in bed if she felt bad and get up if she felt better. Susanna stayed in bed. The real people that came and went seemed less real to her for several days than the man on horseback about whom she dreamed when she slept. The way he had looked, the sound of his voice calling out to her, the momentary sensation of his arms closing around her just before the red world went black— these things recurred again and again as she slept, as her arm healed, as the agony in her head subsided.

While Susanna was recovering, Lilith was re-arranging her affairs. She left Aaron Court's house before he was up, determined not to return. There seemed no likelihood that he would tell her any more about his night with Susanna than he already had; perhaps, as he said, there was nothing to tell. Besides, she found his rejection puzzling. It had never happened before, and she wondered why a wealthy customer should so suddenly have lost interest. It was odd. Not that she didn't appreciate having the bed to herself. She hated sleeping with someone else, hated being touched unless there was a profit in it, hated it even then.

Lilith's first errand in Amnonville that morning was to locate a man named Abner Quincy, a tough old fellow with a reputation as a hard drinker, a reliable employee, and a fast gun. Quincy, after being found in the company of a prostitute who worked out of the little houses on Crib Alley and after being sobered up, agreed readily enough to work for Lilith; he had done special jobs for her before, although he had never been interested in a permanent position on Carlos Mondragon's staff of peacekeepers, both because he did not care for permanent employment and because he cared even less for Mexicans, even Mexicans as tough as Mondragon. He was amused, however, and rather flattered that Lilith wanted him to become a bodyguard to Susanna. His humor was piqued at the idea that he was to keep men away from a famous prostitute's sister and, if he could, keep the sister away from the Fallen Angel. Failing that, he was to see that Susanna came to no harm and that she was told nothing that might disillusion her while she was visiting Lilith at work. To this end, Lilith bullied the management of the hotel into providing a room for him across the hall from Susanna and alerted Clara that he was to be called upon in time of need.

Having settled the problem of her sister's safety and having at least attempted to settle the problem of her sister's well-meant interference in business matters, Lilith immediately forgot Susanna and turned her attention entirely to the reopening of her Moran Land, Cattle, Claim and Fallen Angel Company. She called back her furniture, her gambling equipment, her bar supplies, and her girls from Forbes No. 5; inspected the newly vacated Penvennon house; and by evening was beginning to move in. The new quarters would not be as luxurious, for as the fire advanced, she had had to leave behind velvet hangings and gilded mirrors and other such amenities, but the essentials of a night on the town at Lilith's would be available, and her operation would still be the liveliest in town, fire or no fire, her girls the most beautiful, her gambling tables the most honest, her dance hall the noisiest. The money would flow in; that was the important thing. She opened up again at midnight to a capacity crowd, since she had spread the word through town that the first drink was on the house. By three in the morning, the house next door, vacated only five hours earlier by its horrified occupants, was furnished, and the girls, giggling and flirting, were taking their customers through a gap chopped in the side fence. The festive grand opening lasted until noon the next day and was remembered for years as the best party Amnonville had ever seen. By ten in the morning, Lilith had sent two wagons over the pass to replenish her liquor supplies. Drunks were still staggering through the streets at three in the afternoon. It was a triumph.

10

Several days later when business was booming at Lilith's, Susanna woke up in her quiet room and discovered that her head no longer hurt, that sitting up no longer made her dizzy, that she could hardly wait for her dinner to arrive, and that she was no longer the least bit sleepy or inclined to spend another moment in bed. So she got up.

"Where are my clothes?" she asked Clara.

The woman was astonished. It was the first normal communication the girl had made in days. "Gone," replied Clara, "burnt up. Go back to bed."

Susanna did not go back to bed, but she did sit down. Her legs felt a bit wobbly, even if her head was once again normal. "Where's Lilith?"

"At her place." Clara's mouth turned down.

"But it was on fire."

"She got another."

"Did she really?" Susanna's face lit up with admiration. "Isn't she wonderful? How hard she must have worked. And here I've been lying in bed all these days, not doing a thing to help her. You must go out right now, Clara, and buy me some clothes. Do we have any money?"

"I have to feed you your dinner."

"I can eat my own dinner. Now let me tell you where to go and what to get."

"I can't go nowhere, and you can't go nowhere," declared Clara stoutly. She knew that Lilith did not want Susanna arriving at that brothel, and one way to keep the girl away was certainly to keep her in the hotel with only two nightgowns to her name. Clara could not imagine how the child could be so stupid as not to know what her sister did for a living, but the job as Susanna's nurse and chaperone was turning out to be a good one, better than trying to hold body and soul together seamstressing or serving food to miners in some chop house, and Clara intended to keep the job.

Susanna, however, was not to be deterred. She jumped up from the chair and went to the large wardrobe provided by the hotel. There she found several dresses belonging to Clara, one dress that had been bought secondhand on the street for her by Aaron Court, which she did not recognize, and one dress that had been provided by her sister against the day when she was able to get up. Susanna dressed herself as fast as she could, asking Clara to help her with the buttons in back when she was nearly finished. Instead Clara announced that she was going to get Mr. Quincy and left Susanna to wonder who Mr. Quincy might be. While Clara was across the hall pounding on Abner's door, dinner arrived, and Susanna was eating it with a good appetite when her two protectors returned.

"This is Mr. Quincy," announced Clara. "He's your bodyguard, and he's not going to let you go off anywhere, Miss Susanna. You're sick, and your sister doesn't want you running around the streets and—"

"My bodyguard?" Susanna giggled. "Well, Mr. Quincy, won't you have some dinner to fortify yourself? After dinner you can escort me over to Lilith's Land and Cattle Company. I'm sure she needs my help, and I wouldn't be a very good sister, would I, if I lay around here doing nothing when Lilith has done so much for me and works so hard and . . ."

Neither of her hired guardians were able to dissuade her. At 6:30 in the evening, wearing her demure blue dress and Clara's cape, Susanna flitted into the new Fallen Angel with her bodyguard at her heels. He was looking suspiciously at every man within twelve feet of her; she was all smiles, ready to embrace her sister. Lilith spotted her immediately since there was always a spreading ripple of male interest in Susanna's wake. It had been inevitable, of course, that Susanna would recover and insist on coming in to help again, but Lilith had hoped for at least a two-week convalescence during which she might be able to come up with some really lasting solution to the Susanna-problem, like a kind and respectable husband who would whisk the girl off to San Francisco or Boston or some other place where Susanna would never find out that her sister was Amnonville's most infamous madam.

Instead Lilith had to submit with what good grace she could muster to all the advantages of having a family again—to Susanna's sisterly hug, to Susanna's apologies for being unavailable to help in the reestablishment of the business, to Susanna's offer to make new velvet draperies since the old ones had burned, to Susanna's suggestion that a nice forest green might look more tasteful at the windows than the previous lush red and gold draperies, and to Susanna's insistence that she was now in perfect health and did not need to return to the hotel immediately. Finally Lilith, in desperation, thought she had hit upon the perfect objection to her sister's presence—Susanna's lack of proper formal evening attire. She suggested, as tactfully as possible, that any girl of Susanna's impeccably respectable upbringing should not be asked to appear in public in unsuitable clothing.

Susanna laughed merrily. "Oh, Lilith," she cried, "I don't think your customers will notice. My goodness, some of them are very informally dressed. Many of the men aren't even wearing suits. In fact, Mr. Quincy is not wearing a suit. But you know, a dress like this is really acceptable in any company, Lilith. Well, of course you know that; you bought it." Susanna looked at herself in the new mirror over the bar and smiled with delight. "And it's so pretty, Lilith. I do thank you for buying it for me. It's ever so much prettier than anything Mama ever bought me. Do you want Mr. Quincy to go home and change his clothes?"

"No," said Lilith, giving up. "I hired him to look after you."

"I ain't got a suit anyway," said Quincy.

Susanna glanced at him sympathetically. "I'm sure my sister would be glad to give you an advance on your wages, Mr. Quincy. Would you like me to help you pick out a suit?"

"I ain't wearing a suit," said Quincy. "Lilith, if you figger—"

"Forget it, Quincy," said Lilith. She spotted Grant Penvennon bearing down on her with a thunderous expression. He was a short, dark, rather brawny Welshman with black hair turning gray and a dour expression, a miner who had come to America to make his fortune and who now owned two of the richest mines in the area because, unlike his countrymen, he was not given to hard living and hard drinking. Instead of frequenting saloons as a young man, he had saved his money and invested it in a wife, children, and all the mining claims he could get his hands on.

To forestall whatever ill-tempered complaint Penvennon had come to make, Lilith introduced him to Susanna, who gave him a sunny smile. "Maybe you could see that Mr. Penvennon has a good table and whatever he wants to eat or drink, Susanna," suggested Lilith. "We owe him a great deal since he was kind enough to rent us this house."

"Oh, wasn't that thoughtful," cried Susanna. "Would you like to sit over here, Mr. Penvennon?" Susanna took his arm and led the surprised mine owner away. He had come to complain about the large hole that had been chopped in his fence to allow passage between the brothel and the saloon, and he had certainly had no intention of having a drink at the Fallen Angel; he never drank in saloons and rarely at home, considering liquor a needless expense. "How kind it was of you to come to my sister's aid," exclaimed Susanna, waving over a young woman who was wearing a shocking dress that exposed both her bosom and her knees. "Mr. Penvennon will have a drink of something, Maizie," said Susanna vaguely.

Penvennon, unsure of how he was to treat a madam's younger sister, pulled a chair out for Susanna and asked if she would have a drink also. He was presuming that since he had been offered a free drink, he would not be expected to pay for Susanna's. Otherwise he would not have asked her.

"My goodness, you're very kind, Mr. Penvennon," said Susanna, "but I don't drink spirits. I will have a cup of tea, however, thank you."

Maizie grimaced and went off, and Penvennon sat down across the table from Susanna, feeling quite disoriented. He was not given to spending time in brothels, and the girl across from him hardly looked like a harlot in her demure dress with its high neck and tucked bodice. In fact, the glossy black hair swept back in a proper chignon, the stray curls escaping around her ears, and the sweet blue eyes all reminded him of a beloved younger sister who had died years ago in Wales.

Penvennon cleared his throat nervously. When the devil was Lilith going to return so that he could make his complaint, he wondered.

"What is your line of work, Mr. Penvennon?" Susanna asked politely.

"Mines," he replied.

"Oh, how interesting. Do you prefer a two-handed pick or a single-jack?" She had talked to several miners and felt that she was now knowledgeable enough to introduce topics of interest to Welshmen.

"I *own* mines, Miss Moran," said Penvennon. "I no longer work them myself."

"How fortunate for you," she exclaimed. "I understand that miner's consumption presents quite a danger to men who actually work in the mines."

Penvennon frowned at her. Although many miners did die of the disease, some before they reached thirty, the topic was considered taboo in Colorado, especially by mine owners.

Susanna sighed. Mr. Penvennon was not the easiest man to talk to. Most men at the Fallen Angel were remarkably garrulous and cheerful. "Do you have a wife and children, Mr. Penvennon?" she asked, trying a new subject without much hope, for she had heard that Welsh miners never had families. Of course, Mr. Penvennon did and found himself drawn into a conversation that covered his wife's church activities and Susanna's favorite hymns; his

son's difficulties with mathematics, which boded ill
for the boy's future in the mining business (Susanna
suggested that he purchase the child an abacus); his
losses in the fire, which seemed not so traumatic
once Susanna had commiserated with him over
them, something no one else in town had done; and
his recollections of Wales in the springtime. Penvennon could not remember when he had had such a
pleasant conversation. He was actually having a
second drink, which he had paid for himself without
even noticing it.

"Do you know something that bothers me, Mr.
Penvennon?" asked Susanna with a very solemn
expression. "And I'm sure it must bother you too. I
can't imagine why the town is called Amnonville. I
consider that a shocking name."

Penvennon's mouth dropped open. He personally
did not care what the town was named, but his wife
frequently made the same complaint. In fact, she
and her friends had been complaining for several
years that they did not want to live in a place called
Amnonville, that it was embarrassing. His wife had
even suggested that he form a committee to have the
town's name changed.

"You know, of course, that the name Amnon
comes from the Bible," said Susanna, "from II
Samuel to be exact. Amnon was one of the sons of
David and was evidently not a very nice person. The
Bible says he 'forced' his sister Tamar. I'm not
exactly sure what it was he forced her to do, but it
was evidently a bad thing because she was very
upset. She put ashes on her head and tore up her
pretty dress of diverse colors, that means many
colors, and cried. My goodness. She was in a state,"
said Susanna earnestly. "And not only that but her

brother Absalom was absolutely furious because
Amnon had forced her to do whatever it was—the
Bible isn't always awfully clear—and Absalom had
his servants kill Amnon. So you can see that Amnon
wasn't the kind of person after whom one would
want one's city named.''

Poor Mr. Penvennon was shocked to have a
young girl refer in his presence to that passage of the
Bible since he did understand what had happened
between Tamar and her brother Amnon. In fact, he
was so taken aback that he could not answer her
objection to the town's name. However, he was
saved the trouble, for Susanna's eyes widened and
she caught her breath. When she set her teacup
down on its saucer, there was a slight rattle because
her hand was shaking. The girl turned to him and
said, ''I must go now, Mr. Penvennon. It was certainly been very nice to meet you.'' Her abrupt
departure caused him to wonder if he had offended
her in some way, perhaps by failing to support her
objections to the name of the town; his wife was certainly offended, and frequently, by his indifference
to the subject.

Susanna's heart rate had increased alarmingly,
and she felt short of breath as she moved toward the
bar and paused beside a tall man in a black suit, an
unusual-looking man with hair so light it was almost
white, but with rather dark skin and dark gray eyes.
She put her hand on his arm and murmured, ''Excuse me, sir,'' to attract his attention. Aaron Court
turned from the bar and glanced down at the small
hand on his arm, then into the wide blue eyes.
Looking into his face, Susanna was now sure that he
was the man who had urged her to jump from the
balcony, who had caught her in his arms, of whom

she had dreamed repeatedly since then. "My name is Susanna Moran," she said softly.

"I know," Court replied, unable to take his eyes off her. Seeing her again brought back the delight he had taken in her the night he had had her at his house, the advantage he had taken of her, actually. He wondered if she was remembering the same things.

"I don't know your name," she prompted.

"Aaron Court," he replied. "Didn't Lilith tell you?"

Susanna shook her head. "I'm not sure. I've been asleep a lot. I have a hard time remembering."

Court took her arm and felt her tremble at his touch as she had before. Still he led her firmly toward a table rather than risk the chance of her having any sudden revelations standing at Lilith's bar.

"I suppose you told me your name yourself, but I can't remember anything after you caught me." Court breathed deeply with relief. She might be failing to remember because she did not want to; either way she obviously had not told Lilith any tales of seduction. "I wonder if I'll ever remember," she mused. "The doctor said I might."

"I wouldn't worry about it," said Court hastily. "Would you like a drink?"

Susanna looked at the table in front of her as if she expected to find a drink there. "I had some tea," she murmured, "but I seem to have forgotten to bring it with me."

Court waved to one of the girls and ordered another cup of tea for Susanna and another drink for himself. He had forgotten his also.

"I want to thank you for saving my life."

He found that direct blue gaze disconcerting. "You don't have to thank me," he muttered. "Anyone you had called out to in the street would have helped you."

"Yes, but—but—" Susanna's cheeks had turned a deep rose. "But I couldn't call out, you see." Court raised his eyebrows questioningly, and Susanna looked away from him, stared down at her hands. "I was too embarrassed. I was in my nightgown." She glanced back up, her face burning. "I imagine you were very shocked to see me there. I should have remembered to put on my dressing gown, but I was so terrified, you see. I mean I woke up, and my room was full of smoke, and—and the fire—the fire was on the stairs, so—so—" She swallowed hard, the terror she had felt that night glowing in her eyes. "And when I saw that the stairs were all afire, I just forgot—"

"Miss Susanna," Court interrupted gently, "I hardly think you could have done anything else, under the circumstances, but get down that hall as fast as you could."

"Yes, but—"

"It doesn't make the slightest bit of difference what you were wearing on the balcony. Be glad that you got off alive."

"Yes, but to jump off in a nightgown—" Her eyes were filled with tears.

"What matters is that your burn and your head injury weren't any worse than they were. You are feeling all right now, aren't you?"

"Yes, thank you."

"Good."

Susanna tried to pick up her teacup, but her hand was trembling again. Court took the cup away from her and set it down; then he covered her hand with his own. "If I were you, Susanna, I would forget that night entirely. It can do no good to dwell on it."

Susanna looked directly into his eyes again and replied, "You're a very nice man, Mr. Court. If there is ever anything I can do to repay you for saving my life and for your kindness, I hope you'll tell me."

Court released her hand abruptly, embarrassed to be receiving gratitude from this very nice girl—gratitude he certainly did not deserve. At that moment he fervently hoped that she never remembered any more about what had happened the night of the fire.

"I think I'll go home now," said Susanna. "I just got up today, and I feel rather tired. I wonder where Mr. Quincy is."

"Who?" Court felt a twinge of jealousy that she already had an admirer.

"Mr. Abner Quincy. He's my bodyguard." Susanna gave Court a deliciously merry smile. "Lilith hired him. Isn't that silly?"

"Not at all," Court muttered. It was obvious that Lilith did not intend to leave her sister unprotected during any other nights. Susanna was rising, and Court rose also to pull out her chair for her, but just as he reached out, her face turned white and she began to waver. He caught her and felt again the soft lines of her body against his, and Susanna, dizzy in his arms, was swept with a wave of sweet sensation, the nature of which she could not even identify. Court's arms tightened around her compulsively as the black lashes lifted from her cheeks and revealed eyes that had the same dazed look of surrender he had seen before. Then he caught himself and lowered her into a chair, asking sharply, "Are you all right, Miss Susanna?"

Susanna was confused, warmly flushed, and light-headed—both from having stayed up too long and from the contact with him. "I think I'd better take you back to the hotel," Court said when she failed to reply.

"Quincy will take her," Lilith interrupted sharply. She had witnessed the last part of the scene and did not like it at all. And she was doubly angry when she discovered that Quincy, having seen Susanna in safe conversation with Mr. Penvennon, had slipped over to the next house with Denver Rose for a quick interlude. Quincy was dragged back and sent off with Susanna, and Lilith, once they were gone, turned on Court and demanded an explanation of the scene she had just witnessed.

"Your sister was thanking me for saving her life," Court replied.

"If she was just thanking you, why was she in your arms?" Lilith snapped.

"Because she's still sick. She should have been home in bed instead of over here where she doesn't belong, talking to strangers. She damned near fainted. And your bodyguard doesn't seem to be doing her much good."

"Stay away from her," Lilith commanded, ignoring the rest.

"She's hardly my type," Court replied dryly, but that was a lie. Holding Susanna again had revived his desire for her, and if she had been in his charge, he was not at all sure that he would have returned her to the hotel.

Lilith, however, nodded thoughtfully. "It's

true," she agreed. "Susanna would hardly be able to fulfill your sophisticated tastes, would she, Aaron? Especially since you like to pay for your pleasure and move on."

Court shifted uneasily. Lilith was wrong. Susanna's youth and inexperience had been surprisingly appealing. And he didn't want to pay for her and forget her, his usual practice; he just wanted her again—badly. Had Susanna been for sale, he wasn't sure that he would have been happy about it. Not that he wanted a lasting relationship. He never had, never would.

"So maybe if you're in need, Aaron, I'll accommodate you tonight. After all, we both know that I am to your taste," said Lilith, her eyebrows rising slightly in amused invitation.

For just a moment he considered substituting the older sister for the younger. Then he said abruptly, "Not tonight, Lilith," and turned on his heel, leaving a surprised and suspicious woman staring after him.

Court mounted and set out for his cabin, asking himself why he was no longer interested in the talented Lilith, why he thought so frequently of a girl whose sweetness and innocence were the last things he needed in his life. He was no boy given to fantasies of love. Love, if it existed, was an invitation to disaster in this country, like offering hostages to the enemy.

Then as he rode into the clearing in front of his house, both Susanna and Lilith were driven from his mind by the crack of a rifle shot that lifted his hat and sent him diving from his saddle. Court rolled to the left of his front door. From there he sent two shots in the direction of the gunman who had missed his head by the smallest fraction. Then he rolled again and waited. No more shots were fired, and he heard, in less than five minutes, the receding beat of hooves. Still he waited to see if anyone was remaining behind to have another try at him, and when he finally did enter his house, he did it with great caution.

He was cold and wet from having lain in a hollow that still retained winter snow, and he was extremely irritated. Whoever had taken the shot at him would undoubtedly try again; he could think of several people who might be interested in frightening or killing him, but until he knew, he could do nothing about the threat except to take precautions, which meant barring his doors and windows tonight and moving back into town tomorrow. Cursing, he set about the task of securing his house for the night.

11

With two subjects on her mind, Lilith Moran visited Quincy's hotel room fairly early the next morning. First, she railed at him for having left Susanna unprotected while he went off with one of the whores.

Quincy was unrepentant. He said, ''I cain't watch her twenty-four hours a day. You find someone who can an give him the job. Me, I thought about the safest person in town she could be with was old straightlaced Grant Penvennon. Not likely he'd do her any harm.''

''She wasn't with Penvennon when I found her. She was with Aaron Court. Do you think he's harmless too?''

''Well, Court ain't so bad,'' Quincy muttered.

Lilith's mouth turned down angrily, and it was with reluctance that she dropped the subject of Aaron Court. "I told you that I don't want her over at the Fallen Angel," she continued. "She wasn't even well, and you let her—"

"Lilith, that lil girl may be sweet an innocent, but she's ever bit as stubborn as you. There's no way you're goin to keep her outa there when she thinks she can help you, less you tell her what's goin on over there. Then maybe—"

"Nobody's going to tell Susanna anything. And I don't want her over there fitting draperies either. Dark green!" Lilith grimaced. "I've decided how to handle her. You're going to keep her so busy, Quincy, that'll she'll be too tired by the end of the day to come over here and bother me."

"Don't see how I can do that."

"You're going to teach her to ride and shoot," said Lilith triumphantly.

"That's a stupid idea. She ain't gonna want to learn to ride an shoot."

"She's going to learn because I'm going to tell her it's necessary if she wants to stay out here."

"Well, I cain't teach no lady to ride sidesaddle. I don't know nothin—"

"Teach her to ride astride. She can get some of those divided skirts."

"Women make piss-poor riders," said Quincy, "and ain't no woman can learn to shoot."

"Good," said Lilith decisively. "The worse she is, the longer it will take her to learn. And the longer it takes her to learn, the longer she'll be out of my hair. Take her out and buy her all the things she needs—riding clothes, horses, guns, whatever. That should use up a couple of days. Then take her out-

side of town and start teaching her. I want her so
exhausted at the end of the day—"

"I got the picture," said Quincy gloomily.

"I want you over there in a half hour to take her
shopping. I'll have talked to her by then. Don't
make her sick, of course, but be sure that she's
asleep on her feet by nightfall."

Grumbling, Abner Quincy went over to the
bureau and took his guns and holsters off the top.
"Teachin women to shoot," he muttered. "I ain't
the man I used to be."

Lilith ignored his complaints and swept across the
hall to confront her sister.

Susanna was quite astounded to hear that Lilith
would never have a moment's peace of mind until
Susanna had acquired the essential skills to survive
in the West. Doubtfully she had to agree that
perhaps there were places where one could not go on
foot or in a buggy and that she might need to learn
to ride a horse, but she was not happy to learn that a
lady would not be safe riding sidesaddle over rough
terrain, that she would have to learn to ride astride
like a man. As for shooting, she assured Lilith that
she could never shoot anyone.

"If someone is shooting at you, Susanna, it would
be insane, even suicidal, not to shoot back," said
Lilith.

"But who would shoot at me?" asked Susanna.
"No one ever shoots at anyone in St. Louis. Oh
well, maybe down on the waterfront where—"

"This isn't St. Louis, Miss Susanna," said
Quincy, coming in on the end of the discussion. "I
just heard that someone tried to bushwhack Aaron
Court last night." Susanna turned pale. "An a
course he put three bullets into that thievin bastard

Elias Packard the night after the fire when he caught Packard tryin to steal his safe with all his lawyer papers in it.''

"Is Mr. Court a lawyer?" asked Susanna weakly.

"Yep. Court's a lawyer, and the Packards is outlaws. Hills is swarmin with them bastards."

Lilith was scowling at him for mentioning Aaron Court, of whom she did not want her sister reminded, but Abner assumed that the scowl was because he had used rough language in front of the girl. "Pardon my language, miss," he added without much conviction.

"Oh certainly," Susanna whispered. She was horrified to hear that Mr. Court had come so close to death on two occasions.

"And of course there's hunting," said Lilith. "You might need to shoot your own dinner sometime." Susanna gazed at her sister open-mouthed, having always believed that meat for the table came from a shop.

"Yep," agreed Abner craftily. "Might be we could provide you with some game for your place, Miss Lilith, if Miss Susanna was to get to be a good shot."

Susanna brightened at the idea that she might be able to help her sister by providing supplies for the restaurant, although it made her shudder to think of actually shooting some poor animal. It would probably bleed and—

"I think you'd better start shopping right away for all the things you'll need, Susanna. If you feel up to it, of course. And I don't want you coming over to the—ah—restaurant. The excitement is too much for you."

"Lilith, I can't keep spending your money this

way. Shouldn't we wait until—"

"Money is not a problem, Susanna. Charge what you need to my accounts. Now I have to go."

"But what about the forest green draperies?"

Lilith was already gone.

At four in the afternoon Abner Quincy, having carried out his employer's instructions, returned a very tired Susanna to the hotel, both of them loaded down with packages. They had purchased a gentle horse, a saddle and bridle, a riding outfit and boots, a heavy jacket to ward off the spring cold, and guns and ammunition—the items which had caused the most trouble, for Abner had decided that the one really impossible thing to teach a woman would be shooting from the hip. It ought to take six months just to teach the girl to draw a handgun from a holster without shooting herself in the toe, which, if it happened, would certainly keep her out of the Fallen Angel. Consequently, they had shopped not only for pistols, but for holsters with accompanying gun belts, equipment which was simply not made for small, slim-hipped girls. The gun belts were too long and had to be completely remade for her, with time-consuming measurements that necessitated having the gunsmith's wife brought to do the measuring— this expedient at Susanna's insistence. Then they found that the holsters, if slung low for fast shooting, flapped against Susanna's knees. The problems were endless. It was all Abner could do to keep from doubling over with laughter, while Susanna was hard put to keep from yawning, and the gunsmith from bursting into a furious denunciation of the whole idea of teaching a young girl to shoot the arsenal that Quincy had insisted on buying for her.

Abner managed to get the door of the hotel open for her, and Susanna inched in, her packages obstructing her vision so that she collided with a man attempting to leave. He steadied her courteously, but neither of them moved to recover the packages, for the man was Aaron Court, and for several seconds they simply stood gazing at one another, his hand on her arm while Quincy grumbled and retrieved the scattered purchases himself.

Finally, with difficulty, Susanna looked away. "I've dropped all the parcels, Mr. Quincy," she murmured.

"I seen that," Quincy replied dryly. "Maybe I better git em upstairs myself."

Susanna glanced back at Court. "I understand that you are a lawyer, Mr. Court." He nodded. "I wonder if I might make an appointment to see you at your office sometime," she continued. "I do need to consult a lawyer."

"I'd be glad to help you, Miss Susanna," Court replied, "but as it happens, I don't have an office. Lost it in the fire."

"I'm so sorry. Where do you conduct business then?"

Court shrugged. "Wherever I can. Folks are just glad to make do these days. If you want to go into the dining room, we could have some—ah—tea, and you could tell me what your legal problem is."

"Thank you. That would be very nice." Susanna dispatched a reluctant Quincy upstairs with her packages, promising that she would be up herself in fifteen or twenty minutes.

Court satisfied his immediate desire to touch her by taking her arm as they entered the dining room and then resting his hand lightly on her shoulder as he seated her at a table near the window, and each time he did touch her, he sensed the sharp intake of her breath. He found the awareness between them almost painful and knew that she found it confusing, for she dropped her eyes hastily every time their glances crossed.

"You and Quincy certainly did a lot of shopping today," he remarked to break the tension.

Susanna sighed. "Oh, yes. We were buying all the guns and things."

"Guns?" Court's mouth quirked in an amused smile.

"Yes, Lilith says I must learn to shoot and to ride. She says that every woman in the West should know these things, but Clara—she's my companion—Clara says that's nonsense, but of course I must do what Lilith says. She's so good to me and knows all about everything."

"Indeed she does," Court agreed dryly.

"Yes, but I'm afraid it will take a very long time. I shan't be able to help Lilith with her business, and that seems unfair."

Court grinned. "No doubt Lilith has taken that into consideration." He now understood the purpose of the riding and shooting lessons. Trust Lilith to find some way to distract her sister and keep her as far away as possible from the Fallen Angel without actually forcing her to leave town.

His thoughts were interrupted when their waitress dropped the tray on the table. The tea cakes cartwheeled off to either side; Court's bourbon and Susanna's tea splashed out in a circular ripple pattern that drove both of them out of their seats; and the waitress fell into uncontrollable giggles behind her hand. While Susanna turned a puzzled stare on the girl, the assistant hotel manager rushed up to apologize to Court and hustle the useless waitress off.

"What can be the matter with that poor young woman?" murmured Susanna as Court seated her at another table. "Could she have been having hysterics, do you think?"

"More likely the drummers have been feeding her whiskey," replied Court.

"Really?" Susanna frowned thoughtfully. "Perhaps that also explains why another waitress fell down the other day for no discernible reason. I was getting up to assist her to her feet, but Mrs. Schmidt wouldn't allow it, which I thought very unfeeling of her at the time."

Susanna accepted her second cup of tea and looked inquiringly at Court's new glass. "What are you drinking, Mr. Court?" she asked.

"Bourbon."

"Oh."

"Are you afraid that I'll drop the tea cakes in your lap or that I won't be able to concentrate on business when I'm drinking?" He was giving her a sardonic smile again, and Susanna looked away because she was not sure what the smile meant.

"No doubt you are more accustomed to hard spirits than the waitress, Mr. Court. Now about my problem—it regards money." Court raised his eyebrows with another dry smile, thinking that perhaps Susanna and Lilith had more in common than might have been apparent initially. Susanna met that smile with a serious demeanor. "You see, I inherited quite a bit of money from my mother and father," she explained. "And I need to know about two things. First, I want my sister to have half of it, but I'm afraid she won't accept it because, you see, it wasn't actually left to her."

"In that case, perhaps you should follow your parents' wishes," suggested Court.

Susanna shook her head. "I'm sorry that you should think me a disobedient or an ungrateful daughter, Mr. Court, but you see, my parents were never very kind to my sister. In fact, I always felt that it was their fault as much as hers that she ran away. And she was very young too, no older than I. I would have been so frightened if I had been in her position. And I would like to make up to her for all the years when she had no family and had to make her own way. I love Lilith very much," she concluded softly.

"I see that," Court replied. "Do you mind if I ask how much your parents left you?" Susanna told him, and he stared out the window thoughtfully. Finally he said, "You can afford to give her half, if that's what you want to do. You'll still have enough to live on comfortably."

"And can it be arranged so that the money is transferred to her before she can refuse it?"

"I can arrange a transfer, but not without her consent. For that matter, you must have a lawyer who handled the estate. He could handle the transfer also."

"He's not here," said Susanna simply. "And I don't like him; he wouldn't approve of what I want to do. Then I need to know how to go about having the money transferred here and where to put it."

"You're planning to live here?"

"Of course. Lilith is my family and I hers," said Susanna earnestly. "I wouldn't want to live anywhere else."

"Then if you want me to handle it, you can give me your St. Louis lawyer's name."

Susanna smiled happily at him and immediately took from her reticule a piece of paper that had the lawyer's name and address on it. As she passed it to him their hands touched, and her eyes widened, the color flowing into her cheeks. "I had one other question, Mr. Court." Court waited, staring at her, wanting to touch her again. "My sister has asked me several times about the night of the fire, and I can't seem to remember anything after I jumped from the balcony."

"That's because of your head injury. You were unconscious most of the time."

"All of the time?"

"No," said Court slowly. "When I couldn't find your sister or a doctor, I took you back to my house to treat the burn. You did come to, but you were in a great deal of pain, so I gave you opium." Susanna's mouth rounded in a surprised little gasp, but Court smiled. "The opium didn't hurt you; it just dulls the pain and makes you sleep, although I wouldn't recommend that anyone take it frequently." His smile widened. Then since it was obvious that Susanna was about to ask him another question, he forestalled her by saying, "How is your arm?" He was sitting beside her at the table and took her hand. Although he could feel her tense up, he persisted, "Is it healing well?"

"Yes," Susanna whispered. "Clara says the salve must have been very good."

"It is." Court's voice was low, with a timber that made her feel breathless and light-headed. He unbuttoned the cuff of her sleeve and ran his fingers gently over the scar. "A Mexican friend of mine gave me that salve," he explained. Susanna watched him with rounded eyes, her lips parted. He glanced at her as he buttoned the cuff again and then straightened the curled fingers of her hand to inspect the palm. "You don't know how lucky you are that the fire didn't touch your hand." He touched her hand, running his fingertips lightly over the inner surface. When he looked up to find her eyes dilated, he wondered idly if she would faint if he were to kiss that sensitive palm instead of stroking it. He wondered what she would do if he were to—his attention was abruptly distracted from Susanna when he saw, through the window over her shoulder, a man taking careful aim at them from across the street. Without even thinking, Court swept Susanna with him to the floor as the shots crashed over their heads.

Court did not move, waiting to see if more gunfire would follow. Around them people were screaming and running. In the circle of his arms, Susanna looked directly up into his eyes. "What happened?" she whispered.

"Don't move, and don't be afraid," he whispered back. "Someone shot at us."

"Oh." Susanna did as she was told. She remained on the floor behind the table with his body shielding hers. "Lilith was certainly right," she whispered. "I shall start my lessons tomorrow if people are going to shoot at me while I'm at tea."

Court chuckled softly. "I imagine I was being shot at, not you, Miss Susanna."

"Oh. I'm sorry."

The incongruity of the whole situation overcame Court. He was lying on the floor in the dining room of the Hotel McFadden with at least fifty people milling about, shrieking and shouting, while he held in his arms a girl who shivered when he touched the palm of her hand, a girl he wanted very much to kiss. So he kissed her, exploring again for a brief moment those petal-soft lips, and Susanna's eyes closed as she drifted into a state of suspended delight. Then Court admitted to himself that the other fifty people, plus those who were crowding in, might notice them, so he cautiously rose and helped Susanna to her feet. "Shall I escort you to your room now?" he asked quietly.

"What about the murderers?" she whispered.

Court had recognized the man behind the gun. "Time enough to deal with the Packards later," he replied as he took her arm. And he did have every intention of dealing with the Packards. Once he had seen Elias Packard into jail and ridden out with the posse, he had considered his part in the episode done. Now he intended to kill Hogshead Bates at the first opportunity; it was better, he reflected, to know the face of one's enemy. And as for Elias, Court might even see him to the gallows, if that could be accomplished.

"Good evening, Susanna," he said politely at her door. He was sorely tempted to kiss her upturned face, but he might then have to kill her bodyguard, who was evidently housed across the hall, and Court reasoned that, having acquired the Packard Gang as enemies, he did not need more.

12

Susanna fell asleep thinking of Court's kiss, slept badly, and woke the next morning knowing that she had dreamed of him, although she could not remember the dream, only that she felt troubled and restless. To dispel this uneasiness, she left her bed an hour early and dressed in her new riding clothes, ready to throw herself into activity. A very reluctant Abner Quincy found himself out in the hotel stable with the first light of dawn, trying to show Susanna how to mount a horse. Susanna was determined but hopelessly inept. It was as Abner had predicted: the girl would never be a rider if he gave her lessons for fifty years. In the first place, she was afraid of the horse, a horse that was so gentle Abner would have refused to ride it. Susanna had asked him at least fifty times before they reached the outskirts of the town if horses ever bit people. She also wanted to know if horses became rabid as dogs did. Abner had never heard of a rabid horse and assured her that hers was obviously not rabid since it was plodding calmly along, even under her poor management, without foaming at the mouth or chasing its tail.

As they rode up the valley, Susanna wanted to know if her horse could be expected to suddenly rear up like a horse in a statue in St. Louis did, carrying with it its famous military rider. She was sure that the general must have fallen off and been killed the very second after the sculptor had witnessed the scene. Abner did not bother to answer that question. Instead he insisted that Susanna practice using the reins to turn the horse to one side and the other and to stop the horse. Susanna replied that her horse seemed to do whatever his horse did, and she therefore felt that her horse might be more complacent if not bothered by having its mouth pulled about. Abner insisted. In all this time they had never moved faster than a walk.

"Now we're goin to trot, Miss Susanna."

"What's that?" she asked suspiciously.

"That's goin a little faster."

"I don't want to go any faster. This is as fast as I ever want to go. In fact, I wish we could go slower."

"The only way we can go slower is to stop," said Abner digustedly. "Now you better listen to what I tell you about trottin because pretty soon I'm goin to slap your horse on the rump, an you're going to be trottin whether you want to or not, an it's better to know how to do it." He carefully explained and demonstrated several times. Susanna did not want to try. Abner explained and demonstrated again; then, without forewarning, he slapped the horse, who trotted down the road with her rider bobbing up and down inexpertly. Abner winced to watch her. "Never make a rider," he muttered. "I knew it."

When he caught up with Susanna, who would certainly have stopped her horse if she could, Susanna cried out, "I am going to have to have a softer saddle, Mr. Quincy. I think we should go right back to town and turn this saddle in on a softer model. I feel terrible. I hurt!"

"They don't make softer saddles."

"Nonsense. Chairs come in different degrees of softness. I'm sure saddles do too."

"Now we're gonna try shootin," said Abner.

"It couldn't be worse," said Susanna glumly. Abner agreed. However, before he could teach her to shoot, he had to teach her to get out of the saddle, another operation of which she was terrified, sure that the horse was going to take off at a dead run as soon as she lifted her leg over the saddle horn.

Both Abner and Susanna were so exhausted after the traumatic riding lesson that they moved the lunch schedule up and sat down on a log to eat at eleven o'clock. Both were ravenous and devoured the meal packed by the hotel with little conversation beyond Susanna's ill-received complaint that he ought not to drink spirits when they were going to be shooting guns after lunch. "You might shoot yourself or me," she suggested plaintively.

"*You* might shoot yourself or me," said Abner, taking a deep swallow, "but I ain't gonna shoot nobody I don't mean to shoot. Never have, never will."

"You mean that you have shot someone?" asked Susanna, alarmed.

"Yep. Yer sister wouldn't a hired me if I didn't have a rep as a fast gun, an I wouldn't a taken the job if I wasn't slowin down. You gonna eat the rest of that there chicken leg?"

"Yes," said Susanna.

The afternoon's activities provided Quincy with a shock he would never have expected. He first explained the mechanism of her rifle to Susanna and showed her how to load it, a process which she mastered, although she was lamentably slow about it. Then he explained how to shoot the rifle, demonstrating with great expertise. Finally he set up several bottles on a distant rock, positioned Susanna carefully for a prone shot, and told her to bang away. Susanna shot a bottle off the rock. Quincy blinked. "Beginner's luck," he muttered. He positioned her for a kneeling shot. She shot the bottle off the rock. He positioned her for a standing shot. She shot that bottle off that rock. All afternoon Quincy had to ride his horse back and forth setting up targets on rocks, which Susanna promptly shot off. She shot all of his bottles and remains of his bottles off rocks until there were no bottles or

anything else from the remains of lunch to shoot at.
Then she shot smaller rocks off larger rocks. Finally
Quincy said, "If that don't beat all. Shoot that bird."
He pointed to a bird flying in over some trees to
their left. Susanna missed the bird. "Well, I was
beginnin to think you wasn't never gonna miss
nothin. Let's go home."

"Can we walk?" Susanna asked.

"No." Quincy scowled at her, but he did help her
into the saddle, and he did not insist that she
practice trotting.

When they had left in the early morning, the
streets had been all but deserted, a good thing considering Susanna's lack of talent as a horsewoman.
When they returned, the streets were busy, and
Quincy warned her that she would have to control
her horse rather than counting on the horse to
follow his or figure out what to do for itself. "You'll
sure run over someone, or bump into someone an
fall off if you don't control that horse," he
admonished. "About the only thing you don't have
to worry about is the horse runnin off with you.
That horse ain't got the gumption to run off. If she
had, she'd a done it already."

"Well, that's a blessing at least," muttered
Susanna. She was terrified at the prospect of trying
to ride responsibly among crowds of people, but
when they had come several blocks into town, she
found that she was not having all that much
difficulty. The horse obediently moved to the right
and to the left when Susanna pulled on the appro-
priate rein, and once, when necessary, the horse
stopped on command. Susanna was quite elated by
the time they were approaching the hotel. Perhaps
the horse had been impressed by her talent as a rifle-

woman, she thought complacently. As she edged around the last corner, she spotted Aaron Court striding along the sidewalk; gaily she called out to him and waved, but he failed to acknowledge her greeting.

Court had stopped dead in the middle of the sidewalk to stare at a man coming out the door of a tavern. "Bates!" he called sharply. The man halted in the doorway. "You've been looking for me, isn't that right?" asked Court.

"Don't know what you mean." Bates had paled noticeably.

"You took a shot at me in the hotel dining room and another from ambush out at my place."

Bates shook his head, his hand now hovering near his gun. Citizens were diving for shelter all along the street, and Quincy, seeing what was happening, spurred his horse and cried, "Follow me, Miss Susanna. Hurry."

Court heard her name and, in fact, could see her peripherally, but he did not move his eyes from the undecided outlaw. "I'm going to take you in to jail, Bates. Press assault charges against you." Bates went for his gun then, but as soon as he moved, Court shot him in the chest. Horrified, making no attempt to control her horse at all, Susanna watched as the man wavered, his mouth filling with blood. As he pitched forward, he managed to fire the shot that came too late to forestall Aaron Court. The bullet went wide and grazed the haunch of Susanna's horse, sending it into a terrified burst of speed. As soon as Bates hit the ground, Court whirled in time to see Susanna being carried down the street, clinging awkwardly to her mare's neck.

He glanced down at Bates, whose blood was pouring into a widening puddle on the sidewalk, and then sprang onto his own horse, tethered at a rail in front of the tavern. "Get the sheriff, Abner," he shouted to Quincy, who had turned back. "I'll catch up with her." Quincy did as he was told, for Court was already a block away and more likely to get to the girl before she fell off.

The lawyer was relieved to see that Susanna was still in the saddle when he managed to pull his horse even with hers at the northern outskirts of the town. Edging in on her, he reached across and grasped the reins. Fifty feet further on, he had stopped both horses and lifted her from the saddle. With his hands still resting gently at her waist, Court started to reassure her, but Susanna was staring into his eyes with horror and revulsion, still seeing in her mind that face with blood pouring from the mouth. "You murdered him," she said.

That was hardly what Court had expected to hear from her. He had expected her to be shocked by the shooting, certainly, and to be terrified by her wild ride, but he had not expected to be accused of murder. "Why the hell didn't you get out of there when you saw what was happening?" he snapped.

"Why? So I couldn't testify against you in court?"

"There won't be any trial, Susanna," he said impatiently.

"But you murdered that man in cold blood."

"That man you're defending so hotly was the man who shot at us yesterday, the man who shot at me from ambush last week."

"You killed him."

"Did you expect me to wait for him to ambush me again?"

"You could have told the sheriff."

"The hell I could. If you'll remember, I told Bates I was going to take him in. That's why he drew on me."

Susanna shook her head. Her eyes were filling with tears, and she cried out bitterly, "You're a murderer." She had been romanticizing Court as the handsome stranger who had rescued her from death; whose presence filled her with sweet tension; whose kiss, though brief, had raised a delicious fire in her blood. Now superimposed on her infatuation was the mental picture of a man whose face was tightened in the agony of death with ugly, red blood dribbling, then pouring from his mouth as he collapsed in a crowded street with Court's bullet in his chest.

"Susanna," began Court reasonably, putting a restraining hand on her arm.

She drew back terrified. "Don't touch me," she whispered.

Aaron Court's mouth tightened. "Don't touch you?" he echoed sharply. He found himself suddenly furiously angry that she should so unfairly accuse him, unfairly turn before his eyes from sweet and promising vulnerability to terrified disgust. "Don't touch you?" He clamped hard hands on her shoulders and drew her toward him. "That wasn't what you said yesterday when I kissed you. And that certainly wasn't what you said the night of the fire when we—"

He stopped himself with difficulty. Susanna's cheeks were flushed with humiliation, although he could not be sure whether the humiliation was a result of his reference to the kiss or to—he lowered his head and kissed her again, brutally, his mouth bruising her lips, his arms crushing her soft breasts against his chest. There was no sweet response from her this time. When he finally loosened his hold on her, thinking to reestablish his mastery with gentle persuasion rather than force, she tore herself away from him and, whirling, fled like a frightened child toward town. Aaron cursed both himself and her—himself because, like a fool, he had frightened her when soft words might have won her, and her because he could not very well be seen running after her through the streets of the town or, worse, riding her down. And what the devil was he to do with her horse, which she had left behind?

Susanna ran until the dirt paths gave way to wooden sidewalks under her boot heels, until fire-blackened shambles gave way to untouched structures, until the occasional passerby gave way to crowds of people impeding her way, until the breath rasped burning into her lungs, and still she ran—pursued not by Court himself but by the picture in her mind of a man dying in the street and by the angry kiss of the man who had killed him. Her eyes were still blurred with tears when she tore by Abner Quincy, who had been coming in search of her and had to turn back and dismount to catch her.

"Miss Susanna," he said sharply when she tried to pull away from him. "You all right, Miss Susanna? That horse throw you?"

"No," she gasped. She brushed the tears from her eyes.

"Where is yer horse?" he demanded.

Susanna gulped and tried to order her whirling thoughts. She had forgotten completely about the

horse in her haste to get away from Court. "Mr.
Court. He has the horse."

"Well, where's Court?" Quincy demanded
impatiently. "Why ain't you with him?"

"He's bringing the horse back." The last thing
that Susanna wanted to tell her guardian was that
Aaron Court had kissed her brutally in the street as
if she were some—as if he had some claim on—as if
she would welcome his—her thoughts stuttered dis-
jointedly. "He has the horse," she repeated lamely.

"So he's got the horse. Why ain't you with him?
You shouldn't be runnin round this town by yerself.
There's men who—ah—who nice gals don't—"

"Men like Mr. Court, you mean?" Susanna
demanded defensively. "Did you want me to come
back with a murderer? He just shot down a man in
the street. Didn't you see it? He just—"

"Court ain't no murderer, Miss Susanna," said
Quincy firmly. "That's foolishness."

"But he—"

"He shot down Hogshead Bates, and Bates—he'd
already taken a couple of shots at Court—not face
to face, mind you, neither. And Bates drew first. It
don't make it murder when Court shoots back."

"He killed him."

"Good riddance," replied Quincy shortly. "You
don't know nothin about such things, Miss
Susanna, so better you keep quiet. There's
murderers, an they likes killin, and there's regular
folks, an they shoots if they has to. Court don't
enjoy killin. No more do I, an I killed a few in my
time."

"But—"

"Besides, Bates was one of the Packards, an

they're all murderers. Now let's git back to the hotel."

Susanna could not believe that her protector was defending the actions and morals of Aaron Court.

As Quincy was hustling her up to her room, Court, his mouth tight with anger, led her horse back to town and tossed its reins to the stable boy at the hotel. Then he turned his own horse toward the sheriff's office. He wanted to be sure, first, that Bates was dead; then he intended to see, if he could, that a few more Packards died. Had he stopped to analyze his feelings, he might have realized that his sudden determined interest in breaking the hold of the Packards on the area stemmed not from any sense of civic duty, which might have asserted itself at any time during the last few years, but from the bitterness born of their interference with his own affairs, especially his interest in Susanna and hers in him, for without considering the consequences of his desires, he had been determined to have her again, and his own sense of her attraction to him had been sharp and satisfying—until she had turned on him that afternoon for no just reason.

When Court strode grimly into the sheriff's office, the sheriff was startled at the expression on his face. "Bates dead?" Court demanded.

"Yep. He—"

"You satisfied it was self-defense?" It was more a challenge than a question.

"Well, sure. Folks saw him draw on you. But you shouldn't a rode off like—"

"When's Elias going to be tried?"

"Well—" The sheriff scratched his neck reflectively. "It's always a problem when we got a

Packard to deal with. You know that, Court. Anyways I got a homestead I gotta prove up. I ain't got time for—''

''The judge is in town. When's the trial set for?''

''It was set for next Monday,'' the sheriff replied slowly, ''but now we ain't got a prosecutor. Seems—''

''What about Talland?''

The sheriff grinned. ''Seems his feet was gettin cold when he heard about that shot took at you yesterday. Then today, well—'' The sheriff spread his hands ''—today when you an Bates shot it out in the street, well, Talland's feet just plumb froze. He's on his way to Denver right now.'' Before Court could comment, the sheriff hastened to add, ''Ain't likely no one else is gonna volunteer neither. Might even have a hard time gettin a jury. Don't have to worry about a jury though, when we ain't got a prosecutor.''

''I'll take care of it,'' Court snapped.

The sheriff raised his eyebrows at this announcement, and behind him, Elias Packard, who had been listening and grinning through the whole conversation, although ignored by the participants, called out, ''How you gonna do anything, Court, when my daddy's gonna git you fer shootin' me an fer killin Bates? Maybe I'll git you myself. Sure I ain't gonna be in here much longer. No sir, Daddy'll be comin fer me, and he'll be comin fer you too.''

''Then I don't have anything to lose, do I?'' Court turned abruptly and left.

''Wha'd he mean by that?'' Elias wondered vacantly.

''Maybe he means he's gonna bushwhack you

through the window of the cell," suggested the sheriff.

Elias shifted uneasily. "I'm under yer protection."

"Everybody knows I'm a lazy sheriff," was the amused reply. "Ain't that why you Packards always liked me?"

13

While Susanna, refusing dinner, went to bed and huddled under her covers, pursued in dreams by the dark, angry face and hard lips of Aaron Court, Court was down the hall in the room of Judge Amon Galt accepting a cup of tea from Galt's circuit-riding wife Amanda and politely inquiring as to what the judge intended to do about the sudden disappearance of the local prosecutor.

"I just found out about Talland myself," snapped the judge with sharp ill nature. "Not that I'm surprised. Every time there's a Packard on the docket, something happens to—"

"One lump or two, dear?" asked his wife sweetly, interrupting the anticipated tirade.

"None," said the judge. "I'll have bourbon and so will Court."

"Two then," said his wife, dropping two lumps into his tea and passing him the cup.

The judge glared at her. "If you're interested in the Packard case getting to trial, why don't you prosecute it yourself, Aaron?"

Court suppressed a tight smile. "I might." The judge, who was lighting a thin cigar offered to him by his guest, paused and glanced warily at the lawyer from under bushy gray eyebrows. "Under the right circumstances," Court added.

"What circumstances?"

Court stretched long legs in front of him and blew smoke from his own cigar toward the ceiling. "First off, I don't want any trouble about picking the jury. I want men with guts and men with cause to hate the Packards."

"The first are scarce, the second numerous in this section of the country," said the judge dryly.

"I'll give you a list."

"What else?"

"Just one thing. I want him taken out and hung as soon as he's found guilty."

"A man is innocent until proven guilty, Aaron," Amanda Galt reminded him gently.

"Not a Packard," said Court with grim certitude. He then stared challengingly at the judge. "Do you agree?"

"How many horses did they take that night they hit town after the fire?" asked the judge curiously.

"Thirty, forty."

"Maybe you can get a jury this time." The judge made a steeple of his hands and contemplated them thoughtfully.

"Well?" prompted Aaron.

Galt nodded. "You've got a deal, Court. You'll have your jury, if you can find it, and your hanging, if you can get the verdict."

"Within the hour?"

"The trial?" asked the judge amazed.

"The hanging."

"Within an hour of the verdict," the judge agreed.

"We'll try him tomorrow," said Court.

"Not wasting any time, are you?"

"You can think of some reason to move the trial up," Court replied. "Be just as well if the other Packards don't hear about it till afterward."

The judge smiled. "Then they can come to town after us instead of Elias."

"Sufficient unto the day," said Court indifferently. "I'll worry about the rest of them when I've seen the first one to the gallows."

Court went from the judge's room straight to the Fallen Angel where he commandeered a drink and a corner table in Grant Penvennon's former parlor and began to make up a list of potential jurors and witnesses for the trial, all of whom he planned to contact before morning. As he began the preparations for his night's work, Quincy too had entered the Fallen Angel and was closeted with Lilith, reporting that her sister was safely tucked in bed, shaken by her first experience with gunplay in the streets, although none the worse for it. "But she shore is down on Aaron Court," Quincy concluded. "Figgers him fer a cold-blooded murderer."

"Good," snapped Lilith.

"Bout time someone turned on one a them Packards, I say," said Quincy.

"They always pay their bills when they're in here," Lilith replied.

"The more they git away with, the more they're gonna try," said Quincy gloomily. "Maybe they'll decide yer next."

"That's why I have Carlos—to discourage that kind of thinking," said Lilith confidently.

Quincy grinned. "A few more shootin' lessons, and you can hire your sister as an extra gun."

"Just keep her out of my hair," snapped Lilith. Quincy wandered out of the office and into the saloon to drink and watch the gambling, but his attention was diverted when he saw Aaron in the corner, sipping bourbon and making notes on a piece of paper. The old gunman threaded his way among the restless crowds of whores and waitresses, gamblers and cowboys, miners and businessmen until he came to Court's table and said quietly, "Evenin, Aaron."

Court glanced up, frowning. "Quincy." He nodded.

Without further invitation the older man sat down, putting his hat on the floor and his drink on the table. "How come you sent me off after the sheriff this afternoon, an then you didn't bring Miss Susanna back after you got her?"

"Wasn't my idea," said Court shortly. "Seems she didn't want to be escorted by a murderer."

"Uh-huh. Well, you gotta keep in mind, Aaron, that she probably never seen no one shot down in the street an chokin on his own blood. Likely that kinda spoiled her image of you as a handsome knight, rescuer of fair ladies, an all that foolishness gals likes to dream about."

"Think she'd have been happier if I'd run a sword into the son of a bitch?" asked Court dryly.

"Likely," agreed Quincy, grinning. "But me, I was just as glad to see you used a gun. Mighta been you bleedin in the street if'n you had to wait to git out a sword."

"You ever noticed, Quincy, that where the Packards are concerned, the law doesn't apply, and it's every man for himself?"

"Yeah, I noticed it, but after that horse-stealing raid they pulled the night you shot Elias, I'm not so sure folks wouldn't like to see the law take a hand."

"Enough to testify or serve on the jury? Take you, for instance, Quincy; would you have the guts to testify that you saw Elias shoot down the Roberts boy up above the smelter?"

"We talkin 'Wouldn't it be nice if we could git Elias in court' or we talkin the real thing?"

"Elias is going to be tried—and hung," said Court grimly. "You going to testify?"

"You gonna testify?" Quincy countered.

"I'm going to prosecute."

"Are ya now?" Quincy thought about it. "How you gonna git him tried and hung afore Job gits here?"

"By being quick about it."

"Sounds sensible. Charge him with killin Bert Bob Smith too. I got there in time to take a shot at Elias, but he was already reloadin an into the woods."

Aaron nodded. "Be at the courthouse at ten, then. Who else do you know that can testify? Or serve on the jury? I want men who can keep their mouths shut about the trial, who aren't afraid of the Packards, or at least who are mad enough about losing horses to testify even if they are scared."

"Let's see who you got so far." Quincy glanced at the list and began to suggest names.

14

The next morning Susanna awoke in her hotel room before the sun rose and climbed wearily from her bed to dress for another shooting and riding lesson. As she moved about the room quietly so as not to awaken Mrs. Schmidt, the scenes from the previous

afternoon ran around and around in her mind—the
cold-eyed face of Aaron Court as he called out in the
street to the man coming through the swinging doors
of the tavern; the smoking gun that had appeared so
suddenly in Court's hand; the other man falling,
bleeding; her horse's terrified and terrifying flight
through the crowded streets of the town with the
sound in her ears of another horse thundering up
beside her, crowding close, and then suddenly
Aaron stopping both horses and lifting her from the
saddle; and last his terrible anger when she had
accused him of murder and the feel of his mouth on
hers, punishing her for what was his fault. Susanna
blinked back tears as she pulled her hair tightly over
her ears in the semidarkness and pinned it into a
severe knot at the back of her neck. The light knock
at her door reminded her that Quincy would be
breakfasting with her in the hotel dining room and
that she did not want to be seen with red eyes,
especially since Quincy had been very short with her
about her opinion of Court. "Mr. Quincy?" she
whispered against the door.

"Tell Miz Schmidt to come down too," he
whispered back. "I need to talk to you both."

After awakening an ill-tempered Clara, the girl
joined Quincy in the hall, and they went down together to the dining room where, for some reason,
he refused a seat by the window and insisted on a
table over in an isolated corner.

As Susanna was waiting for the remote table to be
prepared, Court entered the room, looking tired and
grim as the result of a long night spent recruiting
witnesses and jurors, the lists of which he had just
presented to the judge. When their glances met, she
colored and turned quickly away, but not quickly
enough to miss how icy and gray his eyes were, how

grim his mouth as he bowed to her. Susanna fled
to the isolated table that Quincy had chosen, while
Court, strolling casually among the tables in the
more crowded section of the dining room, greeted
friends and ultimately joined a family party near the
windows at the invitation of a laughing blonde girl,
a girl who, for no reason that Susanna had been able
to fathom, had snubbed her one day in the hotel
parlor when Susanna had attempted to strike up a
friendly conversation. Susanna speculated sadly on
the values of a seemingly respectable family who
would let their young daughter smile and flutter her
eyelashes at a man like Aaron Court, who—

"So you see I won't be able to take you fer yer
lesson today, Miss Susanna," Quincy finished.

"What?" Susanna turned a blank look in his
direction.

"If'n you don't like Court shinin up to that
Mayburn girl, maybe you better apologize fer callin
him a murderer," said Quincy dryly. "I don't think
he was any too pleased about that, specially when he
jus rode breakneck through half the town to stop yer
runaway horse."

"My horse wouldn't have been running away if
Mr. Court had not been shooting people down in the
streets," said Susanna resentfully.

"Saved yer skin during the fire too, didn't he?"

"I thanked him for that," she replied stiffly.
"And I am not interested in his relations with
Miss—Miss Mayburn."

"Then suppose you pay attention to what I'm
tryin to tell you. Mornin, Clara." Abner nodded to
Susanna's companion. "We ordered fer you. I was
tellin Miss Susanna, I gotta be in court to testify
against Elias Packard this mornin."

Clara sniffed. "Don't bother about that, Abner.

Jeremy Tallard hightailed it to Denver as soon as he heard that a Packard was comin to trial. There's no one to prosecute Elias.''

"Aaron Court's gonna do that hisself.''

"Is he now? Figgers he's got nothin to lose, I suppose.''

"More like he's a leetle bit peeved with em.''

"Does the judge know that Mr. Court killed one of Mr. Elias Packard's companions just yesterday?'' asked Susanna. "Surely—''

"Don't see Court in jail do you, Miss Susanna? I told you he shot in self-defense. Now you gotta stay in yer room, or you gotta sit with me in the courtroom. Better you stay in yer room.''

"I don't know why you're testifyin, Abner. What possible good kin it do? Job will just—''

"Come too late fer the hangin,'' finished Quincy with a smug grin.

"So that's how it is.'' Mrs. Schmidt nodded. "In that case, I wouldn't mind seein that trial myself.''

"The man hasn't been tried yet,'' protested Susanna. "How can you say he'll be hung?''

Another person who could not believe what he was hearing was Elias Packard.

"Who's yer lawyer, Elias?'' asked the sheriff casually a little later that morning.

"Why, I don't need no lawyer, Sheriff Maxie,'' said Elias.

"Well, ever man's got a right to a lawyer,'' replied the sheriff. "Sure you don't want one?''

Elias laughed heartily. "Pa, he don't hold with lawyers. He'd sure figger I din put no faith in my family was I to git a lawyer.''

"Well, that's yer decision a course. Still, Pinto, I

want you to notice that Elias here din want no lawyer."

"I heard that, sheriff," replied the deputy.

"How about a shave, Elias?" asked the sheriff. "You want a shave?"

"Naw. What'd I wan a shave fer? Less'n some ladies are comin to visit me. You got any ladies wanna visit me, sheriff?"

"Not that I heard of, Elias. Still, you kin have a shave if'n you want one."

"No reason."

"Well, in that case, we better be gittin you over to the courthouse. Yer trial's bout ready to begin."

Elias's mouth dropped open.

When the prisoner actually realized that he was to be tried—the time of realization being when he was ushered into the courtroom with his hands tied behind his back and confronted with half the citizens of Amnonville attempting to squeeze themselves into the few available seats, when he saw Aaron Court turning from a quiet conference with the judge to give him a sardonic bow, and when he saw no Packards and no Packard followers crowding the courtroom to rescue him or to cow the witnesses and jury—at that time Elias demanded the lawyer he had previously refused so lightly. The judge obligingly found him one, but then Elias whispered to the man that he could expect to be promptly killed if he did not get his Packard client off scot-free; the lawyer loudly declined the honor and complained to the judge of the threat.

"Charge the prisoner with threatening an officer of the court," the judge instructed his clerk. "You will testify for the prosecution," he ordered the indignant and frightened lawyer.

"What about me?" demanded Elias.

"Does anyone want to defend this man?" the judge asked the assemblage at large. There being no offers forthcoming, Judge Galt informed the prisoner that he had only himself to blame for his lawyerless status.

"The sheriff said I could have a lawyer," Elias whined nervously. "I got rights."

"Very well," replied the judge, and he appointed the most newly minted member of the Amnonville bar and then appointed a deputy to listen to every word that passed between client and lawyer to see that Elias did not threaten the frightened young man who was so reluctantly attempting his defense. Having protected both the prisoner and his lawyer, the judge read off the list of jurors.

"I protest, your honor," cried the young lawyer.

"Why is that?" the judge demanded.

"Well." The young man turned pink and glanced nervously around. "Could I approach the bench for a private conference?"

Granted that privilege, the lawyer pointed out that all the jurors, as far as he knew, had recently had horses stolen by the Packards.

"You know anyone who hasn't had something stolen by the Packards, or a friend or relative killed by the Packards, or some other injury done them by the Packards?" asked Aaron dryly.

"Well," stuttered Mr. Connard, "I'm new in town."

"That explains your innocence," replied the judge. "Protest denied."

The trial proceeded rapidly with a long list of charges read against Elias Packard, crimes that even Elias himself had forgotten about until reminded in court. Hot upon the charges were the witnesses for the prosecution, one or two for each crime, each witness efficiently questioned by Aaron Court, who occasionally took the stand himself to verify testimony given on one matter or another, particularly on the matter of Elias's having been a party to the stealing of every available horse in town the night after the fire, testimony which elicited waves of hostility from the audience.

Elias's lawyer made little headway in casting doubt on the testimony of so many angry citizens and, when called upon to present the defense, had no witnesses to offer in rebuttal except Elias himself, who was reluctant to testify—not because he minded lying, but because he did not like being outnumbered by an angry mob. Finally after an acrimonious conference with his lawyer, he took the stand and announced, "I didn't do none of them things, and you folks better remember that Pa ain't gonna like this none and sure ain't gonna let you hang me or take kindly to no jurors who vote fer hangin me."

"Charge the prisoner with threatening the jury," said the judge coldly. "Mr. Connard, do you wish to sum up?"

Mr. Connard rose apologetically and remarked that he really had not had time to prepare his case and that the accused was not receiving a fair trial because he had not known, until he was taken from his cell and led to the courtroom, that the trial date had been set forward. Mr. Connard then sat down as Elias said loudly, "That's right; you bastards ain't playin fair, not that it's gonna do you no good."

Court, in his summation, pointed out to the jury

that the Packard Gang was becoming larger and bolder every month and could be expected to completely control the city and all the surrounding territory to the border of New Mexico if something were not done about it immediately. "There's no question that Elias Packard is guilty of all the crimes he's charged with here today and more besides," said Court with a grim countenance. "He hasn't even made any serious attempt to defend himself beyond threatening his lawyer, the jury, and everyone else in sight. If you find him innocent, which is what the Packards expect, it'll be because you haven't got the guts to stand up for yourselves. I suggest that we prove to them that they have miscalculated for once. Maybe they'll hold us a little less in contempt if we hang one of them. On the other hand, if you back down today, what you get will be what you deserve—more theft and more murder." Court sat down, giving Elias a level, hard look as he did so; Elias was still sneering.

"You want to retire?" the judge asked the jury.

The jury foreman looked questioningly at his fellow jurors, then turned to the judge. "We're all fer hangin him," he said casually.

"They ain't voted," Elias called out.

"Any one of you men who thinks Elias Packard is innocent of anything?" asked the judge.

When no man on the jury could think of anything Elias might be innocent of, Judge Galt said, "That's it, Elias. You've been found guilty of murder and all the rest. You want to hear the list of charges again?" Elias was too surprised to answer. "No? Well, then I sentence you to be hanged by the neck until dead. Sheriff, take him out to the big tree by Hobson's Mercantile and hang him."

The sheriff was as surprised at the promptness of the proceedings as Elias. "When did you want me to do that, Judge?" he asked, just to be certain that he had got the gist of the instructions.

"Right now," said Judge Galt.

"We ain't gonna have no dance or nothin while the jury deliberates?"

"The jury has deliberated."

"We always have a dance after a murder trial," muttered the sheriff.

Various members of the audience murmured agreement—especially young people who always looked forward to the festivities that took place while the jury was in the back room debating the guilt or innocence of the accused. One of the high points of such an evening was the hush that fell when the music was silenced and the verdict announced.

"Got fiddlers here an everything," said Sheriff Maxie; he always made a good profit selling liquor to the gentlemen in the back alley.

"You'll have to do your dancing after we hang him," the judge insisted. "I don't plan to wait till Job Packard comes in here and kills a bunch of people while he's rescuing Elias."

"I won't get no last dance," said Elias craftily. In the past, condemned criminals of a romantic inclination had made as their last request the request to have a last dance with the prettiest girl in town. To be so distinguished was enough to make the social season of a local belle. Various young ladies who had anticipated being chosen frowned at the judge's edict.

"You're a married man, Elias," snapped the judge heartlessly. "Take him out and hang him, sheriff. Right now.''

That command brought the townspeople in the audience to their feet, and a buzz of conversation swelled throughout the room as they prepared to rush out to attend the hanging.

''Order,'' roared the judge. ''Sit down, all of you.'' Nearly a hundred questioning faces turned toward him. Several young ladies brightened at the thought that the pre-execution ball might yet be held. Susanna shuddered at the callous offhandedness of the whole procedure. ''The sheriff and his deputies are going out first with Elias to get the rope and the horse ready,'' the judge continued. ''The rest of you give them a few minutes. You aren't going to miss seeing the first Packard hung in Amnonville.'' Murmurs of complaint were silenced by the sight of newly deputized men lining the back of the courtroom, carrying shotguns. Aaron and the judge had made sure, without informing the sheriff of the unusual agreement to an immediate hanging, that there were armed men on hand to forestall any visits from members of the Packard Gang, should any of the witnesses or jurors contacted by Court the night before prove unreliable.

Elias was dragged, kicking and shouting, out of the courtroom by the sheriff and his deputies and set, with his hands tied, upon a horse under the large tree on Copper Street. Since the sheriff had not come prepared with a rope, one had to be borrowed from a visiting cowboy. Once these makeshift preparations had been completed, the judge allowed the courtroom audience to join the crowd already collecting on the street near Hobson's Mercantile. Among the combined throng were Abner Quincy, looking highly gratified; Clara Schmidt, her face

alight with anticipation of such an interesting public
event; and between them, Susanna, who was horrified that a man could be tried, convicted, and
executed in such a cavalier fashion. She wanted to
go back to the hotel; her stomach was churning at
the thought of witnessing the hanging, but she was
afraid to leave Quincy's side and fend for herself.
Everyone in the mob, down to the last woman and
child, looked menacing to her, and the men—Susanna shuddered.

"Don't I git no last words?" Packard cried,
white-faced. "I'm supposed to git a last meal,
an—an a cigarette. Don't I git no last cigarette?"

"All you get is hung, Elias," said Aaron Court.

"You don't wanna do this, Court," said Elias.
"You know Pa is gonna git you fer this, you
especially. It ain't worth dyin, is it, to git even cause
I was gonna blow yer safe? Is it worth dyin fer?"
Packard's voice had risen with fear as it became
clearer and clearer to him that no one was going to
arrive in time to rescue him.

"You're the one who's dying this time, Elias,"
said Court. "Don't worry yourself about me."
Aaron coldly turned his back and walked away from
the tree as a deputy was tossing the noose over a
sturdy branch.

He had planned to turn back to witness the
hanging from the edge of the circle the deputies were
striving to maintain, but as he strode across the open
space, he saw a familiar blue bonnet in the crowd.
Court swore under his breath at the sight of
Susanna's frightened eyes and forced his way
toward her. As the crowd had surged forward,
Susanna had been carried with them and separated
from Abner and Clara. She was staring with fas-

cinated horror at Elias Packard when Court got to
her. "What are you doing here?" he demanded.
"This is no place for a young woman to be by
herself."

"I was with Mr. Quincy and Mrs. Schmidt."
Susanna would have backed away from Aaron if she
could, but the mob behind her was pressing her
forward, and Aaron now had a firm grip on her
arm.

"And you didn't want to miss the hanging, I suppose, seeing as you're—"

"I only went to the trial because Mr. Quincy had
to testify," she cried defensively, looking into his
face and then glancing quickly away from his hostile
stare. In avoiding Aaron's eyes, Susanna saw the
sheriff slap the rump of the horse on which Packard
sat and send it leaping forward. Her face turned
dead white and her hand rose to her mouth.

Involuntarily Court glanced over his shoulder to
see what had frightened her. As Packard's body
plummeted to the end of the rope and began to
twist, Aaron stepped in front of Susanna and put his
arms around her.

"No," she protested faintly.

"Don't look," he advised her, turning her face
into his shoulder so that she could not see Elias
Packard dying. "If you haven't the stomach to see
justice done, you shouldn't have come here."

"Justice?" Susanna tried to pull away from him.
"That wasn't justice. The men on the jury, the
judge—they had all made up their minds that he was
guilty before they heard the evidence. He didn't
have a real chance to defend himself."

Court, retaining his hold on her arm, began to

force her through the crowd. "Where are you taking me?" she demanded.

"Back to the hotel," he snapped. "You say Packard didn't have a chance to defend himself? Well, Susanna, Packard couldn't defend himself; he was guilty of everything he was charged with, and he hung for it—as he damn well should."

"The trial was a farce," she insisted.

"Either you didn't listen to what was said in that courtroom, or you didn't understand anything you heard, Susanna. This isn't any settled, law-abiding community, although there are plenty that would like it to be, and today we finally took a step toward making it one. Every man who took a part in that trial—as a witness or a juror, the judge, me—we all put our lives in the line, because you can be sure that Job Packard will be gunning for us now—just like Bates was gunning for me after I shot Elias and turned him in to the sheriff. In a way, I'd have done a lot of people a favor if I'd just killed Elias instead of getting everyone involved in this trial."

"Am I supposed to find that civic-minded?" asked Susanna sarcastically.

"I don't give a damn how you find it," said Court. "It's obvious that you have no idea what's at stake here. Today some of us had the guts to stand up for community law instead of Packard law, which is what we've had for two years or more. Here's the hotel. Now get to your room and keep the door locked until Quincy gets back."

"I don't have to do what you tell me."

"No, you don't. If you're stubborn and stupid enough, maybe you can manage to be on the streets when the Packards come in to start shooting people down.'' He turned angrily on his heel and stalked off toward the stable where he had his horse.

Susanna stumbled up the stairs to her room and, locking the door, leaned trembling against it, reliving her encounter with Court. He was a horrible man, and yet she could remember every single time he had touched her and the way it had made her feel—his arms catching her as she fell from the burning balcony, his hand covering hers at the table at Lilith's place and his arms around her as she began to faint, the enchanting touch of his mouth as they lay on the floor in the hotel dining room, the brutal kiss when her horse had run away—and then at the hanging when he had put his arms around her and turned her face to his shoulder, she had not wanted to lash out at him as she should; she had wanted to lean against him, to give herself up to the warm trembling that engulfed her when he was near. It was as if there were some wonderful thing between them that she could not quite remember, that drifted through her dreams and waited just out of reach on the misty outskirts of her mind during her waking hours, making her body want to be near Aaron Court while her mind warned her against his cruelty and violence, his sardonic smile and words.

15

The next weeks were depressing ones for Susanna as her sense of isolation increased. All those dreams with which she had left St. Louis seemed out of reach now. She had envisioned a loving relationship with her sister Lilith, whom she had missed so sorely over the intervening years, but it became increasingly obvious that Lilith, although she was fond of

Susanna, looked on her as a responsibility rather than a companion. Lilith seemed bent on making Susanna into some self-sufficient Western pioneer woman rather than allowing her to have a role at the Land and Cattle Company. And in fact, although Susanna tried to ignore the truth, Lilith came to visit less and less at the hotel and was more and more adamant when she did come that Susanna spend all her time with her two chaperones and no time at the Land and Cattle Company, although Susanna had suggested that she could make curtains and draperies for the new place rising on Copper Street; that she could make clothes for the waitresses, clothes that would be more becoming and more socially acceptable than those they wore at present; that she could keep the books, being a skilled mathematician; that she could greet customers, or deal blackjack (which looked quite easy although she did not care much for gambling) or entertain the customers with songs of all kinds or. . . . Lilith would entertain none of these suggestions.

Another dream that had accompanied Susanna from St. Louis was that she might finally get to meet and become friends with people outside her immediate family, but that dream too seemed out of reach. In the hotel parlor young ladies and their mothers, members of families who spent the winter months in Amnonville rather than in cold ranch houses, sat together to sew, embroider, chat, and read to one another, and Susanna, when she was not outside of town wearing one of her now numerous riding outfits and clinging awkwardly to her horse, or blasting away with her rifle at targets pointed out by Quincy, or attempting to draw a pistol from a holster without shooting herself or him, would have

loved to join these ladies. She knew how to
embroider and sew and play the piano, but she was
always pointedly excluded from the circle, until
finally she gave up any attempts to make friends in
that quarter.

And the one friend she had made in Amnonville,
Aaron Court, was now estranged. Although she
thought of him often, and even saw him often, he
still looked at her with cold anger, and she, because
she knew that she should, turned her head whenever
he passed her in the street or at the hotel. To add to
her distress, she read often in the local newspaper of
all the social events that accompanied the court
session. There were dances and plays and musicales,
at all of which, if the newspaper was to be believed,
Aaron Court was a much sought after companion by
marriageable young ladies. Susanna had to read of
this young beauty who had waltzed with him at a
ball and that young beauty who had dedicated a
song to him at a musicale, and another who had
accompanied him to a play. And Susanna, who had
never been to any such events, had to wonder
whether she would have enjoyed these festivities if
she had been invited or whether Aaron would have
danced with her or taken her to a play had she not
called him a murderer and deplored his part in the
trial and hanging of Elias Packard.

One of the hardest things of all for her was Abner
Quincy's attitude, for as they rode together, he
persisted in telling her about every depredation
committed by the Packard Gang over the years,
every escape from justice they had managed until
Aaron Court bravely took a hand in the trial of
Elias. Quincy made it perfectly obvious that she had
done a good man an injustice, whether or not she

was smart enough to see it. And when, ten days after
the hanging, one of the jurors was found shot to
death by parties unknown beside the right of way of
a narrow-gauge mine railroad, Quincy took great
delight in predicting that the vengeful slaughter had
started. "Now if someone starts shootin at me, Miss
Susanna, I want you to head straight back to town.
Don't stick around to git killed. After all, the
Packards don't know you was on their side. They
could just as well shoot you too. They ain't
particular."

"I was not on their side," said Susanna resentfully, "and if they shoot at me, or you for that
matter, I shall certainly shoot back."

"Well, you cain't do that, Miss Susanna,"
declared Quincy. "Why, that'd be murder. That's
what Court did. Bates drew on him, an Court shot
back, an you said—"

"Oh, shut up, Mr. Quincy."

"Well," he advised, grinning, "if you're gonna
shoot back, at least use a rifle. You use a six-gun
an you might shoot me."

"I'm not that bad."

"Hell you ain't, pardon the language."

For his part, Court was having an equally
irritating time. The brief spate of civic interest in
dealing with the Packards that he had managed to
inspire cooled very rapidly. When he had approached the sheriff with the idea of forming a posse
and cleaning out the Packards' headquarters in the
mountains, the sheriff had pointed out that the
Packards habitually lodged out of his county, and
he did not intend to endanger his life or anyone
else's on any illegal expeditions after them. No one

else was interested in pursuing them and asking for trouble either, so Court had to satisfy himself with watching his back trail for bushwhackers and tending to the cases of his clients who were scheduled for that session.

His occasional sights of Susanna returning from outings with Quincy, ludicrously draped with six-guns and bumping along awkwardly on her mare, looking the picture of civic disdain when she saw him, only served to exacerbate his bad temper. To divert himself, he began to attend social functions that he had previously eschewed and to allow himself to be courted by mothers who coveted his wealth for their eligible daughters while fearing his somewhat unsavory reputation with women. Various virtuous young ladies fell in love and took to attending court sessions and eyeing him yearningly at balls and musical events, even looking for him in church where he did not appear. However, once his last case had been tried, once he had danced with the last simpering maiden he ever wanted to see and smiled hypocritically at the last gimlet-eyed mother, once he had even given up on a visit from the Packards to break the montony of a dreary spring, Court closed his house, took up his rifle, and escaped to the mountains to go hunting.

16

Abner arrived in the hotel dining room at his usual early hour to share a cup of breakfast coffee with Susanna and Clara. "Fraid we won't be going out today, Miss Susanna," he announced. "There's snow in the air."

Susanna, who had checked the weather earlier,

laughed. "Why, it looks like a perfectly good day, Mr. Quincy. A little cloudy, but surely this late in the year there'll be no more snow."

Abner shook his head. "It's snow all right. Maybe not till nightfall, but we don't wanna take no chances a gettin caught in a bad storm. Remember the storm in '75, Miz Schmidt?"

Clara had not been in Colorado at that time, but she had heard of that storm, and her experiences with other spring storms led her to agree with him that no chances should be taken.

Having settled that matter, Abner poured himself another cup of coffee and told the ladies the latest piece of gossip he had picked up. "Heard sumpthin that ought to interest you, Miss Susanna," he began. She smiled encouragingly at him as she passed the sugar. "Yep. Heard that the Packards got Aaron Court trapped up in a cabin north of town."

Susanna put down her coffee cup, having turned a little pale. "What does that mean?" she asked.

Abner grinned. "Waal, that means there ain't gonna be no more frontier justice the way Aaron sees to it. Means the Packards is gonna git their revenge like they always does. Too bad too, I say."

"But what do they mean to do?"

"Oh, they won't take no chances. He's pinned down. An they got lots of folks. They'll jus take shots at him if he shows his head, an if'n they don't git him that way, sooner or later he'll fall asleep. He cain't stay awake ferever. Then they'll jus sneak up an kill im."

"But surely someone will go out and—"

"Rescue im? Nope. Who wants to git into it with the Packards? Anybody went out there'd find them-

selves gittin bushwhacked er backshot jus like
Court. Nope, they got im. He must a got careless.''

"Well—" Susanna was horrified, remembering
how Aaron Court had saved her from the fire.
"Well, that's terrible. Something must be done."
She rose to go upstairs for her heavy jacket. "I'll go
to see the sheriff."

"Won't do you no good," Abner told her.

"Still, I shall go." Abner had to scramble to catch
up with her, but he had been right after all, for the
sheriff already knew of Court's predicament and
had no intention of mounting a rescue operation.

"Ain't in my territory. That cabin's in the next
county," he stated flatly to all Susanna's arguments.

Finally, when she realized that there was no help
to be had from the law, she demanded that the
sheriff draw her a map showing how to get to the
cabin.

"Now why would you want that, ma'am?" asked
the sheriff, grinning. "Thinking of going after the
Packards yourself?"

Susanna started to answer hotly, then thought
better of it. Instead she replied, looking as prim as
possible, "I think it is my duty as a citizen to see if
someone cannot be convinced to form a rescue
party. I shall pay men to go if necessary."

"Well, good luck to you, ma'am. Ain't likely that
nobody will be fool enough to take money to git
theirselves into the middle of a Packard feud, which
is what we got goin here. Wouldn't do no good if
you was to git Court out this time anyway; they'll git
to him sooner or later. Still, I'll draw you a map."
Chuckling all the while at the eccentric ideas of
Lilith Moran's sister, he gave Susanna good
directions and sent her on her way.

Abner had not heard this conversation, having stayed outside on the street to talk to an old friend. Consequently he was not suspicious when Susanna informed him with pretended indifference that the sheriff would do nothing, so it seemed that Mr. Court was out of luck. She then suggested that Abner might like some time off, since she planned to spend a cozy day in her room sewing lace cuffs on her best blue merino and otherwise refurbishing her wardrobe. Abner was delighted, escorted her back to the hotel, and promptly disappeared. Then Susanna voiced the same intentions to Clara and asked if she would like to spend the day with her cousin, which would be quite all right since Mr. Quincy would be returning shortly from an errand and could keep Susanna company. Clara fussed a bit, but she was gone also within fifteen minutes.

Having so easily disposed of her chaperones, Susanna turned to assembling the items she planned to take with her—her rifle, food, lots of ammunition in case Mr. Court might be running out, warm clothes, and a canteen in case there was no water in the cabin. She carried all these things down to the hotel stable, packed her saddle bags, left a note to be delivered to her sister at seven in the evening, and, with the sheriff's map in her pocket, guided her horse onto the road north of town.

As she rode along through the cloudy, cold morning Susanna planned her entrance to the scene of the seige carefully. Her sister had once remarked that she never had trouble with the Packards because they did not want to be denied the pleasures of her establishment when they came to town. Consequently Susanna reasoned that the best thing to do would be to ride straight up to the Packards and introduce herself. She felt no compunction about misleading them thereafter. She would tell them that she had come up to pray with Mr. Court so that he might die in a state of grace. Such an idea seemed perfectly reasonable in light of the fact that she owed him her life. Then if the Packards objected, she would simply ride into the cabin anyway and let them shoot at her if they dared. Undoubtedly they would not dare, knowing that they would have Lilith to deal with if they did. In fact, if they did not give up that very afternoon, they would have Lilith to deal with anyway, for Susanna was sure that her sister would send out those mean-looking men, Carlos and the rest, to rescue her as soon as her note was delivered. In the process, Mr. Court, whom Lilith did not seem to like, would be rescued also and Susanna's debt discharged. The corners of her mouth lifted in a small pleased smile, and she rode sedately along enjoying the countryside and worrying not at all that she was about to try to thwart the area's most feared outlaws.

The air was becoming progressively colder, the sky more overcast, and Susanna more anxious for her midday meal when she first began to hear shots from time to time and realized that she was coming close to the scene of the ambush. "Thank goodness," she murmured to herself. "I certainly hope Mr. Court's cabin has a warm fire going." She huddled deeper into her fleece-lined jacket and guided her horse onto the side trail the sheriff had mentioned. It was conveniently marked with a cattle skull planted in the lower branches of a tree. She rode for another five minutes, still hearing shots ahead of her, and then called out in a clear, girlish voice, "Mr. Packard." She was riding, as it

happened, directly toward Job Packard who, even
on a cold day, felt that his position required him to
be out avenging the family honor. "Mr. Packard,"
Susanna called again with no idea whatever of which
Mr. Packard might answer her call. "Mr.
Packard," she called a third time. All shooting had
ceased, and participants were peering nervously this
way and that. Old Job appeared among the trees,
leveling his rifle at her and gaping.

"Would you be a Mr. Packard?" Susanna asked
politely.

"Reckon."

"My name is Susanna Moran. I believe you are
acquainted with my sister, Lilith Moran."

"I am." Old Job looked the girl over. He had
heard of her, and she looked every bit as silly as he
had heard. Once she had told him her errand, he was
convinced that she was mad—or simpleminded.
"That's a mighty Christian idea, miss," said Job,
"but I'm afraid we cain't let you go in there."

"But I must, Mr. Packard," insisted Susanna.
"Mr. Court saved my life during the fire, and now I
feel that it is my obligation to try to save his soul."

"Aaron Court don't care nothin about his soul,"
said Job. "You better jus ride right on back to
town. Reckon if your sister knew you was out here,
she wouldn't like it none. You bring anyone with
you?" Job looked around suspiciously.

"My sister's employees are not that interested in
religious missions, Mr. Packard. Still, I must do my
duty, and I also wish to advise you that should any
harm come to me at your hands, my sister will undoubtedly retaliate in kind."

"How's that?"

"I intend to visit Mr. Court," said Susanna

clearly and loudly so that other Packards could hear too, "and if you feel that you must shoot at me, you should expect that Mr. Mondragon and his men will avenge my death or injury." Susanna then set her whip to her horse's haunch, and the astonished animal bounded away toward the cabin seen among the trees.

"Hold your fire," shouted Job with alarm, deciding instantly that withholding religious consolation from Court in his last hours was not worth a feud with Lilith and her cold-eyed lieutenant, Carlos Mondragon.

Susanna meanwhile was clutching her horse's neck and praying that she would not fall off. She called out, "Don't fire, Mr. Court. I have come to pray with you."

Court was not firing. Although he could hardly believe it, he had heard and identified her voice when she hailed Packard and later when she had loudly stated her intentions. Keeping well back, he watched her stable her horse in the shed with his. Then he unbarred his door and yanked her, her heavy saddle bags, and her rifle in before the Packards could shoot them both.

"What in God's name are you doing here, Susanna?" he demanded, kneeling beside her and holding her firmly to the floor when she tried to rise.

"You're not being very hospitable."

"Keep your head down. Do you want to get it blown off?"

"Oh, they won't shoot at me. They think I've come to pray with you."

"Why did you come?"

"Because no one else would come to your rescue, Mr. Court, and I owe you my life."

"You're mad. You could have got yourself killed, and you probably will get me killed."

"Nonsense. I've brought you food and ammunition." Court glanced at her sharply and then looked through the saddle bags.

"Well, you've brought the right caliber stuff."

"Of course. Can we have lunch now? I'm very hungry."

"You've got to get out of here. Tell him we've prayed."

"I don't intend to leave, Mr. Court. I shall help you defend the cabin until a rescue party arrives."

"Help isn't coming," said Court grimly, "and I don't have a prayer of making a run for it tonight with you on my hands."

"Come on out, miss," shouted Packard. "That's enough prayin."

One of the younger men laughed and called, "Yeah, come on out, pretty thing. All us wanna meet Lilith's sister."

Court's mouth settled into grim lines, and he cursed. Susanne had heard the tone of nasty menace in the voice and looked steadily at Court. "Do you still want me to leave?"

"You're going to get us both killed," he muttered.

"No, I won't. I'm a very good shot. You'll be glad I came." She delved into the food pack and offered him cheese and cold meat.

"Git on out here, miss," yelled Job angrily.

Susanna picked up her rifle, and before Court could protest, she took a quick shot out the window and dropped to the floor. A yelp and cursing were heard outside. "Shall I peel an egg for you while you keep watch?" she asked calmly. "Oh, and I brought a bottle of bourbon for you.'' Court began to laugh, and Susanna's light laughter mingled with his.

"You ain't gonna be laughing by nightfall, Court,'' yelled one of the Packards, "neither you nor your lyin whore neither.''

Susanna's smile disappeared, and she popped a piece of sausage into her mouth and sent another shot through the window, causing several Packards to go sprawling.

"Don't waste your ammunition,'' Court advised, "unless you have a clear shot. And don't show yourself.''

"I am a good marksman though, don't you think?''

"You are,'' he agreed, "but so are they.'' Court showed her how to keep watch without exposing herself, and having eaten, they took up positions at different windows, positions they maintained throughout the afternoon. Susanna became uncomfortably cold and began to feel sleepy, which reminded her of something Abner had said. "Mr. Court,'' she murmured. He glanced over at her. "Mr. Quincy said that they would keep you pinned down here until you fell asleep, and then they would creep up and kill you.''

"That's what they probably figure on,'' Court agreed, "although that's not part of my plans.''

"If you're tired, perhaps I could keep watch while you sleep.''

"I'm not tired.''

They lapsed into silence as darkness fell. Court glanced at her from time to time. He could barely see her, but he knew that her head was drooping and had been since they had eaten more of the cold food around six. "Susanna, you'd better try to get some sleep," he said quietly.

"I can't," she replied.

"Nonsense. I'm not tired, if that's what you're worried about."

"No. It's not that." Susanna sighed. "I'm afraid of the dark," she confessed. "I always have a night light when I go to bed, but I assume that it would be dangerous here."

Court shook his head with wonder. The girl had ridden into certain danger to bring him food and ammunition, she'd been shot at occasionally all afternoon and was undoubtedly very cold and uncomfortable, and her strongest concern seemed to be fear of the dark. Court chuckled to himself. "There are covers over there on the bunk. Did you see where it was?"

"Yes, but—"

"Get them and come over here to lie down," he instructed. "You won't feel afraid if there's someone close by, or are you still bothered by being in the company of a cold-blooded murderer?"

"I'm sorry I said that to you," Susanna admitted. "You were right about the Packards, and I was wrong." She crawled over to the bunk, located the covers, and then moved over beside Court, whom she could now see because the moon had risen.

"Damn bad luck," he muttered. "It will be after midnight before we can make a break for it."

"Why?" she asked, trying to tuck the covers around herself.

Court put his rifle against the wall and showed her how to roll herself up in the blankets for maximum warmth. "We wouldn't have a prayer of getting out in this moonlight. You'd better sleep now while you can."

"Yes," she agreed. "I really don't want to be a burden to you. I wanted to help, not put you in more danger."

"You don't owe me anything, Susanna; I told you that before."

"Yes, but I'm sorry about the way I treated you too. You've always been very nice to me really, but you make me feel so—so uncomfortable."

"I do?"

"Oh, it's not your fault. I think maybe it's the dreams."

Court stiffened. "What dreams?"

"I'm not even sure. I know I dream about you. When I was sick, I did, and I could remember. I dreamed about when you took me off the balcony, but now I can't remember the dreams. I just wake up feeling—oh, I can't describe it—funny all over and not being able to remember. And then I feel uncomfortable when I see you."

Her honesty plus her failure to understand what was happening to her left Court at a loss for words. It seemed to him that Susanna, who could not remember what had happened to her and did not know what was in store for her, was telling him without knowing it that she wanted to make love again, that she dreamed of making love with him, and Court knew that he would accommodate her sooner or later and that there would be trouble because of it, but he was a man who made no effort to avoid trouble, which he assumed would come to him one way or another anyway. In fact, he sensed an inevitability to his relationship with Susanna that was being delayed only for a time by the Packards lying in wait outside.

"What will you do with yourself once Abner has taught you to shoot and ride well enough to satisfy Lilith?" Court asked, turning the conversation aside from subjects about which he could do nothing at the moment.

Susanna sighed. "I guess Lilith wants the lessons to last forever. I had thought that I would help her with her business, but now I'm pretty sure that she doesn't want me over there."

"Oh? What makes you think that?" Court asked the question idly, his eyes again searching the woods around the cabin. The moonlight played tricks on one, and he wanted no surprise attacks.

"A lot of things." Susanna sounded very depressed.

"What things?"

"She's as much as said so. And then she keeps me busy with the lessons, and Mr. Quincy and Clara always try to divert me when I want to go over. But mostly it's the ladies at the hotel."

Court glanced at her sharply. "What ladies have you been talking to?"

"I haven't. That's part of it. The ladies who have been staying there for the winter sit in the parlor and embroider and chat, but when I sit down there, they won't speak to me. I wanted to make friends, but they all ignore me. Some even leave when I come in, and some of them started talking about Lilith one day; they were looking at me out of the corners of their eyes, and they said something bad happens at Lilith's restaurant, something to do with the girls that work there. Do you think something bad happens at Lilith's?''

Court shrugged. "It's all in your point of view,'' he replied. "I wouldn't pay any attention.''

"And Lilith told me not to go to church. I thought that was very strange because I've always gone to church. My parents never let me have any friends or go to school with other girls; I had a tutor. But I did always go to church, and I like it so much. I miss it. But Lilith says the ladies are very stand-offish and wouldn't talk to me, and obviously she is right, but it's very lonely.'' Susanna sighed. "I had thought that I could have lots of friends here and talk to people, but in some ways it's the same as it was at home. I only get to see Clara and Mr. Quincy, and sometimes Lilith.'' She fell silent for a time and then, smiling reminiscently, added, "I like going to the restaurant and talking to people—well, some of them. The girls treat me very strangely. At least I think they do; I haven't known that many girls. But for instance, Mr. Penvennon was very pleasant to me.''

"You must be the only person in town Penvennon was ever pleasant to,'' Court remarked. "What the devil did you find to talk to him about?''

"Well, for one thing I told him what I thought of calling the town Amnonville. You may not be familiar with the passage in the Bible, but as I told Mr. Penvennon, Amnon was evidently not a very nice person.''

"Oh?'' Court repressed a smile. He was familiar with the exploits of Amnon and wondered whether Susanna was about to give him a lecture on the evils of incest.

"Yes. He was a sinner of some sort; it's one of those ambiguous passages, but he forced his sister to do something she shouldn't have done and made her terribly unhappy, and his brother Absalom killed Amnon as a result, and then their father, King David, was very upset because he thought all his sons had been killed and—well, you can see that Amnon isn't the sort of name that reflects well on our community. I think—''

"Actually the town was named after Benjamin K. Amnon."

Susanna turned astonished eyes on Court. "It was?"

"Yes. No doubt he was a sinner like us all," remarked Court tolerantly, "but nothing spectacular that I ever heard of. He made the first gold strike in the valley. Dead now, poor fellow, but he hardly deserves to have his name stricken from history for his sins." Court was laughing softly to himself.

"Oh, my goodness. I had no idea. Naturally, I assumed—I meant no disrespect to Mr. Amnon's memory. You must think me a very censorious person. No wonder Mr. Penvennon—''

Court did not want to hear any more about Grant Penvennon and interrupted her to ask how her shooting lessons were coming.

"Mr. Quincy says it will take a long time for me to learn to shoot from the hip."

"From the hip?" Court laughed softly.

"Yes. It's really rather boring, but I guess it's better than doing nothing."

"Would you like to come riding with me sometime—if we get out of this, that is?"

"Oh, yes." Susanna sat up, and Court quickly pushed her down. "Where would we go?" she asked eagerly.

"There are lots of places you might like. For instance, there's a nice waterfall we could see when the danger of snow slides is past. And in a few weeks there will be fields of flowers higher in the mountains."

"There will? How wonderful. I'd love to see them. We really must drive off the Packards. Maybe we should shoot at them some more, just to let them know they're in big trouble."

"We can't go looking at flowers tonight, Susanna," said Court, chuckling. "And I'm afraid we're the ones who are in big trouble. Why don't you try to sleep?" He leaned over her and brushed her cheek affectionately with his lips.

Susanna gave a contented sigh. "I'm not tired anymore." She sat up and quickly wiggled on her hips until her back was against a wall. "I have an idea anyway."

"If you're going to stay up, keep your rifle at hand," he ordered.

Obediently Susanna laid the rifle across her lap, but she made no move to resume her post across the room. Instead she began to sing in a clear, sweet voice: "Rock of ages cleft for me—"

"Susanna," hissed Court. "What the hell do you think you're doing?"

"I'm just reminding them whose side God is on," she whispered back. Then her voice soared with startling strength and beauty, filling the clearing: "Let me hide myself in thee. Let the water and the—"

"I'll be damned," muttered Court.

"What is it?" she asked.

"You haven't been praying for snow, have you?"

"No, but Mr. Quincy said it would snow today. Is it?"

"It is."

"Oh good." Susanna resumed her song, her voice lifting with pleasure and confidence while outside the shivering Packards were drawing up their collars and drawing down their hats against the damp snow. Job had the uncomfortable feeling that there was a real angel in that cabin instead of a whore's sister and that God was sending him a message.

Susanna was launching enthusiastically into another verse when Job said with disgust to his eldest son, "Well, hell. That does it. We're leavin."

"But Pa—"

"God just ain't with us tonight. If'n we kill that girl, we'll have more trouble than we need, an here it's snowin on me an colder'n a witch's tit. We'll jus have to git Court some other time."

Before Susanna had finished the third verse, the Packards were mounting and riding off. Ten minutes later they were met at the road by a large lantern-carrying party from the Fallen Angel.

"Where's my sister, you old reprobate?" shouted Lilith furiously; she was leveling her pistol at a spot between Job's eyes, having gone through four or five hours of near panic when she discovered that Susanna had tricked her chaperones and disappeared. The person the note had been left with had not delivered it, and Lilith had had to figure out for herself where Susanna had gone by questioning everyone she could get her hands on, from Quincy to the stable boy at the hotel to the sheriff. Even after the conversation with the sheriff, it was hard to believe that the girl had actually ridden off by herself, loaded down with food and ammunition, to single-handedly rescue Aaron Court.

"It's all because he pulled her off that damned

balcony," Lilith had muttered, and then she had rounded up her people to rescue Susanna.

"Where is she?" Lilith shouted at Job.

"You might git Pa," said Isaiah nervously, "but we'll sure git you." Everyone was aiming at everyone else in the two groups.

"Calm yourself, Lilith," said Job. "We ain't touched yer sister. She's probably still up there singin hymns."

"She git any a you all?" asked Abner with interest.

"Jeremiah got winged after she went in there," said Job. "Don't know which one was doin the shootin."

"Told you she was good," said Abner complacently. "I'd never a guessed it, but that girl's got a real talent fer shootin."

"An lyin," said Job bitterly.

"Shut your mouth," snapped Lilith.

"Well, she said she was goin in there to pray with him, but she didn't never come back out."

"Maybe he wouldn't let her go," suggested Isaiah craftily. "Yeah. No tellin what Court's up to."

Lilith shifted uneasily. "How do I know she's even alive? Maybe you just want me to let you go."

"Ain't a matter of lettin us go," said Job. "It's a stand-off. Anyway, no one could be dead or even wounded an sing that loud an that purty. That voice would grace a church. A course, when Court gets through with her, likely she'll only be fit fer singin at your place, Lilith. She's up there alone with him right now, the murderin bastard."

Lilith wheeled her horse and headed up the trail, calling over her shoulder, "If you've hurt her, Packard, I'll have every one of you hunted down and hung from your own trees, and you can forget about trials too.''

When Court had heard the sound of departing hooves on the trail, he had said, ''By God, you've done it, Susanna. I think they've gone.''

''Really?'' She put her rifle aside and wiggled quickly over to look out his window. ''Did you see them?''

''No, but I heard the horses.'' He put his arm around her shoulders as he continued to scan the clearing through the falling snow and moonlight.

''But do you think—''

''Sh-h. I want you to be absolutely quiet for a few minutes, Susanna, so I can listen. I want to be sure, and the snow muffles the sound.''

Obediently Susanna nestled beside him, her head against his shoulder. He was sharply conscious of her soft breathing and the silky feel of her hair beneath his chin as he watched, and he tightened his arm, pulling her closer to him. She made no attempt to move away, but seemed content.

After ten minutes Court was satisfied that no Packards were left in the area. He hugged Susanna, saying, ''You were sure as hell right when you said I'd be glad you came, Susanna. I'd never have thought of bluffing that old ruffian with hymn-singing. He must have thought you prayed in that snow.''

Susanna laughed happily, her face upturned to his. ''What do we do now?'' she asked with youthful exuberance. ''Should we chase them down the trail?''

''God no!'' He laughed. ''We'll leave well enough alone.'' He cupped her chin in his hand and kissed her slowly until she leaned against him, soothed by the gentle pressure of his lips, but Court held her away, kissing her eyelids, cheeks, and throat as he began to undo the buttons of her heavy jacket.

"Aaron, I'll freeze," she protested.

"No. No. We'll warm each other." He slipped his hands inside the jacket and drew her against him, returning his kisses to her lips. She put her arms around his neck and responded yearningly to him, as she would not before when he had kissed her after the death of Hogshead Bates. "Is this what your dreams are like, Susanna?" he murmured against her open mouth.

"I don't know," she gasped. "I don't know." Court touched her breast then, feeling the wild beating of her heart beneath his fingers.

"Don't." She tried to pull away from him, but he used his weight to bear her down on the blankets where she had lain before, and he covered her mouth with his, stilling her protests, as he continued to stroke her, so gently, as if she were a wild young animal he sought to hold in captivity, and she submitted to that gentleness, to that touch that sent pulses of invading heat through her body.

Suddenly Court's hand was still, and his mouth lifted from hers as he listened. "Someone's coming up the road, Susanna," he said quietly. He pulled her up gently and began to rebutton the jacket, for she was dazed and incapable of understanding for the moment. He reached out for her rifle and put it in her hand. "You must go to the other window. All right?" She nodded dumbly. "Don't be afraid. We've come this far. We'll make it home." He leaned forward and brushed her lips with his. "Now." He turned her toward her old post. "And stay low." Court returned to his window and peered through the snow, leveling his rifle toward the trail from which the new threat seemed to be coming.

A party of horsemen broke into the clearing carrying lanterns and making no attempt to hide. The lead rider called out, "Susanna."

"It's Lilith," Susanna cried. "She came for us." The girl began to weep with relief as Court went to unbar the door and admit their rescuers.

Lilith swooped down on her sister, shouting over her shoulder, "Hold a gun on that son of a bitch. Why would you do such a stupid thing, Susanna?" she demanded.

"She saved my hide," remarked Court dryly. "Are you planning to shoot me now that the Packards failed?"

"I ought to. Did you keep her in here as a hostage?"

"Who thought that one up? Job? Isaiah? As a matter of fact, I told her to leave—until the boys out there started making remarks about how much they wanted to meet your sister. Then I figured maybe she'd better stay." Court looked levelly at Lilith. "You know what I mean?"

"I came of my own free will, Lilith," said Susanna, "and I stayed of my own free will."

"You could have talked to me about this. I've been frantic."

"I'm sorry, but I was sure you wouldn't let me go, and it was something I had to do. Aaron was right about good people having to stand up to people like the Packards, and—"

"Who told you Aaron Court was one of the good people?" asked Lilith sarcastically. "Was that your idea, Court?"

He shrugged, but Susanna said, "It's bad enough

living in a place with an awful name like Amnonville. At least we don't have to be hiding in our
houses because of outlaws. Since nobody else would
help, I did. I asked the sheriff, you know." Susanna
was becoming angry, and Lilith backed off; she just
wanted to get the girl home. She had to assume,
because they had both been found at separate
windows with guns in their hands, that Court had
not been up to anything with Susanna. Lilith failed
to notice the long look that passed between the pair
before the group left to ride back to town. But
Susanna could think of nothing else all the way
home. She felt as if his eyes had lit a flame in her,
the burning of which would never subside, and
Aaron cursed the luck that had brought Lilith and
her men riding up that trail so quickly.

17

Court, upon his return from the Packard ambush,
established a temporary office in a room beside
Professor Hockstader's Portrait Salon and above
the Bonanza Tonsorial Parlor and Bath House. He
had had his choice of that location or a room down
the street over the Gold Creek Saloon, and he had
decided that the sounds of clipping and splashing
would be more soothing to his clients than the
sounds of drunks being heaved out into the street or
of dishonest gamblers being shot at the poker tables.
He also surmised that the relative quiet would give
him a better chance of hearing any Packards
stampeding up the stairs to have another try at him.

This office as yet contained only his safe (lumpy,
misshapen, and filled with well-toasted legal docu-
ments) and a table with two chairs moved in from a

restaurant in which he owned a part interest. In these unprepossessing surroundings, Court was meeting for the second time since the fire with Grassback Holbein, so named because his body was completely and thickly covered with a growth of yellowish-gray hair that looked like winter grass. It was said that cattle, finding Grassback asleep on his stomach and shirtless, had attempted to graze off his hair from waist to head.

"An here I figgered myself fer a millionaire," said Grassback ruefully as he settled himself into Court's one client chair. "An now since you managed to git back from that cabin alive, I'm only half a millionaire."

"You really think the claim is that good?"

"I tole you las time I was in that it was good, but, friend, it's not jus good; it's the best vein I even seen. Here's the assay report. I tole em to send the bill to you."

Court nodded and studied the report, whistling softly to himself. "I can see what you mean, Grassback, but it wouldn't have done you any good if the Packards had got me. My heirs would have inherited my half of the claim."

"Son of a bitch. You got heirs? I knew you had ladies all over the place. Hell, two of em showed up to save you from the Packards, din they? But I din know you had babies too."

"Heirs doesn't necessarily mean offspring," said Court dryly and went on to discuss how they should exploit the strike, Court's suggestion being that he arrange for buildings and machinery and that Grassback hire the men and run the mine.

"Ah, hell, Court, I'm a prospector. I figgered on—"

"Selling out to me or someone else and moving on? Forget it. The partnership agreement we signed when I grubstaked you called for you staying. In my experience, a partner's less likely to highgrade me than an employee, and you're a partner. Don't worry. You'll make a good mine operator."

"Don't mean I'm gonna like it," complained Holbein.

A barely audible knock interrupted their conversation, and Susanna appeared hesitantly in the doorway. Grassback acknowledged an introduction to her by saying, "Well, ma'am, you sure din do me no favors when you pulled Court's bacon outa the fire." The prospector slapped a dusty hat decisively against his thigh and, departing, said, "See ya, Aaron. Lemme know when I gotta give up the good life."

Susanna, making no move to enter the room, said shyly, "I received your note," and she gave Court a tiny smile that lighted her eyes but barely lifted the corners of her mouth.

"No chaperone?" Court asked as he rose to take her arm and lead her into his office, closing the door behind her.

Susanna's smile curved up ever so slightly. "Is it necessary for a lady to have a chaperone when visiting her lawyer?" she asked.

"Damned if I know," Court murmured. "I guess it depends on how the lawyer feels about the lady or the lady about the lawyer."

"Mr. Quincy is down the street at the Gold Creek Saloon. Perhaps I should send for him." Susanna's eyes were twinkling so happily that Court almost, but not quite, forgot that he wanted to lock his door, pull his shades, and take up where he had left off with Susanna before her sister had come riding in to the rescue.

"Maybe you shouldn't send for him," said Court, "since he works for Lilith and you don't want her to know about this inheritance business for a while."

"Oh, have you heard from my lawyer in St. Louis? Can I divide the money now?"

Court grinned. "Well, maybe not today, but at least I can give you a more detailed accounting of your assets, and then you can start deciding how you want them split up."

Susanna promptly drew a chair up next to his and bent studiously over his lists of property, her shoulder touching his, silky black curls brushing his face from time to time, and a strange mixed fragrance of horses, gunpowder, and perfume clinging to her. She was certainly like no other girl or woman he had desired, Court reflected sardonically as he discovered another talent he would never have expected in a girl with whom he wanted to spend long hours naked in bed; Susanna had an amazing mathematical ability which she evidently thought everyone had, for she persisted in adding columns of figures almost instantaneously and assuming that he had done the same. It soon became obvious that when Susanna said she wanted to divide the estate with her sister, she meant that Lilith was to have half of everything, half of every investment, half of houses and buildings in St. Louis, half of sets of china, half of a Chinese vase purchased by her father on the occasion of his third wedding anniversary. Court had a hard time convincing her that some assets were worth more if not divided.

"You know, this is all very well," said Susanna suddenly, "but what I really need is some cash money."

"You mean you don't have any?"

"Not a penny. It took so long to get here because of the snow that I spent everything I brought along. Lilith has been supporting me, which is hardly fair or proper."

"Well, I can advance you anything you need, Susanna," said Court, surprised at her predicament.

Susanna flushed. "That wouldn't be proper either. In fact, one thing I need money for is to pay your bill. Am I supposed to borrow money from you to—"

"Don't worry about my bill, Susanna. That's always settled when the estate is settled. As for spending money, I can wire St. Louis, but it may take a few days, and in the meantime—"

"In the meantime I can do without," said Susanna firmly.

"Well, if I can't help you financially, at least I can keep my promise and take you riding."

There was a change in the timber of his voice that caused Susanna to look up quickly into his eyes, which had become almost gray-black under their pale brows and lashes. "I'd have to ask Lilith," she replied in a hushed voice.

"Why?"

Susanna looked confused at the question, and it was obvious to Court that she had never in her life, at least until she rode out by herself to rescue him, done anything without permission from someone. "Why do you have to ask Lilith?" he persisted. "You're independent now. Lilith isn't your keeper."

"But she's my only family. And if I just went, Mr. Quincy would tell her and—" Susanna looked at him helplessly, willing him to understand her predicament.

"Do you think she'll let you?"

Eyes showing clearly the ache of wanting something she knew she might not be able to have, Susanna murmured reluctantly, "I don't know what she'll say."

"Maybe I should ask if you want to go riding with me?"

"Of course. Of course I do, Aaron."

Court's hands went to her shoulders, tightening compulsively as he bent toward her, and her eyes seemed to become huge with both fear and desire. "Ask Quincy," he said, abruptly releasing her. "If you have to ask someone."

"All right," she agreed; her voice was barely audible.

And Susanna did ask Quincy—not Lilith and not Clara Schmidt, both of whom might, in fact would probably, have said no. Susanna wanted to go riding with Aaron Court, and Quincy obviously thought well of him. She quite frankly told Quincy that she was lonely, since she seldom saw her sister and since no one else in town seemed inclined to make a friend of her. Although Quincy did not immediately agree, as she had hoped he might, he did not say no, nor did he insist on taking the matter up with Lilith. He said he would think about it, which he did for several hours after Susanna had retired. Instead of venturing out for his usual evening of drinking, gambling, or whoring, Quincy lay back on his bed in his hotel room and gave Susanna a good deal of thought.

When he had first taken the job as her bodyguard, he had thought her exceedingly young and unbelievably stupid. He still occasionally thought her somewhat dimwitted. But he had also come to admire her. The girl had the courage of her convictions. When she had decided that Aaron Court was a reprehensible person, she had snubbed him persistently, although Quincy knew perfectly well that she had still been infatuated with Court at the time. And when she had felt that Court should be rescued, she had gone out and done it herself—done it with a good deal of courage and ingenuity. The girl had guts. She was also in an unenviable position, Quincy reflected, being as she was friendly, lonely, and unacceptable to any segment of society. There was no place for her in her sister's world because she was too respectable, but there was no place for her in the world of the respectable ladies of Amnonville because of her relationship to Lilith. And the worst of it was that Susanna did not seem to know why she was being rejected on all sides, although undoubtedly she would find out sooner or later. Lilith was deluding herself if she thought Susanna would not eventually realize the nature of business at the Fallen Angel.

Quincy decided to have a talk with Aaron Court if he could find him. With that goal in mind he set out on his usual evening rounds and eventually found Court shooting dice at the Fallen Angel. The two men returned to the bar for a drink, and Quincy remarked casually, "Miss Susanna says you invited her to go riding."

"That's right." Court gave him a level look. "When we were sitting around up at the cabin with the Packards taking shots at us, she mentioned that people hadn't been very friendly to her." His face closed in harsh lines. "Damned hypocritical old bitches," he muttered. That one comment, more than anything else he said, influenced Quincy in his favor. "Anyway I said I'd take her to see the waterfall up at Wailing Squaw Peak and maybe some of the wildflower fields. Girls generally like flowers."

Quincy nodded. "She probably would like um. She ain't much of a rider though."

Court grinned. "From what I saw when she ran that mare across the clearing to the cabin, she shouldn't ever be on a horse moving faster than a walk."

"Ran the horse, did she? She sure must a been set on gettin to you. Generally we have to argue for an hour before I can git her to trot that damned mare." Quincy stared down into his drink for a long minute, and Court made no effort to push the matter.

Finally Quincy said, "Susanna now, she ain't like Lilith. She was brought up respectable, an it took with her." Court still said nothing. "You might think, cause she went out there an bamboozled them Packards an all, that she's got a wild streak in her, but—"

"Quincy, I'm not liable to fault her for saving my life. I'm well aware that she felt she owed me a debt because I pulled her off that balcony."

An are you well aware that she's half in love with you? Quincy wondered sarcastically, but silently. "Well, I'm just pointin' out that she's a gentle little thing, an she's been sheltered—so to speak."

"I was figuring on taking her to see a waterfall, Quincy, not a cockfight or—"

"Okay, okay, Court. Jus so we understand each other. I don't see no reason why she shouldn't go ridin with you; do her good to see someone besides Clara an me fer a change." Quincy threw down the rest of his drink. "Wouldn't say nothin about it to Lilith though if I was you. She don't think as highly of you as Miss Susanna does."

Court smiled a tight, cold smile. "And here I'd always imagined Lilith thought highly of me."

"Not where her sister's concerned," Quincy replied. "Only man, sides me, she ever willingly let near Susanna was Grant Penvennon."

Court laughed and finished his own drink. "Didn't know Penvennon had eyes for Susanna."

"He's a man, ain't he? Susanna's an uncommon pretty girl. Sweet too."

"No question," Court agreed.

Quincy left the Fallen Angel shortly after that, satisfied with the results of the conversation. Although he knew that Court had a fast reputation with women of one sort and because he knew that Court had a great disinterest in all the respectable young ladies who would have been delighted to accept an honorable proposal from him, Quincy had decided that Court might be the very man to marry Susanna, and marriage was the only future Quincy could see for her; she certainly could not continue indefinitely in her present position. Since she was respectable, Quincy reasoned that Court could be trusted not to seduce her, and since she was beautiful and spirited, Court might fall in love with her, and finally since Court was not one to worry about public opinion, he might be willing to marry her, even if her sister was Lilith Moran. Quincy had decided that the odds were in his favor or, to be more exact, in Susanna's. Not that Aaron would make an easy husband, but he would probably be better than none—and richer than most.

18

One crisp morning when the sun had risen in a cloudless sky, promising a clear, lovely spring day for a change, Susanna and Quincy rode slowly along Copper Street, heading out of town in a different direction than usual for her daily lesson. The streets were already busy, crowded with people hurrying about their early morning business and with workmen raising new buildings to replace the old. There were piles of bricks obstructing the street, drifts of sawdust clogging the nostrils of passersby, a train of pack mules heading out for a remote mining camp, a stagecoach arriving to pick up passengers for a destination not yet served by a railroad. Even a week earlier Susanna might have taken a lively interest in all the activity, might have questioned the new direction in which they were heading; that morning she said nothing. Quincy had noticed that she was becoming increasingly quiet, although she obediently rode out with him each day.

As they crossed Tenth Street and entered the north end of town, Susanna suddenly straightened in her saddle and pointed to a building rising on their left. "Look," she cried, "that's where Lilith's Land and Cattle Company used to be. In fact—" She urged her horse into a trot and pulled ahead of Quincy, calling, "Lilith, Lilith, hello."

Her sister turned from supervision of the construction and frowned when she saw her eager, smiling sister. "What are you doing in this end of town?" she demanded.

The smile died from Susanna's face, and Quincy

had to answer the question himself. "We're tryin some new trails. Thought some different scenery might cheer Miss Susanna up. She's been mopin around an not eatin much the last few days." He stared meaningfully at Lilith. "Needs some cheerin up," he repeated pointedly.

"Spring is a bad time to ignore your health, Susanna," said Lilith. "There are fevers going around. I expect you to eat well—and work hard at your lessons."

"Yes, Lilith." Susanna stared at the frame of the new building. "Maybe I could help you here," she suggested wistfully. "Or over at the temporary Land and Cattle Company."

"I have plenty of help. The best way you can help me is to do what you're told. In fact, shouldn't you two be getting along?"

Susanna's brief spurt of animation subsided, and she turned her horse back into the street with Quincy beside her frowning. It seemed to him that Lilith could have been less short with the girl; in fact, her whole attitude irritated him. Prodded by that ill temper, he stopped his horse before they left town, scribbled a brief note, and gave it with a penny to a street boy to be delivered. Then they continued up a winding road that went higher into the mountains toward the pass that took a traveler eventually to Denver.

Since Susanna had shown no curiosity about his note, Quincy had to broach the subject of it himself. "You still interested in goin ridin with Aaron Court?" he inquired.

Susanna turned surprised eyes toward him. "I thought you weren't going to let me. You hadn't said anything."

"Well, I had to think about it, but I don't see no reason why you shouldn't. Maybe we'll see him today. Looks like a nice day to visit Wailin Squaw Peak. Course, you might not feel like ridin that far, but—"

"Oh, yes I would." Susanna's eyes were shining, and she worked particularly hard at her quick-draw lessons, only getting her pistol caught in her holster several times and once even hitting the tree at which she was supposed to be aiming.

When Quincy had had as much of her inept shooting as he could stand, he suggested that they go to Four Mile Branch Meadow for some rifle practice, and Susanna agreed enthusiastically to that suggestion since rifle practice was the one Western skill at which she excelled. When they arrived, Aaron Court was waiting for them, leaning against a tree and smoking a cheroot.

"Aaron," Susanna cried happily. "Mr. Quincy didn't tell me you could come today." Court winced as she threw her leg over the saddle horn and tumbled off the horse, but he could not get to her in time to prevent her from landing painfully on one knee. However, Susanna sprang up smiling and, after dusting off the skirt of her riding habit with her hat, offered him her hand in greeting. Then to his astonishment she drew her rifle from its sheath.

"You're not planning on shooting me, are you?" he asked.

"Of course not," replied Susanna, laughing. "I'm here for rifle practice."

"You forgot to tether your horse, Miss Susanna," Quincy reminded her.

"And you forgot to teach her how to dismount," Court muttered.

"I'd be glad to see how far you git with that," Quincy snapped back.

"What shall I shoot at?" Susanna asked enthusiastically, having taken care of her horse.

"Waal, maybe you kin skip the shootin lessons fer today," Quincy decided. "If you an Aaron's goin all the way to Wailin Squaw Peak, you need to git goin. Why don't you two take the lunch with you, an you kin meet me at the hotel at four. That suit you?"

"Fine," Court agreed immediately.

"Perhaps you could take my rifle back with you, Mr. Quincy?"

Quincy frowned. "No, you keep it, Miss Susanna. Never know who you're goin to meet in the mountains."

"You had any trouble?" Court asked.

"Not so far. You?"

Court shook his head. "But don't worry. I'm watching my back trail these days."

"You want me to go along?"

"No, of course not. I can take care of her."

Susanna was looking from one man to the other, wondering what in the world they were talking about.

"Reckon you can," Quincy agreed. "Waal, enjoy the waterfall, Miss Susanna. I think it's mighty purty myself." He mounted and rode off in the direction of town.

"Maybe we should have asked him along," suggested Susanna. "I wouldn't want Mr. Quincy to think he wasn't welcome to join us."

Court gave her a slight sardonic smile, his eyes traveling over her face and coming to rest on her mouth in a way that made Susanna feel self-con-

scious and unable to meet his glance. Court said
only, "We'd better get going," and putting his
hands around her waist, he swung the surprised girl
into the saddle, then mounted his own horse in a
smooth, easy movement that made Susanna envy his
expertise. "How long did it take you to learn to ride
like that?" she asked as she patted her mare
anxiously in hopes that it would not start up without
warning or embarrass her in any way.

"Like what?" Court kneed his horse forward and
took the lead.

"Well, you didn't even have to kick her to get her
going."

"Him. This is a gelding."

"What's that?"

Court dryly changed the direction of the conversation because he doubted that she would really
appreciate an explanation. "I didn't have to kick the
horse because I used my knees, but that's something
you have to train the horse to understand."

"I'm sure the horse appreciates not being
kicked," said Susanna seriously. "I always feel very
guilty about kicking mine. It's no wonder she isn't
cooperative."

"It's not a matter of what the horse appreciates,"
said Court. "There are times when I don't want to
have to use the reins—when I'm shooting from the
saddle, for instance." Susanna's eyes widened.
Before she could ask him why he would be shooting
from the saddle, he went on, somewhat grimly, to
say that her horse was uncooperative not because it
was being kicked but because Susanna was a poor
rider.

"I'm doing my best," she cut in defensively.

"I wonder. In the first place, you're afraid of the

horse. Why?''

"It's bigger than I am.''

"I'm bigger than you are too. Are you afraid of me?''

He had reined in and was riding beside her on a narrow tree-lined trail, keeping his eyes steadily on her.

"Of course not,'' said Susanna untruthfully. "Anyway, I can talk to you. I can't talk to the horse.''

"Of course you can. For instance, I noticed that when I first put you in the saddle, you were patting the horse's neck and not very gently either. You were nervous, and you were making the horse nervous. If you wanted to soothe the horse, you should have spoken quietly to it. Then look at the way you're sitting the horse.'' Susanna could not look at herself, and it made her very nervous to know that Court was looking at her. "You're sitting there as stiff as a spinster in church.''

"Quincy said I should keep my back straight,'' she answered resentfully.

"You should, but you have to let your body move with the horse from the waist down. Try to imagine that your hips and thighs are part of the animal.'' His hand rested briefly on her thigh, and Susanna stiffened with shock. "And relax,'' he added.

Her head was whirling in confusion. It was hard enough for her to ride, but to have Aaron touching her, commenting on her body, edging his mount closer so that their knees touched—she stared fixedly at her horse's mane, trying to regain her composure, but even that respite was denied her when Court cupped his hand under her chin and turned her face toward his. "Relax,'' he commanded softly, "and close your eyes." Susanna kept her eyes wide open and tried to turn her head away but could not until he said, "All right. You can look now." He turned her face forward as they broke into a clearing at the end of which the mountain jutted steeply upward with a waterfall tumbling merrily over its rock face.

Susanna sighed, self-consciousness leaving her for the moment as she gazed at the lovely scene.

Court had halted his horse, and hers stopped of its own accord as he swung down and came around to put his hands on her waist.

"I can dismount by myself," said Susanna quickly, her eyes darting from the waterfall back to his face.

"I saw you," replied Court with a slight smile, "so I think this time I'll be sure you don't break your neck. Now swing your leg over." Reluctantly Susanna did as she was told. "Take your other foot from the stirrup," he ordered, his voice taking on the warm, husky quality that set her nerves on edge. Obediently she freed her foot, anxious now to be on the ground, free of his hands and the compelling look in his eyes, but Court was standing close to the horse and lowered her slowly, by inches. Dazedly she thought that he must be very strong to be able to do that and that the closeness of his body to hers (for she could not move away from him, not with the horse behind her and his hands still holding her waist firmly) was bringing back all the helpless sensations she had experienced when she had been in his arms at the cabin after the Packards had ridden away and left them alone. It seemed forever to her until he let her feet touch the ground, and then there was no escape from him because, still holding her eyes with his, he bent his head and kissed her in a slow, warm kiss that deepened and deepened until their lips were open and Court's tongue was inside her mouth, lazily exploring, sending shocks of feeling through her. His hands left her waist and his arms encircled her—firmly drawing her against him, and her hands, which had been resting on his arms, moved up to his shoulders and then around his neck, and still the kiss went on with a slow, dreamlike passion until at last Aaron released her mouth and, slipping a hand into her hair, cradled her head against his shoulder and stared unthinking at the waterfall, bemused by the depth of his desire for her. Susanna was content for the moment to rest—eyes closed, mind drifting, her cheek against his shoulder, letting the new, frightening emotions seep away.

Finally she whispered tentatively, "I'm—I'm getting hungry, Aaron."

"Oh God, love, so am I," he murmured against her hair.

"Maybe we should have lunch."

"Lunch?" he muttered under his breath, but he released her and lifted the picnic basket from the horn of his saddle, letting her delay, knowing enough not to frighten her as he had after he had killed Bates.

They ate their picnic lunch by the pool at the foot of the waterfall and afterwards explored upwards, for the mountain, which had looked so steep, could be climbed and had grassy niches, small trees, occasional flowers, miniature worlds dappled with sunlight and mist from the water falling close by. Court let her, in fact helped her, climb halfway up the falls, enjoying her delight. Finally, however, he could let her go no further, and when she protested, he made her look up at the rocks above her. "You see how wet they are? They're also slippery."

"But look at the moss," Susanna interrupted. "It looks like green velvet. I wanted to touch it. And the flower—" she pointed to a blue flower above her head, growing at the very verge of the waterfall but protected from the water which danced around it by the rock out of which it seemed to spring.

"I'll get it for you." Court moved a step away from her and reached toward the flower.

"Oh no," Susanna cried. "Don't pick it; it's the only one."

He laughed and assured her that the mountains would be full of those particular flowers in a week or less. "Come then," he said, "if you won't have the flower, at least you can touch the moss," and he swung her easily upward so that she could reach the next ledge. "But don't scrape it off," he warned. "I know a beautiful girl who doesn't like the mountain disturbed."

As he let her down beside him, she smiled at him and asked happily, "Do you think I'm beautiful?"

"How could I not?" he murmured, slipping his arms around her waist. "Did you like the way the moss felt?"

"M-m. So soft."

Court's lips were on her cheek moving toward her mouth. "As soft as your skin?" he asked.

Susanna started to pull back, and he tightened his arms, murmuring, "Don't move, Susanna. You'll fall," and his mouth came down on hers again, making her feel as if she were indeed falling. "Only a moment," he whispered into her ear. "We have to go in a moment." He kissed her once more, deeply, his hand sliding under her riding jacket to cup her breast. Then he released her and helped her on the downward climb, moving down the ledges first himself, then lifting her down, each time holding her close to him, brushing her hair and forehead with his lips, so that the whole descent seemed like a hot, dazed dream, from which she emerged only when he lifted her once more onto her horse.

That evening, puzzled by Susanna's brief responses to his questions about her afternoon with Aaron Court, Quincy went looking for Court once she had retired for the night. He found the lawyer, as usual, at the Fallen Angel, having a drink. "How'd the ride go?" he asked.

"Didn't you talk to Susanna?"

"She was pretty quiet about it. I think maybe you hurt her feelins." Aaron shot him a quick glance but said nothing. He had seen many a witness in court get himself into hot water by having too much to say. "Reckon maybe she didn't like yer criticizin her ridin," Quincy suggested.

"Better than having her get hurt."

"Maybe."

"Maybe? People get killed on horses, Abner, and Susanna's a prime candidate if she doesn't start improving. Maybe you ought to forget about all this shooting-from-the-hip crap and see that the girl really learns to ride."

"Speakin a shootin, someone took a shot at me on the way back to town this afternoon."

"A Packard?"

"Didn't see. Don't know who else would."

Court nodded. "Maybe we ought to do a little Packard hunting ourselves. I figure it's just a matter of time before they make another try for me."

"Well, you got any ideas that's even moderately sensible, I wouldn't mind. Might even enjoy it."

Court grinned. "Finding your new job a little slow?"

"Slow ain't the word," said Quincy. "You young fellers may enjoy taggin along after pretty girls, but me, I'm of an age I like more spice to life—immediate pleasure, so to speak."

Court smiled to himself, thinking that Susanna was adding a good deal of spice to his life and would add more if he could manage it. "Well, Abner, on your day off, maybe we could head up toward Packard country and see if we can do them a little damage."

"Like what?"

"What would you say to running their horses off and then dynamiting their pass when they come chasing after them?"

"Think we could manage that?"

"Hell, yes. Might even be fun. Might add some of that spice you're looking for."

Abner Quincy grinned. "Might just."

19

During the next days Susanna gave a good deal of serious thought to her relationship with Aaron Court but found that she could come to absolutely no conclusions about it. The deep and frightening feelings of pleasure he stirred in her, the things he wanted to do to her, were absolutely outside her experience. And not only had she had no experience with men, but no one had ever talked to her about relations between men and women. Consequently she had only two criteria by which she could judge her experiences with Court. First she had gathered from her Bible that certain types of conduct involving men and women were sinful; Susanna had no desire to commit any sins, but the Bible was very ambiguous on the exact nature of the sins in question. Second, she had gathered from the attitude of her parents that things that were pleasurable were sinful—the more pleasurable, the more sinful. Being in Aaron's arms, feeling his mouth on hers, melting under the touch of his hands—these were certainly pleasurable sensations, very pleasurable, much more pleasurable than eating all the grapes off the trellis had been, a sin for which she had received a beating. She decided that she would simply have to ask Lilith the next time her sister came to visit. In fact, she marked in her mind certain Biblical passages that she wanted explained, sure that Lilith, who knew everything, would be a reliable source of information.

Her assiduous Bible reading impressed both Clara and Abner with her piety. Abner was especially pleased, his uneasiness over encouraging the relationship with Court put to rest, for he assumed that any girl that lovely and that devout would be more than a match for one lawyer who might mistakenly think he was destined to escape marriage. He felt no compunction about agreeing to another afternoon of sightseeing for Aaron and Susanna, a wildflower expedition, which had been carefully arranged by Abner and Court as a partial alibi for plans they had set up for the night before.

In accordance with these plans, three days before the scheduled raid on Packard country, Abner began to cough and to complain of a cold. By the

afternoon before the raid, Abner had convinced
both Clara and Susanna that he was becoming
rather seriously ill. Yielding to their admonitions to
take care of his health, he agreed to go to bed and to
stay in bed that night and all the next day, assuring
them that a good long sleep, as long as it was unin-
terrupted, always restored him to health. Before he
disappeared into his room for his long sleep, Abner
said to Susanna that Court was expected back from
Denver the next day and had asked to take her riding
in the afternoon. Although her questions were still
unanswered, since Lilith had avoided her all week,
Susanna agreed eagerly to the engagement. No
ambiguous Biblical passages had managed to cool
her growing infatuation with Court, which had only
been enhanced by his sudden departure from
Amnonville.

Aaron's trip to Denver was widely announced
before he left, and he did go to Denver where he
bought mining equipment and explosives, most of
which were sent back to Grassback Holbein in
Amnonville. Some of the explosives, however, were
reserved and stored in Court's cabin in the
mountains while he began a painstaking night recon-
naissance of the Packards' valley. By the time
Abner's cough had reached epic proportions, by the
time several other adventurers had been recruited,
Court knew where the Packards posted guards at the
valley entrance, which guards tended to fall asleep,
which Packards slept in which cabins, what time
they went to bed, and where Grassback thought it
best to place explosive charges so as to drive the
horses out of their corral straight down the valley
and to blow large boulders from the valley entrance
onto the heads of pursuing Packards.

In a brief meeting outside of town the night before
the raid, the four men involved gathered to go over
the plan one last time, to look at the maps of the
valley so carefully drawn by Court, and to divide up
the various jobs to be done. Court took for himself
the most dangerous, the setting off of the explosives
to stampede the horses, which had to be done in the
midst of the whole Packard clan. Benny Ripon, the
bloodthirsty jeweler, chose the midway position
from which the stampede, should it show signs of
slowing down, was to accelerate. Benny made it
quite obvious that he expected to pick off a few
Packards as well.

"So do we all," said Court slowly, "but let's keep
in mind that, if all goes as planned, we should get
their horses and some of the men at the pass, or
maybe some of the horses and more of the men. I
went to a lot of trouble planning the escape routes
for us all, and I'd hate to see anyone hold off using
his till it was too late." Each man, having completed
his mission, was to take off in a different but carefully calculated direction.

Grassback and Abner Quincy, both mountain
men, were to take care of the sentries at the pass and
set off the charges that would bring at least a small
portion of the mountain down on any man or
animal unlucky enough to come through at the right
time. All having agreed on their places and times of
action, the four men shook hands and dispersed.

The next night Court and Ripon worked their way
on foot into the valley, having left their horses
tethered above at the tops of steep trails. They wore
Indian moccasins and buckskin clothes and carried
only their weapons. The explosives, Court had
stashed on earlier excursions. Having been into the

valley under the very noses of his enemies on at least
five previous nights, he had no trouble making his
way undetected toward the vicinity of the corral.
Ripon, less familiar with his territory, took longer,
but he was in his place well before midnight, having
slipped a knife quietly into a Packard follower who
had the ill luck to cross his path. Ripon disposed of
the body behind some rocks.

At the narrow entrance to the valley both Grassback and Quincy, in separate actions, disposed of
the midnight change of guard and placed their
explosives on their respective sides of the pass.

Then at two in the morning when the last drunken
Packard had fallen into his bed, Court moved. First
he slipped the bar that held the gate to the corral in
place and swung the gate wide. The drowsing horses
stamped restlessly but did not attempt to leave. Then
moving to the far side of the corral, he lit a cigar,
took a deep, satisfying lungful of the smoke and
then touched the glowing end of the cigar to a trail
of gunpowder he had laid. He paused only a
moment to watch the swift movement of the white
light in the darkness before slipping into the trees
behind the corral and diving behind some rocks he
had chosen as his shelter. A series of explosions
followed within seconds, and the horses, as planned,
stampeded noisily toward the open gate, running
straight down the road between the cabins before
any Packards could get out of bed and stop them.
However, by the time the lead horses were halfway
down the valley, those Packards who slept light and
had not fallen into bed drunk were up and catching
the last of the herd in order to pursue the first.

Court, satisfied that his part of the operation was
going according to plan, faded back into the heavy

forest and began the climb up the sides of the valley
to the spot where he hoped to find his own horse still
staked out. Benny Ripon meanwhile let the herd,
which was slowing down a bit, get halfway past his
vantage point and then activated Indian noisemakers that Grassback had provided. The huge,
eerie sounds bounced back and forth off the sides of
the valley, sending the horses mad with terror and
increasing again the speed of their flight toward the
ambush at the entrance. Then Benny shot several
Packards out of their saddles, and he too, mindful
of the climb ahead of him and the probable resentment of the gang at the loss of fifty or sixty horses,
faded into the trees and began to scramble up his
escape path.

At the entrance to the valley the herd leaders
began to pass below Grassback and Quincy who,
having no interest in killing the horses, all of which
probably belonged to respectable members of the
community, drew on their cigars and waited until
Packards, shouting and cursing, rode bareback
toward the valley's mouth. Then the two men lit
their gunpowder trails and scrambled away. Again
explosions echoed in the valley, followed by the
crashing of dirt, rocks and boulders—bounding,
leaping, plummeting into the narrow pass beneath.
It was some time before the screams of horses and
men and the shouts of newly arrived Packards subsided, and by that time most of the horse herd was
scattering over the outside trails while the Packards,
penned inside, assessed their losses and the last two
members of the raiding party slipped away.

None of the four night raiders had any idea of
what damage they had actually done, but Quincy
and Grassback knew that the rock slide at the pass

had been more spectacular than any of the group
had anticipated. Even if no Packards had been killed
or injured, they would have a hard time getting out
of the valley to round up the missing horses. Quincy
made it back to his hotel room just before dawn.
Grassback was unable to drop into his bunk at the
mine shack before 7:30. Benny Ripon was late
opening his shop that morning and was pronounced
by the various townspeople who ventured in to be
more short-tempered than usual. Court, who had
the farthest to go, especially the farthest on foot,
barely had time to sluice the sweat and dirt off
himself, change from his buckskins to a black suit,
and get to the McFadden Hotel in time to meet
Susanna for their trip. He complained to her that the
train trip from Denver was a tiring one.

Court had been worried that Susanna might want
a lively account of his trip to Denver—worried
because, having had little sleep in the last week and
none at all the night before, he did not feel up to
giving a lively account of anything, much less of
fictitious activities in Denver. Also he did not relish
telling her a pack of lies to cover his real activities, of
which she would undoubtedly disapprove for one
foolish, ill-conceived reason or another. He need not
have worried. Having made one polite inquiry about
his trip, Susanna was bubbling with news of her
own, for the town had been flooded with rumors
about a disaster in the Packards' valley, rumors of
hordes of stolen horses running loose in the
mountains and other such exciting matters that
Clara had regaled her with on returning from a trip
to the dressmaker to pick up a dress Susanna had
ordered. Susanna was astonished that Court had
heard none of this at the railroad station, the

stables, or the hotel.

Court was very interested indeed to hear that the Packards' valley had been blocked off by a huge rock slide, perhaps brought on by an earthquake; that the tremors had spooked all their horses; that anywhere from six to twenty Packards had been killed or injured in the confusion (figures varied widely); and that hordes of townsmen had taken to the hills to reclaim horses that had disappeared the night after the fire. He was even more interested to hear Susanna's interpretation of these events. She informed him that it was clear that God had caused the rock slide so that the Packards would not profit from their ill-gotten horses. Aaron was content to accept this interpretation of the night's events, much preferring that the Packards take up a feud with God and leave him alone. However, he did not console himself with the idea that the Packards might attribute the explosions, the stampede, the gunning down of stragglers, and the blocking of the valley to divine intervention—not for long anyway. He had to be satisfied that there were a few less Packards ranged against him and that they had many fewer horses to carry them on missions of revenge.

The mountain meadow to which Court took Susanna was perhaps not the most spectacular he could have chosen, but it was in exactly the opposite direction from Packard country and far enough away from the town so that Quincy would have a full day's sleep before Susanna returned to inquire after his health; Court, as he led her over mountain trails, was wishing that he too were asleep. His eyes felt gritty with exhaustion, his head heavy and his mind dull, as if to close his eyes would be to sink immediately into unconsciousness. Susanna noticed how little he had to say and how severe the lines of his face looked, and she began to feel unwelcome on the expedition that had presumably been conceived for her pleasure. Once she had discussed the Packard rumors, she too fell silent, and Court seemed not even to notice. However, when they broke out of the woods, which were as gloomy as her companion, Susanna was enchanted, for a valley stretched out ahead of them that had skeins of blue mountain lupine interwoven with the green of the grasses.

"There must be a million flowers," she whispered in wonder.

"Could be," Court replied. He guided their horses to the left for a half mile and stopped near a shallow stream that bubbled over rocks, making an enticing sound, both soothing and exciting. The area offered sunshine and shade, dry ground and clean water, yellow daisies, and even tiny ground-hugging flowers in the most delicate shades of pink, white and lavender. Susanna was out of her saddle with a frightening, enthusiastic tumble before Court could lift himself wearily from his. As he got the lunch basket down and dropped into the grass where there was a convenient rock against which to rest his back, Susanna was flitting from one delight to another.

"I shall make a daisy chain," she cried happily.

"Have lunch first," he suggested.

"I haven't made a daisy chain since I was a little girl." She plumped down beside him and dropped a handful of lupine on his head.

Court brushed the blue flowers out of his pale hair and mustache and, looking at the blossoms, which had been plucked at the head without stems, remarked, "You still pick flowers like a little girl."

"Lilith used to take me flower-picking. We made violet posies and daisy crowns and clover chains—"

"How do you do that without stems, or did Lilith do the picking?" Court found it hard to imagine Lilith making flower chains. "Don't you want anything to eat?" He had not only had no sleep; he had had nothing to eat since the night before. Much to his relief, Susanna allowed herself to be persuaded to eat, so he then could eat also. He rather hoped that she would not be too hungry, since he could easily have devoured the whole meal himself and was counting on the food to wake him up before he bored her into complete disinterest in him. Even thinking of something to say was difficult until her remarks about Lilith reminded him that they at least had business to discuss.

"One of us is going to have to talk to Lilith about the split in your inheritance sooner or later, Susanna. It won't do her much good if she doesn't know about it."

Susanna stopped eating, a shadow passing over her face. She had been hoping to talk to Lilith all week; dreading and hoping might be a better combination of words, for the subject promised to be difficult. But Lilith had not been to the hotel at all. Susanna had not seen her since the day when she had been too busy to talk at the construction site of the Fallen Angel. "Perhaps I had better talk to her," said Susanna slowly, reasoning that the inheritance would give her an excuse to summon Lilith to the hotel. "A matter of urgent business," Susanna imagined herself saying in a note, although she was not really sure how urgent the questions she had to ask about men and women really were, nor, for that matter, whether the inheritance money was urgent.

She did not know whether or not Lilith needed
money. It seemed that, having lost so much in the
fire, Lilith might welcome the extra income, but on
the other hand, Lilith might very well be angry when
she heard Susanna's plans. "I'll talk to her."
Susanna sighed. She did not anticipate an easy
conversation with her sister. What if Lilith asked
why Susanna wanted to know about men and
women?

Susanna glanced covertly at Aaron from beneath
her lashes. He was stretched out in the grass on his
back now, looking as if he might fall asleep. Was it
polite for a gentleman to recline at full length in a
lady's presence? she wondered. His white lashes
were almost resting on his dark cheeks. Susanna
quickly looked away. Maybe he was bored, she
thought miserably. He had said hardly anything—except to bring up the business matter, and
then he had not even commented on her answer.
Susanna tidied up the remains of the lunch and then
wondered what to do. Aaron was fast asleep. There
was no question. When a man was stretched out flat
on his back with his eyes closed, having said nothing
for ever so long, it was obvious that he was asleep.
Susanna's lips compressed in a hurt line. Well, his
nap offered her an opportunity to explore. *He*
obviously had little interest in the very wildflowers
he had brought her to see.

Resolutely Susanna rose and began to walk away
after carefully marking in her mind the spot where
Aaron lay asleep. As the sun was warm, she took off
the jacket of her riding habit, thinking to use it as a
receptacle for flowers. But when she found that a
jacket made a poor flower basket, she stopped by
the picnic spot and dropped the jacket, taking her

riding hat off instead. The inside of its crown was perfect, and for a half hour or more she wandered, choosing blossoms and putting them in the hat, which she swung happily by its chin strap, humming to herself as she wandered in grass and flowers that often brushed her knees. The meadow, to her mind, was an enchanted place.

When she finally returned, Aaron was still in the same relaxed position, his eyes closed, his breathing even. With a small frown, Susanna sat down cross-legged with the hat full of flowers in her lap. As she began to weave the flowers into chains, she mused on her companion. He had said that the train ride from Denver had been tiring, but he had been asleep over an hour, or so it seemed to her, and he had been so quiet before that, and rather grim. Susanna's hands dropped into idleness, and she raised her glance from the incomplete chain to his face. There were dark circles under his eyes. Had they been there before? Susanna did not even know how old Court was. Maybe he was old enough to always have circles, but with those white brows and lashes surely she would have noticed before. There were also lines there of exhaustion that she had never noticed before, as if he might be sleeping for the first time in a long time. And his mouth—Susanna's eyes were caught by his mouth; there was a sensual, finely cut quality to the shape of his lips. Her own thoughts brought an acceleration of her heartbeat, a flush to her cheeks, and before she could lower her eyes and try to return her mind to earlier speculations, Court had suddenly rolled onto his side and risen on his elbow, his arm streaking out to grasp her wrist and pull her toward him.

"It's not polite to watch someone sleeping," he

said in a husky voice. "What were you thinking about?"

Susanna gasped, her cheeks coloring as if he could tell what had occupied her thoughts. "When did you wake up?" she countered.

"When you first came back," he replied. "What were you thinking about that made you blush when I asked?"

"I was wondering why you were so tired," she replied defensively. "It occurred to me that the things they say happened to the Packards last night might not have been an act of God after all, that you might be so tired because you—"

Court's hand had tightened cruelly on her wrist as he drew her inexorably to him, spilling her flowers into the grass, making her eyes widen in alarm. "What do you think the Packards would do if they even thought I was behind what happened last night?" he asked in a low, tense voice.

"I—" Susanna was staring directly into his gray eyes, her mind whirling. The answer was that they would kill him, of course. "I'll never say that to anyone else," she promised in a hushed voice. Court had drawn her almost into his arms; his lips were inches from hers, his eyes commanding her. "I promise," she said again, as if her promise would deter him. "Aaron." Her voice was a whispered plea, but he drew her upper body against his with one arm and, releasing her wrist, swept the other arm under her legs to slide her onto her back in the grass. In the same motion he stretched out beside her and claimed her mouth in a kiss that wiped all thought of the Packards and his role in their problems from her mind, as he had meant it to.

The brief sleep he had had as she wandered in the

meadow had canceled his exhaustion, and secretly watching her from beneath half-closed eyes as she braided the flowers and then stared openly at his face had fueled his desire for her. But he was prepared to take his time with her, wanted to, in fact. He wanted a long, slow, sweet loving that would sweep her with him, that would put his seal on her, that would surpass what they had had before. Consequently he held her and kissed her there in the grass for long moments until she was soft and relaxed in his arms, accepting the warm pressure of his lips and the hot searching of his tongue in her mouth that followed. Gradually her arms tightened around him and she molded herself to him as her mind relinquished control and her body surrendered. Then he slipped the buttons of her silk riding blouse and moved his fingers in gentle caresses to her breasts and finally his lips to a pink nipple that was already full in passionate response to his touch. When his lips touched her breast, drew the rosy circle into his mouth, when she felt the gentle suction, the touch of his tongue on the painfully sensitive tip, her body arched and her arms tightened convulsively in response to a shaft of aching sensation that started between her thighs and spread and intensified into her legs and her pelvic valley. Susanna's wild response wiped all calculation from Court's mind. Without relinquishing her breast, his hands went to loosen her riding skirt, and then his mouth was at her waist, his tongue teasing her naval and his hands under the skirt sliding over the soft skin to trace her pelvic bones with light fingertips toward the silky nest of black hair that he wanted so much to probe again. However, that touch ignited not passion but terror in Susanna, and she turned from him, drawing herself into a ball that denied him access.

Cut off so abruptly, Court paused in confusion. "What is it, Susanna?" he asked gently.

"I'm afraid," she answered truthfully, her voice barely audible. "I don't understand what's happening."

"Oh, love," he murmured, "you don't have to be afraid. I wouldn't hurt you." Court sat up in the grass and scooped her tightly curled-body into his lap. "You don't have to be afraid." She was trembling in his arms, and he rocked her, pressing light kisses into her hair and onto her forehead. "You don't have to be afraid, love. There'll be other times." Court tipped her chin up and smiled into her eyes. "Other times. There's no hurry, and no reason to be afraid of me." Then he kissed her lips lightly, running his tongue across the sensitive joining as he began to button her blouse, tucking it into her skirt as if she were a young child who needed to be dressed. When he was done, he turned her against his chest and held her with her face pressed into his throat, his hand tangled in her hair—just held her until all the tension ran out of her body, and she snuggled peacefully against him. Then he said quietly, "We'd better get back before we worry Quincy."

"Oh, Mr. Quincy has been sick in bed," Susanna replied.

"Has he?"

"Or maybe instead of being in bed last night he was—"

Court stopped that speculation with a kiss that was not at all gentle. "Sick," he assured her and then drew her to her feet and lifted her into her saddle for the ride home.

20

Once Court had left Susanna at the hotel, he rode on to a chophouse where he ate dinner with various business acquaintances who happened to be there and who found him rather uncommunicative, considering the interest of the latest Packard tale. In fact, Court seemed so indifferent to the whole matter that his fellow diners never thought of connecting him with the event; they assumed that he had lost interest in bringing the Packards to heel once he had managed to get Elias hung.

Such was not the case. Court was simply preoccupied with thoughts of Susanna, whose rejection of him that afternoon, instead of irritating him as a similar experience with any other woman might have done, had served only to increase his desire for her. Every moment with her was a delight; every passage between them acted on him as an aphrodisiac, cemented his certainty that she belonged to him, that he would have her again and that she would be fully willing the second time. The memory of her wild reaction when he had kissed her breasts, of her delicate hip bones and of her silky skin and hair beneath his exploring fingers, made him ache for complete possession, and he knew it would come soon. Susanna belonged to him.

With his thoughts still full of her, Court dismounted at his cabin and soon fell into his bed and into deep, exhausted sleep while it was still early evening. For hours he lay unmoving, sleeping off the effects of nights without adequate rest. What his dreams might have been, he never remembered, and he might never have awakened from that sleep had his own wracked coughing not jarred him into consciousness well after midnight.

Court rolled off the bed onto the floor where the smoke was not so thick and then crawled out into the hall, after taking his guns from the bedside table. He saw that he could not leave by either door, for fires had been built outside each threshold. He lay flat on the floor, breathing the clearer air and thinking out his next move, which had to be an attempt to escape through a window with the hope that the arsonists had assumed they could leave and allow their fires to do their work for them. Unfortunately, they had not been so careless. The cabin had only two windows, and Court's shots from them brought return fire. He calculated that there were several ambushers hidden in the woods waiting for him to burn or suffocate but ready to pick him off if he should attempt to leave.

Cursing the Packards for the murdering swine they were, Court dragged on his pants and assessed his chances. The probability that he might be able to shoot the men and get out a window before the fire or smoke got him was slim indeed. That left the old tunnel the original owner had built when Indians were still a menace to isolated settlers. Court had no idea whether it was still usable. When he first bought the cabin, he had explored half of it and then backed up the way he had come rather than risk having the filthy tunnel cave in on him. Now it seemed he had no choice but to try it all the way. Without donning boots or shirt, stopping only to reload his guns and grab a rifle, he crawled back into the hall and pried up the trap door. The fire had now eaten well through the outer doors, and he doubted that he would be able to return should the tunnel prove impassable—providing always that he was not buried alive down there before he had a chance to move to one end of the escape route or the other.

There were no steps down into the passage; he had to drop the guns down and then jump himself. Once on the dirt floor, he realized, cursing, that he had brought no lantern or candle and would have to return or to feel his way. Impatiently he reached up and pulled the trap door closed to keep the smoke from the cabin out of the tunnel; then, on hands and knees, he began to feel his way along the gritty passage. His slow movement brought dirt sifting down on him, and he had to take the utmost care lest he jar one of the supporting timbers and bring the whole roof down on himself through his own carelessness. It seemed to him that the air was barely breathable. The taste of dirt in his mouth, the sound of his own rasping breath, the smell of the musty tunnel and of his own sweat, the unexplained rustlings, and the soft fall of dirt around him all combined to make his mind cringe with claustro-phobic aversion, but still he forced his body to move on. He wondered if he was running out of air. Had he brought a candle, as miners did, he would have known. He continued to crawl, sucking dust-filled air into unsatisfied, laboring lungs. What if the tunnel were blocked off ahead of him? What if, dazed, he blundered into a support and the roof caved in? He would die down here, gasping for breath, choking and gagging like a hanged man. He continued to crawl. How far was it to the end? He had never been to the end. He knew only that the tunnel came up somewhere in the woods beyond the clearing, but he had never bothered to search for the exit outside, had simply remembered what the first owner had told him. The exit might be unusable. The Packards might be waiting there to blow his head off. Better than dying down here, he thought. He continued to crawl. Never had liked mines. Cold. Wet. Dark. How could men go into the mines day after day? Penvennon. Remembered Penvennon saying once that a mine was a peaceful place. Wrong. Bloody, black hell. Never liked Penvennon. Penvennon never liked anyone. Except Susanna. He continued to crawl. Susanna. He fastened his mind on Susanna. Silky, curly black hair. Wide, wide blue eyes. Pink cheeks, pink lips, pink-tipped breasts. Susanna. Precious. Soft. Warm. Susanna. Barely moving, he continued to crawl. Susanna was his, and no Packard was going to kill him before he could get to her, and no tunnel, and no—his head touched gently against a wall. With caution he extended the fingers of his right hand, rifle still clutched in the left. Exploring like a blind man, he touched walls on three sides, and the wall ahead—it seemed fairly solid. Not smooth, but not like a pile, not like a cave-in. Breathing in shallow gasps, he laid down the rifle and rose to his knees, exploring above his head with his hand, then to his feet with arm partially extended. Wood. Rough, rotting wood. He bent for the rifle and used the butt to exert cautious force against the outer edges of the wooden square, hoping to lift it if it was another trap door. Light pressure accomplished nothing. Heavy pressure pushed the rifle butt through and brought dust and rotting chunks of wood down into his upturned face, brought scouring tears into eyes already blinded by the darkness of the tunnel. Court found it hard to think. If he attacked the roof, he might call down the attention of the Packards on himself while he was still trapped. But if he did not get out soon, he might not have the strength left to get out at all. Gritting his teeth, closing his eyes, he swung the rifle butt again and again at the roof until he had cleared a hole big enough for his body. Then shoving the rifle ahead of him, he grasped the splintered edges and hauled himself up, but the handholds crumbled, tearing his palms and fingers and dropping him back into the tunnel. Ignoring his own pain, he tried again, and a third time, until he had his upper body sprawled on the ground and his legs dangling into the tunnel. From there, he inched carefully forward, praying dimly that the Packards were elsewhere attending to their fire and that he would not be plunged back into the tunnel.

When at last he was free, with his rifle clutched in one bleeding hand, he lay sprawled under the trees, fillings his lungs with the clean air, letting tears clear his eyes of the blinding dust until he could see the moonlight filtering through the branches. Packards he could neither see nor hear, so he rested, unmoving, breathing as quietly as he could, gathering his strength. Some minutes had passed before he began to think clearly about his situation, which now seemed to him to be good, to be wonderful.

In the darkness Court smiled a wicked smile. If the Packards were still around, they must think that he was dead or dying in his house. Perhaps they were waiting hopefully for screams. Court moved silently out of the dim moonlight into darkness, letting his eyes adjust before he tried to move again. There was no hurry now. If they were still about, he would get them. He slipped from tree to tree, watching, listening, moving back in the direction of his cabin, then circling cautiously the edge of the clearing. Finally when he had come a half circle, he first heard the voices.

"Think the smoke got him?"

"Likely," was the answer. "Too damn bad it wasn't the fire."

"Well, Job said we gotta be sure. Shit, we may have to sit around here till the whole damn cabin burns down."

"Almost wish he'd tried to git out. Didn't git off too many shots, did he?"

"Smoke musta got him."

"Likely."

Court took careful aim at the speaker who had wished him in flames and shot the man in the back of the head. The second one whirled but was too stunned to dive for cover in time. Court shot him in the throat and then slipped back into the heavy trees to await a possible third member of the gang. None appeared, and the two he had shot, when he nudged them over on their backs with the butt of his rifle, both proved to be dead. He dragged the bodies into the clearing and went to inspect his house, noting with contempt that Packards were not very efficient arsonists. The fire at the back had died out with damage only to the door and frame, and they evidently had not even noticed it. The front door was gone; part of the parlor wall and some of the furniture were smoldering fitfully. Court drew water from his well and tossed it on the embers till they seemed to be dead. Then, barefooted, he picked his way through the debris to his bedroom where he put on the rest of his clothes in preparation for a trip in to the sheriff's office with the two bodies. He found, as he slung them over a horse's back, that he did not know their names, although he had seen them around and recognized them as Packards. One he thought was a Packard cousin.

Court arrived at the sheriff's door about four in the morning and pounded loudly with the butt of a pistol until the man came grumbling to answer the summons, cautiously inquiring as to who was there before he opened. The answer caused him to say angrily as he drew the bolts, "This here's the second time, Court, you got me out of bed this spring. This better be important."

Court unceremoniously dumped the two bodies into the street in front of the jail. "Brought you two Packards," he said briefly.

"Drunk?"

"Dead."

"Hell." The sheriff, holding up his lantern, peered down at the corpses. "Packards," he agreed. "Dead Packards is nuthin but trouble. Nuthin but trouble. An what the hell am I supposed to do with two corpses this time a night?"

"Leave em in the street, for all I care," was Court's reply.

Peering down again, the sheriff said, "This one's been shot in the back."

"Right. I shot him from behind and the other from in front—while they were watching my place burn, wondering whether the fire or the smoke had got me."

"Shot in the back," muttered the sheriff dubiously.

"In the back," Court agreed. "You go out and look at my place. Then if you want to arrest me, you can try. I'll be at the McFadden." Court swung into his saddle and rode off, leaving the sheriff muttering.

Under the pressure of having two late-night corpses dropped on his doorstep, Sheriff Maxie had not paid much attention to Court's appearance, which he could not see very clearly in the dark street anyway. The night clerk at the McFadden did notice. Court looked like some apparition from hell, his pants, face, and fair hair covered with soot and dirt, his shirt clean but carelessly buttoned and showing a chest as filthy as his face and hands. The terrified clerk could hardly be convinced that the person before him was a prominent local lawyer who might cost him his job if he did not come up immediately with a room, hot water for bathing, and a bottle of whiskey.

"I'll be in the room within fifteen minutes," said Court sharply, once he had been given a key. "Have the water, the tub and the whiskey up there. In the meantime I have to see someone."

"Not one of our guests?" asked the horrified clerk. "At this time of night, Mr. Court, and looking as you do, I'm afraid—"

"I realize you're afraid," said Court dryly. "Don't worry; your guest won't be." He whirled on his heel and left the man stammering while he took the stairs two at a time on his way to Abner Quincy's room. Grim-faced, boot heels striking the floor sharply, he stalked down the silent hall and raised his fist to pound on Quincy's door. Then, however, he paused and dropped his hand. If the desk clerk had been shocked at his appearance, how much more so would Susanna be if she were awakened by his pounding at Quincy's door and came out into the hall to investigate a possible threat to her bodyguard? Court grinned. He would not put it past Susanna to come out armed and take a shot at him if she failed to recognize him in his satanic coating of soot. Having reconsidered, Court knocked twice, quietly, and then waited until muffled wisps of sound from inside told him that Quincy had left the bed hastily and was now standing against the wall to the left of the door with his gun drawn, in all probability. "It's Court," Aaron said quietly.

Instead of admitting him without question, Quincy released the lock and said, "It's open. Come in with your hand away from your guns."

Raising his eyebrows in sardonic comment on that cold welcome, Court did what he was told and allowed Quincy time to inspect him in the dim light coming through the open door. Once Quincy was satisfied that his visitor was indeed Aaron Court, unaccompanied by companions in the hall with drawn guns, the older man closed and relocked his door, lit a lamp, and held it high to inspect his friend's grimy exterior. "I shore musta missed somethin interestin tonight," he remarked, setting the lamp on a table and waving Court to the room's only chair as he himself took a seat on the rumpled bed.

"I wouldn't feel too bad about it," Court replied. "The next move should be more fun, if I can work it, and I figure to include you in."

"What was the last move?" Quincy asked.

Court described the night's events and went on to suggest that they set an irresistible trap for the Packards.

"Well now. This here feud's really heatin' up," said Quincy. "What you figger would be irresistible to a Packard?"

"The chance at a lot of gold and my hide at the same time." Quincy agreed that the combination might well appeal to old Job, who seemed to have developed a special fondness for the idea of killing Aaron Court. Court went on to suggest that Grassback be enlisted to come into town and, while drunk, drop hints about a gold shipment from the new mine, a shipment that Court was going to slip into town by pack train in the middle of the night.

"If they believe it, and I expect they will if you're right about the bastards here in town who's feedin em information, they'll probably go for it," Quincy agreed, "but I also figger they got a fair to too-damn-good chance of gittin you when the shootin starts."

Court shook his head. "Maybe. It's a chance I'm prepared to take. In the first place, I know every piece of cover on that trail. I think the odds are with me, and I know the odds are against them. We're going to get a lot of Packards just by loading down a bunch of pack mules with worthless rocks."

Quincy nodded reluctantly and then, having looked Aaron over while they talked, said, "You better do somethin about them hands or you won't be up to this plan."

Court nodded. "I got a bath and a bottle of whiskey waiting in my room. You want to come up and take the splinters out for me?"

"We gonna drink the whiskey?"

"No, we're going to use it on my hands."

"Hell of a waste," said Quincy, as he pulled on his boots and took out a vicious-looking knife which he planned to use for splinter removal.

21

Susanna heard nothing of the latest abortive attempt on Court's life, for Quincy did not mention it, Clara did not hear of it, and Susanna talked to no one else that week. As she had planned, she sent a note to her sister urging that Lilith visit her to discuss an "urgent matter of business." Since Lilith assumed that the business in question was some new idea of Susanna's for helping her at the present Fallen Angel or at the construction site of the future Fallen Angel, help which Lilith did not want, she sent an answer promising to come as soon as she could. But she had no intention of actually visiting her sister. Instead she called Quincy in and demanded that he keep Susanna busier.

Thereafter Quincy watched Susanna waiting for her sister's visit and becoming more thoughtful and withdrawn when the visit did not materalize, and his irritation with Lilith increased. As a result, the next time he saw Court, he suggested that Aaron spend the day with Susanna while Quincy was out at the mine site rehearsing Grassback in several scenes of drunken indiscretion he was to play for the benefit of Packard informants. Court agreed with only slight hesitation. Şusanna would unquestionably be a distraction from a plan that needed careful attention to every detail if it was to work. On the other hand, he wanted to see her again before he went out with that mule train, for there was always the possibility that he might not be alive afterward to take advantage of the opportunity, or even that Quincy might not be alive to offer it to him.

Susanna was told that she could go riding again

with Aaron in four days time, and a tiny frown
creased her forehead as she agreed. Surely, she told
herself, Lilith would have come to see her before
then. Lilith's answer had said "as soon as possible."
That had to be within the next few days since several
days had already passed. After her last overwhelming afternoon with Court, her questions
about the morality of what was happening to her
were more urgent than ever. While she waited for
her sister's visit, she continued her program of Bible
reading without finding any clear answers to her
questions—until she came to an astonishing section,
one she had either not read before, although that
seemed impossible, or had found so meaningless
that she had failed to remember it. In fact, it was
still very hard to understand as she read and reread
the words in her room after dinner, but it said things
that touched her heart and her new experience with
Aaron. It seemed to celebrate the very things that
were happening, yearnings that were overcoming
her. And it said nothing whatever about morality.
Throughout the Bible were passages that offered unambiguous moral strictures, or at least strictures
that would have been unambiguous had she understood all the words, but this passage was entirely
different. Having read it, she read no further, never
got to St. Paul, who would have told her, "It is
good for a man not to touch a woman."

In St. Paul's stead, she drank in the sensual love
poetry of the Song of Solomon, which said nothing
of not touching, which cried instead, as if from her
own heart, "Stay me with flagons, comfort me for I
am sick of love. His left hand is under my head, and
his right hand doth embrace me."

Which said, "Let him kiss me with the kisses of

his mouth; for thy love is better than wine. / A bundle of myrrh is my well beloved unto me; he shall lie all night betwixt my breasts"—putting into poignant words the desires she had hardly acknowledged. Susanna shivered to think of lying all night in Aaron's arms.

The words of the verses sang in her mind as she waited to see Aaron again, as she waited for Lilith to come and confirm her own feeling that that spring was for her and for Aaron what springtime had once been for Solomon and the nameless woman in the poem. She turned again and again to the words:

> Rise up, my love, my fair one, and come away.
> For, lo, the winter is past, the rain is over and
> gone;
> The flowers appear on the earth; the time of
> the singing of birds is come, and the voice of
> the turtle is heard in our land.

Susanna looked no further for answers; she never got to the New Testament that governed the world around her.

22

Court's plans to entrap the Packards were going well by the day he arrived to pick Susanna up at noon at the hotel stable. Grassback was taking a professional interest in the performance he was to give: he tried out different lines on himself as he worked at the claim; later he insisted on rehearsing with Court or Quincy acting the parts of "Packard suckers," as Grassback insisted on calling the informers he would seek to hoodwink. Also, once the news of the fire at

Court's cabin had got around, various men in town, who had become sensitive about fires and Packards, discreetly mentioned to Court that any worthwhile ideas he had for retaliation would receive their support. Court had recruited some of them. Even his hands were healing—without infection, thanks to Quincy's skill with a knife and a liberal soaking in whiskey. He expected to have the bandages off the next day and be ready to take his part as primary bait in the ambush. However, when he swung Susanna into the saddle, she noticed only the bandages and asked what had happened to him. Court explained with as little detail as possible the attack that had been made by the two Packards, and Susanna exclaimed in horror, "They set fire to your house? With you in it?"

"Right."

"They ought to be shot!"

"I shot them," he admitted.

"Well, they ought to be hung."

"You've sure changed," Court remarked dryly.

"It's a miracle you're alive." Her obvious distress at the thought of his death caused Court to reach across the distance between them and awkwardly trace the lines of her lips with an unbandaged thumb, smiling at her in a way that made her feel dizzy. "And your house?" she whispered.

"Cabin. It's just a log cabin."

"You live in a log cabin? Isn't that wonderful!"

Court was not sure what was wonderful about a log cabin. Most women preferred milled lumber and brick, although sensible folk knew that a well-constructed cabin was warm in winter and cool in summer, which could not be said of a good many more expensive houses in the area. "I've been living at the hotel since the fire," he said in answer to her remark that his living in a log cabin was "wonderful."

"Oh. Was the cabin badly damaged?"

"Well, it was a lot more comfortable before the Packards set fire to it," Aaron admitted. "I've had people out there cleaning and repairing it, but I haven't had a chance to see how they did. You want to stop by and take a look? It's not much out of our way."

Susanna agreed enthusiastically, and they set their horses southward.

When they reached the clearing, it was empty, and Court remarked with surprise, "They seem to have finished the work, more or less." The cabin presented an incongruous patchwork appearance, for the workmen had repaired the damaged doors, frames, and surrounding areas with boards that contrasted strangely with the original weathered logs of the cabin. "Look around inside if you like," said Court, helping her down from her saddle and opening the front door for her. "I'll tether the horses."

Susanna entered hesitantly, peering first into the smoke-blackened sitting room on one side of the hall, then into a room that Court seemed to use both for eating and business. When he came into the house, however, she was in neither of the front rooms where he had expected to find her. Instead she was standing motionless in the middle of his bedroom.

"Susanna?" He spoke to her quietly, but she seemed unaware of either his voice or his presence in the room. When he spoke to her again, she failed to turn. Finally he took her gently by the shoulders, turned her toward him, and saw the stunned aware-ness in her face. "Do you remember being here before?" he asked.

Her eyes cleared and she saw him instead of the dreamlike memories. She swallowed painfully. "Here with you," she whispered. "Yes. I remember now." Her eyelids lowered over her eyes as he drew her in against his chest. "Being with you," she finished.

"It was very beautiful, Susanna," he said, smoothing her hair. "Very perfect."

"I didn't remember anything could be like that," she answered hesitantly. "Even when I was with you the other times—I didn't remember. I turned away—afraid."

"Oh, love." Aaron swept her up into his arms and carried her to the bed, burying his face in her hair and putting her down gently on the coverlet. "Take the bandages off my hands," he told her.

"But you'll be in pain," she objected. "It will hurt your hands."

"The pain will be in my soul if I can't touch you," he replied.

How strange that he should say it that way, she thought as she unwrapped the bandages. The words of the song ran in her mind: "By night on my bed I sought him whom my soul loveth." Then Court slipped the pins from her hair, and running his fingers through its silken lengths, spread it out on his pillow, and Susanna lay absolutely still, watching him, but that stillness became charged with tension as she realized that he planned to undress her in the dim light of the room, watching her. Piece by piece, he removed her clothing, touching her in feather-light caresses as he bared each part of her body, but it was not only his fingers that made her skin tingle and grow warm, it was his eyes looking at her so intimately. Everywhere his glance touched her, waves of sensation followed, making her want to move, to turn away; she did not know what would ease her, and it did not matter because she was caught, helpless, in the passionate threads of his weaving and could not move. When he had taken all her clothing away, leaving her naked under his gaze, he began to take off his own clothes, still watching her with that terrible intensity as she watched him with helpless fascination. His boots fell by the bedside. He stripped away his shirt, revealing a tightly muscled, brown chest covered with curling, pale hair. Then, as he stood by the bed, his hands went to his belt, and Susanna's eyelashes drifted down on her cheeks. She knew what was there, remembered, but she could watch no more; her own tension was now past bearing. It was a release when finally he pulled the bedclothes from under her and stretched out beside her, pulling the sheets back up over them, taking her into his arms so that she could feel the whole, hard length of his body.

The kissing and touching seemed brief to her, hardly a flicker of time until his fingers were again tracing the lines of her hip bones down to her inner thighs where so very gently, so gently that she never thought of protesting although she quivered under his touch, he drew her legs apart, laying her open to him, then sliding his fingers into her, arousing a terrible deep ache that made her long to cry out, but she lay still, accepting, letting him do what he would.

Finally when it seemed to her that she could stand no more, he whispered, "I can't wait any longer,

Susanna.'' In answer she put her arms around his waist and drew him down to her, and he entered her slowly, a little way, then withdrawing, and deeper, and withdrawing, and though Susanna was in agony, she could do nothing to assuage her own hunger. She was like a woman under a spell, able to draw him deeper into her only with fluttering contractions of those involuntary inner muscles that caused him exquisite pleasure and finally overcame his careful control and drove him into reckless, heated frenzy. And before he could regret that loss of control, he felt the beginning of her climax coming and his own, and Aaron stopped thinking beyond the overpowering desire to take Susanna with him beyond even the peak of sensation they had reached before. For Susanna, that last deep stroke drove her beyond yearning acquiescence to mindless, shuddering surrender, and finally to a floating, boneless peace. Still sprawled beneath Aaron, still holding him, she dropped abruptly into deep sleep, leaving him, in the aftermath of his own mind-shaking pleasure, to think about her.

With neither maturity nor experience to fuel it, Susanna had a sensuality that took complete possession of him and of herself, and unlike her sister's, her love was not selfish, nor grasping, nor brutal. She gave and gave, holding nothing back, making him feel, as he had never felt before with another woman, that they had been fused, completely, deeply melded together in the fire of their passion. Involuntarily, his arms tightened around her in jealous possession, and she, whose hold on his body had loosened in sleep, turned to him without waking or opening her eyes and nestled her face into his throat and her breast against the side of his chest, curling her fingers into the hair that grew thickly from his throat to his belly. He relaxed then and buried his face in her hair, letting himself drift into sleep.

They left the cabin late in the afternoon to ride back into town, and Susanna was virtually silent, wrapped in a dreaming contentment that seemed to isolate her from everything around her and focus her attention on the sensation of deep-rooted, inner awareness which was an ambiguous amalgam of slaked sensuality and the desire to be taken and satisfied again. She said nothing herself, and when Court spoke to her, she turned a shy, radiant smile on him, often as not without replying. The look of her, had he recognized it, was that of a new bride, deeply in love and newly awakened. However, Aaron Court had had little enough to do with weddings and new brides and knew only that when she looked at him that way, his guts twisted and he was hard put not to turn her around and take her back to the cabin. To stifle his own impulses, he made conversation.

"Have you spoken to Lilith about the inheritance?" he asked.

Susanna shook her head. "I sent her a note, but she never came to see me," the girl replied after a pause. During that pause, the thought drifted into her mind that she no longer needed to talk to Lilith, that the talk would come too late, that there could hardly be anything beyond what had happened to her that afternoon about which to ask her sister. In fact, she felt, in a vague way, that there was some hard and unloving quality about her sister now that would render Lilith unable to understand what had happened to Susanna.

"Do you still want to talk to her yourself?"
Aaron asked.

"No." Susanna shook her head indifferently.
"You might as well, if you don't mind doing it."

Aaron did not really want to see Lilith. The
memory of her was like the taste of sour wine in his
mouth, but he promised to bring the matter of the
inheritance up with her because he sensed that
Susanna was too hurt by her sister's indifference to
insist on seeing Lilith. Well, that much money
should bring Lilith around to the hotel for one
reason or another, he thought.

23

Court may have meant to see Lilith immediately, but
he harbored a reluctance beyond his personal
distaste. He really had no desire to bring her more
fully into Susanna's life, for he saw Lilith as a
threat. Consequently the pressures of the
approaching confrontation with the Packards were
reason enough to avoid Lilith. Later would do—if
he were still alive. Court found risking his life to
trap more Packards less a matter of indifference
than it had been when he first conceived the plan in
the rush of anger caused by the burning of his cabin
and his traumatic trip through the Indian tunnel.
Now that he had Susanna, he did not want to give
her up—either to her sister or to death.

Still, the plan was moving forward with its own
momentum. Grassback had drunk himself into
seeming idiocy just the night before and had
revealed to two secret Packard cohorts that his
canny partner, Aaron Court, was going to sneak a
fortune in gold nuggets out of the mine and into the

safe of the Amnonville First State Bank without anyone being the wiser. In the meantime, Grassback had chuckled, no one would ever find that treasure at the mine where it was so well hidden that God himself could not have found it, had he had a mind to steal it. Cackling with drunken cunning, Grassback had refused to mention the night when the secret transfer was to take place, although his companions had bought him enough liquor to float secrets from a deaf mute. He had, however, promised to return for another night of joviality with his new friends.

"There's just one damn thing wrong with this plan of yours, Aaron," Quincy had said when the three met at the mine after the first successful phase of the plot, "and that's how the hell you can be sure that the Packards are goin to take you at Red Sky Canyon."

"If you were going to take me, where would you do it?" asked Court with calm certitude.

"What you an me would do is one thing," said Quincy sourly. "We're smart. What the Packards'll do is another. They ain't had much luck with you so far—mostly because of dumbness."

"Job isn't that dumb. They'll be at Red Sky Canyon."

"You better hope," muttered Quincy. "If they make a dumb move, you're dead."

"That's just what I don't intend to be," said Court. "Dead."

Abner, having less confidence in the intelligence of his opponents, decided to make contingency plans of his own. Court was, after all, the only prospective husband he had for Susanna, and he could not see himself as a doddering old man and her a sour spinster going out every day together for the next twenty years to make minor improvements in her ability to shoot a six-gun and ride a horse.

24

Court rode slowly along the trail, peering warily into the darkness, listening to the quiet night noises overlaid by the creaking of harness, the snorts of the animals, the dull plodding of hooves. He had several miles yet to go before he entered Red Sky Canyon and faced the attack that he was sure would come, and he used the time to go over in his mind the features of the terrain where he would have to seek cover. If he survived the initial onslaught, he could stay alive long enough for his men, and there were fifteen distributed at points of vantage in that canyon, to massacre the Packards, who would think that they had shot him from the saddle and would be blundering carelessly about in the dark looking for his body and appropriating the mangy mules and loads of worthless rocks he had prepared for them. Court grinned. If they lived long enough to inspect their loot, they were in for a galling disappointment. As satisfying a thought as that was, on the whole he preferred that they did not live that long. The irony would be if he broke a leg—while acting the part of a man who had been shot out of his saddle—and could not then get away from them, the only greater irony being if they actually did shoot him out of the saddle. The thought of Susanna flashed through his mind, but he put it away and returned to his catalogue of hiding places in Red Sky Canyon. The Packards' best point of attack would be about five hundred yards beyond Stinking Beaver Creek, and

from there his best cover would be the jumble of
rocks at—

He felt the burning impact of the bullet at about
the same time he heard the shot. After that first
instant of angry confusion because the Packards had
not done as he had anticipated, his mind began to
function again. He controlled immediately the
impulse to set spurs to his horse's flanks; he could
not afford to remain in his saddle, an easy target.
Therefore he pitched off the horse in a fair imitation
of a dead man and hit the hard ground, rolling away
from the dimly moonlit stretch of trail. Almost immediately he was into an area of low brambles that
tore at his skin and clothes, exacerbating the already
searing pain in his left shoulder and making the
devil's own amount of noise as he continued to
scrabble through crackling thorns toward a stand of
trees looming not ten yards to his left in the darkness. The noise of his passage was not cause for concern because Packards were now appearing on the
trail, swearing and grunting at one another. Court
cursed himself for a fool as he slipped in among the
trees. The Packards, instead of choosing the place
where they were least likely to lose any of the pack
train, had chosen a place where they would have the
benefit of what little moonlight there was, one of the
few places on the trail not shadowed by heavy forest
or towering cliffs. They had been more intent on
getting him than the gold, as their conversation on
the trail proved. Court leaned back against a tree
and felt his shoulder gingerly after checking for his
rifle, his knife, and his two pistols. The jacket was
sticky with blood, but he could not tell in the dark
how bad the wound was. It hurt enough to make
him nauseated, but previous experience had taught

him that pain was not always an indication of a mortal wound.

"Where the hell is the body?" he heard a voice say down on the trail. "I saw the bastard fall."

"It wasn't here. It was futher up the trail by a couple a hunnerd yards."

"Well, find im," came a hard voice, addressing the first two speakers.

"I wanna look at the gold."

"It ain't gonna go away. Hey, all of you, start combin the trail, the woods, wherever you gotta look." Court surmised that Isaiah Packard was giving the orders. He moved further back into the forest.

"He's dead, Isaiah. I know I got him right in the chest."

"Pa wants the body this time," said Isaiah ominously. "He said no slip-ups. He wants to see the body."

"What's he gonna do with hit?" called another voice. "Scalp hit?"

Laughter greeted the suggestion. "Nah," cried the man who had claimed the kill. "Old Job, he wants to cut off Court's balls, he's that mad."

One part of Court's mind was filling with brutal rage while the other part stood back like a spectator, reminding him that the whole bloody mess had started because of a half-melted safe full of papers, a fool who thought there might be some treasure in it, and a girl who did not know the difference between self-defense and murder. However, it had started, and as soon as the Packards began to fan out, Court reminded himself, his chances of winning this round or any other round would become phenomenally thin because the counter-ambush he had so

cleverly planned was two miles down the trail where
it could do him no good, and in the meantime all he
could do was move in that direction, killing as many
Packards as he safely could until they killed him or
blood loss dropped him unconscious or dead. With
his rifle in one hand and his knife in the other, Court
began to move—quietly, pausing frequently to rest
and listen, finally freezing against a tree as he heard
footsteps coming up behind him. Court gripped his
knife, glad that the searcher was taking so little
trouble to conceal himself. The man must be sure
that he was on a fool's errand. Like all of us, Court
thought sardonically. He stopped breathing entirely
as the dark figure passed within inches, but once the
searcher was in front of him, Court leaped,
snapping a hard forearm across the man's throat
from behind to prevent any cries for help. With his
other hand he drove his knife into the man's chest
and felt the body slump silently to the ground.
Cautiously, as quietly as possible, Court propped
him up against a tree and felt for the artery in the
neck with his fingers. The man was dead. One down,
thirty to go, he thought bitterly and moved southwest again toward Red Sky Canyon, a destination he
never expected to reach.

He heard a voice behind him shout, "We gotta
light the torches."

"Hey, I ain't gonna make myself no target,"
came a complaining reply.

"Ain't no one round here to see you, lessen
Court's still breathin."

"He ain't."

"Right, so let's go home with the loot."

"Mighty mangy mules these are."

"Don't matter. We ain't in the mule business. Pa don't care none for mules."

"Maybe not, but he wants Court's body. Now light them torches."

Cursing their persistence and their damned torches, Court moved steadily southwest away from the babble of Packard voices, his rage almost overcoming the pain and nausea. When they got those torches lit, he was a dead man, he thought bitterly.

Had he but known it, Isaiah's insistence that torches be lit to aid in the search was what saved Court. Abner Quincy had never been as sure as his friend that the Packards would strike the mule train in Red Sky Canyon. Because he accepted the logic of Court's contention, he had stationed the men earlier in the evening just where Court and he had agreed that they should be stationed, but to satisfy his own misgivings, he had hired a disreputable Indian acquaintance and promised him a full week's drunk if he could pick up the Packards as they left their sanctuary, trail them to wherever they went, and then hotfoot it to Quincy's position in Red Sky Canyon and pass the information on—all without alerting the Packards and getting himself killed. Chief Elk's Butt, as the Indian was called by his white friends, had no problem accomplishing his mission; he claimed to be able to track a bird through a blizzard if there was something in it for him. Consequently Quincy had forewarning and was moving his men out before the Packard bullet hit Aaron Court's shoulder. By the time Court jumped his first unwary pursuer, Quincy and his men were infiltrating the area where the Packards were searching. In the dark Quincy worried that his men would not be able to tell friend from Packard, but the Packards, in lighting torches, obligingly identified themselves.

Soon Aaron was hearing shots. He paused in confusion. The gunfire seemed to be all around him, coming in sporadic bursts, punctuated by shouts. The noise made it hard for him to hear pursuit, but a bobbing torch and a voice cursing alerted him to an approaching Packard. "What the hell? What the bloody hell?" the man was mumbling. Court shot him as he appeared between two trees and then dove to extinguish the torch before it drew other Packards. The jarring contact brought on a wave of pain and dizziness that held Court motionless on top of the man he had shot. Warm moisture was soaking his clothing, and he could not be sure whose blood it was, but it *was* blood—sticky, too hot to be dew. Court took a deep breath of the cold air in an attempt to clear his head. Had the Packards been shooting at one another? The gunfire and voices had died away. God help him if he had to put a knife into anyone else. He was not sure that he could get up again, and not enough time had passed for Quincy and the others to have heard the shots and got here from Red Sky Canyon. No use to count on that. The Packards must have blundered nervously into each other in the dark, and now they were being more careful, which meant Court could not shoot either without bringing the whole mangy pack of them—pack of Packards—his thoughts trailed off in mental chuckles. Pack of Packards. How soon would Quincy get here? How much time had passed? There was an old saying, "Time flies when you're having fun." Could have been hours since he had been shot, he told himself, laughing. Had he

laughed aloud? Stupid. "Just shut up and sit here
against the tree and shoot down Packards till Quincy
comes," Court admonished himself. He tried to lift
his rifle and found it too heavy—too heavy. He let it
fall and dragged out a pistol. Hoofbeats. Were they
going to ride him down? Circle the wagon train,
howling like Indians? More gunfire. Court hoped
vaguely that Packards were shooting more Packards
in the dark than he was. "God, Susanna," he
muttered.

25

The Indian, finally, was the one who found Court.
He had refused to leave Quincy's side until he was
paid off for bringing the information and, being
available, was put to work again. When the vigilantes were reasonably sure that all Packards were
dead, unconscious, or driven from the area, they
used discarded Packard torches to begin a search of
the area for loose horses, dead bodies, and the
wounded—with particular emphasis on Aaron
Court. Elk's Butt had pursued the project
methodically with patience, thoroughness, and
expertise, having been promised ten days of drinking
instead of a week if he could locate Court alive. As
he plodded along, reading signs by torchlight, he
tried Quincy's patience sorely with comments such
as "Here man fall from horse and tear up hide in
thorn bushes," "Here man drop blood on ground,"
"Here man put knife in back of noisy fool," "Here
man rest and bleed on tree," "Here one dead man
and one still breathes. I find right one?"

"Jesus," exclaimed Grassback. "He looks as
dead as the dead one."

"Well, he's breathin." Quincy was kneeling beside Court, who was still propped up against the tree, unconscious, gun in hand. "An the wound's stopped bleedin on its own."

"Maybe blood all gone," suggested Elk's Butt.

"If his blood was all gone, he'd be dead," snapped Quincy. "And if he's dead, you don't git the extra three days."

"Get white warrior to medicine man quick," said Elk's Butt.

They did. The procession back to Amnonville included nine extra Packard horses, ten Packard corpses, and Aaron, carefully carried in the arms of a solicitous Indian.

26

When Job Packard heard the news that he had lost ten men, that his eldest son Isaiah was seriously wounded, and that he had neither the gold nor the corpse of Aaron Court to show for the effort, his watery eyes turned cold and full of wrath. He sent the others away and kept with him his son Jeremiah. "There's two things yer gonna do fer me, Jeremiah," said Job.

"Okay, Pa."

"First yer gonna git in town an git a doctor fer yer brother, Isaiah." The young man nodded, figuring that he could kidnap a doctor without too much trouble, the new one in town having no reputation as a gun hand. "The second thing is Aaron Court. If he's dead, that's good, but I been told before Court was dead an he wasn't. This time I want to know, an if he ain't dead, I want him watched. You do hit yerself, Jeremiah—soon as you git that doctor. Cause the next time us Packards goes after Court, he is gonna be dead. My honor is at stake. So you watch him, you hear. I don't think he is dead. My old bones say, 'Court's still alive,' but this time I'm gonna git him. I'm gonna figger out a foolproof killin scheme, an yer gonna hep, Jeremiah.''

"Yes sir, Pa. If he ain't dead, we'll git him fer sure.''

27

Court, immured in his hotel room, was far from dead. The bullet had gone through his shoulder cleanly, causing much pain and copious loss of blood but little damage. Court was weak from the blood loss and exceedingly bad tempered from the enforced stay in bed and from Quincy's refusal to let him see Susanna, lest Lilith hear of it, but he was in no danger of anything but a charge of assault on his doctor. That young man had suggested bleeding Court to hasten his recovery, and Court had suggested bleeding the doctor to hasten his departure. Court's suggestion was the more effective; the doctor left hurriedly, and when he failed to reappear the next day to check on his patient, Court simply assumed that the young idiot was afraid to show his face. Whether or not the doctor would have returned after the threat was a moot point; Jeremiah Packard kidnapped him on his way to deliver a baby, and neither Court nor the expectant mother nor anyone else saw him again for some time. Court took the doctor's timely disappearance as permission to get out of bed, which he did.

His first impulse was to visit Susanna, but Quincy

refused to let him see her until he was strong enough to protect her should the need arise. Both men admitted that the Packards would be more vengeful than ever when they discovered that they had not only been ambushed in their own ambush but that Court had escaped.

28

Sitting behind her desk, Lilith opened the conversation by saying contemptuously, "I see you got yourself shot."

Since Court could hardly deny it, his arm being in a sling and the story of his being caught in his own trap having spread all over town and for miles in every direction, he remained silent and satisfied his ill temper by biting the end from a cigar and spitting it onto her carpet.

Lilith's lips curled. "Your manners seem to be going the same route as your intelligence, Court. Time was, if you'll remember, you'd have been smart enough to mind your own business and not get mixed up in stupid feuds with the Packards. There's not a damned thing you can get out of this but killed. There's sure no money in it."

"You all that sure you're immune, Lilith?" Court asked.

"I take care of myself if I have to, and I know when to mind my own business. What are you here for anyway?"

"Business," said Court. She eyed him suspiciously, and Aaron grinned. "Don't worry, Lilith. This isn't going to cost you a penny. In fact, your sister Susanna has asked me to—"

"You don't have my permission to see Susanna,"

Lilith snapped. "I thought I made it perfectly clear that I didn't want you near her."

"I'm her lawyer, Lilith, and I'm here representing her."

"The hell you are. If Susanna had anything to say to me, she wouldn't hire you to—"

"According to Susanna, she asked you to come to see her on a matter of urgent business, and you have yet to arrive. Just how long has it been since you've seen her?"

"I've been busy," Lilith snapped.

"Well, you don't want her to come here for obvious reasons, and you don't go there for less obvious reasons, so she finally had to ask me to come and see you. Now do you want to hear about this, or do I have to write you a letter?" Lilith looked flushed and furious and did not reply, so Court went on. "Susanna inherited quite a bit of money from your parents. She has decided that the fair thing to do, since you are her beloved sister and since she feels that your parents treated you unfairly—" Court's voice had a sardonic quality through all this that further infuriated Lilith "—is to divide that money and property evenly with you. Here is an accounting of the full amount and of your share. If you'll let me know where you want the money and deeds deposited—"

"I have no intention of taking a penny from Susanna, especially not money that came from our beloved parents." Her voice dripped venom at the word *beloved*, and her face was white. "Not a penny. And you don't have to tell Susanna. I'll tell her myself. Now get out of here, Court, and stay away from her. I'll also tell her to find another lawyer."

"What's the problem, Lilith?" asked Court, watching her with narrowed eyes through the smoke of his cigar. "Are you trying to keep from establishing any ties with the girl? Are you afraid that letting her do what she wants about the inheritance will put you under an obligation to her?"

"I'm taking care of her," said Lilith angrily. "I pay her bills; I've hired people to—"

"Hired people to keep her company," he agreed. "Because you don't want to see her yourself. You really ought to consider letting her help you over here, Lilith." Lilith's fists clenched, and she drew breath to tongue-lash him. "Oh, not as one of the girls." He grinned. "But she'd be a hell of a bookkeeper. She's a lightning calculator—and honest. She probably wouldn't charge you much either."

"Get out."

Lilith's humor steadily worsened as the evening progressed. Finally Carlos suggested sharply that she leave the Fallen Angel to him and stay out of sight in her office rather than cost them any more business. She swore at him too, as she had at a number of surprised customers during the evening, but she did leave. A fact that was known to no one else in Amnonville was that he was a full partner in Lilith's enterprise and had been since its inception. Their original agreement had been that his investment was to remain unknown, since investments made by Mexicans had a way of meeting ill fortune. The agreement did explain, in part, the fact that when Carlos Mondragon made a suggestion, especially a suggestion related to business, Lilith usually took it. Many townsfolk suspected that she was susceptible to personal suggestions from him too, but few ventured to bring the subject up with either party, since Mondragon had a reputation for quick violence when he considered his privacy invaded in any way.

When business had slowed to a sleepy, early morning hum, Mondragon went to her office and asked blandly, "What was it Court said this time that made you so angry, querida?"

Lilith glanced up at him with surprise, but she did not bother to deny that Aaron Court was the source of her bad humor. Instead she tossed the accounting sheets that Court had left with her across the desk to her partner. "Read those," she commanded.

Carlos dropped his long frame into a chair and gathered up the papers. For some time there was silence in the room as he read them through. Finally he said, tossing them back on the desk, "And she wants to give you half of all that? You must be pleased."

"Why should I be pleased?" snapped Lilith. "I don't intend to take a penny of it."

"Why not?" Carlos was sprawled in his chair smiling slightly at her, like a dangerous animal in a playful mood. "It's a lot of money. I'm glad for you, my love."

"I wouldn't take anything that belonged to them," Lilith hissed.

"But why not? Think of how angry they would be if they thought you had any of their money."

"It's Susanna's money," said Lilith sullenly. "Do you think I'd take it from my sister?"

"Not even when she wants you to have it?"

"I can take care of myself. She can't."

"Ah, sí. Now we come closer to the heart of the matter. She can't take care of herself, and you don't want to do it for her, do you?"

"I am taking care of her."

"And wishing she would disappear."

"That's a damn lie."

Carlos laughed. "You tell lies to yourself sometimes, Lilith, but I don tell lies to you. Susanna is a responsibility you don want. You don wan her love, you don wan her help—"

"I can't have her helping here."

"An you don wan her money—because that would double your obligations to her. No? What you feel for your sister is guilt, Lilith. You ran away an made yourself a life the way you wanted it, an she stayed home an paid the price for your freedom. Isn't that how you feel?"

"No."

"You're wrong, of course, because it was your parents who made Susanna pay for your freedom, not you, but it doesn't do any good for me to tell you that, does it?"

"You're talking crap," said Lilith angrily.

Carlos laughed again. "I think you feel guilty because of what your parents did to her, an then you feel guilty because you don wan her here, an now she wants to give you all that money an make you feel more guilty. An what are you going to do, querida?"

"I'm not going to take the money."

"Too bad. It's not going to erase the guilt, an you won have the money either." Lilith took the papers Court had left and angrily ripped them into shreds. "I always have thought, my love," said Carlos musingly, "that your parents are still controlling your life. Guilt is a powerful weapon."

Lilith had risen from her chair as if to walk away from his ideas. "You don't know what you're talking about, Carlos. Stick to keeping the customers and the whores in line."

"You don think I'm right?"

"I don think you're right," she mimicked.

"But look at us, Lilith." He had risen too and put his hand on her arm, drawing her to face him. "What you feel for me is as close to love as you'll ever come—"

"You flatter yourself," she muttered.

"An yet what you want from me is not love," he continued softly. "You want punishment."

"Stupid Mexican," snapped Lilith.

"You prove my point," he murmured. "You seek to anger me. Would you not be disappointed if I responded with tenderness?"

Lilith turned her back to him, but Carlos laughed and put his arms around her waist, whispering in her ear, "What do you want from me tonight, my beautiful Lilith—violence or tenderness?" She shivered.

29

"Susanna's talkin like she thinks you don't want to see her," Quincy admitted. He had just refused to let Court meet her secretly in any of their rooms at the hotel, including Quincy's own room, on the grounds that it was not proper for a girl to see a man in a bedroom, even the bedroom of a third party.

Court restrained a sardonic comment on Quincy's ideas of morality being now beyond the point. "I hope you told her that I do want to see her, that you're the one who won't—"

"Well, don't you think they're watchin you?" Quincy demanded angrily.

"I told you I found tracks out at the cabin."

"You want her hurt if they ambush you?"

"If we're careful, it won't happen."

Finally they agreed, Quincy reluctantly, to meet at a place outside of town to which Quincy was to bring Susanna, taking care that they were not followed, Court coming a roundabout way and taking even more stringent precautions.

"An if you even think someone's on your trail, you'll turn back," Quincy reminded him one last time.

"They're just as likely to be following you."

"They ain't half as interested in killin me as they are in killin you."

"Thanks.

30

"Have you seen Susanna yet?" Carlos asked Lilith as they stood at the bar surveying the early evening crowd.

"No," Lilith snapped. The slight smile that her answer brought to his lips made her add, "I've been busy. I'll see her tomorrow or the next day."

31

In a stand of trees so dense that it made midday seem dusk, Quincy delivered Susanna to Court, asking tersely, "Anyone on your back trail?"

"Not that I can tell. You?"

"Nope. We been ziggin and zaggin for the better part of two hours. Where you two goin?"

"Donnell's Glen."

Quincy nodded. "Take the old trail in," he advised, and he turned his horse away and disappeared almost immediately into the surrounding forest, leaving Susanna and Aaron to stare at each other, she self-consciously with the memory of their last meeting in her mind.

"I wasn't sure that you wanted to—"

"See you?" he finished for her. "Quincy wouldn't let me."

"Does he know—"

"He thinks it's not safe," Court interrupted again. "It isn't, for a fact. I'm the number-one Packard target now."

"Oh, Aaron." Susanna looked helplessly at his arm, immobilized in a sling. "You mustn't pursue this feud any longer, even if you do think it's the right thing to do. They'll surely kill you if you—"

"At this point I can't really call it off, Susanna," he remarked wryly. "I don't think old Job would be willing to accept a truce."

"It's not funny, Aaron," she cried.

"I'm not laughing, Susanna," he replied seriously enough, and he kneed his horse closer to hers and leaned across to kiss her. "God, but I've missed you, sweetheart. I think about you all the time." He kissed away the beginning tears on her cheeks. "I was thinking about you just before—" She had put up her hand to curl her fingers across his throat and around the side of his neck. "We better stop this before you fall off your horse," he said abruptly, his voice low and harsh. Court shifted his body away and stared straight ahead for a minute. Then he resumed in a normal tone of voice. "I saw your sister yesterday. She doesn't want the inheritance."

"We anticipated that," Susanna replied.

"Did she come to see you?"

"No," said Susanna sadly.

"She will, if only to insure that I don't. Let's head out." He turned his horse, saying over his shoulder, "Watch for low-hanging branches."

Susanna followed him silently until they came out

onto a trail where they could ride abreast. Then she asked, "What did she say about my seeing you? I didn't even know that she knew we—"

"She doesn't, as far as I know," Court replied. "She doesn't want you using me as your lawyer. Now I don't want you to say anything else till we get where we're going. I'm sure no one's following, but I want to stay sure."

Susanna nodded and obediently fell silent. Twenty-five minutes later Court drew rein in a small glade that contained a spring, a tiny pond fed by the spring, and warm flickering sunlight that reached the ground in the patterns of the leaves around which it shone. To one side the land sloped up abruptly, covered with trees and broken by rocky ledges.

Susanna sighed and said, "You must know every beautiful place in the mountains."

"And every ugly one," he agreed, laughing, as he dismounted. "You should see the the place where the Packards ambushed me and Quincy and the others ambushed them. Don't think I'll ever see much to like about that stretch of trail." Susanna shivered.

They ate by the pond and then Court showed her how to skip rocks, a pastime she found new and fascinating, and which he regretted having introduced, the pond being too small to accommodate many skips.

"Look, mine skipped twice," Susanna cried enthusiastically.

"I saw it, and that means you've just exhausted the number of skips you can accomplish on this particular body of water. Another day I'll find you a bigger pond."

"Can you skip rocks on an ocean?" Susanna asked earnestly.

"I'm sure you can," Court replied. "Have you ever seen an ocean?"

"No, but—"

"In that case why don't you forget those arrogant ambitions of yours, come over here, and sit down beside me."

Susanna giggled and obediently dropped down beside him on the blanket they had spread. "Undo the sling for me, will you?" he asked.

"But surely—"

"It's just there to remind me to keep my shoulder still. I can remember that on my own." Susanna undid the sling that was tied behind his neck, allowing him to ease the confined arm away from his chest. Thus freed, he slipped his good arm around her and pulled her down beside him on the blanket. His mouth was gentle at first, but more demanding as he continued to kiss her. Finally, pressing his lips against her throat and then moving them slowly into the valley between her breasts, he turned his head to rub his face against the silk over one soft curve. "Unbutton your blouse, Susanna," he murmured, his own fingers beginning to open his shirt.

Susanna drew away from him, flushing. "But Aaron, we can't do—that."

"Make love," he prompted gently.

"Make love," she repeated. "Not here—not outdoors where—"

Aaron could have told her that love would be as sweet in the sunshine as it had been on his bed in the half-light of his house, but cautiously he chose to prove this to her in slow steps. His own shirt fell open over his chest, and he reached up to begin on her blouse. "I want you to lie against me, Susanna," he coaxed softly, and Susanna acquiesced, helping him with the buttons and then slipping down on her side so that her breasts brushed his chest, the nipples aroused by the teasing contact with his pale, wiry hair. She made a small sound in her throat and pressed against him, and Aaron began to kiss her, caressing the inside of her mouth with his tongue, slowly rousing her, making her forget where they were.

He freed his right hand to begin a gentle re-exploration of her body, but eventually her riding skirt stopped him, and he whispered, "I want to touch you, love. Undo the skirt." She was trembling with desire, losing her sense of anything but his hands and mouth, and unthinking, she obeyed him and slipped out of the skirt without ever noticing, until he began for the first time to guide her hands, that he had freed himself from his trousers. The shock of touching him intimately dissipated as she was caught up in their mutually building passion. Then suddenly he moved his hand away from her and pulled her close against his body. "Susanna—love." His voice was hoarse with desire. "I want to be inside you again. Lord, sweetheart, I need you."

She lay against him a long, silent moment before she said, "We can't do that. Your shoulder—you can't move it. It would hurt your shoulder terribly."

"Not if you do what I tell you." Rolling her with him, he turned onto his back, and there was a husky, compelling quality to his voice that kept her silent, unprotesting. "Kneel over my hips," he ordered softly. Susanna flushed, understanding then what he wanted, and though she might have protested, he was already urging her with his hands to do as he told her. Half unwillingly, she let him

command her body, and before her knee came to
rest on the other side of him, she felt again the
electric shock of his beginning entrance, and her will
was gone. His hands on her hips pulled her down,
and he filled her with a radiating, pulsing excitement that spread outward from his slow penetration. Susanna's eyes closed, and she shuddered as
he pressed up into her. Then he pulled her body forward to lie on top of him, letting her rest there while
he murmured love words into her hair.

Susanna was content, but Aaron was not. He
wanted to give her pleasure upon pleasure. Again he
put his hands on her hips, curling long fingers
around her soft buttocks which he began to press in
a persuasive rhythm that quickened her breathing.
He taught her hips a motion that brought both of
them greater excitement in inner and outer
contractions and frictions. The movement of her
own body against Aaron's rigid passion sent
Susanna shuddering once more toward ecstasy, but
he held back a second time, calming and stroking
her again. He felt instinctively that behind that sweet
sensuality he had aroused in her lay a wilder, more
exciting abandon, and he wanted to loose it. He
wanted her pleasure more than his own, which was
not his usual goal with a woman.

When finally he was satisfied that his intensifying
caresses had taken her to the edge of abandon, he
slid his right hand between them and lifted her away
from him, letting her feel the hard shift of his
position within her and the deepest penetration. She
moaned and a flush spread, tingling, through her
veins, washing away thoughts, fears, inhibitions.
Again he schooled her body until she was moving
wildly above him, her hair whipping in a concealing
silken curtain around them. Then Aaron too began

to lose control, and they spun together over the boundaries of delight to a rare explosion of pleasure before they spiraled down to gasping, stunned quiet.

And when she had returned to normal time and control, to warm sunlight and cool mountain air on sweated skin, when she might have felt humiliation at her own abandon, he held her close and caressed her with gentle hands and loving words, and she was content to be where she was, having done what she had done. Court, as awed as she, wondered what instinct had guided him to give and receive a kind of joy he had never imagined, much less experienced before.

32

"Lemme kill him now," said Jeremiah Packard, eagerly sighting down the rifle from the ledge and caressing the trigger in anticipation.

"Don't be a fool," snapped his older companion. "Likely you'd kill her, an he'd git away again."

"Yeah. She's too purty a piece to kill, ain't she, even to git Aaron Court. I'd sure like to spend an afternoon with her like he jus done."

"Maybe you will, Jeremiah," said the older cousin, "cause I jus seen how we can git us Aaron Court right where we want him. Dead." The man rose from his position and began to edge backward toward the horses. "Les git on back and talk to your daddy."

"An let Court git away?"

"Nah. Let him have today. He ain't gonna have many more."

III
Packard Valley

33

    •

It took the Packards several days to entrap Susanna, and then they had to take her out of her own room at the hotel, waiting until Quincy had gone for his nightly visit to the Fallen Angel, tying and gagging Clara so efficiently that she was not discovered until late the next morning. By that time Susanna, who was still clad only in her light cotton nightgown, was imprisoned in a filthy cabin in the Packards' valley, listening with growing comprehension and terror to the plans that her hosts had for her and Aaron Court.

When she first arrived, already bruised and terrified by the callous treatment of Jeremiah Packard, the patriarch of the clan had stamped in to inspect her.

"Why have you brought me here?" Susanna demanded, tears streaming down her dirty face. "You—you can't just go around kidnapping women."

"Generally speakin I ain't much for woman stealin," Job agreed, "but I don't have to be concerned about you, do I, Miss Susanna—you bein a liar? You remember lyin to me? You remember comin to pray an stayin to shoot?"

Susanna wiped a hand across her eyes like a child and quavered, "I did pray. Why—why do you think it snowed?'' That seemed a strong point to make.

"Whores cain't pray up snow," said Job. "An yer a liar an a whore. Aaron Court's whore."

"What's a whore?" asked the frightened girl.

"A fornicator!'' roared Job. "You been fornicatin with Aaron Court. That bein the case, it ain't as if we're stealin a virtuous woman."

"Give her to me, Pa," said Jeremiah eagerly. "I don mind what she's been doin with Court. I could do with a little fornicatin myself."

Susanna cowered away from him in terror, but Job ignored her and turned cold, scheming eyes on his son. "Since you stole her, Jeremiah, I reckon maybe I will give her to you."

Susanna felt that she would faint when Jeremiah reached for her eagerly.

"But not right yet," Job cautioned. "We'll wait till Court gits here." He turned to Susanna. "You're gonna bring him here; did you know that? When he hears we got his little whore, he's gonna come in nice an peaceful cause he knows if he don't, we'll all share you an then we'll kill you an spread the word that he didn't have the guts to pertect his woman."

"What about Lilith?" asked Susanna desperately.

"Don't matter no more," said Job. "If she knows what's good fer her, she'll stay outa this. Maybe we'll even give you back when we've got what we want from you. But if she wants to interfere, we'll kill her too. She's just another whore when you git right down to hit."

"Why can't I have her now, Pa?" demanded Jeremiah, more interested in claiming his prize than in the strategy in which Susanna was a pivotal factor.

"Well, I'll tell you, son; if'n I give her to you

now, you'll have her all wore out an tamed down afore Court gits here, an that ain't what I want. I got it in my mind to tie him up right here in this cabin before we kill him an let the bastard watch you rapin his woman, so we want her lively and scared, don we? Lively an strugglin an shriekin. Think you can manage that, boy?" Susanna had turned gray-white. "Lock her up in the other room. I don want her pukin in here," Job ordered callously.

"Lemme take her," suggested Jeremiah, his voice tight with pleasure at the prospect of the promised rape.

"Nah, boy," said Job. "You save yerself up. Maybe we'll all watch tomorrer with Court. That wouldn't slow you down none, would it?"

"Nothin would," Jeremiah assured his father.

"Good boy."

34

Court had stayed up gambling at the Fallen Angel until long after midnight. It was ten o'clock the next morning before he awoke and found the note that had been shoved under the door of his hotel room the night before. In fact, he had heard the footsteps that paused outside the door and had automatically rolled off the far side of the bed, taking his gun from the nightstand as he did so, but the footsteps had moved on down the hall, and Court, hardly waking for the whole maneuver, had replaced the gun on the table and himself in his bed. When he read the note the next morning, he wished desperately that he had awakened enough to investigate, but by then it was too late. Had he known it, he was given more time to plan and to act than Job Packard had wanted to give him, for Job had instructed Jeremiah to have the note delivered late the following night, not on the night of the kidnapping, but Jeremiah, anxious to get back to his captive, could not be bothered to arrange the delivery and had slipped the note under Court's door himself as soon as they had Susanna safely out of the hotel. He reasoned that Court would not find it until morning when Susanna would be safely imprisoned in the Packards' stronghold. He was right.

The note informed Court that Susanna would be held unharmed until noon Wednesday and that he was to enter the valley Wednesday morning armed with only one gun and unaccompanied if he wished to effect her release. Otherwise she would be raped and killed. The note also warned him to tell no one of her whereabouts. Court was offered a fair, face-to-face shootout with a Packard of his choice once Susanna was free.

After the first powerful surge of rage and fear was past, Court sat down to think the situation through. It took him only a few minutes to come to the conclusion that they would kill her whether or not he showed up, that they could not afford to let her go even if they got him. His second conclusion was that he was more likely to be given a shot in the back or worse than a "fair, face-to-face shootout." His third conclusion was that organizing a group of men, and he had no doubt that he could recruit them to storm the valley, would be the second surest way to get Susanna killed. His final conclusion was that, acting alone, he had to get her out of the valley himself if he could and that if he failed, others would have to try more direct methods. It never occurred to him to ignore her plight.

Court shoved the note into his pocket and went to find Quincy, who would have to organize the second effort that would go into effect should Court fail to free her. His mind, as he strode through the halls of the McFadden to Quincy's room, was swinging wildly between blind rage that made him almost incapable of rational thought and a brand of cold-hearted fury that made him the most murderous of opponents. In those semi-rational moments he calculated that his advantages were his great familiarity with the valley and almost a full day of time. In fact, he was astonished that the Packards had given him that time, being unaware that Job had had no such intention, that Job had been intent on giving his own men time to get her safely back to the valley before letting his enemies know of her whereabouts. Court also calculated that his greatest disadvantage was that any plan he conceived tended to veer away from its objective, getting Susanna and himself safely out of the valley, toward a desire to accomplish that objective with the greatest loss of Packard life, which would be unwise at best, fatal at worst. Any sensible plan, he had to keep telling himself, would be carried out with no loss of life, with no knowledge on the part of the Packards, until after the fact, that anyone had been in their valley.

Quincy, who had been sleeping late on his day off, was as furious as Court when he realized that the Packards had taken the girl, and he agreed with Court's conclusions in all respects but one, and that was that Court should go into the valley alone to get Susanna. He insisted that two rescuers would be more likely to succeed than one.

"If I'd stayed away from her, she wouldn't be in danger," snapped Aaron angrily. "I put her there;

I'll get her out.''

"If we're passin out blame," said Quincy dryly, "then maybe you ought to keep in mind that I'm paid to look after her. If I'd been here doin it instead of over at Lilith's place drinkin, Susanna wouldn't be in their hands. Howsomeever, it ain't gonna do her no good—us sittin around decidin who's to blame. What we gotta figger is that two of us is more likely to git her out alive than one of us. If you git killed, I kin still git her outa the valley, an this ain't gonna be no picnic, Court; gittin killed is as likely as not. An let's say both of us git out with her. If they're followin, it wouldn't hurt none to have one to peel off an distract the pursuit, so to speak. Then there's—''

"Who's going to organize the raid if we fail?" Court demanded.

"We'll leave that up to Lilith an Mondragon. I'd say you git on out there an start scoutin the valley. We gotta know where she is before dark. I'll go tell Lilith an work out her part of it, an then I'll meet you before sundown at the branch in that trail that comes over the top on the southwest side of the valley.''

Court stared at him with blank, ferocious eyes. Finally he said, "All right. Sundown then.''

"Gitta hold a yerself," said Quincy sharply. "Anger ain't gonna git her out; smart thinkin is.''

Court's eyes cleared as he rose. "You better check on Clara Schmidt too. I never thought to look for her when I checked Susanna's room. God knows what they did with her.'' Then Court was gone—silently, like a large, very dangerous predator, and Quincy thought to himself that perhaps Job Packard had made his greatest mistake when he decided to use Susanna to trap Aaron Court.

35

Susanna was kept locked in the back room of the cabin for most of the morning—shivering, terrified, and desperate. Although spring was well advanced with most pockets of snow finally gone from the mountains except in the higher elevations, the temperature had begun to drop as the morning advanced. Susanna, in her thin nightgown, could find nothing in the room to protect her from the cold—no blankets, no clothing, no fireplace—and her physical discomfort added to her terror. From time to time she could hear laughing remarks in the next room between Jeremiah, who stopped by the cabin frequently, and her guards, who made disgustingly explicit suggestions to him about what he could do to her the next day to amuse himself, humiliate her, and pay out Aaron Court for his interference in Packard affairs.

At first these conversations made her faint with terror and nausea, but finally her fear turned to desperation and resolution. She had to do something to get away, to thwart the Packards before Aaron arrived. Would he come, she asked herself fearfully. Better if he did not. Then his life would be spared, and her lot might even be easier. But he would come. If only he did not come alone and virtually unarmed, as they had specified. If only he came with lots of men, with Quincy and Carlos Mondragon and all those hard men who worked for him at the Land and Cattle Company, with the men who had trapped the Packards trying to ambush Aaron and the pack train; if only he would—"But I have to do something myself," she thought desperately. She prowled the room like a caged animal looking for an avenue of escape and could find none. The one window was high above her head; there was no furniture, nothing—nothing to use as a weapon, nothing, and beyond the one door were the guards and from time to time Jeremiah saying terrible things, increasing her desperation and the dreary sense of futility that was creeping over her.

Finally Susanna thought of prayer. "God will help me," she tried to assure herself. "He won't let them hurt Aaron or me." She fell to her knees and, with tears streaming down her face, began to pray ardently, if incoherently, that God give her some weapon to use against them, some way to escape from them.

In a sense, the very act of praying had an effect on Job Packard when he found her on her knees in the barren room. "Git up," he shouted furiously. "God ain't gonna listen to the likes of you."

Susanna's heart began to beat with excitement when she saw how disturbed the old man was. Obediently she rose, but she said with quiet certainty that made him more uneasy than ever, "God listens to me. And God will protect me from you—because you're evil. Evil!" Her voice rose, and Job grasped her shoulder and flung her into the other room.

"You're gonna work, you hear," he shouted. "Yer Packard property now." Then he forced her outside. "Put her to work, Marrymay," he instructed his daughter-in-law, the widow of his late son Elias.

The woman, who had suggested in the first place that Susanna be forced to work for the family, dug her ragged nails into the girl's upper arm and dragged her toward the surrounding forest. "Court's woman, are you?" she hissed to Susanna. "Well, Aaron Court saw my man hung, an I'll be right there tomorrow to see him get his, an you too. When Jeremiah gets through with you, you'll wish they'd killed you in yer fancy hotel room."

"I need something to wear," said Susanna, chosing to ignore the woman's vicious words. "Something besides this nightgown."

"Do you? Maybe one of them fancy dresses like yer whorin sister Lilith wears, Miss High-an-Mighty?" Marrymay laughed and veered from her original path, dragging Susanna with her to one of the cabins where she had a short, snickering conversation with a huge man at the door. Grinning, the man handed her a garment which she flung at Susanna. "How's that suit you?" she demanded. Susanna stared in horror at the thing—an immense apron encrusted with dried blood. "Put it on," snapped Marrymay. With a shudder, Susanna did so, overcoming her horror by reminding herself that it at least gave her some protection from the chill of the overcast day and from the stares of the men in the camp.

Elias's widow forced Susanna to stumble ahead of her into the forest, threatening the girl with a knife when she did not move fast enough. Susanna was to gather fallen branches for firewood, and she did as she was told, scratching and tearing her hands and arms in the process and hardly noticing, so intent was she on watching for a chance to get the knife away from Marrymay. But the woman was cautious. She watched Susanna at all times, and as the load of firewood became heavier, Susanna's heart became heavier with it. She knew they would soon return without there being an opportunity for her to escape, and then she would probably be locked up in that horrible room again with no hope but prayer.

She put down her bundle of sticks and branches and knelt obediently when Marrymay told her to gather more. "Please, God, help me," she prayed desperately under her breath, squeezing her eyes shut in concentration, holding back the tears.

"Hurry up there," snapped her guard.

Susanna opened her eyes again and saw, as if through a rain-splashed window, a scattering of tiny reddish-brown mushrooms in the grass. In her mind she heard Aaron's voice, almost as if he were standing next to her: "They may look tasty, Susanna, but just one of that kind would make you sick as a dog, and two would likely kill you."

"Git to work before I kick yer butt," threatened Marrymay.

Instead of the threat Susanne heard Aaron's laughter. "They say when a Ute squaw felt herself ill used by her husband, she'd grind a few of those to powder and drop them in his food. Depending on how mad she was at him, she could kill him or just make him sick enough to wish he was dead." Shielded by her own body, Susanna's hand crept out and snatched up four of the precious mushrooms before Marrymay's foot sent her sprawling.

"I warned you," the woman shrieked. She kicked Susanna again, but Susanna hardly noticed. She was slipping her hand into the pocket of the filthy apron, hiding her four little red-brown weapons. Had she dared, she would have picked them all, poisoned every Packard in the valley, but four would be

enough for Jeremiah—maybe even Job—if she got
the chance. She scrambled back to her knees and
began to sweep up dry branches and twigs as Marrymay laughed. "That's what you needed, wasn't it,
bitch? A good kick."

"Thank you, God," said Susanna softly. "Thank
you."

36

It was afternoon before Quincy arrived at the Fallen
Angel to inform Lilith of her sister's disappearance.
He had first assembled the supplies that would be
needed to carry out the rescue. Court did none of
the buying since they assumed, on the basis of the
warning in the note, that the Packards might have
people watching him to see that he told no one of
Susanna's kidnapping. If the Packards did have
watchers, they saw nothing, for Court was long gone
before the time when he was supposed to have got
the note. Around noon Quincy had delivered the
supplies to him outside of town and sent him on his
way.

Then Quincy remembered Clara and, in checking
Susanna's room for clues, found her tied up and
stuffed in a wardrobe. Finally, reluctantly, he
headed for the Fallen Angel to break the bad news
to Lilith, insisting that Carlos Mondragon
accompany him into the office.

The first burst of Lilith's fury was directed at
Quincy because he had let the Packards take
Susanna. Since Quincy admitted his own culpability,
he accepted this tirade in silence. Then abruptly
Lilith concentrated on another aspect of the
situation. "Why did they think Aaron Court would

care about her?'' Lilith demanded. "Because he's her lawyer?'' She glared at Quincy. "I don't believe that. What's been going on between those two behind my back?''

Quincy shrugged. "Maybe you should a come to see her when she asked you to. That was a couple of weeks ago, ain't that right?''

"I hired you to—''

"To what? To protect her from ruffians was my understandin. I did a damned poor job of that. But Court ain't no ruffian. I figgered if Miss Susanna was ever to git married—''

"Married!'' cried Lilith. "Aaron Court isn't the marrying kind.''

"—she had to have a suitor. If you got any better prospects for her, maybe you should a trotted em around—er at least come around yerself.''

"You bastard! You idiot!'' Lilith was beside herself with fury, and Quincy's face was turning hard.

"This is not getting us anywhere, Lilith,'' said Mondragon. He had been leaning negligently against the wall, smoking and listening without comment.

"That's right,'' said Lilith, throwing him an angry look. "Court will just have to give himself up. I'll deliver him tomorrow morning myself. I'll—''

Quincy rose furiously to leave, but Mondragon shook his head; then he turned to his partner. "Sacrificing Aaron Court might make you happy, Lilith, but it will not get your sister back.''

"Glad someone around here's got some sense,'' muttered Quincy.

"Court does know about this?'' Mondragon directed his question to the old gunfighter.

"Sure. He got the note.''

"Why?" demanded Lilith. "That's what I want to know."

"It doesn't matter now," Mondragon answered her. "What does Court think should be done?"

"I don't care what Court thinks," Lilith cried. "This is none of your business anyway, Carlos."

"Yer gonna git Susanna killed, the way yer goin at this, Lilith," said Quincy. Then he answered Mondragon. "Him an me are goin in after her tonight. That's all arranged. He's already on his way to scout the valley, try to find out where they got her locked up.

"Jus you two?" Mondragon looked skeptical, but Quincy grinned and replied that they had been there before.

The Mexican studied Quincy thoughtfully and then smiled. "The rock slide," he murmured. "So. And if you fail?"

"Give us till four tomorrer mornin. If we ain't got her out by then, you kin storm the valley. Think you kin get together enough men?"

"It will be no problem." Mondragon's face was expressionless. "We will storm the valley even if you do get her out. I think we have all had enough of the Packards."

"Don't be stupid," snapped Lilith. "It would cost us a fortune to hire the men. If we have to do it, of course—"

"I know at least fifty men who'll ride fer nothin," said Quincy. "Ain't no decent man gonna like the idea that they're takin little gals hostage now."

Mondragon nodded and the two, over Lilith's protests, began to decide who would be recruited and how the plans could be kept quiet so that the Packards would have no word of the impending attack. Ultimately they decided to simply capture and tie up the informers before recruiting the vigilantes.

37

By midafternoon Court had tethered the horses, cached supplies outside the valley, and established himself high above the settlement with a pair of army field glasses, but he was too late to see Susanna shoved, stumbling under a heavy load of firewood, out of the woods and then locked up again in the small cabin where she had been kept previously. He could, however, deduce her whereabouts easily enough, since there were two guards to keep her from escaping, one in front of the door and the other sprawled under a tree with a rifle across his lap, keeping an eye on the cabin's one window. No other areas of the settlement were under guard. Having established her place of captivity, Court began to chart the rest of the cabins, checking as best he could which were occupied and by whom. The cabin in which he assumed Susanna was being kept had once been used by an older cousin of Job's, a trusted lieutenant who had been killed in the pack train ambush. Other cabins were now empty also, he noticed with satisfaction, but Job still occupied the large structure near Susanna's prison.

As Court continued to observe and plan, Susanna huddled in the corner of the locked room, trying to decide how she could use the mushrooms. Aaron had said that the Ute squaws made a powder of the mushrooms, but Susanna saw no way to do that. They were not dried and could not be dried by nightfall, after which it would be too late, nor did she have any tools for reducing them to powder. She slipped her hand into the pocket of the apron, which she had been allowed to keep, and touched them to be sure they were still there. Her eyes traveled hopelessly around the empty room once again; nothing but trash was—

Susanna straightened and stared at some bits of crumpled paper in the corner, cigarette papers they appeared to be. She was reminded of picnics Lilith had taken her on as a child. The cook had always twisted small servings of sugar into little papers so that they could sweeten their tea. How Susanna had loved to untwist those papers and let the grains of sugar slip down the fold and into the cup. Then Leah (Lilith, she reminded herself) had let her lick the paper. It had been such a treat, something her mother would never have approved had she known, which had always made the taste of the few last grains of sugar on her tongue that much sweeter.

Susanna's eyes sparkled as she crawled quickly across the floor and swept up the trash, her hand shaking with excitement. She would pick the mushrooms into tiny, tiny grains with her fingernails, and then she would twist the grains into the cigarette papers just as Cook had the sugar—one mushroom to a paper, and then somehow, sometime before morning she would put those mushrooms into something that Jeremiah ate or drank. If she could feed him one mushroom, he would be sick. If she could feed him two, she could kill him. And Job—maybe she could kill him too. She carried the treasured papers back to her corner and sat down to take out the first mushroom. Tiny, tiny grains, she reminded herself, so tiny they would never be noticed. The Packards had not fed her since she had come to the valley. Surely tonight she would be given food, and they would eat and she would have the opportunity. But what if she was kept locked in this room until Court came? She forced the thought from her mind. Patiently Susanna nipped small bits from the mushroom with the tips of her fingernails and dropped the lethal particles into the folded paper. Finally she twisted the first serving and slipped it into her pocket, smiling, thinking that Cook at home would never have approved putting anything to eat into such a dirty paper, or taking it out of such a dirty pocket. Cook had been very meticulous about clean kitchens and clean food. Susanna giggled. What would Cook have thought of unclean poison mushrooms? She began to pick apart the second mushroom.

38

By six in the evening Court was sure that he knew how many people were in the valley at that time and where they were housed. He also knew that the Packards had more guards out, especially night guards, for he had seen them move off to their positions as the light began to dim. He made a note of the guard posts in his mind. There was much to tell Quincy; there were plans to be revised and agreed upon, but where the hell was Quincy? And where was Susanna? She had not been out of that cabin since he had taken up his post above the valley. Again he focused the glasses on the guard at her door, if it was her door. The man was slumped against the frame, looking toward a cabin with smoke drifting from the chimney, thinking about his dinner, no doubt. Court heard movement behind him now and slipped into the trees, just in case it might not be Quincy.

"Where the hell is he?" Quincy muttered as he padded into the area on almost silent moccasins. "I know damn well this is the place where—"

"It is," said Court quietly as he took up his post again and refocused the glasses.

Quincy lowered the pack he was carrying and dropped down to catch his breath and watch with interest as Court's hands turned white on the glasses and he began to swear viciously.

"What's the matter?" Lemme see," said Quincy.

"Susanna. I just spotted her."

"She okay?"

"How the hell can I tell from here? She can walk."

"Then what's the problem?"

"Jeremiah Packard's the problem. The bastard has his hands all over her."

Quincy's face tightened in grim lines. "Well, we cain't do nothin about that now, Aaron, so git holda yerself."

Aaron's face was white and strained. "My God, we can't just leave her down there. Can you imagine what's going to happen to her later tonight? Jeremiah's—"

"Stop thinkin about it!" snapped Quincy. "We cain't go in now; we cain't go in till after midnight."

"He's—"

"I know what he is. Now we got plans to make, so stop thinkin about it." Quincy was eyeing him narrowly. "How do you feel about Susanna anyway, Court?" he asked.

Court glanced away from the field glasses toward Quincy and then resumed his survey of the camp.

Susanna had been hustled into Job's cabin. He felt that she was his property, that she had been stolen from him by scum, but he could not very well say that to Quincy, so he said only, "I don't want her in their hands; that's how I feel about her."

"That all?"

"What else?" Court shrugged.

"How do you think she feels about you?" Quincy asked, continuing to press for answers he wanted.

"She'd probably like to shoot me," replied Court bitterly. "She must know by now that I'm responsible for the fix she's in."

"I doubt that Susanna would look at it that way," said Quincy. "In fact, I figger the girl's more than half in love with you, Court." Aaron glanced at him again and then away. He did not like the direction of the conversation, never having really been willing to probe his feelings for Susanna nor hers for him—at least not beyond their mutual passion. "If any of us gits outa this mess alive, maybe you should give her feelins some thought. Young girls in love, they kin git hurt purty easy."

"Especially when they're being held by Packards," snapped Court. "I thought you wanted to make plans."

"Yeah." Quincy had been taking food out of the pack he had brought, and he tossed bread and jerky to Court and helped himself. "Yeah. I got an idea bout takin out the sentries as we go. You seen Eben Packard down there?"

"You mean the old man with the harelip? He's there. Last cabin on the north side of the trail."

"How's this fer an imitation of Eban?"

39

Susanna allowed herself to be dragged along by
Jeremiah to the larger cabin where a plate of food
was shoved into her hands and she was pushed unceremoniously down beside him on a bench. She
kept her head hanging, her eyes lowered, as if she
were cowed by her rough treatment, but beneath her
eyelashes she saw everything, everyone in the
room—Job, Marrymay, six or seven strangers, all of
whom sneered at her and made threatening remarks
about what was in store for her the next day.
Susanna said nothing; she ate—because she had
been ordered to and did not want to call attention to
herself by disobeying and because she was
agonizingly hungry by then, but each bite she took,
she took with fear, miserably aware that her fingers
might, probably still did, have the poison on them
from those hours of picking the mushrooms apart.
She had little appreciation for the irony that she
might die from the very poison that she meant for
Jeremiah. Still she ate, her stomach quailing at each
bite, and she watched. Jeremiah's plate was so close
to her. Given the opportunity, she could have
slipped the mushroom particles into the beans, and
he would never have seen them, hopefully would
never have known the difference until he had eaten
them.

That afternoon after she had picked apart the last
mushroom, she had practiced for hours undoing a
paper twist and shaking out a bit of dust that she
had rolled in it. She could release the contents with
the twist concealed in one hand, virtually invisible.
Would he notice if she passed her hand over the

plate? Would he see the reddish-brown fragments on top of the food, since she could not stir them in? She continued to eat her own serving, the first twist concealed in her left hand, and she continued to watch for her opportunity.

"Tomorrow you gonna fool around with her first, Jeremiah," asked a young cousin, "or you just gonna ram it in?"

Jeremiah turned to the boy and Susanna stiffened, her hand clenching on the paper, but Jeremiah felt the movement next to him and turned to her, grinning. "Kin hardly wait, kin you?" The other men laughed raucously, and Susanna said nothing, keeping her eyes lowered so that she would not have to look at their leering faces.

"Go git me some coffee," Jeremiah ordered. "You bring it to me nice an hot an I might even give you a little feel tonight."

Susanna's heart started to pound as obediently she put down her own tin plate and took his cup in her right hand. She knew just how she would do it. She had made plans for every contingency she could think of. She walked to the hearth where a large coffee pot rested on the fender. Putting the cup down as she knelt before the fire, she passed her left hand over it, just as she had practiced, while she lifted the pot with her right. The handle of the pot was hot and burned her skin, but she held it tight, and she poured without a sound.

"The bitch is so scared she don't even know that handle is red hot," cried Marrymay, who had been standing to one side, hands on hips, watching the girl.

Susanna said nothing. She could not now put in a second twist, not with the woman watching her so maliciously. She rose and carried the cup back to

Jeremiah and sat down again beside him. What if all the mushroom particles floated to the top and he saw them? She had been afraid to look as she carried the cup back. Or what if they all sank to the bottom and he got none of them?

Jeremiah drained the cup and handed it to her. "More," he commanded, grinning at her.

Susanna looked into the cup. It was empty. He had got it all. She returned to the hearth and repeated the whole sequence. Two mushrooms, she reminded herself, would kill him. Then he could never do to her the things he was describing to his young cousin. Filth, she thought as she watched him drinking down his own death. Filth! She turned her head away, closed her ears, concentrated on Job. Jeremiah was dead. If she could kill Job too, it would surely throw the camp into chaos. Maybe in the furor she could get away. Court had said the mushrooms made for an unpleasant death. Maybe— Job had just finished his own coffee and put the cup on the table at which he was sitting. Like a sleep-walker, Susanna rose and moved toward him.

"Here now. Siddown, you bitch," Jeremiah shouted.

"Can I get you a cup of coffee, Mr. Packard?" Susanna asked, her face expressionless under its coating of tear-streaked dirt.

Job frowned up at her as she stood so humbly in front of him, her hair straggling in black clumps down her back. "You think gittin me a cup of coffee is gonna make one smidgeon of difference in what's gonna happen to you tomorrer, girl, you're wrong."

"I was taught by my mother and father that a young woman should wait on her elders and show them respect," she said in a low, toneless voice.

Job continued to frown at her. "That's true," he

muttered, oddly disturbed that she should say that to him, that Aaron Court's woman and Lilith Moran's sister should—he cut off his own uneasy thoughts by shoving the cup at her.

Silently she moved again to the hearth. "Hey, I think we got her tamed already," remarked Luke Packard, the cousin who had first thought of kidnapping the girl to trap Court. He laughed loudly while Susanna knelt and put down the cup.

"Maybe we ought to make her shoot Court herself," suggested Jeremiah, "after I git finished with her." Susanna released the mushrooms smoothly into the cup and poured the coffee. "What do ya think about that, Pa? Think he'd like to die at the hands of his own woman, after he'd watched her bein raped?"

Job glanced uneasily at Susanna as she handed him the cup, and he did not answer his son. Susanna returned to her place by Jeremiah.

"How do ya like that idea?" he asked her.

Susanna stared at the floor and slipped her hand into her pocket to touch the last twist. She didn't have to answer Jeremiah; he was dead, she thought without feeling. But there was the last twist—and Job, his father. From beneath her lashes, she watched Job.

"You ain't nearly so much fun as you was this morning," Jeremiah grumbled. "Reckon Pa was right; you need a good night's rest to liven you up."

"Hey you, girl. Git me that whiskey," ordered Luke.

Obediently Susanna rose again, but she went to Job. "Can I get you another cup, Mr. Packard?" she asked softly.

"Never drink no more than two cups," was the

answer. "Git Luke his whiskey." The old man pointed to a jug on the hearth.

Susanna's eerie calm disintegrated into panic-stricken indecision. In the split second as she stood in front of the old man asking herself whether she should wait to see if she could give him the mushroom in something else or whether she should try to give it to someone else, she felt the full danger, the horror of what she was doing. Then the emotion passed, clamped down into some inaccessible portion of her mind as she moved toward the whiskey jug into which she would pour the last of the mushroom particles. Job might drink some, and a little more might kill him. Others would drink it; they probably all drank hard spirits. They might all become at least a little sick, and if they were all sick, Susanna could slip away. Without looking to see if anyone as watching her, she calmly bent over and uncorked the jug. She could not even slip in the mushroom fragments unobtrusively because the opening was small, but she tipped the last portion carefully in from its paper container and let it slide down while behind her Marrymay shouted, "Hey. What are you doing there?"

Susanna dropped the paper on the floor and bent close to the jug. Then she looked over her shoulder at Marrymay and replied, "I'm smelling it to see if it's hard spirits." She rose and walked to Luke, swirling the liquid in the jug around and around as she moved. The Packard cousin snatched the jug from her hands. She was acting so peculiarly, swirling it that way, her eyes looking as blank as the eyes of a corpse; Luke was afraid she might drop the whiskey before he got his drink.

"Give her some if she likes the smell of whiskey so much," sneered Jeremiah.

Susanna had dropped down beside him, weak with relief that she had at that point done all that she could do. At his words she stiffened with horror. Was she to die in the trap she had set for them? she wondered desperately. "My father would never allow such a thing," she said, staring into Job's eyes. "He watches me from heaven; he won't allow me to drink hard spirits."

Jeremiah hooted and started to force a cup of whiskey to her lips, but she kept her eyes on Job—staring at him, willing him to protect the rights of her father, as he protected his own patriarchal rights. "Leave the girl alone," Job muttered.

"Ah, Pa. A dead daddy ain't gonna mind a little whiskey—not after what him an me seen her doin with Aaron Court over by Hiller's Pond." Jeremiah snickered.

"Leave her alone," Job snapped angrily.

The son subsided with sullen ill nature, refusing to drink the whiskey himself, and Luke, reminded of the day when he had watched the girl making love with Court and of tomorrow when he would watch Jeremiah rape her without ever having the opportunity to do so himself, lost his desire for drink. He too refused the jug. Instead he passed it to his young cousin. Susanna looked down at the floor, satisfied. Jeremiah had had his share of the poison. Luke might change his mind, and now the others would have their share. She sat back to wait.

Each minute seemed to stretch on and on, and still no one became ill. Jeremiah said disgusting things to her and to his relatives, who laughed raucously, and she continued to stare at the floor, willing him to become ill, to fall dead beside her, anything. Job sat talking to an old man with a harelip. The others drank. And none of them looked sick, even a little sick. How long did it take? Court had not said. If it took two days, Aaron would be dead before them, and she—Susanna shuddered. And still the minutes passed like the slow drip of molasses. Maybe she had got the wrong mushrooms and the Packards would not fall ill at all. Maybe the mushrooms were poisonous only if they were dried. Maybe she was indeed a sinner as Job had seemed to be saying with all his strange words that he hurled at her so contemptuously, and if she was a sinner, perhaps God had turned away from her, and the Packards would never feel the results of the poison. But surely God would not protect the Packards—surely—

"Lock the girl up again," commanded Job.

Susanna's eyes flew up in shock. They were going to put her in that room again, lock her in before they fell ill and she could escape. Then even if Job and Jeremiah and all the others in the room died, she would still be imprisoned, and there would be other Packards to kill Aaron and to—Susanna, panicking, fell to her knees and cried, "Oh God, please, please strike them down. Please—"

"Get her out of here," Job shouted. The others were gaping at her, taken by surprise since she had been so quiet and docile all evening.

"Please, God—"

"God don't listen to you!" Job was now standing over her, his face flushed with anger.

"Please, God," she begged hysterically. "Strike down Jeremiah. Strike down—"

"Pa—" Jeremiah had fallen to his knees beside her.

"What're you doin, boy?" demanded Job. "Git yerself up. You praying with her fer yer own—"

"Pa—" Jeremiah's face was gray and covered with sweat, his arms crossed over his belly. "Pa, I cain't—"

"Git up."

"My—my guts is on fire." Jeremiah began to retch violently.

Susanna, still on her knees, turned to stare wide-eyed at him, brushing her black hair back from her face. "Thank you, God," she whispered.

Job was staring at her wildly as Jeremiah fell forward into his own vomit.

"Marrymay, look to your brother-in-law," Luke ordered.

"Thank you, God. Thank you," Susanna continued to whisper over and over.

"She's a witch!" said Job in a low voice filled with superstitious horror. "I always said woman-stealin were dangerous. Now you dun talked me into bringin a witch into my valley, Luke."

"Now, Job. She's jus a girl," said Luke. "A plain, ordinary girl."

"Witch. She's a witch." Job was still staring at her, ignoring his son, who was then moaning on the floor. Susanna hugged herself and rocked back and forth, staring at Jeremiah with wide eyes from which tears flowed and flowed. "Lock her up in the cabin," Job commanded. Luke and the young boy dragged her, struggling and screaming, from Job's cabin. "I'm gonna burn you," Job shouted after her. "Yer a witch. You'll burn. Tomorrer." He was already beginning to feel knifelike cramps in his own belly, but he ignored them and turned to his son, who was twisting on the floor at his feet. "I'll burn her, Jeremiah," he promised. "It wasn't God did this. It was her. Witch. Witch," he continued to mutter. "Git that doctor we caught for Isaiah."

"We set him loose when Isaiah died," Marrymay

reminded him. She was kneeling on the floor beside her brother-in-law, but she did not know what to do for him.

"I told Elias to leave Court alone," mumbled Job. "An he disobeyed me an he's dead, an all the others, they died. An now we got a witch among us. A witch. She's set her spell on me too. She's—"

"Jeremiah—he'll be okay, Pa. He just et sumpthin disagreed with him." Marrymay did not believe in witches. In fact, she believed in very little after her years in the Packard valley.

"Witch," muttered the old man over and over.

40

"Those bastards!" Court had been lying for hours surveying the Packard settlement through the field glasses. Even in the darkness after nightfall, he had still continued to scan the huddle of cabins, using the weak moonlight that shone occasionally through the heavy clouds and the light of the campfires to keep watch for Susanna. When she came out of Job's cabin again, he had to know it. And he wanted to know, as accurately as he could, where all the others were when the Packards finally settled down for the night.

"What is it?" Quincy asked.

"Susanna. My God, what are they doing to her? What have they done?"

"What da ya mean?"

"She's struggling and fighting them."

Quincy sighed. "She's still alive."

"But it's taking two of them to get her back to the other cabin. What—?"

"Don't think about it," said Quincy sharply.

"Have they posted guards again?"

"Yes."

"Then likely she'll be there the rest of the night. We'd best start movin closer." Quincy gathered the weapons. "I'll move down to the next place an then I'll keep watch. Give me fifteen minutes before you start." Court nodded, continuing to scan the valley, wondering what was happening to her inside the cabin. The two men who had brought her there, neither of whom looked like Jeremiah, had left and gone back to Job's place, but Court could not be sure who might have been waiting inside for her. While he was watching Job's cabin and the rest of the camp, someone could have gone into hers. His mouth set in grim lines, and he shifted his body slightly, hoping he would not be too stiff from cold and inaction to move quickly when the time came.

41

Luke and the boy hurled Susanna roughly into the back room of the cabin and threw the bolts of the door, then hurried back to Job's with hardly a word to her guard. For a few minutes after she heard the bolts click home, Susanna lay still on the floor. Then she crawled into the farthest corner of the room and curled up, weeping, her courage and hope gone. She had killed a man, maybe more than one, and it had been for nothing. She was locked up again and could not escape. It had been for nothing—worse than nothing. Job was going to burn her as a witch, and if he did not live to do it, the others would. They would carry out his wishes. And they would kill Aaron. Would they make him watch her burn? With Jeremiah dead and unable to attack her, they would probably burn her in front of Aaron for revenge. She prayed that he would stay away. She wept—in terror at the idea of being committed to die by fire. Outside, giant bolts of lightning flashed in her small, high window, but she did not notice. Thunder rolled across the valley, but she did not hear. Wild rain began to slash onto the cabins and the trail, bending the trees in the forest, rolling rocks down the mountain, but Susanna only shuddered and wept and finally dropped into exhausted, haunted dreams.

42

Job heard it all and muttered, "Is it her? Does she command the storm? Or is it God? Has she turned God against me?" He looked to his son Jeremiah who twisted and turned, covered with sweat, vomiting blood and moaning as the storm howled through the valley.

43

"We'll move now," said Quincy. "Under cover of the storm."

"Pray God it doesn't let up while we're down there," muttered Court.

"Pray God it does let up once we're got her away," Quincy replied. "Else it'll be hell gettin her up the hill to the horses—if they ain't bolted."

44

Susanna awoke from a terrifying dream to a more terrifying reality. There was a hand—wet and cold—over her mouth and another at her waist holding her down. Icy water was falling onto her. Her body stiffened and she began to struggle wildly. Then the man who was holding her dropped his full weight onto her without removing his hand from her mouth, and she was pinned under him—helpless, speechless, freezing as the cold, wet body on hers soaked her nightgown and her skin. Had Jeremiah come to attack her after all? she wondered, her mind spinning in wild circles. No, he was dead, dead. They had come to burn her.

"Quiet, Susanna," said a voice in her ear. The man's breath was warm, the only warm thing in that terrible, cold room. "Don't struggle, love, and don't cry out. It's me—Aaron. Quincy and I are going to take you out of here."

Susanna's body went still under his. She raised trembling fingers to touch his face in the dark. "Aaron?" she breathed against his hand.

He took the hand away from her mouth and lifted her with him to a sitting position. "We have to go now—right now. Don't you have any clothes?"

"No," she whispered as he drew her to her feet. "The guard?"

"Dead," said Court. It had been simple enough when it came to it. They had just walked into the settlement in a rain that cut into them like sabers of ice. As far as they could tell, no one was about except the guard at Susanna's door, and Quincy had limped up to him and told him, in the lisping voice of his cousin Eban Packard, that Job wanted to see him. While the guard was agreeing eagerly to turn his post over, Court had walked up behind him and put a knife into his back. Then they had taken the body into the cabin with them, and while Quincy

stood guard in the dead man's place, Court roused
Susanna. The three of them were out the door and
into the surrounding forest within five minutes of
the time that Court and Quincy had left it.

"She has no shoes and no clothes but a nightgown
and some sort of apron," said Court once they were
among the trees.

"We'll take turns carryin her," Quincy had
replied. They moved up a trail they could not see in a
rain they could hardly make headway against—hoping
it would slacken, hoping they were not becoming
lost.

45

"He's dead, Pa," said Marrymay.

Job turned from the fire to look at the still figure
of yet another of his sons. "Git the witch," he said.

"It's rainin out there, Job," Luke objected. "We
cain't have no burnin in a storm like that."

"Git the witch!"

Luke shrugged and went out into the storm to get
Susanna. In a few minutes he was back. "She's
gone," he announced angrily. "The guard is
dead—knifed. An she's gone."

Job's shoulders slumped in defeat. "Flew away,"
he muttered. "She musta flew away."

"Flew hell! I told you Simon was knifed. Someone got her outa there."

"Satan," said Job. "Satan got her out."

"We gotta catch em," said Luke stubbornly. He
did not want to see his plan come to nothing just
because the girl had got loose. "Ring the alarm
bell," he ordered a young nephew.

"No use," said Job, who was being overcome by

the effects of the mushrooms himself. "She done got me too."

"Ring the bell, boy," Luke ordered. "Take care of your pa, Marrymay." He left Job and went to order the search party. The girl could not have been gone long, and even if she got away, they might still get Court. The girl would never get to Amnonville in that storm, not in time to keep Court from coming —unless it had been Court who rescued her, in which case they could just catch Court a few hours earlier. The brazen bell began to clang above the diminishing sound of thunder.

46

"They've discovered she's gone," said Quincy when he heard the alarm. He stopped wearily and lowered the girl to the ground. "You take her from here, Court. I'll stay an cover yer trail. If they come this way, I can slow em up, lead em wrong."

Court shook his head. "It's a good idea, but since I started this mess, I'll—"

"Not if you want to git her out," said Quincy wearily. "I'm jus plumb too old to git her up to the horses by myself. But I ain't too old to hold off Packards. Now git goin. The further you two are away, the better."

Court hestitated only a moment. What Quincy had said made sense. He stooped to swing the shivering girl over his shoulder. "See you back in town, Abner," he said quietly.

"Yep." Quincy turned to leave, then thought of something. "Court!" he called. "She's gittin too cold. If the rain don't let up, git her to Bedlow Caves an light a fire. She won't make it else." Court nodded, put his hand briefly on Quincy's shoulder, and then started up the mountain again. Abner Quincy, picking up his rifle, turned back toward the Packard settlement.

47

All his life Aaron Court remembered that nightmare struggle out of the Packards' valley. Although its force had slackened somewhat, the rain continued—hard, drenching, and cold, so cold he ached with it deep into his bones and his body felt numb and clumsy. The night was a smothering black hell, impenetrable except when an occasional bolt of lightning gave him fleeting sight of his surroundings, and then although he could check his path, he had to remember that each garish explosion of light might be the one that killed them. Only the fact that he had been into that valley so many times before on that path and in the dark allowed him to continue accurately toward the place where he had tethered the horses and left the supplies. And as they moved closer to the top, they became exposed to sharp gusts of wind that made the cold and rain harder to bear and Susanna harder to carry.

To add to his fears, when they were less than half-way up by his calculations, he heard gunfire from below, but he had no idea what was happening, whether Quincy was still alive, whether the Packards were closing in on them. He tried to move faster, but the way had become steeper, and Susanna, who had tried to help at first, became more difficult to handle. She stopped holding onto him, and the rain made it hard for him to hold onto her. When he put

her down for a moment's rest, she stumbled and fell,
even when the path was smooth. When he gave her
orders, she failed to obey. When he asked her
worried questions about what had happened to her,
she mumbled, did not seem to understand. Had it
been so bad for her that night in the valley that she
was no longer sane? What had they done to her? he
wondered anxiously as he struggled upward with
Susanna shivering violently in his arms.

48

Quincy was in no hurry once he had left Aaron and
Susanna. He advanced cautiously because he did not
know the trails and because he needed to think out
his next move. He could hear voices calling back and
forth below him now, but he was not yet close
enough to distinguish the words, and those voices
did not seem to be moving closer to him—which did
not mean, he reminded himself, that there might not
be some smart Packards coming his way quietly
without any stupid announcements of their presence. Still, in this rain they would have no chance to
read sign and, consequently, could have no idea of
which way Susanna and her rescuers might have
gone or how many rescuers might be in the valley.
He continued to edge down the mountain, having
decided to see if he could eavesdrop on their
councils.

When he finally worked his way almost to the
main cabin area, he was surprised to find that Luke
Packard rather than Job seemed to be in charge of
the search party and that none of the Packards were
showing much inclination to cooperate.

"Maybe old Job is right. Maybe she is a witch."

A witch? Quincy puzzled.

"We sure ain't gonna catch her if'n she flew off," continued the witch theorist.

"Don't be a fool," snapped Luke. "Someone came in here, knifed Simon, and took her off. Now we gotta find her."

"How the hell are we supposed to do that in this rain?" complained another member of the gang. "I'm soaked already."

So am I, thought Quincy gloomily, a hell of a lot worse than you, you bastard.

"We're gonna find em by each takin one of the trails up the sides of the valley. I don't figger they was dumb enough to try the pass, but we'll cover that too."

As Luke began to assign various unenthusiastic pursuers to various areas, Quincy slipped off toward the corral, where he limped up to a man who was saddling horses and lisped into his ear that Luke wanted two. Grumbling, the man turned over two saddled horses to the hunched figure he took to be Eban Packard, and Quincy disappeared into the rain with them, back the way he had come. He intended to wait until the men assigned to the trail Court and Susanna were on came close to him. Then he would burst past them, heading for the entrance to the valley with both horses. If he could convince enough Packards that the girl and a rescuer had gone that way—well, it might work.

And he did just that—calling out, "Make for the pass, girl. Maybe we can get by the sentries in the rain." He, with the riderless horse on the far side of him, dashed by within twenty yards of three men who were fumbling around looking for the trail that Aaron Court had been able to locate more easily than they and grumbling because they were afoot in the dark in a driving spring rain.

Eagerly the three pursuers took the bait. "That's them," shouted one, and he fired the signal shots that had been agreed upon at the meeting. Then the men ran back toward the corral to get horses and pursue the girl and her rescuer down the valley. They shouted the news enthusiastically as they ran and stopped to tell it when they met other Packards. All this passing of news and answering of questions and revision of plans allowed Quincy to ride as far as the point at which Benny Ripon had rushed the stampeding horses on their way with the Indian noisemakers. Quincy could hear the pursuit now and wished that Ripon was beside him on the empty horse. The two of them, holed up behind some rocks up there, could have cut down a good many Packards.

The gunfire had begun again, and these were not signal shots. The bullets were beginning to get close; the Packards were getting the range, beginning to catch glimpses of him through the rain. Quincy released the other horse and, reining in his own horse slightly, hit the riderless mount sharply on the haunch, sending it careening aside into the night. He did not care where it went as long as it avoided the direction taken by Aaron and Susanna. Then he began to send shots back at his pursuers, not with any hope of hitting them under such adverse circumstances, but to slow them up if possible. He had no idea that he would make it through the pass—not with Packards ahead of him and behind, but he intended to hold their attention for as long as he could and hoped that the two horses, one running loose in the rain, might further delay them—even add to the confusion if and when they caught the horses and discovered the animals to be their own.

Quincy had made it to a point halfway between Ripon's post and the valley entrance, with the Packards closing fast, when a bullet burned into his arm, his right arm, which went numb. He gritted his teeth, both against the beginning pain and against the ill luck of it, for although he could shoot left-handed, he did not do it well, and he could not both shoot and control the horse with only one arm. Making his mind up instantly, he kicked his feet loose from the stirrups and dove off, rolling as soon as he hit the ground. Then he drew his gun and put a shot across the haunches of the horse, which had been slowing down in confusion. It broke into a wild run, and Quincy, congratulating himself on being a better left-hand shot than he had thought he was, crawled away from the road and into the trees. The Packard pursuers thundered on by in the rain, unable to see that they were now chasing two rider-less horses, their own at that.

49

When Court finally climbed out of the valley, his relief was much less than he would have anticipated. One of the horses had broken loose and was gone, not that Susanna could have ridden if he had chosen to take both of the remaining horses and leave Quincy without the means to escape a situation that was bound to be more dangerous than their own. Susanna had stopped shivering and was by then barely conscious, and Court had realized with dread that she was suffering, as Quincy had warned, from cold. In fact, if the descriptions he had heard from men who had seen others die of exposure were accurate, she was in danger of dying. Much as he wanted to head straight for the safety of the town, he decided that he would have to follow Quincy's advice and try to find his way to the caves, for Quincy had evidently realized early what was happening to her, clad only in a thin nightgown in a cold, driving rain.

In the wet darkness he struggled to get her into the extra clothes that Quincy had brought along for her. Why the hell hadn't the Packards given her at least something warmer to wear? he wondered.

"Bastards," he muttered to himself. By the time he had her dressed, the new clothes were wet through too, but at least they were heavier, made of wool, and would offer her more protection than the cotton nightgown. He chose the better horse for himself since it had to carry double, checked to see that the horse he hoped Quincy would return for was tightly tied, and then lifted Susanna into the saddle in front of him and set out to pick his way, if he could find it, to Bedlow Caves.

50

"How many men?" asked Lilith tensely.

"Forty, maybe forty-five."

"It's not enough."

"It's more than the Packards have since Court started attacking them."

"Bastard. If he'd left well enough alone—"

"Forget it, Lilith."

"The informers?"

"One is dead. The other two tied up in back."

"And the sheriff. Is he going?"

"Of course not," said Mondragon. "He says it's not—"

"In his county," Lilith finished coldly. "I want to leave now."

"It's only midnight, querida. Give them time to get her out. That's the best chance she's got. Then if—"

"Then it may be too late."

"It may," Mondragon agreed.

51

Court stumbled into the cave carrying Susanna, dragging the horse behind him and praying there would be dry firewood stacked against the wall, as he had heard there often was. The wind was blowing the rain so badly he had to feel his way in fifty steps or so before he could put her down on dry stone, and then he had no idea how close they were to the first drop-off since he had never been inside the place before, only heard of it. Somehow, with the few damp matches in his possession, he had to find wood in the darkness and build a fire. The lantern. Quincy had brought a lantern, but was it on his horse or on the one he had left behind or on the one that had got loose? Court was so tired he found it hard to decide what to do first—look for the lantern, look for the firewood, get the wet clothes off Susanna and roll her in blankets. God! Did he have blankets? Wearily he began to unpack the saddle bags by touch in the unrelieved darkness. The lantern was there, thank God. But the only blanket was the one on the horse, and it was wet. Court leaned against the horse. Susanna or the fire? He knew that ultimately he had to get the wet clothes

off both of them and hope that, once they were
wrapped in the blanket, his body heat would save
her. In a sudden panic he leaned down to be sure
that she was still alive. She was breathing, but
cold—so cold. Fire! He lit the lantern and dragged
himself in search of wood. It was there, as he had
heard, and still dry because it had been piled just
beyond a curve in the cave wall so the rain could not
get to it. With the last of his strength, he built the
fire and drew off their clothes, scattering them carelessly about because he was now past realizing that
he should place them carefully to dry. Then he rolled
himself and Susanna into the one damp blanket in
front of the fire. She was as cold and unmoving as a
dead woman in his arms. "Let it be enough," he
muttered as he drew her closer to him, and he
dropped into a sleep as deep as her unconsciousness.
He had even forgotten that the Packards might be
pursuing them—that they could be found by the
light of their fire and killed as they slept.

52

Once the Packards were passed, Quincy had
propped himself up under a rock ledge and tied a
bandana tightly around his arm, hoping to stem the
bleeding he could not see. He had no idea how bad
the wound was—only that it hurt more than it had
before and that the arm was next to useless. Sighing,
he tipped his hat over his eyes to keep the rain out of
his face. Then he prepared to wait, since he could
think of nothing else to do to insure the safety of
Susanna and Court and since he was not sure that he
could manage to do anything else if he could have
thought of anything else to do. Therefore he dozed,

coming awake from time to time as confused, shouting Packards rode by in various directions. It was obvious that their search was getting them nowhere; otherwise they would not have continued to search, he deduced with satisfaction. Quincy had no idea what time it was, but sooner or later Mondragon would arrive with a posse from town. Perhaps by then he would be up to moving out to tell them that Susanna was probably safe somewhere. The information, if Court had not managed to get it to them, might save some lives on one side and lose some Packard lives on the other if the townsmen did not have to worry about Susanna being killed in the attack. Quincy wondered idly from time to time, as he woke and slept, whether he was dying—of loss of blood or of the cold. It did not seem to matter too much at the moment; maybe it might seem more important later.

53

Susanna came awake very slowly, her mind functioning in a sort of drugged, creeping confusion. Her first clear realization was that she was warm, whereas she had been cold before. For several minutes she was afraid to move, governed by the vague idea that if she moved, the terrible cold would return. Once she had become accustomed to the feeling of a warmth that continued, she became aware of other bodily sensations—her own bare skin, the unfamiliar experience of sleeping naked, a rough blanket against her back, hard ground beneath her shoulder, hip, and leg. And finally there was the source of the heat—a naked body lying full-length against her own—warm; rough, curly hair against her breasts and stomach; hard legs; muscled arms holding her; measured breathing and warm breath stirring her hair; the face of Jeremiah Packard in her mind—Susanna came fully awake with a strangled cry and all muscles convulsing in terror.

Pulled instantly from deep sleep, Aaron instinctively tightened his arms around her and rolled on top of her to hold her down. "Quiet!" he hissed.

She lay beneath him, shuddering. "Get away," she cried in a voice cracking with horror.

"Quiet, Susanna." He put his hand over her mouth. "You're all right. We got you out of there." When she continued to struggle, he put his mouth to her ear and whispered over and over, "It's all right. It's all right, Susanna. You're with me now. The Packards are gone. It's all right." Over and over until the words penetrated, and she recognized the voice, and she went limp, her breathing at last calming, slowing. Then she put her arms around him and began to cry.

Court would never have thought anyone could cry that much—choking, wrenching sobs that went on and on, and she told him all the things that had happened—the brutal, contemptuous treatment; the strange names Job had called her, "whore" and "fornicator"; the threats to rape her, to kill him, to burn her; and the mushrooms, the twists of paper, the poisoning of Jeremiah who had collapsed screaming, and of Job, and of those who had drunk the whiskey; and then the final horror, that they had locked her up so she could not escape after she had committed murder to get away. Her crying went on and on, and she told him the same things over and over again, seemingly unable to stop talking, to stop confessing—until Court had to stop her himself because he could bear her anguish and terror no longer. So he stopped her with his mouth, and his hands, and his body—making love to her until her tears dried and her mind slipped away and she wanted only to be thrust into, and to be forced into sensual delirium, and to be lost in him—and this he did for her. He erased Jeremiah and Job and all the others, and when the last shudder of passion had passed, they were the only ones left in that cave and in their own minds. Then they slept—at peace, still joined, under a rough blanket, before a dead fire.

54

At one o'clock the Fallen Angel was the meeting place not of gamblers or drinkers or men intent on purchasing the time of one of Lilith's girls, for all these had been unceremoniously run off to make room for forty grim, heavily armed men, all of whom knew that no word had been received from Susanna or her rescuers and that in all probability they would be riding out within the hour to clean the Packards out of the area for good and to rescue the girl themselves if they could.

Lilith's face was white, her eyes flashing. "They've failed," she cried accusingly to Mondragon. "I told you—"

"We don't know that they've failed," he interrupted calmly. "We may meet them on the road."

"They probably never went after her. That damn Court was just giving himself time to get out of Amnonville. We should have left hours ago."

"Near to dawn is better," he replied.

"And what's happening to her in the meantime?"

"Leave it alone, Lilith. We'll go in after her, and you'll know by morning."

"I'll know when you do. Did you think I'd stay here? I'm going with you."

This declaration caused uneasy grumbling among the men gathered for the raid. They expected to be hampered enough by having to watch out for Susanna. The prospect of having Lilith too—but she would not be dissuaded, and finally the effort was abandoned since the time was needed to plan the raid. The most practical suggestion was offered by Grassback Holbein, who had received word of his partner's involvement in a new Packard atrocity and had come in to help if he could.

"No use us all gittin cut down in the pass by the sentries. Since me and Benny know where they's at, we'll go in with a few others an clear the way."

"If they hear you, they'll kill Susanna before any of us get into the valley," Lilith objected.

"The whole idee, ma'am, is fer all of us to git in without the folks around the cabins bein none the wiser. I ain't plannin on shootin the sentries. We'll kill em quiet-like."

"Don't interfere, Lilith," snapped Mondragon, his patience with her slipping. "You can be sure that if they hear gunfire at the valley entrance, they'll kill her or take her away before we can get to her. It's several miles from the pass to the encampment."

With Lilith silenced, the plans moved forward, and Holbein, Ripon, and several confederates left before two, the others to follow shortly but enter the valley only when they had word that the way was clear.

Up until the moment they received that word,

Mondragon had expected to be met by Court or
Quincy and told that Susanna was free. Instinct had
convinced him they would get her out and that the
attack on the valley would therefore be a less touchy
problem, for one thing because Lilith could be sent
home. Mondragon did not want her interference,
and even more important, he did not want her hurt.

However, they received no word. At the time the
larger group rode quietly into the valley, Quincy was
asleep again under his sheltering rock ledge, and
Court and Susanna were free. Fortunately, three
hours of fruitless searching in the rain had exhausted
the Packards and weakened the already loose
control Luke had over the group. Job was by that
time too sick to give any advice or issue any orders,
and other closer members of his family who had
been in his cabin earlier and drunk the whiskey into
which Susanna had put the last mushroom were also
sick to lesser degrees. Consequently, disgruntled,
exhausted, and virtually without leadership, the
Packards simply drifted off to their beds, refusing to
implement any more plans made by Luke. He was
able only to replace several of the guards stationed
on the slopes of the valley, and he still had men at
the pass. With that he had to be satisfied. Ill and
exhausted himself, he went to his own cabin to make
plans for the morning and was so engaged when
forty men from Amnonville rode into the settlement
and began to root stumbling Packards out of their
cabins, shooting down any who offered resistance.
The few guards on the slopes, all of whom had been
dozing at their posts, were taken completely by surprise when gunfire erupted, for the continuing rain
had muffled the sounds of horses entering the
valley, and the riders had been absolutely silent.

Instead of attempting to help their relatives from their superior positions above the camp, the guards fled.

"Where's Susanna?" Lilith screamed at the first men to be brought to her.

"She ain't here," was the sullen reply.

"Liar!"

"Search all the cabins," Mondragon commanded one of his own men.

The men returned in fifteen minutes, by which time most of the Packards were standing in the middle of the area, hands tied, guns trained menacingly on them.

"She ain't in any of the cabins," Mondragon's man reported. "Couldn't find no sign of her."

"Where are Job and Jeremiah Packard?" Lilith demanded. "They must have her."

"Jeremiah's dead. Looks like he died of natural causes—but hard. Job's in his cabin—real sick. He can't even git up."

"You sure he's not faking?" demanded Mondragon.

"We got guards on him an his daughter-in-law, but he ain't fakin, Mr. Mondragon. He's real sick."

"Where is she?" Lilith demanded furiously of Luke.

"As you can see, your sister ain't here, ma'am," said Luke respectfully. "Why would she be with us?"

Lilith's eyes narrowed. "Aaron Court got a note yesterday morning saying he had to come here or you'd kill her."

"We didn't send no note. Job, he don't approve of woman-stealin. Everone knows that." Luke looked her straight in the eye. "Maybe Court writ the note hisself an run off with her. I heard tell he's been seein her.''

''He's lying,'' said Mondragon.

Lilith looked up at him sharply. She could almost believe what Luke said since they had had no word from Quincy or Court, but she could not be sure. If Court had written the note, how did Quincy fit into the scheme? Was he fool enough to think that Court would marry Susanna once he had run off with her? ''We'll see,'' said Lilith coldly. ''Maybe if we hang a few of you, we can get some answers. I think I'll hang you one by one till we learn the truth.'' Her eyes were searching the group of men standing before her. ''Him,'' she said, pointing to the boy who had sat next to Jeremiah that evening. ''Hang that one first.''

Two of the vigilantes dragged the boy from the crowd of his relatives and boosted him up onto a horse. Another man tied a noose and tossed it over a thick tree branch nearby. Carlos made no move to halt the proceedings, and within two minutes the trembling boy had the noose drawn tight around his neck with only the horse beneath him to keep him from strangling.

''Where is she?'' Lilith demanded of the boy.

''We ain't seen her,'' he replied in a quavering voice. He could not believe that they were going to hang him, that anyone would hang him. They were bluffing, and he would not be forgiven by his kin if he was weak and failed to call the bluff, but he was afraid. ''She ain't been here,'' he reiterated, his glance darting to Luke.

''Hang him,'' Lilith commanded.

From the corner of his eye the boy saw the man holding the reins drop them and another raise his hand to strike the horse. "Wait!" he cried, terrified.

"Well?" Lilith continued to stare at him with implacable eyes. It was obvious to him that she did not care whether he or anyone else lived or died.

"She was here," the boy cried, trying not to look at his Uncle Luke, whose mouth had tightened in lines of anger and contempt. "She was here, but someone took her."

"Who?"

"We don't know. We looked everywhere, but—"

"Liar."

"I ain't lying," cried the boy desperately. "I was sitting next to her in old Job's cabin, next to Jeremiah anyways. It was after that she was took."

"Someone took her right out of Job's cabin? With three of you Packards there? Hang him," snapped Lilith.

The man behind slapped the horse and the boy died, his neck broken.

"Well, Luke?" Lilith turned to him.

"The boy was lying, trying to save his neck," Luke replied. "We never had her."

"Let's see how you like the feel of the rope around your neck."

Luke died without changing his story, and Lilith wondered. Had the note been a trick of Court's? The Packards were shifting uneasily, two of their number having been hanged before their eyes. They had assumed before Elias's death that they were immune to the law. The deaths since then had at least been in running fights of one kind or another, although the toil had been heavy. But this summary justice, without trial, without delay, being dispensed by Lilith Moran—each man was trying to figure out whether he stood a better chance of escaping the rope, at least temporarily, by telling the truth, which she did not seem to believe, or by telling Luke's story, which made them all out to be innocent, although she did not seem to believe that either. And in fact there was no one in that motley crowd of outlaws who could save himself by giving Lilith what she demanded, the sight of her sister alive. And so the hangings continued, and all the bodies were left dangling—the trees festooned with gently swinging corpses, limp and dripping in the rain.

"Wha's happenin, girl?" mumbled Job weakly from his bed. Marrymay was kneeling by the window, watching her kinsmen die in the wind as their horses were kicked out from under them.

"They're hangin em all, Pa," she whispered.

"Caught em, did they? Good." Job twisted uneasily under the sweat-soaked covers. "Wan her burned though, not hanged. Burned."

"It's Packards are hangin, Job," said his guard, a faro dealer from Lilith's place. "One by one, Lilith is stretchin the necks of all yer kith and kin. You wanna go out an tell her where her sister is, maybe she'll quit. Then again maybe she won't."

"Wassa whore doin in my valley?" mumbled the old man, trying to rise. Marrymay ran to him, and the faro dealer allowed her to help Job to the door of the cabin, where he stared, unbelieving, at the corpses of his kinsmen. "Lilith," he called, still leaning almost his full weight on his daughter-in-law.

Lilith turned in her saddle and fixed her eyes on Job outlined in the doorway by the light from his own hearth. "You come to take your turn at the rope, Job?" she called. "Like the rest of your lying family. Or maybe you'd like to tell me what you've done with my sister.''

''I took her to git Court. That's what I done. We don't care none about her. Jus Court. Was she still here, you could have her back soon as we git Court.''

''Well, I don't care about Court,'' said Lilith, her voice venomous with determination. ''And I'll hang every last one of you until I find her.''

''She ain't worth the life of one of my boys,'' said Job. ''Not one of em. She's a liar. And she's Aaron Court's whore.''

''You're a liar,'' cried Lilith furiously.

''I ain't lyin. Jeremiah an Luke saw her fornicatin with Court—''

''Liar,'' hissed Lilith.

''—right over to Hiller's Pond. In broad daylight.'' Job leered at her. ''Said she seemed to be likin the whole thing more than most.''

''Hang him,'' cried Lilith.

''Twistin an squirmin like a good little whore,'' Job continued. ''Heard tell you don't like it that much, Lilith. Maybe you oughta use her in yer whorehouse. No use Court gittin all that, an fer nothin—''

Two men pushed Marrymay away from Job and began to drag him toward a tree where a horse was brought to put him on, but Job kept his eyes on Lilith. They glared with a fanatical light. ''And she's a witch, Lilith. Yer lil sister's a witch an a murderer.'' They hoisted him onto the horse. ''She called down the wrath of Satan on Jeremiah an he fell an died, an she called a curse on me an more of my folk, an we been sick. The girl's a witch.''

''Get the noose on him,'' Lilith ordered.

''Be sure she don't curse you, Lilith. God ain't

gonna pertect you from her—no more'n he did me an mine. She's a whore an a witch, that sister o—'' Job's ravings were cut off by the rope, and he died quickly with one hard jerk of his heavy, old body.

Lilith wiped a wet hand in front of her eyes and turned to Carlos. "What he said about Susanna and Court—''

"Do you believe your sister's a witch?'' he asked sharply.

"No, of course not.''

"Then why believe the rest? The only thing you know at this point is that she was here and that she is gone now.''

"I don't even know that,'' said Lilith wearily. "Why doesn't this damn rain stop? I might know more if I could see their faces.''

"The dawn is coming.'' Carlos pointed to graying sky in the east.

Lilith turned her head quickly when she heard her name being called by voices from the road. Soon two men who had been searching the valley came in carrying Abner Quincy between them. "We found Quincy,'' they called. "He's been hit—not too bad, but he like to froze waitin for us to get here.''

Lilith dismounted immediately and knelt beside the man she had hired to guard Susanna. He seemed hardly able to talk. "Get the man some whiskey!'' she ordered impatiently. "We've got to revive him.'' One of the vigilantes handed over a flask, and Lilith held it to Quincy's lips, spilling the liquor sloppily down his throat, onto his chin, and into his already soaked clothing.

"Don't choke me,'' Quincy muttered, coughing. "I ain't dead, jus damned cold.''

"Where is she?'' Lilith demanded.

"We got her away. Here, lemme sit up. Sleepin in the rain don't do ole fellers my age no good." Quincy struggled into a sitting position. "We got her away—outa the cabin where they had her locked an part way up the mountain."

"Why didn't you let us know, Quincy," asked Mondragon, "as we agreed?"

"They found her gone and started huntin, so I led em off on a false trail while Court carried her up the mountain. I got shot—couldn't git word to ya."

"They never got back to town," said Lilith suspiciously.

"Try the caves," gasped Quincy, having helped himself to another drag at the flask. "That's better. Beginnin to feel like I might live. Told Court to take her there if the rain didn't let up."

"Why?" Lilith demanded angrily.

"Fraid she'd freeze to death."

"Rot! It's spring."

"It's cold, an her in only a lil thin nightrail. She was dyin a the cold. I know the signs."

Lilith looked questioningly at Carlos, who nodded. "Could be," he agreed. "Cold wind an rain, no protection. What caves would he have gone to, Quincy?"

"Bedlow. I'll take ya." Quincy rose slowly.

Lilith was staring at him with hostility. "Job said Court had—had seduced her. What do you know about that?"

"I know the Packards treated her bad," replied Quincy, giving her back a stare as hostile as her own. "Don know what they done to her. She could hardly talk when we got her outa that cabin. As fer Court, if she's alive, it's cause he got her out. If she's dead, it ain't cause he din try."

"What about—?"

"Maybe we better find them an ask the questions later," Mondragon interrupted.

"The Packards done hurt her," said Quincy stubbornly. "Not Court."

Lilith planted her hands on her hips and looked around the clearing as the light became stronger. Various vigilantes and Packards in their custody were standing in the crowd, attempting to hear what was being said. Lilith's mouth drew down at the corners. "I want my own men to go with me to find my sister," she said in a loud, clear voice.

"What about the rest of the Packards?" asked Holbein. "We supposed to take em in to jail?"

"My advice is to hang them right here," said Lilith, "but suit yourselves."

"Some musta got away," Ripon pointed out. "We take these in, the others will break them outa jail, and we'll have the whole thing to do over again."

"But we ain't even had no trials," said one citizen uneasily, having suddenly come to the realization that he had just participated in a good many illegal hangings.

"We kin vote to hang em," said Ripon.

As Lilith, Mondragon, Quincy, and the rest of the group from the Fallen Angel were mounting up, the multiple trial of the remaining Packards in the valley began.

Job's words kept resounding in Lilith's mind as they rode: "Aaron Court's whore . . . fornicatin with Court . . . right over to Hiller's Pond. In broad daylight." Never, Lilith's mind told her. Susanna would never let him seduce her out in some meadow, and what would they be doing in a meadow alone? ". . . likin the whole thing more than most. . . . Heard tell you don't like it that much," came Job's voice. But with Court! God, Susanna couldn't have let Court do those things to her! "Twistin an squirmin like a good little whore," sneered the ghost of the old man. Susanna was a virgin, didn't even understand what happened at the Fallen Angel. ". . . use her in your whorehouse . . . Court gittin all that, an fer nothin . . ." Court refusing Lilith when she had reminded him of her price—after he'd spent a night with Susanna, but Susanna—it had to be a lie, couldn't be Susanna Job had seen. Lilith shifted uneasily in her saddle, pictures in her mind of Court in her room at the Fallen Angel, of things they had done, wild things she had taunted him into, his contemptuous eyes, his anger, Susanna saying he had rescued her like a handsome prince, his cruel hands and mouth—

"Do you believe she's a witch?" asked Carlos softly, as if he could read her mind.

"No, of course not," came her tortured reply.

"Then why believe the rest of it?"

"Because I know him," she whispered.

"The man you know, the man she knows—they could be different people, querida. You and I know things of each other that no man else knows. Don't think of them. Jus hope she's safe—alive."

When the sound of voices woke him, Court was almost too tired to move, to think, or even to care, but the smooth warmth of Susanna's body against his reminded him that he had to care—if caring would help. Lying naked in a dark, unfamiliar cave with a sleeping girl to protect and only his pistols at hand did not put him in the best position to defend himself, he thought sardonically as he put one hand gently over her mouth and his lips to her ear. "Wake up, Susanna," he whispered. He felt her move and closed his hand more tightly over her lips. "Don't say anything; just listen." His voice was the barest stir in her ear, and she nodded. "There's someone outside the cave. I'm going to put a pistol in your hand, and I want you to roll to your left. There are rocks there. Get behind them and move toward the back of the cave." As he spoke, he was freeing them both from the blanket and closing her fingers around the gun. "Feel in front of you every step in case there's a drop-off." She nodded against his hand. "You have six bullets. Don't use them unless you have a clear shot. Don't use them at all if they don't know where you are." Her hand had come up to clutch his shoulder. "I'll be right behind you," he finished, hoping that would answer whatever question she had. When he released her, she brushed her mouth softly against his, bringing their bodies again into brief contact; then she rolled away as she had been bidden. Court's mouth drew down in pain at the thought that there might never be another time when he felt her against him, that they might both soon be dead.

The habits of years allowed him to wash his mind clear of those thoughts as if he could drown his own emotions in freezing water. Then with his mind cold and concentrated on the front of the cave, his pistol pointed in the direction of his thoughts, he too began to move left. He was almost to the wall when the lantern light flashed across him. Reflexively he shot out the light and reached backward with his free hand to feel for cover.

"It's Quincy. Don't shoot again." Court froze

against the wall, then let his breath out in a long sigh and relaxed against the cold, rough surface.

The light of two more lanterns swung in, casting eerie shadows in the cave, highlighting Court, naked against the wall, his gun resting in one fist against his thigh; the scattered clothes on the floor; the dead fire; the tumbled blanket.

Lilith held her lantern high and surveyed the scene. "Where is Susanna?" she demanded.

"She's here," Court replied, straightening and walking forward to pick up the blanket, which he took into the shadows to wrap around Susanna. "She's alive." His voice was unutterably weary as he put his arms around the girl, lifted her over the rocks behind which she had been hiding, and set her on her feet, still keeping an arm around her shoulders.

"Where are her clothes?" Lilith's voice rose sharply. Mondragon had come up behind her with the other lantern and, sensing trouble, tried to head it off.

"Maybe we better go back outside and let them—"

"Let them what?" Lilith demanded. "What have you been doing to her, Court?"

"Don't be an ass, Lilith. We were freezing to death."

"If you were freezing to death, why are you both naked?" Her eyes were narrowed with fury. "I ought to kill you, you son of a bitch," she hissed.

"Lilith," Susanna cried. "How can you say that? Aaron got me away from them. You don't know what they were going to do to me."

"Probably the same thing he did to you," snapped her sister cynically.

"Nothing's happened between Aaron and me that wasn't good," said Susanna, her voice gentle and sure.

"You're a fool," snapped her sister.

"Lilith," cautioned Carlos, a warning note in his voice.

"*Good*? You think what Court did to you was *good*? Will it be *good* when you're pregnant?"

"What do you mean?" Susanna's eyes were filling with tears.

Tightening his arm around her, Court said in a cold, threatening voice, "Shut up, Lilith. You wouldn't know anything about—"

"About you?" she asked. "Why, I know all about you, Court. I know all about the *good* things you do to women."

"Lilith—" Susanna cried.

"Shall I tell you how I know all about Aaron Court, little sister?" Lilith demanded.

"You—you shouldn't repeat gossip," said Susanna. Her voice was trembling. "Mama always said—"

"Mama always kept you away from men, didn't she? And with good cause, evidently. The reason I know all about what happened with you and Court, Susanna, is that Court and I have done all the same things."

Susanna's eyes opened wide and she stared, stricken, from Court to Lilith, pulling away from him, backing away with the blanket clutched tightly around her body, the tears slipping down her cheeks.

"I know all about Aaron Court, more than you do, I'll wager, my foolish sister. Isn't that right, Court?"

His mouth was set in grim lines. "The relationship was hardly the same," he replied coldly. He stooped, calmly picked up his clothes, and began to dress. "Nobody could ever accuse me of harboring any strong affection for you, Lilith, or you for me. Wouldn't you say that's correct?"

"I'd say that no one could accuse you of harboring any affection for anyone but yourself, Court."

Susanna's small indrawn sound of grief reminded both of them that she was listening to their bitter exchange.

Court turned to the girl as he was buckling on his gun belt. "Susanna," he said gently, "I'm sorry that you had to hear about this, but my relationship with your sister was purely professional."

"What does that mean?" She was still holding his gun clutched in one hand, and he removed it, opening each of her fingers as if she were a child, then shoving the gun back into the holster when he had it.

"You'll have to ask your sister about that," he replied.

"Bastard," Lilith snapped.

"Susanna—" Court put his fingers caressingly to the side of her face.

"You made love to my sister?" she asked, drawing sharply away.

"Yes, but—"

"And a hundred other women besides," said Lilith coldly.

Susanna's face was white and sick in the lantern light.

"I think enough's been said," Quincy interrupted quietly. "How much you two think she can take? Now all a you git outa here. Miss Susanna, you git your clothes on; I'm gonna take you home."

"The hell you are." Court moved toward her, but Quincy stepped between them.

"Git out, Court."

"Susanna goes back with me," said Court grimly.

"If you don't git outa here, Aaron, I'm gonna hafta shoot you," said Quincy, his voice still quiet.

"Or I," added Mondragon.

"Well?" Lilith turned triumphant eyes on Court.

"You leave too, Lilith," said Quincy. "I don't reckon Miss Susanna wants to see you neither, not right now."

Mondragon drew Lilith forcefully away, his fingers biting into her arm when she resisted. Court directed a demanding glance at Susanna—more than ready to kill to keep her. She turned her back on him, but not before he saw the pain and the rejection in her eyes.

IV
The Fallen Angel

55

"Dios! How could you say those things to your sister? Do you know how much you hurt her?"

Carlos had cornered Lilith in her office at the Fallen Angel once Susanna had been safely returned to Clara's care. The girl had ridden beside Quincy on the way back to town, saying nothing to anyone, her eyes bleak and tearless, and Quincy would let no one near her—not Court, not Lilith.

"I'm tired, Carlos," Lilith said sullenly. "If I'm to run this place tonight, I need some sleep."

"I'll run the place tonight. For now, I want to know why you told your sister that Court had been your lover—or should I say customer? Ask yourself, Lilith, why you did that."

"I don't have to ask myself. Everything I said to her was true. What did you want me to do, let her become Court's mistress—until he gets tired of her and—"

"I'm not arguing that she should continue with Court—if they were intimate, which we don't know."

"He didn't deny it. She said it was true."

"She said that what happened between them was good. What the devil makes you think that means he seduced her? It could be anything from a kiss to—"

"To a bastard nine months from now. Do you

think that's what I want for her?''

''Do you want for her the misery you caused her by telling her that you have been with Court yourself? You told her that hundreds of women have been with him. How do you think that made her feel? She was in love with him.''

''Well, she's not now. It's not as if he would have married her,'' said Lilith defensively. ''He wouldn't. He would have broken her heart, maybe left her pregnant. My God, she's got to toughen up. She can't go through life thinking every man she meets is a white knight.''

Mondragon sighed. ''I don't think your sister is a woman who's going to toughen up, as you put it. She's one of the gentle ones—not like you, querida.''

''I know that. I know it. What I don't know is what to do about her, what's to become of her.'' Lilith brushed her hair away from her face wearily. ''She shouldn't be here at all. She shouldn't be anywhere where anyone knows that I'm her sister.''

''She has no one else to go to. We can only hope that none of the men outside heard what was said in that cave about her and Court.''

''What difference would it make? Everyone heard what Job Packard said about them.''

''No one believed that but you, Lilith. Any more than anyone believed it when he said she was a witch and killed his son. I think the worst damage done to Susanna was done by you, querida. I think maybe you didn't care what you said because you were jealous. You and Court have been attracted to each other for a long time, but he lost interest after he met your sister, isn't that so?''

''I'm not attracted to him,'' Lilith snapped. ''I hate him.''

"Love and hate are so close, Lilith, especially with you."

"If you think I love Court, why do you want me, Carlos?" Lilith's eyes glittered with the desire to hurt him.

"I always want you," he said in a low, grim voice. "Always. Even now when, like a jealous bitch, you've attacked your own sister." His hand went out to fasten menacingly in her hair. "You'd better think about your feelings toward her, Lilith." He twisted the hair around his hand, pulling her head back, compelling her to look directly into his eyes. "If you hate her, if you're jealous of her, you'll do her more harm."

"I don't hate Susanna," Lilith cried.

"Good. Then be careful what you say when you see her." Lilith tried to turn away, and Carlos forced her to look at him. "When will you see her?" he demanded.

"How can I? God. She's going to ask me what he meant when he said our relationship was strictly professional."

"You brought the question on yourself. You must answer it."

"We're going to open the new place this week. I can't—"

"I've never known you to be a coward, Lilith. If you haven't seen her by the time we open the new whorehouse—"

"Don't call it a whorehouse. I hate that word."

Carlos smiled coldy. "I know. When you give up whoring, you won't have to hear the word again—from me."

56

When Quincy turned the girl over to Clara at the hotel room, the woman had thrown her arms around Susanna and cried, "Thank God you're safe, Miss Susanna."

"I hope they did not hurt you, Clara, when they took me away," said Susanna, sounding very formal, each word pronounced carefully as if she might make some mistake. She had said nothing for hours.

Clara and Quincy exchanged glances over her shoulder, and Clara said, "Oh, my poor child, what have they done to you?"

"I don't want to talk about that," said Susanna. "Ever." She moved with short, careful steps to her bed, lay down, and turned her face into the pillow.

Clara looked curiously to Quincy, but he only shook his head and closed the door quietly behind him.

In the three days that followed, Susanna wept when she was awake because her mind tortured her with pictures of all the times she had spent with Aaron Court and all the happiness she had felt, but superimposed on each memory was the sound of her sister's voice telling her other, different, cruel things about him. She could not believe that he had felt so little and she so much, but he had denied nothing Lilith said. She could not believe that what they had done was sinful, but that was what Job Packard had said and what Lilith's anger had meant. And so her thoughts ran around and around in pain and confusion, and she wept.

When she slept, she dreamed—of the Packards,

the brutality, the threats, the terror, and the mushrooms; of Jeremiah threatening to hurt her in front of Court; of Job calling her terrible names; of Jeremiah pitching forward in agony; of Job threatening to burn her, locking her up in the dark. She slept in exhaustion of body and spirit, and dreamed in agony, and cried out in those dreams.

Poor, mundane Clara Schmidt had no idea what to do for her charge. Susanna would not talk to her—about anything that had to do with that time or with the dreams. She hardly talked at all. Her chaperone was left to imagine what had happened, and her imaginings were in some ways worse than the actuality, but they fell far short of the mark in the pain that Susanna was feeling. And Lilith stayed away.

Since Susanna could not talk, Clara did. Trying to distract the girl, she talked endlessly. Clara told Susanna that her sister and the vigilantes had seen every last Packard in the valley hanged. Susanna stared at her with haunted eyes; she had seen Elias Packard die of hanging and Jeremiah of the mushrooms. Of the two deaths, Jeremiah's was the worse.

"Why did she bother?" Susanna asked idly.

"Why? Why because they kidnapped you," Clara responded. Susanna shook her head. That did not explain it; if Lilith cared, why did she not come to visit now? Why had she sounded as if she hated Susanna at the cave? Susanna turned away.

Clara told Susanna of the impending opening of the new Fallen Angel, of the rumors of its luxurious fixtures and the money that Lilith had spent on it.

"What do they do there?" Susanna asked. Clara stuttered and turned pink and never answered, and

Susanna lost interest. She fell asleep again, and the nightmares began again, unaffected by the news that the Packards were dead, hanged by Lilith and Mondragon.

Aaron, maddened by the thought that she had turned away from him at the cave because of things her sluttish sister had said, unable to get word of her, came to the door of the room and demanded to see her.

"Oh, thank God, Mr. Court," cried Clara, much to his surprise. "Maybe you can do something for her."

"What's the matter?" asked Aaron anxiously, his own resentments forgotten. "Is she ill?"

"She won't talk to me. She cries an cries. An when she sleeps, she has terrible nightmares. I don't think she hears a half of what I say to her." Aaron cursed and started to push past the woman. "No. Let me tell her you're here," Clara insisted. "Surely, she'll want to see you—you havin saved her from those terrible people."

Clara closed the door and went in to Susanna, who was lying on the bed, her face turned to the wall. "Mr. Court's here to see you, dear. Isn't that lovely? He's such a handsome, brave gentleman." At the mention of Court's name, Susanna had turned eyes filled with agony toward Clara, and Clara's voice faltered. "I know you'll want to see him, to thank him for savin you."

"I owe him no debts," said Susanna. "He's taken his payment."

"What do you mean, child?"

"Send him away. Never let him in here."

"But—"

"Is he out in the hall? Make him go away."

Susanna's voice rose in near-hysteria. "Make him go away and never come back." She turned her face to the pillow and began to weep.

Not knowing what to say to Court, Clara went out into the hall and closed the door behind her. "Maybe she's not up to seein anyone yet, Mr. Court. She's still very—upset."

"What did she say?" Court demanded.

"She—well, she—"

"Exactly, Mrs. Schmidt. I want to know exactly what she said."

"She said to—to make you go away an never come back," quavered poor Clara.

"What else? Is that all?"

The expression on his face so frightened Clara that she dared not refuse to answer. "Well, it's just that I said I knew she'd want to thank you for gettin her out of the valley—an—an she said she owed you no debts."

"No debts?" Court frowned.

"She said you'd taken your payment." Clara looked at him anxiously as his face flushed and his eyes became cold, the gray turning to angry charcoal, his mouth settling into grim lines, all its sensuality turned to bitterness. "I can't imagine what she meant," Clara faltered. "She's so upset. She doesn't seem to know what's goin on. She—"

Court turned abruptly and strode away.

57

Quincy came to see Susanna on the fourth day when she had stopped crying. He had come to her door and talked quietly to Clara every day before that. He had kept to his room to be near Susanna in case she asked for him or needed him. He knew to the last detail how things were with her. When he decided that it was time for him to talk to her, he did not ask. He simply sent Clara downstairs and went in. Susanna sat by the window staring, empty-eyed, seeing nothing.

"Miss Susanna," he began, drawing a chair up beside her, "I come to beg yer forgiveness."

"There's no need, Mr. Quincy," she replied in a lifeless voice, not even turning from the window.

"Oh, yes, ma'am, there's need. Lettin you ride out with Aaron Court was like lettin the lamb ride out with the lion. I made a bad mistake. I may have meant well, but I made a bad mistake. An it wasn't a mistake what hurt me, like it shoulda. It hurt you, an I'm sorrier fer that than fer anything I ever done in my life. An the worst of it is, there ain't much I kin do to make amends."

Finally she turned to him and sighed, life coming back into her eyes. "Truly you shouldn't concern yourself, Mr. Quincy. I know you meant well. It was Aaron who didn't mean well, and I was foolish, such a fool—"

"It ain't foolish to be innocent, Miss Susanna. It ain't foolish to be lovin neither. I'd be glad to kill him fer you if'n it'd help. That's about all I can do."

Susanna's eyes filled with pain. "Oh no. There's been so much killing. I—I killed Jeremiah." Quincy's eyebrows lifted in surprise. He had been told what Job had said of her and had laughed. "I poisoned him to keep him from—from—"

Quincy nodded. "We do what we has to, Miss Susanna. No use dwellin on it." They both fell silent for a time, Susanna turning back to the window, erasing Jeremiah, as she had gradually learned to do, from her mind. "What will you do now, Miss Susanna? Go back to St. Louie?"

"No. How could I? I'm not the same person I was."

"Might be best. You must know good folks there."

"They wouldn't know me." She bit her lower lip and turned to him once more. "He—Aaron—said his relationship with my sister was professional. What did he mean?"

"Reckon you better ask Lilith that," said Quincy.

"Then I will." She stared straight at him, and there was a determination in her eyes that had been missing before.

Quincy thought to himself that she was going to be all right. "I'm across the hall when you need me, Miss Susanna."

"Thank you."

"Don't leave the hotel without me. Might be folks would want to talk to you you wouldn't want to talk to."

She nodded. "I understand." Quincy rose, feeling himself dismissed, but Susanna thought of something else. "There is one thing you could do for me."

"Shore."

"I want you to talk to Mr. Court for me." Quincy's face hardened, his reluctance obvious. "You must do this, for I don't want to see him again. You must tell him that he is no longer my lawyer. Tell him to turn my affairs over to some other local lawyer; you can choose one for me since I know none. Tell him to send his bill to that man."

Quincy stared at her for a minute. "I'll take care

of it.''

When Clara went to Susanna's room, she was astonished to be ordered to go out and bring back the dressmaker Susanna had patronized before.

''Well,'' stuttered the flustered woman, ''Abner did you a world of good, I can see, but Miz Reynolds, she don't make calls. She only works outa her shop.''

''Offer her twice the money, three times. It doesn't matter, but have her here today.''

''Three times!'' Clara was horrified.

''Why not? I have it.''

58

Once outside in the hall, Quincy was tempted to go back to his room, for he had no desire to carry out the commission Susanna had given him. ''Might as well git it over with,'' he muttered to himself, and hitching up his gun belt, he headed out to Court's office. However, he did not find the lawyer there. In fact, Court's neighbor, the owner of the barbershop downstairs, after trying to sell Quincy the Saturday-evening shave and bath special, told him he had not seen Court since the previous morning. From there Quincy went across the street to the Gold Creek Saloon to make discreet inquiries and was told that Aaron Court had indeed been there and in a number of other saloons in the last few days, drinking hard and in a mean mood.

''Ah'd wait a few days afore Ah talked to him,'' advised the bartender, ''if that's what you aim to do. He don't seem to be talkin to nobody, an he don't want nobody to talk to him.''

Quincy then limited his search to saloons and

finally heard in another that Court had won three thousand dollars gambling at the Bonanza the night before and then had shot the cards out of the hand of a cardsharp who was trying to cheat him. The bullet, having destroyed the cards, came close to killing the gambler and put a damper on enthusiasm in the place for the rest of the evening. "Hope he don't come in here to play," muttered the saloon owner who told Quincy the story.

It was late in the evening before Quincy found him in a rowdy dance hall on the north edge of town. Court was sitting at a corner table by himself drinking, and Quincy went to the bar and watched him in the mirror. He knew the man well enough to know from the expression on his face that he was feeling as ready to fight as a man could be, and Quincy was himself in a mood for trouble. Consequently, remembering that Susanna did not want any more killing, he finished his drink and turned to leave. Tomorrow would be soon enough for his business—when Aaron Court had less liquor under his belt and maybe less sand in his craw. Quincy spoke briefly to a friend several places down the bar and then headed for the door.

"Quincy." The voice behind him was quiet enough, the hand on his shoulder easy.

Quincy turned and looked at Court, who was leaning a little against the bar—not so much that he seemed unable to stand.

"Court."

"Have a drink with me."

"I won't do that," said Quincy, hard-faced. "But I do have business with you."

"Do you? Well, don't have a drink. Sit down. Or would you rather stand too?" Court started back for his table, walking steadily, although Quincy was now sure that he was very drunk, for all he gave little sign of it.

"I have a message for you from Susanna."

Court looked up, his eyes clearing, focusing sharply.

"She wants you to turn over her lawyer affairs to Bard Shapely."

"Does she?" Court's mouth settled into angry lines. "Anything else?"

"She doesn't want to see you. That's all. Says send your bill to Shapely."

"Damn her."

"Damn you," said Quincy coldly. "You betrayed her. I trusted you to take care of her, an you used her fer yer own pleasure."

"My pleasure?" Court smiled sarcastically. "The pleasure was mutual, my friend, I assure you."

"I'm not your friend, Court. An what yer sayin don't impress me none. You know an I know she'd never been with a man afore you got a hold a her."

"And she liked what we had, Quincy. If she hadn't, she wouldn't have kept coming back to me."

"You ever plan on marryin her?"

"Don't be a fool. You know I'm not the marrying kind."

"I was a fool. Only a fool would have trusted you with a woman, Court. But you're a hell of a lot wors'n a fool. You're a blackguard cause we both know you took advantage of her, an now she's hurtin bad."

"She didn't have to be. Lilith—"

"Right, Lilith. Lilith's your kind. You should a stayed with Lilith an left Susanna alone. Be sure you turn her papers over to Shapely."

Quincy rose abruptly and stalked out, leaving Court behind, pale with anger.

59

Lilith was standing on the staircase looking at the whirling crowd below her with satisfaction. The music coming from the dance hall; the laughter of the women in their bright, provocative dresses; the sound of male voices (every male for fifty miles around, she thought with satisfaction, was at the new Fallen Angel spending money); the rich velvet draperies; the sparkling mirrors surrounded with ornate, gilded frames; the cigar smoke rising toward crystal chandeliers; the muted click of dice; the calls of the dealers; and the gamblers' exclamations of joy and despair—Lilith took it all in, breathed it in deeply like the bouquet of rich wine, and like wine it went to her head, loosed her laughter. She had created her own fantasy world—lush, sinful, rich, and violent—it had every attribute that her parents would have hated, and she had made it all herself in ways that would have appalled them. She caught Carlos's eyes on her from where he stood at the mahogany bar, and she gave him a slow, promising smile. Later, she thought. Later there would be time to be with Carlos, who gave her what she wanted—whose loving was like the Fallen Angel—as lush, as sinful, as rich and violent as—

"Your energy is amazing, Lilith. I don't know how you can have accomplished so much in so short a time."

Lilith turned sharply toward the voice that came from behind her where Susanna was standing several steps higher up the staircase, her hand resting on the railing, her eyes taking in the scene below. She was

wearing a dress of deep blue silk that matched her
eyes, accented their startling color. Around her neck
was a demure velvet ribbon with a heart suspended
from it, a gift Lilith had given her when she was a
small child, but beneath this childish trinket the neck
of the dress was cut away deeply to reveal the lovely
curves of her breasts.

Lilith gasped in surprise. She had always considered her sister a beautiful child and girl, but in
that dress— ''Why are you here, Susanna?'' she
asked, turning, but glancing nervously over her
shoulder at the crowd below.

''I came to your opening.''

''In that dress? It's cut much too low.''

''It's cut no lower than yours, Lilith,'' Susanna
replied without any particular inflection in her
voice. ''I thought it was very becoming.''

''So will every man in the room. You'd better
come to my office.'' Abruptly Lilith took her hand
and hurried her back up the stairs and into the
office, closing the door behind them and locking it.

''I'm not planning on trying to leave, Lilith,'' said
Susanna, smiling at the gesture. ''After all, I came
to see you, since you haven't been to see me.''

''I don't want anyone to disturb us.''

Susanna nodded. ''Or overhear us,'' she suggested. ''I have some questions to ask you.''

Lilith's lips compressed. ''And I have some of my
own.''

''Very well. What did you want to know?''
Susanna glanced around at the room and chose a
straight-backed velvet chair to sit in, folding her
hands in her lap.

Lilith could remember her sitting just so as a child
in their mother's parlor, and she found it hard to

phrase the question she wanted to ask. "Carlos feels that perhaps I have misjudged the situation between you and Aaron Court, Susanna. I want you to tell me exactly what did happen."

A slight flush rose in Susanna's cheeks, but she stared into her sister's eyes, her own wide and unflinching, and she said, "Aaron kissed me and he touched me and he—he pushed a—a part of himself into me. He gave me more pleasure than I would have ever imagined possible. Is that what you want to know?" Susanna's chin was held high, her lips in a defiant line and her eyes wide, as if she were willing her tears away.

"And didn't you know you weren't supposed to do that with a man?" Lilith asked.

"How was I to know? Do you think Mother or Father ever talked to me about such things?"

"No, but—"

"When—when things began to happen between us, I didn't know what to do. I was going to ask you, Lilith. I wrote you a note. Do you remember? I said it was important, but you didn't come. And I read the Bible."

"The Bible!" Lilith exclaimed. "The Bible certainly never told you that—"

"I read the Song of Solomon. Have you ever read it?"

"Yes, of course."

"I hadn't. Or if I had, I didn't understand it, but it seemed to be about the very things that were happening to me. I thought what was between Aaron and me was beautiful, special—like what was between Solomon and his beloved. I didn't know, until you told me at the cave—how could I?—that—that—that there was nothing special about it at all.

That you and he had done the same things. That he had done those things with everyone who would, I guess." Susanna finally dropped her eyes to her hands.

"It's criminal," muttered Lilith. "It's criminal that they let you grow up to be that ignorant."

"I suppose so, but it's also too late for regrets. Now I would like you to answer some questions for me, Lilith." Lilith stiffened, but she intended to be as blunt as Susanna had been. Nothing else would do if she was to exert any responsible influence on Susanna's life in the future. "Aaron said his relationship with you was professional. What did he mean?"

"He meant that I never let him touch me unless he paid me, and it cost him a lot," said Lilith coldly. "No woman who knows any better or who isn't a fool gives herself away to a man. She makes him marry her—or pay her."

"Did you want Aaron to marry you?" Susanna asked.

"I don't want to marry any man. I belong to myself and always will."

"But you sell the use of your body, is that what you mean? Why, since it gives you pleasure too? Is it because you might have a baby? I gather that that's how it happens—when a man and a woman—"

"That is how it happens, but I know how to take care of myself. You, unfortunately, don't."

"Perhaps you should tell me."

"You don't need to know, Susanna. I expect you to stay away from men in the future, unless you marry."

"But you don't—stay away from men: You let Aaron make love to you—well, do that—as long as he paid you. And you let other men—"

"Occasionally," said Lilith sharply. "Not often anymore."

"Is that what Job Packard meant when he said I was a whore like my sister? He thought I was making money?"

"Job Packard was insane and evil. Forget what he said, Susanna."

"How can I? I still dream of him and Jeremiah. They threatened to do things to me in front of Aaron—rape, they said. Is that what Aaron did to me?"

"That's when the woman is unwilling. If you were willing, then Aaron didn't rape you," said Lilith honestly.

"I was willing, with Aaron," said Susanna just as honestly. "But I was terrified of Jeremiah. What he was talking about had nothing to do with pleasure. He meant to hurt me."

"Susanna." Lilith rose to go to her, but Susanna turned away.

"I killed Jeremiah. Did you know that, Lilith?"

"That's nonsense."

"No, I put poison mushrooms into his coffee so he couldn't hurt me. And into Job's. But I guess, from what Clara said, you hanged him before he had a chance to die."

"Did you tell anyone else this?" asked Lilith anxiously.

"Only Aaron—and Quincy. I may have killed some of the others too. I put the last mushroom into the whiskey. I must be damned—because of what I did with Aaron and because I killed all those people and—"

"You're not damned, Susanna. You didn't even

know what you were doing with Aaron—that bastard. And as for the Packards, people have a right to defend themselves against scum like that. In fact, I'm proud of you."

"Proud of me?" Susanna stared curiously at her sister. "I thought you hated me. At the cave, I thought—"

"I don't hate you, Susanna." Lilith's heart twisted. Carlos had thought the same thing, but it was not true. "I don't hate you. I just want to protect you. Now you must go home."

"No, I'm going to work here. You can hardly object now on the grounds of my innocence, can you? Wasn't that why you objected before? Because you didn't want me to know what was happening here? I suppose all the girls that work here get money for being with men, don't they?"

"There's nothing for you to do here."

"You're wrong, Lilith. There isn't anything here I couldn't do. I can keep books, make drinks, dance with men, work at the gambling tables. Do you know I can remember every card that's been played at whist? That should be useful in some of those games. I could even work for Carlos." She smiled slightly. "After all, you had me taught to shoot. I could even be a whore, couldn't I, if I—"

"No."

"Aaron seemed to like being with me. Of course, he didn't pay me, but—"

"Stop it, Susanna."

"Then find something for me to do, Lilith. I can't spend the rest of my life sitting in a hotel room, going out every morning to take silly lessons."

60

Court came into the Fallen Angel around midnight to see for himself the wonders being described all over town. He was reasonably sober and more than reasonably angry, having been tortured with mental visions of Susanna ever since his talk with Quincy. He took in immediately the opulent interior of the place and muttered under his breath, "Quintessential Lilith." The second thing he noticed was Susanna, standing at the bar, talking to Arnold Schweibrunner, a rancher from the southern part of the state. She looked pale and beautiful—stunningly beautiful, with her hair piled in careless black curls on her head and that accursed dress that no young girl should be allowed to wear anywhere, much less in a place full of ruffians, drunks, whoremongers. Court strode purposefully toward her, putting his hand possessively onto her arm as he stood behind her and said quietly, "I know you'll excuse us, Arnold—"

"Well sure. Sure, Court." Looking into that grim face, Schweibrunner would not have dreamed of protesting.

Susanna, at the sound of Court's voice, had stiffened. Once the rancher had strolled away, she whirled on Court, but he forestalled whatever she might have said by asking in a low, tense voice, "What the hell do you think you're doing here, Susanna?"

Equally angry, she flared back, "This is my sister's place. I have a right to be here. Didn't Clara tell you I don't want to see you again? And Quincy? Didn't he tell you the same thing?"

"He gave me your message," said Court with dry irritation. "I've had your files delivered to Shapely, as you requested. Now let's get back to my question. This may be Lilith's place, but she doesn't want you here."

"There's no reason for her to object anymore, is there? After the—the education you gave me, I have nothing to learn here."

"Don't be stupid," he snapped. "In that dress you're wearing, every man in the place is looking at you with lust. You'll find there's a great difference between rape—if you provoke it—and what we had."

"What was it we had, Aaron?" she asked bitterly. "Your lust and my stupidity? Well, I don't want the first, and you can no longer count on the second."

"Susanna." Court reached out for her; his hands curved gently around her shoulders, and his eyes glittered with the desire and tenderness she well remembered and wanted to forget.

"Go away," she cried in a low, choked voice.

"I'm afraid the lady doesn't want to see you, Court." Carlos Mondragon had come to stand beside them. "Quincy is waiting at the door to take you home, Susanna," he said quietly. "Court, will you have a drink with me?" Carlos signaled to the bartender for two drinks as Court watched Susanna hurry away through the crowd. Then he turned angrily to Mondragon, who said, "Let us find a table. I think we need to talk." The Mexican handed a glass to Court and, putting his hand on Court's elbow, steered him toward a table across the room where they would have at least a little privacy.

Yet when they were seated, Mondragon leaned back, sipping his drink and studying the lawyer; he said nothing for a long time, and Court returned the stare with narrow, hostile eyes.

Finally Carlos sighed and put his glass down on the table. "Aaron, you might as well forget her. You've lost her."

"To Lilith?" asked Court contemptuously. "You're wrong. Susanna belongs with me."

"You might have been right about that once, my friend, but it is no longer true—because you took more than you gave. Susanna gave you not just pleasure but love. You gave her only pleasure in return, and it was not enough when she finally understood the nature of the exchange."

"That sounds like the thinking of the master of a whorehouse," said Court in a cold voice.

Mondragon only laughed. "Ah yes, I know about such women too. For some, money is enough; for some, money and passion. But Susanna is neither of these. Surely you didn't think that that one had the soul of a whore?"

Court scowled. Actually he had thought she was a whore the first time he had been with her, and after the first time he had no longer cared what she was as long as he could have her again.

"So admit to yourself what kind of woman she is. Then you must also admit that you can't afford her. You won't give her what would keep her at your side, so like a poor man, you must do without what you cannot afford."

Aaron lit a cheroot and stared with a wry smile through the smoke at the man sitting opposite him. "That's more words than I've heard from you in all the years I've known you, Carlos. Why are you telling me all this?"

Mondragon too smiled slightly. "Since you seem

set on pursuing her, you give me the choice of talking to you or shooting you. Lilith might have preferred that I shoot you." He chuckled; then the laughter died off his face. "Still, if you listen to my words, maybe I won't have to shoot you."

"Do you think she belongs here—at the Fallen Angel?" Court asked sharply, ignoring the threat.

"No. I think her presence here can only mean trouble. But because she is hurt, she has decided that she does belong here, and none of us can change her mind. Nor can you, my friend, because you are the one who has hurt her."

"Lilith is the one—"

"Had Lilith never found out what was between you two, still there would have come a time when Susanna realized she could never count on you beyond the desire of that day. And when that happened, it would have been over. Better to get it over with before she is hurt any more. And you, Court. You'll forget her soon enough—with another woman who pleases you." Mondragon rose and put his hand on Aaron's shoulder. "Stay away from her, my friend. Forget her."

"The hell with that," Court muttered grimly as he watched Carlos stroll away.

He himself left shortly thereafter, brooding on Susanna's bitter reception earlier but giving little thought to Carlos's remarks. He had no intention of being warned away from her if he decided that he wanted to take the trouble to get her back, but did he? If he and Susanna were to resume their relationship, he would have to make her his mistress, install her in her own house in order to keep her away from her protectors—at least until such time as he and she tired of one another. Although he was sure he wanted

her—at the moment—he was not sure he wanted to
become that entangled, wanted to mortgage any part
of his future in order to possess her for the present.
Already his passion for her had precipitated him
into an uncharacteristic and profitless feud with the
Packards and had given them a dangerous hold on
him as long as they had held her. The voice of his
own experience told him that she was not worth the
danger she exposed him to. No woman was.

Court mounted his horse and rode off toward
another house to see a girl named Amelia, with
whom he had maintained an intermittent relationship for several years—a pretty girl who laughed
easily and performed with skill in bed. Amelia was,
as always, delighted to see him, kissed him warmly
in greeting, drank and laughed with him, and was
both surprised and disappointed when he left
without going upstairs with her. Court was no less
disappointed to find that he had lost all interest in
her, that he could think of no woman with whom he
wanted to be—except the one who claimed that she
never wanted to see him again.

Then he had to consider Carlos's words, and ultimately he rejected them. The very fact of making a
decision steadied him. He decided that he wanted
Susanna and that, one way or another, he would
have her. From then on, he stopped the heavy
drinking and gambling. In the day he went back to
business, going to his office, keeping his appointments, making the final arrangements for the
opening of his mining venture with Holbein. At
night he went to the Fallen Angel—nowhere else. He
intended to keep the pressure on Susanna, sure that
if he could get her alone, he could influence her. In
the meantime, if his presence disturbed her so much,

he would use it to drive her out of the Fallen Angel, where he did not want her to be, and away from her sister, whose influence he sought to undermine. And if Susanna refused to stay away from the Fallen Angel, at least he could see her there, and he admitted to himself that he was hungry even for the sight of her.

She appeared each evening wearing gowns that aroused and infuriated him, almost respectable ball gowns that swept the floor and were cut too low in the neckline for a man's comfort, gowns that left her arms and shoulders bare, that exposed curves of breast that he had once touched, kissed, treasured. He watched her dance in the arms of other men, smiling and chatting as if she were a debutante at a ball, and he wondered with grim self-mockery whether her presence was not putting more pressure on him than his on her. He knew she was aware that he watched her, but she would not catch his eye; if he moved toward her, she slipped away—or Mondragon or Quincy moved between them. So he watched, and he moved in on her when the opportunity presented itself, making her turn pale, keeping her on edge so that the smile she reserved now for other men failed her and her laughter died. We torture each other, he thought bitterly, when we should give each other joy, when we should be together instead of separated by fools and strangers.

61

One night she came down the stairs late, wearing an unusually daring gown. She must be spending a fortune on clothes, he thought, worrying about her financial condition. Had she given half her money to Lilith? Was she using up her capital buying those dresses that each seemed calculated to make him angrier and more frustrated than the last? This dress was dark red—whore's colors, he thought bitterly —with fringes of black and a black-fringed shawl that had been allowed to slip down her arms so that it concealed nothing; the dress was cut so low it barely covered the tips of her breasts.

He was standing at the bar staring at her openly, as were a number of men, but for once she stared back and swept him a sardonic curtsy which revealed so much that he started forward in anger. However, she straightened and turned away from him in one quick, dismissing movement, flicking open a black fan that covered the earlier display, and then she was smiling a happy girl's smile at Grant Penvennon, who had just entered in search of Lilith. Suddenly the décolletage disappeared beneath the pretty shawl, as the bitter smile disappeared beneath her glad greeting to the Welsh mine owner. Court controlled his rage with difficulty and watched her lead Penvennon to a table. He remembered that she had once told him how nice Penvennon had been to her. It galled him that that cold-hearted miser could talk to her, evoke her happy smiles, and he could not even get near her; he turned away to the bar and ordered another drink.

Susanna was genuinely pleased to see Mr. Penvennon. She had sensed his goodwill from the first time they had met. Knowing he liked her, she liked him in return; she asked after the health and happiness of his wife and children, inquiring particularly about the progress of the son with problems in mathematics. She also inquired as to his own well-being and the prosperity of his businesses, and to all this Penvennon answered, gratified at her interest. What a lovely young woman she was, he reflected, although he was sorry to see her back again at the Fallen Angel, particularly wearing that shocking dress, which he assumed her sister had picked out for her.

"Since you have been so kind as to inquire about my businesses, Miss Moran—"

"Won't you call me Susanna?"

"Well, certainly, if you wish." How surprised his wife would be if she were to hear that he called this lovely young girl, the sister of the notorious Lilith Moran, by her first name. "As I was saying, I am here on business. Is your sister, by any chance, available?" Susanna looked at him warily, wondering what he meant by *available*. "I am here on behalf of my neighbor about a piece of real estate," he added hastily, so that there would be no misunderstandings about the nature of his business, although he had heard, and believed, that Susanna did not really know much about the goings-on abovestairs at the Fallen Angel.

"I haven't seen Lilith this evening, Mr. Penvennon, but perhaps I can help you. I've a much better head for figures and business than my sister anyway."

The mine owner was quite surprised to hear this. "At least you might deliver a message to your sister for me Miss—ah—Susanna. You may be aware that your sister rented my house and the house of my neighbor until she rebuilt her establishment."

"Yes, I knew that," Susanna replied. "Although I rarely went to the Land and Cattle Company during that period."

Nor should you be going now, thought Penvennon disapprovingly. "Yes, well of course, my family has now moved back into our house, but Mr.

Claver, my neighbor, has a problem relevant to his house.''

"I hope no damage was done to it," said Susanna sympathetically.

"Not in the physical sense," said Mr. Penvennon, wondering how in the world he was going to phrase what he had to say without being ungentlemanly. "Perhaps I should talk to your sister herself."

"Not at all. I shall be glad to deliver the message. What is the problem with Mr. Claver's house?"

Penvennon sighed. "The problem is his wife. She refuses to move back in because of—ah—"

Susanna was looking him calmly in the eyes, a slight flush on her cheeks. "Are you trying to say that Mrs. Claver objects to the nature of the business that was carried on in her house?"

"Yes. As a matter of fact, that is the problem."

"I suppose that house was where the women sold themselves," said Susanna bluntly.

Penvennon blushed, quite shocked that she knew what was going on and, worse, had actually mentioned it to him.

"Mrs. Claver's feelings are understandable, I think," said Susanna, "but since she does feel that way, why did Mr. Claver rent the house to Lilith in the first place?"

"Mr. Claver feels that your sister misled him. He thought that that—ah—activity was to go on in my house, not his own."

"That seems a minor distinction to me," said Susanna, "if he and his wife feel strongly about the matter. Was he not adequately compensated for the use of his house?"

"Quite," said Mr. Penvennon. "Still, since he can no longer use it, he wants your sister to buy it."

"I rather doubt that she would," said Susanna. "She lives here. She does not need a house."

"So I pointed out to Claver," agreed Mr. Penvennon. "However, if you would mention the matter to your sister, I will have kept my promise to my neighbor."

"What is Mr. Claver asking for his house?" Susanna inquired curiously.

Penvennon mentioned a figure. "It is a good price," he added.

"I suppose he anticipated trouble selling it, considering the use to which it was put," Susanna remarked.

"I suppose so," Penvennon agreed.

"I might buy it," said Susanna, her voice soft and thoughtful. She was strongly aware that Aaron Court was standing at the bar staring at her and that she saw him with unhappy frequency coming and going at the hotel. If she were to buy a house, at least she would not have to see him where she lived. Rapidly she calculated the financial advantages. "At that price, I think it would be less than three years before my hotel bills amounted to the same figure. Perhaps Mr. Claver's house would be a good investment for me."

Penvennon was quite taken aback; in his experience, young ladies never talked of, or even thought about, investments. "If you will tell me what your hotel rate is, I can quickly do the figures for you," he offered.

"Oh, I have done them in my head. Is the house large enough for myself, and for Mrs. Schmidt and Mr. Quincy, my chaperones?"

"Yes, certainly."

"And I should doubtless save money on food by

not eating in the hotel dining room. Mrs. Schmidt could cook and keep house.''

"Yes, there should be a considerable saving there,'' admitted the astonished mine owner, more and more surprised that so young and beautiful a female should be so sensible.

"You seem quite surprised, Mr. Penvennon. Perhaps you would object to having me for a neighbor, or your wife and friends would object.''

Mr. Penvennon flushed. "I would certainly not object to you, Miss Moran. However, I cannot tell you that the ladies in the neighborhood would welcome you. They would not, although they would do nothing to—to—''

"You mean they would snub me because of my association with Lilith and the Land and Cattle Company—they have already done that—but they would not cast stones at me as I passed or set fire to my house?''

"No, certainly not. It is a quiet neighborhood.''

"Perhaps then, Mr. Penvennon, you would mention to Mr. Claver that I have some interest in purchasing his house. In the meantime, I shall consult my lawyer. I cannot say that the price is agreeable without professional advice.''

"Mr. Court is right over there at the bar,'' Penvennon pointed out.

Susanna's cheeks flamed unaccountably. "Mr. Court is not my lawyer,'' she snapped. "I have a new one.''

"But Court is an excellent lawyer, the best in town. I hope you have not changed the better for the worse.''

"That is my business, is it not?'' she replied angrily.

Penvennon was quite surprised, unable to think of how he had offended her. He had understood that Aaron Court had put his life in jeopardy to save the girl from the Packards when she had been kidnapped. It seemed hardly gracious in her to so reward him for his trouble.

"If Mr. Claver is interested, he may contact Mr. Shapely who will act in my behalf in this matter," said Susanna. Having controlled her anger, she rose, smiling, and bade Mr. Penvennon good evening.

Again he had a clear view of her immodest dress and shook his head as she walked away. What could Lilith Moran be thinking of to let her sister wear such a gown? It could only provoke trouble, since the girl was not prepared to offer what the dress seemed to promise.

At the bar Aaron Court was not the only man watching Susanna. A miner who had come in looking for a woman had spotted her immediately and decided that he would have her as soon as Penvennon finished with her. He was prepared to sit at the bar for as long as it took her to service her present customer. Consequently, when she left Grant Penvennon without going upstairs, the miner was delighted. He thumped his beer down on the bar and cut through the crowd toward her, coming up behind her and swinging her around with an enthusiastic, "I'm next, sweetheart," and a wide, leering smile. "Let's us hustle right up the stairs."

A number of things happened at once. Susanna stared at the man with white-lipped horror. Aaron Court started up from the bar in a killing anger, his hand already on his gun. Carlos Mondragon and Abner Quincy, who had both been keeping an eye on her from various parts of the room, converged on the two. And Susanna, recovering from her shock, said, "If you don't take your hands off me immediately, I shall have you killed." There was so much violent contempt and determination in her eyes that the startled man did release her immediately.

Quincy had arrived then and murmured into the fellow's ear, "This one ain't for sale, friend. Better git outa here before someone kills you fer tryin."

"If she ain't for sale," stuttered the miner, "what's she doin here?"

"A question for which there is, unfortunately, no answer," said Mondragon softly. "You will find what you are looking for in the next room, my friend." He turned the man in the right direction. "Susanna, perhaps you should go home now," Mondragon suggested.

"No," said Susanna with determination. Her eyes had been held by Aaron's, who was standing not three feet from them. She knew without doubt that he would have killed the man who had accosted her, had not Quincy arrived. Turning to Mondragon, she said, "I'm going to buy you two a drink—to celebrate." She linked her arms through theirs, smiling up at each in turn. When she glanced in Aaron's direction, he was gone.

"This here's nothin to celebrate, Miss Susanna," said Quincy reprovingly. "That fella—"

"I'm going to buy a house," said Susanna. "We're not going to live in the hotel anymore, Mr. Quincy." And I'm not going to have to see Aaron in the halls and lobby anymore, she thought.

Court, glancing back as he opened the doors to leave, saw her smiling up into Mondragon's eyes and felt his heart contract in jealousy and anger.

62

Susanna rarely left the hotel without Clara or Quincy at her side, but the next morning Quincy had gone off after breakfast to see about having his horse shod, the horse having suddenly developed its problems when Quincy heard that Susanna was planning yet another visit to her dressmaker. Then to her dismay Susanna discovered Clara suffering from such a headache that she could not in good conscience insist on the woman's company that morning.

Well, I'm not going to let him keep me from my appointment, thought Susanna with determination. He can't spend all his time lying in wait for me anyway; he has business of his own to take care of. Having thus convinced herself to take a practical view of the matter, Susanna gathered her parasol and gloves and descended the stairs to the lobby, where she was happy to see no sign of Aaron Court. She breathed a sigh of relief and walked with lighter steps and heart toward the door which she was just about to open when an arm covered in familiar black cloth forestalled her.

"Susanna," he said quietly, "what a pleasant surprise to see you up so early."

Susanna whirled on him angrily, her eyes stinging with tears of dismay and frustration.

Aaron smiled at her in a most formal, friendly fashion and took her arm. "You don't want to make a scene here in front of all these respectable citizens, do you, Susanna?" he murmured in a low voice. "They might wonder why you were being so rude to a man who risked his life to save yours." Then at an ordinary conversational sound level, he said, "Will you do me the honor of having coffee with me?"

Susanna took a deep breath and raised her chin stubbornly. Not to be outdone in maintaining appearances, she replied, "That's very kind of you, Mr. Court, but I'm afraid I'm already late for an appointment with my dressmaker."

"Indeed." Aaron opened the door for her politely. "Then perhaps I shall walk a few steps with you." Much to her distress, he took her arm again and turned her down the street. "So you're being fitted for another dress, are you? I can't imagine how you could possibly surpass the gown you wore last night—unless perhaps the new one leaves you bare to the waist." Susanna flushed painfully and her head snapped up, but Court forestalled her protest. "Of course, that would be an enchanting sight, I must admit." She had expected to see the usual sardonic smile on his lips, but his face and eyes were very serious, his forehead tightened in a small frown. "Still, it is hardly a sight that I would care to see exhibited publicly."

"You're being unbelievably rude," she cried.

"Of course, I thought you looked very beautiful last night, Susanna, just not very respectable. I was quite overcome by the sight of you, of your breasts, perhaps I should say." Susanna, the tears rising in her eyes, tried to pull away from him, but he tightened his hand painfully on her arm. "Don't you like to be complimented, my dear? You're a very beautiful young woman, but when you display your charms so—blatantly, shall we say, you must expect other men to be as much overcome as I was—that poor miner, for instance."

"Poor miner!" she exclaimed. "He—he wanted—"

"To take you upstairs? Of course, he did. He thought you were a whore. If you dress like a whore, you must expect men to think you are one, Susanna."

"In that case," she cried defiantly, "maybe I should just—just be what people think I am." She pulled her arm out of his grasp and turned abruptly into another street to get away from him. Court let her go, watching her moodily until she was out of sight. He hoped that the things he had said to her, unpleasant as they had been, would make her a little more circumspect in what she chose to wear. In fact, perhaps he had made an impression, he thought, smiling slightly. The direction she had taken was not the direction of the dressmaker's shop.

Susanna had indeed changed her mind about going to the dressmaker's. She was heading for the office of her new lawyer to make sure that he negotiated seriously for the house beside Mr. Penvennon's. The sooner she could move in there and out of the hotel, where she was constantly running into Aaron Court, the happier she would be—no matter how many respectable ladies snubbed her. How could he have said such cruel things? she wondered, blinking back her tears. Had he always felt such contempt for her? Susanna brushed the back of her hand against her eyes and turned into the stairs that led to Mr. Shapely's office. At least his office was not above a barbershop and down the street from a rowdy tavern. Mr. Penvennon must have been mistaken in saying that Court was the best lawyer in town. I should have asked him if Mr. Shapely is any good, she thought distractedly. She had never even met the man.

63

That evening Court was again at the bar watching her as she came down the stairs. He studied the neckline of her gown without any attempt to conceal his interest; it was less revealing than the one she had worn the night before, and he raised his glass to her, smiling slightly. Embarrassed and furious, Susanna continued steadily down step by step, longing to turn and run, his words repeating and repeating in her mind: "If you dress like a whore, you must expect men to think you are one, Susanna."

"Miss Susanna, may I have a word with you?" Grant Penvennon was standing at the bottom of the steps.

With difficulty, Susanna tore her thoughts away from Aaron Court. "Of course, Mr. Penvennon."

The mine owner escorted her to a table and politely ordered her a cup of tea. "I had a conference with Mr. Claver and Mr. Shapely, your lawyer, this afternoon, and I think there should be no problem about your purchasing the Claver house, if you still wish to do so." Susanna nodded, her mind entirely elsewhere. Penvennon went on to discuss the price and the details of payment and transfer of the deed, the date of possession and other matters he assumed would be of interest to her.

"Mr. Penvennon," said Susanna, her lips trembling, her eyes defiant. I'll show Aaron Court! was her last thought before she continued with what she had to say. "Mr. Penvennon I have decided to go into my sister's profession."

"What?" Penvennon could not believe she had said what he thought he heard.

"Yes! I have decided to become a—a—" Susanna could not bring herself to use the word that Court had used to her, but he would see! He would have to watch her take Grant Penvennon up the stairs! Then he would leave her alone. What was the difference, after all, she thought wearily, between what Court had wanted and done with her and what would happen shortly with Mr. Penvennon? It was all the same, surely. "Since you have always been so kind to me, Mr. Penvennon, I would like to invite you to become my first customer." Susanna sincerely hoped that Mr. Penvennon would accept her offer; she could think of no one else to whom she could make it without fainting from fright. Still, Mr. Penvennon might not be interested; Susanna had no idea whether all men bought women for their pleasure, or only some men. "If you are interested, of course," she added politely.

Penvennon was glancing around wildly, hoping no one had heard what Susanna had just said to him. "I think we had best discuss this in—in private," he stammered.

"Well, yes of course," Susanna replied. "Upstairs is—is—"

"I know that." Penvennon took her arm and hurried her toward the steps.

Evidently he was accepting the offer, thought Susanna without any feeling but sadness. Since she had not planned her actions beforehand, she did not know where she could take him. "I shall have to find a room," she said.

"We can use your sister's office," Penvennon replied shortly.

"I don't think Lilith would like that." Susanna spotted Denver Rose coming down the stairs and asked if there was a free room. The prostitute, looking from one to the other of that unlikely couple, was quite astonished.

"Last one at the end of the hall, dearie. It's empty."

"Thank you," said Susanna, and she continued up the stairs, Penvennon still holding her elbow and hurrying her along—before more people than necessary saw them together, heading in such a compromising direction. Susanna, of course, was only interested that Court should see her and draw the obvious conclusion.

He did see her from his station at the bar, had watched her whole conversation and departure with Penvennon; however, his conclusions were not what she would have wished. He had heard that she was negotiating for the Claver house, that Penvennon was involved in the negotiations, and he assumed that they had gone up to Lilith's office to settle matters, Claver being too big a hypocrite to come to the Fallen Angel himself. Court was, in fact, pleased that she was putting her money into property in a respectable neighborhood instead of into clothing that could only get her into trouble. Satisfied that their morning talk had had a good effect on her, he finished his drink and left.

Upstairs Susanna opened the door to the last room along the hall with a trembling hand and invited Mr. Penvennon in. Neither of them had ever seen one of these rooms, which were small but lushly appointed. Susanna took in with embarrassment the bed, the basin and ewer decorated with rosebuds and cupids, and the oil painting of a coyly posed naked woman which hung on the wall. Penvennon had expected the first two items, having been to a house in Denver in his youth, but was somewhat surprised at the picture and the abundance of plush and gilt that met his eye. Must have cost Lilith a fortune to furnish the place, he calculated.

"Won't you have a seat, Mr. Penvennon?" Susanna asked.

"Thank you," he replied, thinking wryly that the girl seemed quite at a loss as to how to behave in her new profession and should, therefore, be easy enough to dissuade. "Am I to take it, Susanna, that you have only just decided to become a—a lady of ill repute?"

"That's right, Mr. Penvennon." She looked at him anxiously as she took a seat on the edge of the bed. "However, you need feel no compunction about accepting my offer. I have already been dishonored."

"I see." Penvennon was at a loss as to what to say after that revelation.

"I must admit that I did not knowingly fall into sin," she continued, not wanting him to think too badly of her, "but that's all one now, isn't it?" The expression on Mr. Penvennon's face was hard to interpret, and Susanna did not know how to proceed. "I mean since I am already a fallen woman, I might as well just—just—" Her sentiment trailed off lamely. She wished he would do something. Aaron had taken off her clothes. He had taken the initiative entirely, but Mr. Penvennon just sat there, and Susanna had no idea what was expected of her.

Penvennon realized this, and although he found the whole situation very painful and embarrassing and was sorely tempted to give her a lecture and insist that she leave the Fallen Angel immediately, he thought that letting her flounder a bit might force her to convince herself that she was making a decision she would regret. So he waited in silence, and Susanna glanced up at him from time to time, becoming more and more nervous.

"I don't know what to do next, Mr. Penvennon," she finally admitted. "Perhaps I should take off my clothes?" She looked at him questioningly.

"Certainly, if you think it best," he replied. He seriously doubted that the girl could undress in front of him. What could have happened to her to bring her to this room, for which she was so obviously unfitted? The Packards were responsible, no doubt.

Think it best? Susanna's mind echoed in confusion. What did that mean? Did he think they could—make love—with their clothes on? Why was it called making love, she wondered sadly.

Susanna looked so close to tears that Penvennon almost relented, but he reminded himself that his most effective tactic with his own children was silent disapproval. He was accustomed to inviting a recalcitrant child into his study, mentioning without comment some unseemly behavior, then falling silent. His unmathematical son had been persuaded in this fashion to exert himself in school. Stern fatherly silence had also influenced a chubby daughter to desist from slipping apple pies out of her mother's pantry. Penvennon had no doubt that Susanna could be diverted from prostitution by the same homely methods.

Goaded by his silence, Susanna rose and glanced around the room. "There—there doesn't seem to be a screen—or—a dressing room," she faltered.

"No, there doesn't," Penvennon agreed, continuing to watch her.

He's not even going to turn his head, she thought with despair. She tried to smile at him as her fingers went to the small buttons that marched down the back of her dress. She realized then that she might not even be able to get out of the dress by herself, that she was proving to be the most inept of—how had he put it?—ladies of ill repute. A terrible failure. Perhaps he would get tired of waiting and go away. Susanna unbuttoned, with difficulty, the first button of many. Mr. Penvennon calmly sat in his chair without offering to help.

Down the hall Abner Quincy had just gone into one of the luxurious little rooms with Denver Rose, and no one in that room was hesitant about how to accomplish the business at hand. Rose was out of her dress and into bed in a twinkling with Quincy not far behind, although he only bothered to remove his boots and pants, figuring he might not have much time before Susanna finished buying her house. He supposed they had gone to Lilith's office to settle the deal. And Quincy thought it was a good idea. It made him nervous to have Susanna living in the same hotel with Aaron Court, and he knew it hurt her to have to see Court so frequently—poor girl.

"You'll never guess what happened," said Rose, giggling.

"What?" Quincy was not really interested in conversation.

"It's about Lilith's sister."

"What about her?"

"She and Grant Penvennon just took the room at the end of the hall. Imagine old skinflint Penvennon paying for something he can get at home."

"Shut yer dirty mouth," snapped Quincy. "She an Penvennon are talkin business in Lilith's office."

"Well, she asked me which room was free, an she took him in the room at the end of the hall, an no one talks business in there," snickered the prostitute, "unless it's some dummy who don't know Lilith sets the price—"

"God almighty," Quincy swore, and he was out of bed in an instant. What the devil could the girl be up to? He pulled on his pants and, ignoring his boots, raced down the hall in his stocking feet and pounded twice at Lilith's door before flinging it open.

Lilith had been talking to Carlos and turned on Quincy furiously, saying, "No one, Quincy, comes in here without—"

"She's down the end of the hall with Grant Penvennon—up to God knows what," Quincy interrupted.

"Who?" Lilith demanded, her face turning white.

Mondragon did not bother with such unnecessary questions. He was on his feet immediately. "Which room?" he asked.

Before they got to Susanna's door, Mondragon, who was ahead of her, turned to Lilith and said, "Whatever's happening, keep your voice down. The little fool doesn't need a noisy scandal." Then he tried the door, which to his surprise was unlocked, neither Penvennon nor Susanna having thought to lock it. Mondragon opened it without knocking and closed it just as quickly, once Lilith and Quincy had entered.

"Just what is going on here?" Lilith demanded, her voice quivering with outrage. Mr. Penvennon was still sitting in his chair, and Susanna was sitting on the bed with tears slipping down her cheeks. She had finally managed to struggle out of her dress, only to discover she could not undo by herself the strings of her corset, which had always been tied and untied by Clara.

"Nothing is going on here, Miss Moran," said Penvennon calmly. "Your sister had decided to become a prostitute, and she offered to take me as her first customer. However, I hope and believe that she has now changed her mind."

"You needn't worry, Lilith," said Susanna miserably. "I am an utter failure as a lady of ill repute, just as I was as an ordinary girl. I don't seem to be able to do anything well. I couldn't even get my clothes off." She began to cry in earnest.

"I don't know how you could do this, Susanna," exclaimed Lilith angrily.

"I hardly think you should blame your sister for this unfortunate incident, Miss Moran," said Penvennon. "Much of her pain and confusion is a result, you can be sure, of the ambiguous social position in which she finds herself here in Amnonville. She is unacceptable in normal society because of her relationship to you, and yet she hardly has the temperament to follow your profession, as this unfortunate experience should point out quite clearly. I had only to sit here and say nothing in order to let her convince herself that she could not do what she had meant to do. Your sister should not be in Amnonville, much less in this establishment." He looked at Susanna and his eyes softened. "Now, child, if you will put your dress back on, I will see you safely to your hotel, and I urge you to never in the future make the offer to anyone that you made to me this evening. It would be very unwise indeed."

Susanna wiped her tears away with the back of her hand and said meekly, "Yes, sir."

"Quincy can see Susanna back to the hotel, Mr.

Penvennon," said Mondragon quietly, "and we thank you for your forebearance in this matter."

"Certainly," said Penvennon. "We can conclude the sale of the house tomorrow afternoon at your lawyer's office if you like, Susanna."

"Yes, sir. Thank you."

"I'll bid you good evening then." Penvennon walked calmly out of the room as if nothing unusual had happened there and went home to a good night's sleep.

"What do you mean by thanking him for his forebearance?" Lilith demanded, rounding on Mondragon.

"Ask yerself what would a happened if she'd brought someone else up here," said Quincy.

"Very true, my love," Carlos agreed dryly. "Any man but Penvennon might have insisted on getting what he paid for."

"He hadn't paid yet," sniffed Susanna. "But I would have insisted," she assured her sister.

Lilith turned on her and cried, "Don't you ever, ever—"

"Let her alone," said Quincy.

"And don't you tell me what to do. I pay your salary."

"Susanna pays my salary now," Quincy replied. "Get dressed, girl. I'll take you down the back way. No use anyone else seein you up here an gettin ideas."

"I can't get the buttons." Susanna had already stepped into the dress but was fumbling ineffectively with the buttons.

"Well, I ain't no dress buttoner," said Quincy. "For God's sake, help the girl, Lilith."

"I have a few more questions for you, miss, before I allow you to leave."

Carlos cursed under his breath and said, "Turn your back to me, Susanna."

"Get your hands off her," Lilith cried involuntarily, for when Susanna had demurred, Carlos had simply turned her and begun to fasten her dress—quickly and with a rather grim expression on his face.

"What's this about your buying a house?" Lilith demanded, afraid to protest further when Carlos looked so angry.

"I'm going to buy the Claver house," Susanna mumbled.

"I forbid it," Lilith cried. "The only smart thing Penvennon said was that you shouldn't be in this town at all."

"Well, I don't intend to leave, and I don't intend to stay at that hotel any longer, so unless you want to give me a room here, I shall just have to buy a house, shan't I?"

"The house is a good idea," said Quincy.

"And if I can't be a—a lady of ill repute, I'll just have to find something else to do here. I told you to find something for me, didn't I, Lilith?"

Susanna, having been efficiently dressed by her sister's lover, said, "Thank you, Mr. Mondragon, for your assistance," and she swept angrily out of the room.

"Not at all," Carlos replied with a dry smile. Once the door had closed behind Susanna, he turned back to Lilith. "I'd think of something for her to do if I were you, Lilith," he said, "before she gets herself and you into more trouble."

"I don't want her here at all," snapped Lilith sullenly.

64

Before Quincy would allow Susanna to go to her room, he insisted that she come into the hotel restaurant, now nearly empty, for a cup of tea and a talk, which she dreaded.

"Now, Miss Susanna, I think you'd better tell me why in the world you ever did such a thing." Susanna's lips began to tremble again and her eyes to fill with tears. "Cryin ain't gonna do no good, Miss Susanna. I'll jus sit here till you're through, an then I'll still want an answer."

"He—he said that I dressed like a whore."

"Who?" asked Quincy frowning.

"Aaron. He made me walk with him on the street, and he said if I dressed like a whore, people would treat me like one. And—and then tonight there he was, staring at me with that—that nasty smile, and I thought—I thought—well, if that's what he thinks, I'd just—just—"

Quincy nodded. "You did it to spite him."

"I guess so."

"It wasn't a very smart thing to do, Miss Susanna. You're mighty lucky it didn't turn out no worse than it did."

"I know."

"An I want you to promise you won't never do nothin like that agin."

"I promise," said Susanna in an almost inaudible voice. "I don't think I could have."

"I don't think you could have neither—not willin, anyways." He stared at the shining black hair, which was all he could see of her since her face was buried in her hands. "You gotta forget about Court, Miss Susanna."

"How can I when I see him all the time, and he—he won't leave me alone?"

"I'll take you over to the lawyer's tomorrer to see about that house you want. That should help—movin outa here. You got the money to buy it?"

"I have plenty of money," said Susanna bitterly. "Much good it does me."

"The poor's sadder'n the rich, I reckon," said Quincy. "Best you git to bed now. Tomorrer we'll see about yer house. Sooner we git you moved in, the better."

"It's empty now," said Susanna. "Mrs. Claver won't live there—not since Lilith used it as a whorehouse. Isn't that ironic?" she added sadly. "I'm going to buy my own whorehouse, and I couldn't even—"

"That's enough," said Quincy. "Maybe we kin find another house if that bothers you."

"Why should it?" Susanna's face hardened. "I ought to get a good price. Probably I'm the only person in town who would buy it."

Quincy saw Susanna to her door and then went to Court's room. He intended to talk to Court that night, even if he had to comb every saloon and whorehouse in town to find him. That did not prove necessary, however, for Court had been asleep in his own bed and, after identifying his late caller, appeared at the door wearing only his pants and asking brusquely what Quincy wanted.

"Wanta talk to you."

"That's a change, isn't it?" Court opened the door wide enough to let his former friend in.

"No change. I feel the same way about you as I did before." He was staring coldly at Court, thinking it was easy enough to see why Susanna had let herself become involved. Court was a striking

man with that pale hair and dark skin and eyes, and
that powerful body. Quincy cursed himself again for
a fool. He had known well enough that Aaron Court
exerted a magnetic influence on any woman he chose
to notice, and knowing that, Quincy had still given
him access to Susanna.

"Well, what is it you want to talk to me about?"
Court asked impatiently.

"Somethin happened tonight that you oughta
know about," said Quincy. "Seems Susanna
decided she was gonna become a whore. Offered
herself to Grant Penvennon." Court's face turned
white. "Took him upstairs to one of the rooms."

"Jesus Christ. What was she thinking of?" The
lines of pain had formed around his mouth. To
Quincy, his eyes looked tortured, and Quincy was
glad to see it.

"She was thinkin of what you said to her."

"I said to her?"

"You told her she looked like a whore an she
should expect to be treated like one."

"I said the dress—"

"Susanna wouldn't look like a whore if she was
stark naked on Copper Street," said Quincy angrily.

"I was afraid she'd get herself in trouble."

"Well, she did. Seems you hurt her feelins this
mornin, an you laughed at her tonight, an she jus
decided if she had the name, she might as well have
the game."

"Dear God. What happened?"

"She picked on Grant Penvennon. That's what
happened. And he didn't like it one lil bit. Seems he
trotted right upstairs with her, sat down an left the
whole thing up to her, and she didn't know what to
do. Finally she tried to git her clothes off—" Quincy
observed with satisfaction that Court was looking

more and more stricken. "—an she got hung up on some of them female strings an such. By the time Lilith an me an Mondragon got there, Miss Susanna was in tears, an Penvennon give Lilith a lecture—"

"Sounds like a comedy of errors," said Court with relief.

"You think it sounds funny? I want you to think a minute what would a happened if she hadn't gone upstairs with Grant Penvennon. She might a picked anyone."

"She would have backed down," said Court.

"Maybe. But maybe she wouldn't a been given the chance. What I'm sayin to you, Court, is that none a this would a happened if you'd left her alone. You pushed her into this. Now stay away from her. She's had as much as she kin take."

"I don't intend to stay away from her," said Court, his eyes narrowed. "I mean to have her."

"How?" asked Quincy. "You want her dead? Beat to death by someone who didn't get what he thought she was promisin? Dead because you broke her heart?"

"She'll not be hurt by me."

"You already have hurt her. Leave the girl alone now before she decides she don't wanta live no more. This child has had more tears an humiliation already than she should a had in a whole lifetime."

"If you keep her away from the Fallen Angel, she'll be all right," said Court.

"She's already said no to that," said Quincy. "She says since she wasn't no good as a whore, she's gonna try somethin else. God knows what she'll come up with next."

"Couldn't be worse," Court muttered as Quincy disappeared down the hall.

65

For several weeks Susanna was occupied with her
house and did not go to the Fallen Angel. Her
absence was a source of relief to Lilith and Carlos,
who appreciated the tenor of business as it used to
be; and to Quincy, although he hated being drafted
to help in the buying and placing of furniture; and
even to Grant Penvennon, although he now had to
listen to the complaints of his wife, who did not
want a woman of dubious reputation living next to
her and could not understand her husband's unsym-
pathetic attitude about her remarks. But to one
person Susanna's absence from the Fallen Angel
brought sharply conflicting emotions: Aaron was
torn between the fear that his very presence would
precipitate her into some more foolish venture than
her last and the simple desire to see her, which he no
longer could do, now that she lived elsewhere and
never came to Lilith's anymore. He moved back to
his cabin, pursued his business, and thought about
her, no less determined to get her back somehow or
other.

Susanna, seeking to drive from her mind the pain
of her memories of Aaron and the humiliation of
her venture into prostitution, worked night and day
on her house. She spent money lavishly on
furnishings when she could find something to
buy—most things had to be ordered from
Denver—and she moved into the house as soon as
she had paid for it, before she had even a bed to
sleep on. She bought fabric and made draperies and
curtains. She held long conferences with Quincy and
Clara on how they would like their rooms decorated.

She drove Lilith mad with demands for advice,
which she never accepted since her taste ran to the
understated and subdued while Lilith's ran to the
overstated and colorful. She made elaborate plans
with Clara for canning and pickling, for stocking
her cupboards, for menus and laundry schedules
and cleaning days. She even ventured out into the
countryside with Quincy for the first time since her
last trip with Aaron, and she insisted that the
reluctant gunfighter help her dig up wildflowers, all
of which died when planted in her yard. And last she
purchased a piano at the auction of the estate of a
deceased saloonkeeper and personally painted out
the disgusting pictures that had been commissioned
by the previous owner.

The piano gave her something to do while she
waited for her purchases to arrive from Denver, and
it also gave her an idea. What Lilith needed at the
Fallen Angel, she decided, was entertainment. There
was a girl there who sang from time to time and was
reputed to have a huge repertoire of songs that
appealed to miners and other patrons of the Fallen
Angel, but the girl had a poor voice and was usually
poorly received. As a result she found it more profitable to pursue her other calling, and the Fallen
Angel, which offered everything else, rarely offered
singing. Susanna decided that she herself was the
person who should add that last item to the list of
her sister's offerings.

Knowing instinctively that Lilith would argue, as
she did at every suggestion that might bring her
sister back to the Fallen Angel, Susanna did not tell
Lilith her plans. She simply dropped by the
establishment one afternoon and engaged Ellie, the
seldom singer, to visit her new house and teach her
as many popular saloon songs as possible. Since

Ellie had her eye on a beautiful length of bright yellow brocade at the Arbuthnot Mercantile Store and since Susanna was offering a generous sum for an afternoon's work, Ellie was glad to oblige. She knew enough songs to last as long as Miss Susanna—who wasn't a bad sort when you got right down to it—had money to pay for them.

Ellie had certainly expected the arrangement to last longer than it did. She had expected she might be able to teach Susanna a song an afternoon, but she found that Susanna not only wrote down the words but also the little black circles and lines that allowed her to play the music on the piano, and that after an afternoon of taking down songs, Susanna was able to play and sing them the very next day. Ellie could not imagine how she managed to learn them that fast. Could Susanna be staying up all night to do it? She certainly did not look it. In fact, she looked better than Ellie herself, who had been used, after a night at the Fallen Angel, to sleeping away not only the morning but a good part of the afternoon. And Ellie found it somewhat disconcerting that Susanna sounded so much better singing the songs. Susanna had a beautiful voice and, even better, a loud voice. Susanna could have sung at the Fallen Angel and made money, thought Ellie wistfully. It never occurred to her that that was exactly what Susanna had in mind—not until Lilith called her in and upbraided her furiously for going to Susanna's house and teaching her all those songs without getting permission.

"She's your sister," said Ellie in an injured tone. "I thought sure you knew what she was doin."

Lilith just glared at her and told her to get out. She was tempted to fire Ellie, but the girl was a successful whore and hardly to blame for Susanna's dreadful ideas. Being a fair, if choleric, woman, Lilith allowed Ellie to remain.

When Susanna had appeared in Lilith's office to suggest that she was ready to become a singer at the Fallen Angel, Lilith dismissed the notion out of hand. "You're supposed to be decorating your house," said Lilith.

"There's just so much that can be done to one house," Susanna had replied. "Until the furnishings from Denver arrive, I've done what can be done—and learned a number of songs that Ellie assures me are popular with your customers, even when she sings them, and she has a terrible voice. I have a very good voice, and you have a stage and no one to occupy it. Obviously this is an area in which you really need me." Susanna smiled mischievously. "And my price is attractive. You can pay me whatever you think fair in view of the extra business I bring in."

"Susanna, you have no idea how a singer in a place like this is treated."

"Presumably the audience will listen or not listen as it suits them."

"They shout, and they expect—"

"Well, they'll soon learn that they can't expect more than songs," said Susanna stoutly. "Aren't you even going to listen to me sing?"

"I don't need to listen to you sing," said Lilith. "You learned to sing in church. That's not—"

"I have learned at least fifty songs that would never be sung in any church, some of which Ellie said were very popular and I considered perfectly horrible. The least you can do is listen. I even bid on a piano with appalling pictures painted on it so I could help you. It took me two days to paint out the pictures."

"What are you talking about?" Lilith demanded.

"I bought a piano that belonged to the late Alfonso 'Turnip' Bragg."

"You didn't!" Lilith started to laugh helplessly. Turnip Bragg's piano was infamous for its lascivious caricatures. People had come from hundreds of miles just to look at those pictures. "You bought that piano?"

"Yes, I did. It was the only piano in town. I don't know why you're laughing. You can't have seen what Mr. Bragg had painted on it. Women with monstrous—"

"You don't have to tell me, Susanna."

"Well, the pictures in your rooms are—are bad enough, goodness knows. Poor Mr. Penvennon must have been shocked."

"I imagine he was more shocked to be invited up there by you, Susanna, than by my pictures—"

Susanna blushed and wished she had not brought the matter up. "Well, the pictures on the late Mr. Bragg's piano make yours seem absolutely tasteful in comparison."

"Thanks," said Lilith dryly.

"So are you going to listen to me sing?"

"Are you going to give me any choice?"

"No," said Susanna. "Shall we go downstairs? I can also accompany myself on the piano, of course."

"I have a pianist," said Lilith. "You'll have to sing with him. It's customary." Lilith was hoping Susanna might have difficulty if accompanied by the rather eccentric playing of Eddie Minsk, her seldom sober pianist.

And at first Susanna did, for Minsk took her to be another talentless job applicant, having never noticed her before in the place or paid the slightest attention to gossip about the owner's troublesome sister. However, when he heard Susanna sing in a fine, sweet voice that resounded through the room and caught the absolute attention of the sparse early-afternoon crowd of drinkers, he sat up and began to play in such a way as to complement her singing. She turned a happy smile on him and finished her song. The drinkers applauded enthusiastically, Susanna asked Eddie if he knew the music to "Beautiful Dreamer," and Mondragon, who was standing behind Lilith, said, "She's got you. She can sing."

"I don't like it," Lilith replied forebodingly.

"It's better than the last thing she tried."

"I wonder."

66

Lilith made no attempt to spread the word around town that she had a new singer. In fact, she hoped that no one would notice, and Susanna opened to the usual crowd—who loved her. Although Ellie had taught her a number of songs, Susanna chose to sing only the sentimental ballads; she ignored the songs she considered naughty. By the third night the house was packed with men who had come for the express purpose of hearing her—packed at nine o'clock, for Susanna never stayed past midnight and gave only two performances. The liquor sales had doubled among the listeners as had the need for bouncers on Mondragon's crew to take care of the patrons who wavered between teary sentimentality when Susanna was singing and drunken belligerence among themselves when she was not. Mondragon definitely considered her a mixed blessing. Lilith was on tenter-

hooks until Susanna went happily home under the
guardianship of Quincy after her second program.
The time between programs, she spent chatting
companionably with patrons who seemed to be
sober—listening sympathetically to their tales of
hardship in the mountains, families left behind,
dangerous adventures with Indians, blizzards,
avalanches, and such. Susanna was feeling almost
happy again. And no reminders of Aaron Court had
been forced on her since she had moved from the
hotel.

On Susanna's fourth night as a singer at the Fallen
Angel when she had just finished singing "My Old
Kentucky Home," for Stephen Foster was a favorite
of hers, she suddenly noticed Court among the
rather rowdy audience. The others were cheering,
smiling, clapping—if somewhat drunk. Aaron was
neither smiling nor clapping. He looked to her just
as he had looked the morning he had commented on
her clothing, had told her that people would take her
for a whore; her heart plummeted. Had she known
it, Court was remembering the time that she had
come to rescue him from the Packard ambush and
her hymn-singing had frightened off superstitious
old Job Packard. Susanna, however, took his
expression for disapproval, and she resented it that
he should spread gloom over the one source of
happiness she had found—her one success. Her chin
came up and her eyes flashed. "Mr. Minsk, do you
know . . ." She whispered into his ear the name of
the naughtiest song she had learned. Eddie looked
astounded and advised her not to sing it.

"Don't you know it?" she demanded.

"Well, sure, but—"

"Play it, please." Susanna sang the song, using

all the coy gestures that Ellie had used when she taught it to Susanna. The audience was absolutely silent as she sang; the reception was terrifying when she finished. They howled and shouted and surged toward the stage. And Susanna was rooted to her spot in the middle, unable to move. Then suddenly an arm encircled her waist, and she was behind the curtain. Her disappearance caused a riot that took Mondragon a half hour to quell, that prevented Quincy from getting to her, from even searching for her. He could not even get out of the tumultuous crowd.

"You idiot," said Court as he dragged her out into the alley behind the Fallen Angel. "You little idiot." He put his arms around her and leaned weakly against the wall. He was shaking; Susanna was in shock.

Court had guessed what might happen before she was halfway through the song and had worked his way backstage so that he could get to her before the crowd did.

"Let go of me," she whispered.

"Susanna, my God. Don't you know what you did?" He tightened his arms around her. "You made everyone of them fall half in love with you when you sang all that sentimental slop, and then you as much as invited them to come and take you with that last piece of trash. Why in God's name did you sing that? Where did you learn it?"

"Ellie. Ellie taught me," she faltered.

One of his hands was in her hair, pulling her head back, the other at her waist, pulling her body against his. When he kissed her, she felt as if the world were dropping out from under her feet. Nothing had changed. The waves of heat and desire engulfed her as they had before. That reaction filled Aaron with a vaulting joy, Susanna with despair.

"Do you believe me now when I tell you that we belong together?" he asked when finally he had released her lips.

"I wish the Packards had killed me," she replied in a broken voice.

"God damn it, Susanna—" He cut himself off. "I'm sorry, love," he said more gently. "I know you're upset by that mob scene. I'll take you home."

Unable to protest, to do anything, Susanna allowed herself to be led to his horse and carried to her house in his arms, but the touch of him was agony to her; her tears slid in silent rivulets down her cheeks, and he tasted them like bitter wine when he kissed her at her own door.

"Don't cry, love," he begged. "It will all come out right." Susanna let him hold her without protest, but she continued to cry. "We'll talk tomorrow. I'll come here tomorrow and—"

"No."

"Yes, sweetheart, it has to be. You and I belong together. Now go in. I'll tell them you're safe—Lilith and Carlos—and I'll be here tomorrow morning." His mouth found hers in the dark and stilled her protests, her very thoughts. Then he released her and sent her in.

To the Fallen Angel he sent a messenger. He did not want to quarrel with Lilith. He had won, and that was enough.

V
The Cabin

67

Lilith received Court's message that Susanna was safe at home, but she never knew or even questioned, in the midst of the chaos that confronted her at the Fallen Angel, who had sent it. She did, however, go to Susanna's house once order had been restored to see for herself that her sister was unharmed.

Susanna had been in bed for several hours by then, but she had been sleepless, tormented by her encounter with Court. Her overpowering response to him had proved to Susanna how vulnerable she was, but worse, she knew that it had proved to him that he still had a hold on her, a hold which he intended to take advantage of the next morning. She had only a few hours before she had to face him again, and what did he expect of her? Nothing that her self-respect would allow her to grant, Susanna told herself hopelessly.

When she heard Lilith's vigorous knocking at the front door, she was sure that the intruder was Aaron, too impatient to wait for morning. She was so relieved to hear that it was Lilith instead who wanted to see her that she entirely forgot that Lilith might be angry about the incident at the Fallen Angel. She saw her sister as an ally, not an enemy. Perhaps Lilith could be persuaded to spend the night. Perhaps—Susanna leapt eagerly from her bed to welcome her sister.

Meanwhile, Lilith occupied herself as she waited downstairs by looking around her curiously, having been in the house only once before. The room in which she sat, although it had beautiful draperies, a piano, and two chairs, had no other furniture and no carpet. It gave the appearance of a room in transition, a room whose owner was moving in or out. Then she heard her sister on the stair and went to the door to watch Susanna come down to her. Lilith experienced a feeling of wonder, of disorientation. She knew what had happened at her place as a result of Susanna's performance, but as she looked at the girl now, it did not seem possible that Susanna could have caused that sort of havoc. Her hair was plaited demurely into one long braid, and she was wearing a loose, all-concealing robe. Her face was gentle, tired, and sad—and very young.

"Are you all right, Susanna?" Lilith asked anxiously. "You weren't hurt?"

"I'm fine," Susanna replied, her voice emotionless, muted.

Lilith sighed and returned to her chair. "You wouldn't believe what happened. There was a riot—fourteen people hurt—I don't know." She shook her head wearily.

"I'm so sorry, Lilith. I didn't mean—"

"Don't worry about it. It's all part of the business." The words were gallant, and Lilith essayed a gallant smile to match them but was not quite able to bring it off. She leaned forward earnestly and said, "Susanna, you've got to get out of town for a while. I'm not trying to send you away for good, but I'm afraid you'll get hurt. Too many men got—got ideas about you tonight." She looked at Susanna hopefully, but her sister said nothing;

Susanna was staring, bemused, at her own hands. "You could go to Denver, see about your furniture. They don't seem to be in any hurry about shipping it. The stores are wonderful there. I know you'll see lots of things you want to buy for the house. If money's a problem, I'd be glad to—"

"Money isn't a problem." Nothing had ever actually been said between the two sisters about Susanna's plan to divide the inheritance from their parents. This silence was a relief to Lilith and also insured that Susanna would remain a very wealthy young woman. "I have plenty of money."

"Good. Well, then there's some business you could conduct for me, if you want to. I—"

"When does the train to Denver leave?"

"Tomorrow morning at nine," Lilith replied. She could not believe it was going to be so easy. Susanna had been so stubborn in the past.

"How early could I board?"

"Why—why, at seven, I think."

Susanna nodded. "I'll pack tonight." Aaron had said he would return in the morning, but it would not be that early, Susanna reasoned. He would expect her to sleep late; he would be tired himself. And she could be gone before he arrived.

"Do you want to take Quincy with you? He's still over at the Fallen Angel—"

"It won't be necessary. I got here from St. Louis by myself. I guess I can get to Denver."

"Of course you can." Lilith was not about to argue and jeopardize the whole arrangement. Quincy had not been that effective a protector anyway. "I'll give you the names of a good hotel and of business associates of mine to contact. Anything you need there, Caldwell Mason will be glad to take care of."

"You'd better write the names down now. I want to be on the train as soon as it comes in. Will there be any problem about a ticket?"

"I'll take care of it tonight and pick you up myself in the morning."

"You don't have to do that, Lilith. Quincy can—"

"Of course I will."

They continued to discuss the practical details of the trip, Lilith still amazed that Susanna was being so agreeable, Susanna tense with fear and foreboding, keeping tight control of herself. All she had to do was get to Denver, she told herself over and over that night—pack her clothes, board the train, and get to Denver.

"I'll telegraph you when I think it's safe for you to come home," Lilith had said.

"Yes." Susanna had nodded, not thinking about returning, thinking only about escaping, getting away before Aaron came for her.

68

"Is Miss Susanna up yet, Clara?" Court asked.

"Oh, Lord, yes, Mr. Court," said Clara cheerfully as she wiped her hands on her apron. "What a night we've had, but Miss Lilith got her off in plenty of time after all. They left not a half hour ago."

"Left?" Court controlled his expression carefully. "It's quite important that I speak to her. I wonder—"

"Well, I expect she's on her way to Denver by now, Mr. Court. I'll tell her you called, though, when she gits back."

"When will that be, Clara?" Court asked politely, biting back his fury.

"Well, she didn't say. She promised to write, an I heard Miss Lilith say she'd telegraph her when it was—how did she put it?—time to come back?—safe to come back?—maybe that was what she said. I think maybe there was some trouble at that place Miss Lilith runs."

"She took the train, did she?"

"My yes." Clara sighed. "How I envy her. Do you know, Mr. Court, I've never been on a train."

"Is that so?" Court took his watch from his pocket and glanced at it, his mind originating and rejecting plans with lightning speed, his anger growing to a white heat behind calm gray eyes.

"It's going to be lonely here without Miss Susanna. She's such a sweet thing."

"Yes," said Court in a tight voice. "Well, I'll bid you good morning, Clara."

"An good morning to you, Mr. Court." Clara watched him mount and ride away toward the south edge of town. She remembered then that Miss Susanna had said that no one was to be told of the trip. Still, it could do no harm if Mr. Court knew. What a fine-looking man he was, Clara reflected. And he had always shown such a kind interest in Susanna. Clara had once harbored a hope that they might marry, he having rescued Miss Susanna so romantically from the fire and all, but it didn't seem to have worked out. Still maybe. . . .

Court trotted his horse down the quiet street under Clara's eyes and, once around the corner, set spurs to the animal and headed south toward his own cabin at a dead run. He had a half-hour.

Having made two very brief stops, one at his cabin and one at his bank, and with neither luggage nor a ticket, Court swung onto the last car of the train to Denver just before it left the station. In the confusion of departure, his presence went unnoticed by anyone, including Abner Quincy, who was lounging against the wall of the station opposite the middle section of the train. That anonymity was something Court had counted on.

His first act was to catch the conductor and buy a ticket, not an unusual procedure on that train. Then he announced that he must find his sister, who had not expected him to accompany her, and he started forward on a methodical car-by-car search. He discovered Susanna sitting by herself in the dining car staring out the window. She looked exhausted.

"Susanna," he murmured quietly, sitting down at her table as if she had been waiting for him. She turned and looked at him with weary dismay, passing her hand over her eyes as if he were an apparition that could never be explained in any reasonable way. And so he seemed to her; the one thing she had been sure of when the train pulled away, after a tense and sleepless night, was that she was leaving Aaron Court behind her, and yet there he sat, calmly asking her if she had ordered. She shook her head.

"You'd better have a good breakfast. You look very tired," he remarked sympathetically.

He did not even seem to be angry with her for leaving when he had expected to see her at her house later that morning. He was acting as if they had planned the trip to Denver together, Susanna thought with confusion. Had she mentioned it to him? Of course not. The whole idea of going had been to get away from him.

Court waved the waiter over to the table and ordered for both of them, and Susanna had not the strength to argue or protest. Her mind felt numb.

"Have you made this trip before?" he asked.

"No. No, I came in by another route."

"Oh yes, I remember. You were held up by a blizzard, weren't you?"

"Yes."

"In a minute you'll see a siding near a lake. Yes, there it is." Obediently Susanna looked out the window as he told her of a train from Denver that had been engulfed in a snow slide there five years before. He interrupted himself to ask if she took cream or sugar in her coffee, which had been delivered just as he called her attention to the site of the winter disaster he proceeded to describe.

"Neither," said Susanna.

"Five people died in the first car," he continued, "and the engineer and fireman. They managed to dig the rest out alive, but only after thirty-six hours, and many of them were in bad shape by then." He handed her the cup. "Drink it up," he advised, "and I'll pour you another. It will make you feel better."

Holding her coffee cup in both hands, like a small child trying to manage a cup of milk, Susanna drank some of the coffee.

"Too hot?" he asked.

She shook her head. He made it all seem so normal. Susanna did not know what to do. She did not know what he planned to do.

"That's a very becoming suit. The color is good on you."

She thanked him, thinking anxiously that she was all by herself, traveling to a strange city with Aaron Court on the same train. Why hadn't she brought Quincy along?

"Many women look washed out in gray. But with your blue eyes—" He was smiling at her, his own eyes friendly, as if there were no bitterness, no—

"Finished with your coffee? Here, let me pour you another cup."

Susanna passed her cup to him, and he refilled it. I'm supposed to be pouring the coffee, she thought. Why is Aaron doing it? She almost wished he would ask why she had left without telling him. That at least would seen normal instead of this—

"Well, here we are. This train has excellent food. I think you'll be pleased." The waiter was placing covered dishes in the middle of the table. "Now, what will you have? Sausage?" Aaron helped her to sausage and then eggs and toast. "Good. They have strawberry jam this morning. You have to try that."

He spooned jam out on her plate and passed it to her. Susanna looked at it with dismay. Suddenly she felt terribly dizzy and a little sick.

"More coffee, Susanna?" he asked.

It must be my going without sleep, she thought, drawing a deep breath to try to overcome the vertigo.

"Susanna, are you all right?"

Susanna was aware that he was staring at her with concern. She put both hands to her head. "I don't feel very well."

"This is a rough stretch of track. The motion—"

"I—I think I'd better go to my—" She could not finish.

She felt his arm around her shoulders as he helped her up. "Come on. Maybe some fresh air will revive you."

"Somethin the matter, sir?" asked the waiter, hurrying toward them.

"She's feeling ill."

The man nodded sympathetically. "Not used to travelin in the mountains most likely. It affects lotsa folks that way, specially young ladies and children."

Court nodded and helped Susanna toward the door of the car. It opened just as they arrived to admit the conductor. "Found her, I see," he said cheerfully.

"Yes, and not a minute too soon. She seems to have been taken ill."

"Fresh air is just the thing." The conductor held the door for them. "Let me know if I can help."

"Thank you. I will." Court let the door close behind them, then leaned against the back of the swaying car, holding Susanna easily against his chest. "Breathe deeply." He rested one hand soothingly on her shoulder, the other arm around her waist. "Any better?" he asked. Susanna shook her head. "Do you want me to take you to your compartment?"

"Please." One part of her mind warned her not to tell him where it was. The other found nothing threatening about his conduct, wanted only his help in getting to the compartment, which she would never be able to reach on her own.

"You'll have to tell me where it is, Susanna," he prompted.

"Any better?" asked the conductor, opening the door and peering out.

"Worse, I'd say," Court replied. "I'd better get her back to the compartment. Could you tell me where it is?"

The conductor laughed at the idea that Court would not know the number of his sister's compartment. Perhaps the girl had been running away from home. "B, third car. Need any help?"

"I'll manage," Court replied. However, Susanna became less and less able to walk, and Court wished, before he got her to the compartment, that he had accepted the offer of help. She was hardly conscious by the time he put her on the seat and sat down with his arm around her. For ten minutes he stared out the window, watching the familiar scenery go by. This interlude was interrupted by a knock at the door and the entrance of the friendly conductor.

"Any better?" he asked again solicitously.

"She's dozed off," said Court quietly, "but if she isn't feeling any better by the time we get to Caldwell, I'm going to get off and take her to the doctor."

"Didn't know they had one. Won't be another train till Wednesday."

Court nodded. "Looks like she may be back at home tonight instead of in Denver."

"Bad luck," said the conductor. "I'll stop in before we get to Caldwell. It's only ten minutes."

"That close?" Court settled back in the seat to wait, and the conductor left.

At Caldwell, Court carried her off the train, and the conductor obligingly arranged with the clerk at the station to check her luggage until they could return for it. "Lucky she's a little thing," said the conductor. "You'll have to carry her across the street to the hotel unless you know where the doctor's office is." Court nodded and thanked the man for his help. Then he made his way to Caldwell House and explained to the desk clerk that his sister had been taken ill on the train and that they would need a room for a couple of hours until he could arrange transportation to get her back home. The clerk was as helpful as the conductor had been, escorting them upstairs and opening the room for them. Court laid Susanna gently down on the bed and sat down beside her for several minutes. She was breathing normally but was very deeply asleep. Satisfied, he went out and locked the door. In less than two hours he was back with a sturdy horse, a mule, and a load of supplies which he distributed in packs and lashed to the mule. Then he paid for the room, telling the clerk they would be on their way.

"Hope it ain't nothin serious with your sister," said the clerk. "Yer welcome to stay the night. We got another room right down the hall."

"I would if there were a doctor," said Court, "but as it is, I'd best get her home. Mother will want to look after her."

"Yer probably right," the man agreed. "My ma was always better at doctorin than any two doctors I ever seen."

Court carried Susanna down the back stairs of the hotel to the alley where he had tethered the animals, and they were well into the mountains within an hour. By sundown they had arrived, even allowing for the mule's slow pace, at the cabin where the Packards had ambushed him and where Susanna had come to his rescue. He laid her down on the bunk, wondering whether she would regret that now, wondering whether he would have been alive to bring her here if he had been left on his own to get out of that situation. He stared thoughtfully down at her for a few minutes, then went to lay a fire in the fireplace and start a stew in the pot that hung there. While it cooked, he stowed the supplies and stabled the animals. Susanna still slept.

Stretching weary muscles, Court went to sit in a large rocking chair that was the only other piece of furniture in the one-room cabin besides the bunk and a rough table with two benches set at it. Not a very luxurious place for a romantic abduction, he thought humorously. Still, it held some pleasant memories—a sweet interlude between them before her thrice-damned sister had arrived, and before

that, before the Packards had left—he laughed
softly, pictures of Susanna drifting through his
mind—Susanna calling, "Mr. Court, don't shoot;
I've come to pray with you," and riding straight
across the clearing, hardly able to stay in the saddle;
Susanna with a piece of sausage in her mouth,
taking a quick shot at the Packards and winging
one; Susanna confessing in the middle of a gun
battle that she was afraid of the dark; Susanna, just
before the snow started, bursting into a hymn and
convincing Job Packard that God had deserted him.
Court grinned. Surely there was no girl in the world
quite like her.

He rose from the chair and took a bucket out to
the stream to bring back water, making the trip
several times until he had filled the coffee pot and an
old chipped ewer and still had a bucket to spare.
Then he took the ewer over to the bunk and set it on
the floor. He gently stripped the sleeping girl to her
chemise and petticoat, after which he used a damp
rag to wipe the dust from her face, neck, and hands.
The cool water caused her to stir restlessly in her
sleep. Soon, he thought, she'll be awake. He went
over to check the stew, which was bubbling and
thickening in its pot. He added a little water, threw a
cover over Susanna to ward off the chill of nightfall,
and went back to his chair to wait, drawing off his
boots and propping his stocking feet up on the
hearth. He wondered how she would take it—not
well at first, perhaps, but later it would be all right.

She was stirring again. He went over to stand
beside the bunk, patiently letting her take her time
to wake. There was plenty of time now. Susanna's
eyes fluttered open and closed again. He thought of
speaking to her but held his peace.

To Susanna only one thing stood out in that awakening—the tall figure standing beside the bed on which she lay, illuminated from behind by firelight. Everything else was blurred by the dull pain behind her eyes. She tried to reach back in time to the last moment of consciousness she could remember, but her mind seemed to skip confusingly, flashing brief pictures that were gone before she could understand them. The only stable point of reference was the figure beside the bed, but she did not know where she and that person were or when. She closed her eyes again, perhaps in the hope that the pain behind them and the confusing problem and even consciousness itself would go away. For a time she drifted, and Aaron waited with calm patience. When she opened her eyes again, one picture from the past had steadied in her mind. She knew that she had become sick on the train—in the dining car—with Aaron chatting pleasantly across the table from her, pouring coffee, showing concern. Aaron. There was nothing between leaning weakly against Aaron on the platform outside the car and—now. And now there was nothing but Aaron, standing beside the bed.

She put her hands to her head, frightened, and whispered, "What have you done?"

"Only what I promised, Susanna. I came for you." Her hands were then over her eyes, fingers digging into her temples. "What is it, love?" he asked. "Are you in pain?"

"Why did you bring me here?"

He had sat down beside her and was frowning thoughtfully. "We can talk about that later when you feel better. You're acting as if your head hurts." He put the tips of his fingers to her temples and began with a hard firm pressure to massage them in small circles. Then with his fingers pressed still at the sides of her forehead, he ran his thumbs from the bridge of her nose under her eyebrows to the outer edge of the eye sockets—again and again, pressing, stretching the skin. "You'll have to tell me what helps," he said in a low voice, his face set in serious concentration. She wanted to tell him to leave her alone, but the pain seemed to flee before his touch. Then he had slipped those long fingers underneath her head and began to knead the back of her neck and the base of her skull behind her ears, and it was hard for her to keep her eyes open, hard not to relax and let him help her.

When finally the pain lines had smoothed away on her face and she was acquiescent to his touch, tension gone, he lifted her and carried her to the rocking chair beside the fireplace where he held her sideways on his lap with his left arm around her. "You have to eat something now," he said quietly. She made a sound of protest, but he insisted. "You've had nothing since breakfast and little enough then. You'll feel better if you eat." He speared a piece of meat from the stew, let it cool, and fed it to her, and although she allowed him to put it in her mouth, she did not chew it. Court helped himself to ladles of the stew while he waited. Finally he had to give up on getting her to eat the meat and vegetables; he fed her only sips of the thick gravy. That she swallowed obediently, half asleep. When he was satisfied that she had eaten enough to ensure that she would not be ill the next day, he put her back in the bunk, washed out the tin plate from which he had eaten, banked the fire and, after undressing, slipped in beside her. She awakened briefly and protested when he took her into his arms, but he ignored her, telling her to go back to sleep, which she did. God, it feels good to lie beside her again, he thought as he drifted into sleep himself.

69

Susanna awoke abruptly with the first cold light of dawn, and with that awakening she knew exactly where she was and with whom—even if she could not imagine how he had managed to get her there. Under the blankets with Aaron's body sprawled beside hers, his arm around her, it was warm. His body heat seemed to radiate through her, making her a part of him in that warm cocoon—even while the air of the cabin was cold against her face and her mind was frozen in revolt against the position in which he had put her. She jerked away from him, sat up, and shook his shoulder roughly.

"You've kidnapped me!" she exclaimed, her voice tight with accusation.

His eyes opened; his smile came—easy, lazy, and contented. "You're letting in the cold air, sweetheart. Come back under the covers." Court reached out for her.

"No!" Susanna wiggled away from him until her back was against the rough wall of the cabin, a foot of space between them. Careful, she cautioned herself. Don't let him see that you're afraid; don't quarrel. "Kidnapping is a crime, Aaron," she pointed out reasonably. "You could go to jail."

"Um-m." His smile was amused; he made no move to reach for her again. "What do you think I should do?" he asked idly.

"I won't tell anyone," she promised. "If you'll

take me to the nearest train station, I won't tell anyone. I'll just go on to Denver as if nothing happened. No one has to know. Just—"

He laughed—not sarcastically, as he had often enough in the past, but with genuine amusement and seeming affection. "I didn't go to all the trouble of bringing you here, Susanna, just to take you back to the train the next morning."

"Why did you bring me here?" she asked, and regretted the question as soon as she had voiced it. She did not want to hear why he had kidnapped her. "You can't have thought about the consequences of doing this," she hurried on, "or—"

"I brought you here, Susanna," he said patiently, "because it seems to be the only way I can be alone with you. Between your sister and Quincy and Mondragon—"

"They were only carrying out my wishes," said Susanna desperately.

"Those weren't your wishes before your sister started to interfere."

"That doesn't matter. Before I talked to Lilith, I thought—I didn't know—"

"I think we've had enough talk," said Aaron, frowning. He sat up and wrapped his fingers around her shoulders, forcing her away from the wall and onto her back.

Her eyes, looking up at him, went dark with fear, and she trembled in his grip. "I don't want this," she whispered, her voice a plea.

"You will." Aaron slid down beside her. The weight of his body half covering hers, the hard muscles of his arms around her, the pressure of his lips allowed her no room to struggle against him.

When finally he released her mouth, pulling her

chemise down around her waist so he could put his lips to her breast, she cried, "You mustn't rape me. You can't. You're doing what Jeremiah wanted to do."

"No." He took the nipple between his lips and felt it harden against the pressure of his tongue, as passion flooded through them both in a drenching wave. He took away her petticoat and slipped his hands between her thighs, pulling them gently apart, and she could no longer move to defend herself. When he began to stroke her, it was all she could do to keep from arching her hips to increase her own uncontrollable excitement, but she did hold still, trembling.

"Aaron, I'm not willing," she pleaded.

He ignored her words and responded to her need—guiding his own entrance into her body, penetrating her quickly, sending her mind spinning and conquering all her resolutions to hold back. When they came together, it was in the desperation of desire too long repressed. Delving deep, pressing close, holding hard, they each sought a complete possession of the other, a giving and a taking in equal measure that would ease the hunger of the body and the empty loneliness of the heart.

When finally, reluctantly, Aaron drew out of her, he kissed her tenderly and murmured against her mouth, "You were willing." She turned her head away, bitter humiliation replacing contentment, bitter tears replacing pleasant exhaustion. "Why cry, Susanna?" he asked gently. "You're where you should be—here with me."

"For how long?" She turned her body away from him, rolling into a protective ball.

Court sighed. "What does it matter?" he asked.

"None of us has more than today." He slipped his arm around her waist and pulled her into the curve of his own body. "It's cold. We'll sleep until it warms." His own contentment was slipping away as she remained tense in his arms, the shudders of her weeping quivering through his nerves, but he held her until she calmed and slept. She'll accept this, he thought. It's too good between us; she has to accept it.

70

When Susanna awoke for the second time that morning, she was alone in the bunk. Not daring to move or to open her eyes, she listened for the sound of him, but she heard nothing. She had the terrible feeling that he might be standing beside the bunk staring down at her as he had been the night before, waiting to remind her that, for all her protests, she had come to him willingly in the end. Her mouth tightened with grief and humiliation, and her eyes flew open. He was not there.

Cautiously she probed the far corners of the cabin, which she now recognized. Her heart leaped with hope. She knew exactly where she was and how to get home if she could just get away. She sprang up and ran to the windows but could see him nowhere. Did she dare hope that he had left for good? Or would he return any minute now? Desperately she began to pull on those pieces of her clothing that she could find, her eyes darting to the tempting water in the pitcher. She felt that his touch was everywhere on her like a stamp of possession, and she longed to wash it away but dared not waste a single precious second.

With her hair streaming wildly around her, her
blouse only half buttoned, her jacket clutched in one
hand, she burst out the door and ran across the
clearing toward the road that lay beyond the trees.
She was so panic-stricken that she forgot Court had
a horse she might have ridden. Afraid of falling, she
kept her eyes on the ground as she entered the
woods, and the thunder of her heartbeat in her own
ears seemed deafening. As a result, she was taken
completely by surprise when Court's arms closed
around her. He had been coming back, naked, from
a bath in the stream when he saw her dash from the
cabin and moved to head her off.

"Leaving without saying good-bye?" he asked,
tightening his hold on her. "You surely didn't plan
to return to town in a state of such disarray? Why,
your blouse isn't even buttoned, Susanna." She had
been pushing against his chest, but her fingers flew
automatically to the forgotten buttons. "Shall I help
you?" He pulled her hands away and stripped the
garments from her. "And you seem to have forgotten your chemise and petticoat. Couldn't you
find them among the bedclothes?" Susanna backed
away from him, embarrassed under his gaze,
intimidated by the anger that seemed to underlie his
sarcasm.

"Look at me," he commanded.

"I have a right to leave," she mumbled. "You
shouldn't have brought me here."

"When you leave, it will be because I'm ready to
let you," he replied, his voice cold. Then
moderating his tone, he placed a hand gently against
the side of her neck. "You mentioned rape this
morning, but the truth is I've never forced you;
you've always come to me willingly, although it

sometimes took a little persuasion." He smiled at her with whimsical humor, and Susanna blushed. "Our pleasure in each other is something special," he continued. "You don't seem to understand how unusual and beautiful it is."

"Pleasure isn't enough," said Susanna, turning her eyes away from him resentfully.

"It's all there is," he retorted. "That's obviously something you need to learn." He picked her up, holding her against his chest, and carried her back to the cabin, where he set her down and threw the bolt on the door. "I'll have to be more careful about leaving you alone, won't I?"

"My clothes are still out there."

Court smiled rather grimly. "Let them stay. Without clothes, I think you'll be less likely to try to run away from me."

"You—you can't keep me completely naked." Her face flushed with humiliation and dismay.

"I can't think of anything more pleasant," Court replied sardonically. He was pulling on his own pants and boots as the tears began to slip down her cheeks. "Here." He tossed his white shirt to her. "You can put that on."

Bare-chested, he went to the fire to lay more wood. Susanna dragged on the silk shirt, which covered her only to the thighs and clung to her revealingly.

"Very fetching," said Court as he turned to stare at her. "Even if your mood fails to improve, the sight of you should provide me with some enjoyment."

Susanna did not know what to do with herself. To hide under the covers on the bunk seemed like an open invitation for Court to join her. She had to

settle for huddling in the rocking chair with her feet
and legs tucked up and her arms crossed protectively
over her chest. To Aaron, sitting at the table
cleaning a rifle, she looked like a child who had
offended and was trying to remain inconspicuous, if
not invisible. He said nothing for an hour or more,
giving himself time to get his temper and disappointment under control. Twice now she had run away,
although he knew that her feelings for him were as
strong as his were for her. Her behavior was
irrational and infuriating. He hardly trusted himself
to touch her, regretted having said she could not
have her clothes back, for her nakedness under the
shirt kept his desire simmering.

Finally he rose, unable to stay cooped up with her
in the cabin any longer. "I'm going to chop wood,"
he announced brusquely. "Don't try to run. I'll be
just outside." He left and in the next hour enlarged
the clearing by one tree, making a good start at
reducing it to firewood. When he returned with a
load of split logs, his restlessness somewhat
assuaged, Susanna was still in the rocker.

"Don't you know how to take care of a house?"
he asked. "You should have made the bed by now
and started the stew."

She glanced up, longing to defy him but afraid,
and he saw the defiance and chuckled. "Of course,
you may prefer other domestic pursuits," he
drawled as he pulled her to her feet. "Is that it?" He
slipped his hands under the tail of the shirt and
cupped her buttocks, lifting her up against him
without force, but with a studied intimacy. Susanna
pulled back sharply from the contact and stumbled
because he had lifted her almost off the floor.
Laughing again, Court steadied her. "I guess you

prefer housework, after all." He gave her a gentle
push toward the hearth. "Swing the pot over the fire
and put more water in," he suggested; "that is if
you want to eat dinner tonight. If not, I'll let you
suggest a better pastime."

Susanna did what she was told, putting the stew
on to simmer and then making up the bed. In the
process she found her chemise and petticoat and
quickly started to draw on the latter.

"Leave it alone," said Aaron from the other side
of the room, where he had begun to mend a worn
saddle strap. Susanna stopped, her bare foot poised
to step into the cambric skirt. "Put the petticoat on
the bed, Susanna," he ordered. "I like to look at
your legs."

"You're abominable," she cried.

"Very likely," he replied, grinning.

"I'm not your slave."

"More's the pity." He rose, gave her a good-
natured kiss on the nose, and went to check the
stew.

That night after dinner, he taught her poker, and
they sat prosaically at the table playing by firelight.
Court watched her closely as she became more
nervous and distracted, as she glanced from under
her lashes at the bunk they would share later in the
evening. Let her stew, he thought. He was determined that the lovemaking she dreaded would occur
the next time because she initiated it herself.

71

In the morning Court was moody and silent. He
fixed the breakfast and assigned her no tasks. After
they had eaten, he went out to chop wood, leaving
her in the rocking chair. Susanna's tension was so

great that she wanted to scream or weep. She thought it would almost be a relief if he took her to bed again—just to get it over with. But one more time wouldn't necessarily satisfy him, she reminded herself. He could keep her here as long as he cared to and do whatever he wanted with her whenever it suited him. Shivering, despairing, she rocked and stared into the fire, which hardly served to warm her when she had only his silk shirt to wear. Still, she dared not move toward the petticoat that lay on the bed for fear he would return.

It wouldn't have been so bad, she thought with shame, if she could submit coldly, but it seemed that once he began with her, she was helpless. Just thinking about his lovemaking caused that twisting ache in her loins. Finally she heard the axe strokes cease, and Court returned to the cabin. Without glancing at her, he went to the washbasin and splashed the sweat from his face, chest, and arms. Then he turned and said quietly, "I have to go hunting if we're to have meat." Susanna remained silent, stared at her hands. "I'm going to have to tie you." He did not sound pleased about it, but his tone was matter-of-fact.

"T-tie me?"

"Yes. Your wrists and ankles. You can sleep while I'm gone. You won't be uncomfortable."

"You can't," Susanna gasped, her eyes widening with fear.

"You leave me no choice," he replied in the same quiet voice. "Lie down on your side on the bunk."

"No." Her refusal was a bare whisper.

Court did not care to argue with her. He swept her up out of the chair, deposited her on the bed, turning her on her side, and pulled her arms behind her. He was gentle enough, but his grip was firm, and when she tried to pull away, he said, "Hold still now, Susanna. I don't want to hurt you." Then he tied her wrists together.

"What if someone comes?" she asked, her voice high and frightened.

"No one will come here," he replied as he bound her ankles. Then he turned her so that she faced the room, and kneeling by the bunk, he kissed her lips as he smoothed the hair gently away from her face and pulled the covers over her. "I'll be no more than a couple of hours," he told her. "Why don't you try to sleep?"

As he left the cabin, her eyes, wild with fear, followed him. Oh, God, she thought, is he doing this to punish me for trying to escape? He had drawn shutters over the windows before bolting the door and leaving her in the dark with only the embers of the fire on the hearth to shed a small glow in one section of the room. Her body had gone rigid with fear before the sound of his horse's hooves faded. Her eyes began the first of hundreds of desperate searches of that dark room. Her ears strained for sounds in the silence.

The terror that overwhelmed her was not based on any unformed, undefined child's fear of the dark, but on fears that had pursued her ever since her imprisonment in the Packards' valley. She had dealt with the recurring episodes of terror and the night-mares after her return to Amnonville by working— on her house and at Lilith's place. She had never let herself rest or think; she had slept little during that time.

Here there were no distractions, nothing to protect her from memories of the threats and abuse she had endured at the hands of Jeremiah and Job. She knew, of course, that those two were dead—Jeremiah because she had poisoned him and Job because Lilith had hung him. But not all the Packards had been caught that night. Others must be loose in the mountains. Perhaps they had been watching the cabin—waiting for Court to leave, waiting for a chance to take vengeance on her. Job had said she would die by fire. What if they set fire to the cabin while she was tied and helpless? They had set fire to Court's house. Her thoughts went around and around in spiraling horror. Every sound heralded their arrival. Her sweat soaked the shirt and bedding. She strained against her bonds until her wrists and ankles were raw. Her breath came in frantic gasps, making her dizzy and light-headed.

Then she heard the horse's hooves in the clearing. She heard boots strike the ground outside the door. She heard the bolt loosen. She heard everything magnified a hundredfold by terror. And she lost consciousness. Court had been gone one hour and ten minutes.

"I got a couple of rabbits," he remarked as he dropped the animals on the hearth and went to open the shutters. "They'll only last a meal or two, but I didn't want to leave you too long since you seemed nervous about it." He sat down on the edge of the bunk. "Susanna?" Her eyes remained closed, and he could see that her hair was wet. "What the hell is this?" he muttered. He flung the covers back and discovered that his shirt was soaked and plastered to her body. Frowning now with sharp worry, he lifted her eyelid; she was unconscious. His hands were shaking as he undid the ropes at her wrists and ankles. He had tied them loosely enough; he had taken special care, and yet the skin over those delicate bones was chafed and raw.

My God, what can have happened? he asked himself, but there was no answer. Her skin was cool, damp, so it couldn't be a sudden fever. He looked around the cabin but found no sign that anyone had been there.

What if she's dying? he thought in a panic. Could he get her into town in time to find help? And that stupid young doctor—would he know what to do? What if she were already dead? No. He could feel the warm breath coming and going at her nostrils and the slow, even beat of her heart when he pressed his fingers between her breasts.

Court rose from the bunk and went over to the hearth to get water, a rag and a towel. When he returned, there was still no sign of consciousness, so he unbuttoned the wet shirt and stripped it off her. Gently he wiped the sweat away from her body. Then he took the chipped bowl outside and emptied it, pouring clean water in. With that he sponged off her face and neck, lifting her damp hair away to give access to the nape, then running the rag around to slide it over her collarbones and the slender column of her throat. At last she stirred, and Court felt almost weak with relief.

There was confusion in her eyes at first, then terror—wild animal terror. Just seeing it accelerated his heartbeat. "Susanna, what in God's name happened?" When she seemed unable to speak, Court rose quickly, got water in a tin cup and fed it to her drop by drop. "There's nothing to fear, Susanna," he assured her. "Can't you tell me now what happened?"

"Packards," she whispered in an unsteady voice.

"That can't be," he replied.

"They were coming to hurt me, to burn the cabin with me in it after—"

"Susanna—"

"Jeremiah, and Job, and some I don't even know."

He remembered well enough then how terrified she had been as she lay in his arms after their escape to the cave, how she told him over and over the things they had done and said to her, the threats they had made. He cursed himself for leaving when she had begged him not to. He had simply dismissed her fears that someone would come while she was tied and helpless. Still, how could he have known that she thought there were members of the Packard gang left in the mountains?

"Susanna," he said, swallowing his own dismay, "the Packards are gone now." He took her cold hands into his and began to massage her fingers. "Most of them are dead. A lot of them I killed myself, and the few that were left after Quincy and I got you out of there and after all the hangings—they ran for their lives."

"No, some must have—"

"They're gone, all of them. Believe me. If I'd known you were still afraid, I would have told you."

Blinking back tears, Susanna turned away, still shivering.

"Well," said Court, hoping to distract her, "we'd better clean those rabbits if we're going to eat tonight."

She twisted back in panic. "Where are you going?"

"Just outside," he replied reassuringly. "You can—"

"No." She caught at his wrist before he could move. "Don't leave me."

"Susanna."

"Please." She tightened her fingers frantically.

"Sweetheart, we can both—"

"Bolt the door," she whispered urgently. "You've left it open." Frowning, he glanced at the door. "And the shutters," she whispered.

"Susanna, I'm not going to close the shutters. It's a nice day. You can come outside with me." When he leaned over to brush his lips against her cheek, she drew him down to her with desperate strength.

"Don't leave me, Aaron. Please. Please." She turned her face up to catch his lips, rolling completely onto her side until they were lying against each other on the bed, kissing deeply.

"Susanna, I can't hold you like this and not make love to you," he groaned.

She tightened her arms and pressed against him. "I don't care," she whispered against his mouth. "I'll do whatever you want if you'll just stay with me. Promise, promise."

Court's eyes closed with pain. She was offering herself to him as he had wanted her to—but not because she was willing to stay with him, only because he, with callous disregard, had terrified her into submission. His desire slipped away in sadness of heart, in dismay and disappointment, and Susanna, feeling against his body the evidence that he no longer wanted her, was afraid that she would be abandoned again, and she began to cry.

"Sh-sh, love," he murmured quietly. "I'm not going away. Be still." He undressed and lay down again to hold her, their bodies touching lightly from chest to knee, and he began to stroke her back—long, slow, gentle strokes that inevitably aroused his own desire and hers too, he thought. Or was she just afraid to object? Testing her, he moved his hand to her thighs and ran his fingers along the

backs of them up to her buttocks where he felt the
muscles tighten. He moved his hand down again and
repeated the caress, sliding his fingers between her
legs and stroking up until he was stopped in the
warm valley where her thighs joined. He did this
again and again until she shivered and all the
muscles under his touch went slack. Then he lifted
her knee to his thigh and caressed her more
intimately until she began to moan softly and her
legs closed on his hand, trapping the fingers that had
driven her almost beyond sanity. Quickly he rolled
her onto her back. When he was poised over her
with his knees between hers, with her breath coming
in gasps and her head tossing, he tangled his fingers
in her hair and held her face turned up to his. "Look
at me, Susanna," he commanded. Her eyelids
opened over blue eyes, dazed with passion. "Tell me
that you want me. Say it! Admit that you want to
stay here with me."

"No." Her eyes closed and her hips arched up to
him; he took her because he could not stop himself.
Although Susanna responded ardently as she always
did, to Court it was a bitter triumph at best, for she
had come to him in fear and would leave him if he
allowed it. He had wanted more than mere physical
response. He had asked for more and been refused.

With that bitterness of spirit eating at him, he
said, "If you think you can let me go now, I'll do
something about our dinner."

Susanna said nothing, let her hands fall away
from his back where she had been dreamily savoring
the feel of the hard muscles beneath her fingertips.
He lifted himself away and stared down at her for a
moment. At last turning quickly, he picked up the
lantern and his clothes and left the cabin.

Susanna was not hurt by what he had said to her; she knew she had provoked the bitterness by refusing to tell him what he had wanted to hear. Why, she wondered idly, did he want to believe that she stayed with him willingly when, for his part, he would make no commitment to her and wanted nothing beyond the pleasure of the moment? He had told her himself that was all there was. Could her acquiescence enhance that pleasure? She thought not. The pleasure was physical—lay in the repeated lovemaking, which seemed to improve each time. He had so sated her that day that her body felt heavy with contentment. She had no energy left for emotion or for movement—no fears, no desires, even no regrets—only the sad knowledge that it would all come to an end. Everything he said meant that he would not stay with her, and the longer she stayed with him, the worse it would be for her when she returned. Were it known that she had been with him in the cabin, she would be fair game for any man who wanted her. How could Lilith and Quincy protect her? And why should they want to? What would there be to protect if she gave herself willingly, repeatedly, knowingly to a man who had made and would make no promises to her? And Lilith had said she might become pregnant. Surely the longer she stayed here, the more likely that became. What would happen to her and to the poor child in Amnonville when Aaron had tired of her? Bad enough that she was an outcast herself. How could she raise a child that way?

Still held in the calm and dreamlike thrall of her physical contentment, Susanna explored the possibilities of escape. The key must lie in Aaron's insistence that she admit—what? That she belonged with him for as long as he wanted her? That there was a rightness in their being together? That she wanted to be with him—not just when he had aroused her into mindless passion, but before and after and at all times? And if she gave him what he wanted? If she said what he wanted to hear and never resisted his touch or her vulnerability to it? What then? Would he tire of her and release her? Would he become careless and let her escape? It was only two hours—or was it four?—to town if she could take the horse. How stupid she had been to run when she could have ridden yesterday. But then perhaps he had been watching her all the time.

And what if he still kept her, and there was no chance to escape? Susanna stared at the ceiling above her, her body still floating on the lapping sea of spent passion and her mind planning her escape from the whip that had driven her there. If Aaron did not let her go through knowing indifference or through carelessness, she would have to find some other way.

She rose and went to the door of the cabin which he had left open. There was a moon low over the trees, and by the light she saw, hanging from the peg on the wall, the carcasses of the two rabbits he had skinned. Aaron was not there, but she knew he had not gone for good. She could hear the horse moving restlessly in the lean-to. Was he walking off his anger? Perhaps he wanted to frighten her with his absence. She leaned against the door, aware of her own nakedness only in that the evening air was cold against her skin. She did not think of going back for the shirt, a flimsy covering at best.

Court saw her immediately as he came out of the woods. He had only a towel around his waist, and she watched him as he strode toward her, thinking how handsome and powerful a man he was with the

moonlight catching the gold-white hair on his chest
and head and highlighting the smooth muscles of his
body but darkening the already dark skin.

"Where are your clothes?" he demanded. He had
been shocked at her nakedness in the doorway and
at her beauty, which seemed greater than ever.

"I don't know," Susanna replied. "You took
them." She put her arms around his waist and
leaned her head against his chest.

For a long moment he was too surprised to reply.
"This is a change," he growled.

"Will you take me to the stream to bathe?"

His hand came to rest hesitantly at her waist. "It's
cold."

She moved her cheek against his chest. "You're
warm."

Court hesitated a moment longer, then swung her
up in his arms and carried her across the clearing
and through the trees to the stream, no more than
two hundred yards away. When they reached the
bank and Susanna could see the glint of the moonlight shining through the trees into the water, she
turned her head and kissed his shoulder. Court
stiffened and his arms tightened around her. Whatever he had had in mind before, his reaction was to
put her feet briefly onto the ground while he
loosened the towel around his waist and dropped it.
Then he picked her up again and waded into the
water until he reached a depression in midstream
that was waist-deep. Already the icy current swirled
around her hips and feet and she shivered. "I
warned you," he said softly. But he let her down all
the same, keeping his hold on her waist when her
feet touched the rocky bottom. "I have no soap."

"It doesn't matter," she said, her teeth
chattering. "I just want to get wet all over."

"Well, you are now. Have you had enough?"

"No. I have to wash my hair."

"God damn it, Susanna. You'll catch your death."

Holding tightly to his hand with one of hers and holding her nose with the other, she ducked under water before he could stop her. "Would you swish my hair around in the water when I go under this time?" she asked, coming up for air.

"Hell no, I won't. You can wash your hair tomorrow if it's sunny. In the meantime you're going back to the cabin." He swept her up again and moved in long strides out of the water and through the trees and clearing in about half the time he had taken to make the trip before. Susanna was shivering violently by the time they reached the cabin, and Court was muttering angrily under his breath about the foolishness of women.

"Why my foolishness? Who kept me in bed making love until the sun was gone?" she demanded humorously when he set her down in front of the hearth.

Again the look he gave her was wary and puzzled. Because he could think of nothing to say in the face of that undeniable remark, he built a roaring fire as quickly as he could after tossing another towel to her and wrapping one around his own hips. But he did not dress; instead he ignored his own discomfort to go out for the rabbits he had skinned. Susanna dried herself slowly, watching him as he spitted the rabbits and put them on a rack over the fire in the huge hearth.

"Are you satisfied that I can cook well enough to keep you from starving?" he asked sharply; he was somewhat disconcerted by her close observation of him, since he was not that used to being semi-naked himself.

"Of course," Susanna replied. "Do you have another towel?"

Court took another from an untidy pile on a wall shelf and handed it to her.

"I meant for you." She stepped behind him and began to dry his back, saying, "I'm afraid I'm not yet shameless enough to do the rest of you."

Court found it hard to believe that she was willing to dry any part of him. He quickly finished the job and drew his pants on. "Do you want the shirt?" he asked.

She sighed. "Is there anything else? It must be stiff with sweat."

He looked around. "I should have gone to get your clothes," he admitted. "Some damned animal may have carried them off by now."

"At best they're full of ants," she sighed, putting her hand on his arm to forestall him when he started toward the door.

"Well, there are a few more blankets."

Susanna smiled. "I've never worn a blanket. I'm not quite sure how to go about it."

At her smile, his face relaxed into tenderness, and he cupped her chin in one hand and brushed his lips across hers. She willed herself not to become tense; this was what she had planned, to give him what he wanted, or what he thought he wanted. She let herself relax against him so that her nipples brushed into his chest hair and hardened. Heaven help me, she thought. It doesn't take much pretending.

Surprisingly, Court let her go and turned the two rabbits on the pit. Then he got the softest blanket and wrapped it under her right arm, tying the two upper corners over the opposite shoulder, and belting the whole affair with a neckerchief. "Modified Roman," he remarked.

"Really? Roman ladies must have felt remarkably itchy." They both began to laugh, and in that easy mood, Court pulled her down on his lap in the rocking chair and rubbed her hair dry in front of the fire while the rabbits roasted.

As they shared the larger of the two animals, the smaller being reserved for the next day, Court said, "Tomorrow we'll have to go to look for roots, leaves, berries, that sort of thing." She glanced up at him in alarm. "Both of us," he said soothingly.

Susanna looked down again. "Roots and berries? I thought bears ate those."

"Well, they'll keep us from getting scurvy," said Court dryly.

Susanna giggled. "Only sailors get scurvy. Everyone knows that."

"Sailors and people who try to live exclusively on rabbit meat."

"Maybe you should shoot a bear," she suggested. "If the bear's already full of roots and berries, we can just eat the bear."

Smiling at her fanciful ideas of nutrition, Court tossed the rabbit bones into the fire and wiped out the plates. Then he took her back onto his lap and combed out her hair, which was hopelessly tangled after several days of inattention and hours of love-making. When she discovered his gentleness, for he took his time and disentangled all the snarls without ever hurting her, she relaxed against him trustingly, her mind floating back to childhood when her mother had washed her hair and then dragged the comb through it roughly, as if the tangles were some sin that had to be atoned for with pain. In many

ways sin was less painful than virtue, Susanna
thought wonderingly. Why then did anyone bother
to be virtuous?—when heaven seemed so far away, a
distant dream, and pleasure was warm under her
cheek, a steadily beating heart in her ear, a gentle
hand creating small shivers of pleasure along her
scalp as the comb ran through her hair from her
head to her waist.

"What shall I do with it now?" Aaron asked
when he had combed it all out.

Susanna murmured in contentment and turned
her body into his, slipping her arms around his waist
and rubbing her cheek sensuously against his bare,
warm shoulder. It doesn't matter what I do, she
thought dreamily. It's all part of the plan to escape.

"Take it to bed, I guess," he muttered, and he
picked her up and carried her to the bunk, divesting
her of her Roman blanket before he slid her under
the covers there. Susanna curled her body into his
and raised her mouth for his kiss.

72

Warmth permeated every inch of her body with a
slow fire of well-being when Susanna awoke the next
morning and reached out for Aaron. Even his absence from the bunk did not penetrate for some time
her drowsy lethargy; she snuggled back under the
covers and drifted, savoring a thousand deliciously
abrasive sensations of a woman who had been so
well loved that her body hovered on a fine line
between past satiety and present readiness to be
rearoused by the smallest touch or glance. For long
minutes both her mind and body focused completely
on that blank, intense awareness of Court. Only

when she heard through the unshuttered windows his approach across the clearing did she realize that he had been gone and that she might have missed a chance to escape had she been less wrapped in sensuality. Her mind moved slowly, telling herself she would never get away if she allowed him to submerge her aims in his own, but physical satisfaction overcame mental alarm. The very fact that he had left her alone and untied indicated that his defenses were going down, she assured herself; there would be other chances, other—

"I only found your skirt," he told her.

Susanna opened her eyes and smiled at him lazily. He was standing beside the bunk holding the tattered remains of the garment. "You don't seem too upset to be left just a skirt to wear—and not one that's likely to cover very much of you," he remarked dryly.

She tried to think about what he said, but she was looking at him; he was wearing knee-high moccasins, buckskin trousers, and a buckskin shirt carelessly unlaced over his chest. He looked so different from the black-suited lawyer she was used to confronting—he seemed half savage, half clothed, half again as exciting. Without thinking, Susanna rose on her elbow, skeins of silken black hair swinging across her face. She pushed it away—over her shoulder—revealing sleep-flushed cheeks and, where the covers had slipped down around her hips, rose-tipped breasts. Court's breath caught sharply, and he moved a half step toward her, dropping the ragged skirt. As Susanna's head went back and her eyes opened wide, lips parted in quick, short breaths, her hand came away from her hair to reach out to him. Her fingertips touched the

wiry curls, the hard muscles just below his waist. A
shudder passed over her body, and he swore with
soft wonder and dropped down beside her to take
her into his arms. He had long since realized that he
never seemed to be able to get enough of her, but
now—now Susanna seemed driven by the same
compulsions.

They came together with a slow, hot passion, and
afterwards Susanna felt the most irrational
happiness, a happiness that refused to acknowledge
the fact that she had herself initiated that lovemaking without the slightest concern for how it
might affect her chances of getting home. She was
lying against his chest with her arms loosely clasped
around his waist and one leg sprawled over his when
she was overcome by that wave of pure, heedless
joy, and she responded to it by hugging him tightly,
planting a wet, noisy kiss on his shoulder and
laughing aloud with delight.

Aaron, who had been half asleep, raised his head
in surprise and asked, "What was that all about?"

"Breakfast," said Susanna. "Aren't you going to
give me any breakfast?"

"Good Lord, woman," said Court, laughing and
sitting up abruptly, "is there no end to your
demands?"

"None whatever," Susanna assured him. "And
right now I demand my breakfast."

"Then you'll have to catch it yourself." He stood
up and pulled her out of bed after him. "Here, put
on your skirt, hussy." He tossed her the ragged skirt
and pulled on his trousers. Then without bothering
to provide any other garments for either of them, he
grabbed a hide bag from the table with one hand and
Susanna's wrist with the other and began to drag

her, laughing and protesting the damage to her feet, across the clearing.

"Well, I can pick you up, but I won't stand responsible for what that might lead to," he replied, "especially with an insatiable baggage like you."

"What's an insatiable baggage?" she asked, skipping along beside him over soft pine needles toward the stream.

"That's a woman who keeps her man in bed when he should be out hunting and fishing."

"I haven't done anything." Susanna gave him a look of exaggerated innocence that delighted and amused him. "You're just trying to excuse yourself for not feeding me."

"Look at you," he said. He had stopped on the path and was smiling at her with eyes narrowed speculatively. "Not a stitch on you above the waist, and when I touch you, you catch fire." He touched her breast lightly as if to demonstrate, and she shivered. "Just as I said," he muttered, sweeping her into his arms and kissing her until her mouth opened under his. "You've forgotten all about breakfast, haven't you?" He tipped her face up. "Haven't you?" he demanded.

"M-maybe you'd better provide me with a blouse and stop touching me," she replied, stumbling over her words.

"That's not likely on the one hand or possible on the other." He muttered as he released her.

"What happened to my clothes on the train?"

"They're checked at the town where I took you off."

"I never did understand what happened to me or how you happened to be there," said Susanna, frowning.

"I don't imagine you did," Court muttered.

It occurred to Susanna that Lilith might discover that her sister had disappeared on the way to Denver. Maybe the railroad would inform her about the luggage. Maybe she would think to look here. Someone might describe the man who had taken Susanna off the train. Maybe—

"First we've got to dig up some worms," said Court.

"Worms?" Susanna forgot about a possible rescue and gaped at him.

"That's right. We need worms to bait the hooks."

"Why?"

"Because fish like worms. They try to eat the worms and get caught on the hooks."

"That's disgusting."

"I thought you wanted breakfast."

"I certainly don't want to eat any fish that have been eating worms. Would you eat worms?"

"I'm not a fish," snapped Aaron. "You're being illogical. The most delicious trout come from streams like this that are ice cold and fed by melting snow." Aaron sat down cross-legged beside the stream and began to tie lengths of string to metal hooks, all of which he took from the rawhide bag. Then he used a flat stone to turn over the soft earth by the stream, revealing fat, wiggling worms. The expression on Susanna's face when he looked up set him to laughing. "If I bait your hook and drop it in for you, do you want to fish, or would you rather hide behind a tree?"

Susanna took a few steps closer to him. "Well, I've never been fishing," she said wistfully. "Won't the hook hurt the worm and the fish?"

Court sighed. "I don't know, Susanna, but that's how it's done."

"What should I do?"

He put a fat worm on a hook, wound one end of the string around her hand and, after stretching her out on her stomach on a flat rock that hung over the water, dropped the hook upstream. "Now just lie still, be quiet, don't fall in, and if a fish bites, pull in your line or, better yet, tell me."

"How do I tell if a fish—"

"You'll feel a tug."

Aaron baited his own hook, took a position further down stream, and promptly caught a fish. Susanna soon forgot her hook and became fascinated with the water. In some places where the rocks were submerged just below the water line, the water ran over them in satin swells; in others where the rocks jutted up into the air, the water turned to white, lacy foam, flinging little drops of ice into her face; where the stream bed was deep, the water looked black, smooth, and almost still; at shallower depths it ranged from deep green to pale green to white, and there were silver coins of sunlight dancing on its surface, and everywhere it changed— the currents, the textures, the colors; the water was never still and never the same, and Susanna was mesmerized by its beauty and variety. She had been staring for several minutes at the movement of the water around a particular rock when she realized that she was looking at a fish swaying languidly back and forth in the shelter of the boulder.

"Aaron," she whispered excitedly. "A fish." She never took her eyes from her find.

He glanced up from his place, having caught three fish while she was water-watching like a daydreaming child. "Good for you," he murmured, smiling. He rose to his feet in an easy motion, checking first to see that the lines of the fish he had caught were firm. Then he walked upstream and knelt beside her, ready to help her pull in her catch. He took her hand, the one around which the fishing line was wrapped, and tested the tension. To his surprise there was none.

"There it is," she whispered. "Can you see? Right in front of the big rock."

Frowning, Court followed the direction of her pointing finger and saw the little fish. "Susanna, you haven't caught it," he pointed out. "It's not enough to just spot one. He's not going to jump into the pan, you know."

"Oh, I know." She half turned and smiled up at him. "I just wanted you to see it. Isn't it pretty? I'll bet it's a baby. How big are they supposed to be?" She had turned back on her stomach and was resting her chin again on her hand, smiling and watching her fish. Aaron shook his head and leaned over to drop a kiss on her cheek just in front of her ear. He might well have caught another fish or two and thus secured their breakfast in the time it had taken him to come to look at her little, uncaught fish, but how could he be angry with her? He shook his head again and drew in her line to see if it still had a worm on it. Then he threw it back and returned to his place.

"Aaron," she called excitedly a little later, "I've got a bite."

"So do I, love," he muttered, carefully working his fish in.

"But I don't know what to do."

He sighed and secured his line without bothering to check to see that the hook was well set, hoping his catch would not get away.

He discovered, when he got to Susanna, that there

was indeed tension against her hand, tension that did not give at all. He frowned and studied the position of the line.

"What have I caught?" she demanded excitedly. "Is it a big one? I can't pull it in."

"It's a big one all right," Court informed her. She was squirming with excitement. "You've got the hook caught on that rock out there."

"I caught a rock?" Susanna began to laugh and could not stop, sitting cross-legged on the bank with her ragged skirt hiked up, doubled over, laughing and laughing.

"Very funny," said Aaron. "How do you think I'm going to get my hook back?"

"Well," said Susanna, going off into fresh peals of merriment, "maybe if you ask the rock nicely. Or you might wade out and wrestle him for the hook."

"What am I going to do with you?" He cut the line and turned to look at her, beginning to grin.

"Feed me," she suggested. "I get light-headed when I'm hungry."

"I ought to throw you in."

"Okay," said Susanna promptly and threw her arms around his waist. "But I won't go in by myself."

"Come on," said Court, pulling her up with him. "Before the ones I caught get away."

When they had pan-fried and eaten their fish for breakfast, the sun was already directly overhead, and Aaron announced that if they were going to gather things for dinner, they had better start.

"We've living like Indians, aren't we? Spending all our time finding things to eat."

"Not all our time," said Aaron slowly, his eyes reigniting the restless ache in her. "We've spent a lot of time making love." Then he let it drop. "But you're right. When you're providing your own food and shelter, it does take a lot of time. And it's not a bad life."

"Would you be content to live this way?" she asked curiously. "Always?"

"I am content," he replied.

Susanna looked down; he had not answered the question. "Well, I can't go running around the woods with no shoes; the rocks hurt my feet. And I'd just as soon not go half naked. So maybe you should go by yourself." She wondered without any real tension how he would respond. Would he leave her alone?

"Put on my shirt." He tossed the silk shirt to her, and she grimaced.

"That doesn't help my feet," she reminded him.

"I have some moccasins I bought from an Indian for the child of a friend. Maybe they'll fit you." He rummaged in a corner and came up with some moccasins that laced up to the knees as his did.

Susanna accepted them and measured them against her feet, finding them large enough, but having no idea how to tie them on with the hide thongs. Aaron pushed her into the rocking chair and knelt in front of her to fasten them on, and she sighed and leaned back, unthinking, to enjoy the touch of his fingers on her feet and calves as he bound the soft hide against her skin. When he had finished, Susanna stretched like a hearth cat who had been petted and scratched, and she curled her toes luxuriously against the palms of his hands. "M-m-m," she murmured low in her throat. "They're so soft."

Aaron eyed her thoughtfully. "Do you know that you're a thoroughgoing sensualist?" he asked.

She smiled at him with heavy lidded eyes. "What's that?"

"Something that would surprise your very strait-laced parents, I imagine," he murmured, half to himself.

They set off after that into the woods with Susanna slipping her hand into his and skipping from time to time to keep up with his long-legged stride, chattering happily, stopping to pick up pine cones and peer at wildflowers, which caused him to comment that they could eat neither.

"Well, what should I look for?" she asked happily, not to be discouraged by practical considerations.

"Berries, wild onions, mushrooms."

"No," she cried sharply.

Court looked at her with surprise. "No, what?"

"Mushrooms." Her voice was shaking.

"You're thinking of toadstools," he said quietly. "I can tell the difference, sweetheart."

Susanna just shook her head, her eyes haunted. "You didn't see him double up. You didn't put them in the coffee, spend a whole afternoon fixing them, pick them right in front of Marrymay. You didn't—"

"All right, Susanna. No mushrooms." Court was appalled that her lighthearted happiness had dissipated so suddenly. "Can you recognize a wild onion?"

She was trembling and could only shake her head. He described the narrow green shoots to her and soon managed to interest her in looking for them and for berries. She first discovered chokeberries with a cry of delight. "They're better for jelly and wine than for eating," he admonished, but Susanna had to try them and was surprised at the pungent flavor. "We'll find something you'll like better," he assured her.

Next she found a patch of squawberries, which Aaron again told her were good for jelly—and bears.

"Bears?" Susanna eyed him dubiously.

"They love squawberries," he assured her. "Shall we eat them till a bear comes up to protest and then try to catch the bear?"

Susanna threw a handful at him and jumped up to continue her search. Soon they were climbing, the ground rising steeply under their feet, rocks jutting up among the trees, and Susanna began to feel ill—mildly nauseated, dizzy, and short of breath—but she persisted, dancing ahead of Aaron, who climbed at an even pace. Finally when they came to a flat section of ground covered with spruce, she stopped, a little frightened at how weak and sick she felt. "Aaron?" she murmured, putting her hands to her head. "Have the berries made me sick?"

He caught up with her and drew her into the circle of his arm. "You're taking it too fast," he explained. "It's high here, higher than you're used to. We call it mountain fever, what you're feeling."

"I'm sick?" she asked, alarmed. "What can we do for it?"

"Lie down," he ordered, pulling her down beside him. "If we had mountain sage or Oregon grape-root, I'd brew you tea."

"How do you know such things?" she asked, resting her face against his shoulder.

"My mother," he replied shortly, and his tone of voice invited no questions. "Since we have none, you'll lie quietly till you feel better. The air is thinner up here. That's what's making you sick."

She nodded. "I feel as if I can't catch my breath. But what about dinner?" she asked, sitting up.

"There's time." He pulled her down beside him again, and they lay on their backs, looking up at the sky through the boughs of the trees. "If you'll stop talking and frightening them away, you'll see birds."

Obediently Susanna fell silent and watched. When she saw a flash of blue, she touched his cheek and he whispered, "Bluebird."

"I know that. I can see it's blue," she whispered back. "What about the brown one?" Aaron identified the ptarmigan for her, telling her that it was only brown in summer, that in winter it was white with protective coloration. After that she lay contented in the circle of his arm, marveling at the depth of his knowledge of the area, its plants and wildlife. Finally they began to climb again, this time slowly, and they found wild onions and dropped them into an ugly flowered bag Aaron carried.

"What is that?" she asked.

"It's a flour sack. Haven't you seen one before?"

"Why does it have that ugly design on it? If it's just to carry flour, they could as well have used some decent, plain—"

Court grinned. "Women all over the West buy their flour in these and are perfectly happy to wear the sacks."

Susanna's eyes opened wide. "I don't believe you."

"Well, it may not be as elegant as the gowns you wore at Lilith's," said Aaron, "but a good flour sack would cover you up more decently—more decently than what you're wearing now, for that matter," he added, glancing at her ragged skirt, which offered tantalizing glimpses of her legs.

"Well, take the onions out of it," said Susanna sharply, "and I'll put it on."

"I think I like what you're wearing now better," he replied.

"You would." She sniffed and strode out ahead of him.

"Not too fast," he cautioned.

"Look, look what I found," she cried. "Those are raspberries." She dropped down beside a patch of the dark red berries. "Aren't they? Aren't they?"

"They are," he grinned. Susanna picked a whole handful and stuffed them into her mouth. "Aren't you going to put any into the bag for dinner?" he asked.

"I haven't had lunch."

"You just had breakfast."

"That was hours ago, a whole mountain ago." She plucked more and pressed one to his lips, ordering him to open his mouth. Soon they were laughing, feeding each other, stained with the dark juice, having forgotten completely that they were supposed to be scavenging for their dinner.

Finally Susanna sighed and said, "We haven't put anything in the bag."

"We have lots of supplies at home," he replied.

"Then why are we climbing all over this mountain?"

"Because the supplies will last longer if we live off the land."

"How long?" asked Susanna, reminded that she should be planning her freedom.

Court shook his head, unwilling to look beyond the moment. He put a berry between his lips and bent over her, kissing her and sliding the fruit into her mouth. Then with his tongue exploring, flicking tantalizingly, the juices of the berries mixing, her thoughts of the future slipped away in a sweet, overwhelming surge of desire to feel his touch, but more, to touch in return. She slipped her hands under his loose buckskin shirt and ran hesitant fingertips and sensitive palms from his waist to his shoulders where her small hands closed spasmodically on the smooth, powerful muscles. She was trembling, her breath coming in uneven, fluttering gasps, and her wild response to his teasing kisses made Aaron's heart melt with tenderness for her.

He pressed his mouth to her throat, whispering huskily against the pulse, "You're like slow, sweet honey in my veins, Susanna; you're a gentle fire warming my heart." His teeth teased her shoulder. "My Susanna, my angel," he murmured.

The last words were muffled in the soft hollow below her collarbone under the silk shirt, which he had unbuttoned and pushed aside. His tongue had begun to trace exquisite patterns on her skin, but Susanna caught the word *angel*, and her restless fingers stilled on his back. "Angel?" she echoed.

He repeated the word caressingly against the first swell of her breast.

"Like Lilith?" she questioned. "Like the other women at the Fallen Angel? Am I—"

"No." His hand, which had been cupped gently under her breast, raising its peak toward his descending lips, tightened possessively. "No. You're my woman. No one else's."

"That's what that means, doesn't it? Fallen angel, fallen woman? Wh-whore?" Her breath caught on the last word.

"Susanna." His voice held a warning as he raised his lips from her silken skin, abandoning with reluctance the sweetness of her body. "Be quiet now."

Susanna caught the warning note but ignored it. "I—I'm a—a sort of private whore."

"God damn it, Susanna."

"B-better than most be-because you can have me in your own b-bed or—or out in so-some—"

"Shut up." Court's face was flushed.

"And I'm cheap. You don't have to pay me. Lilith said only a fool would give herself away. And you've found a bargain, a—"

Suddenly Susanna found herself pressed back against the ground with Aaron's hand over her mouth. "Don't talk to me about your sister," he hissed. "You're nothing like Lilith. I've never said you were." Court's voice grated and he moved away from her, his hands shaking. "Lilith." His voice shook with anger. "That bitch—"

The tears were flooding Susanna's eyes, and she looked at him with such anguish that in an instant he drew her back into a protective embrace. "I don't think of you as a whore, Susanna," he whispered to her. "Never." He could feel the tremors of misery shaking her still. "My God," he muttered, "I swore I'd never hurt you." He had her in his lap and could feel her tears soaking his chest where just minutes before she had been caressing him. "Look at me, Susanna," he begged.

In answer she buried her face against his shoulder, unwilling to see those gray eyes that had held such fury. At her? At Lilith? Both, she thought. And what if the reassuring words that followed were a lie?

Susanna would not look at him, and Aaron could not force her, not when she was so distraught and he so angry. He slipped his fingers into her hair and cradled her head against his shoulder. "Don't you know how I feel about you? I haven't wanted another woman since the first moment I saw you. I haven't been able to stop thinking about you. I can't get enough of you no matter how many times I make love to you. You're—God, Susanna—" His lips were in her hair. "You're an obsession." He was silent for a minute as his arms tightened around her.

"I'm bewitched, Susanna," he said seriously. "You have the face of an angel, but Job was right. You're a witch. You've cast a spell on me."

Her lips trembled. "Job said I'd burn."

"Not alone, Susanna." His voice was low and rough with emotion. "We burn together, my lovely witch. We set each other aflame."

His mouth moved from the valley between her breasts where her heart beat against his kiss—to the wild pulse point at her throat—to her lips. And he murmured one husky word at each pause, his words like a brand on her skin: "Beloved—wanton—witch."

With the word *witch* hanging between them like a flame and his lips searing her, Susanna's eyes closed and her arms slipped up around his neck.

They did not rise from the grass to return to the cabin until the sun was low in the sky and the woods were beginning to grow dim.

73

Court and Susanna ate the second rabbit in a stew mixed with onions they had found and potatoes he had brought. Then remembering how little attention she had paid when he had taught her to play poker, he taught her to throw dice instead, and she took to it immediately, laughing, bouncing the dice against the hearth, and losing consistently.

"You'd make a terrible gambler, Susanna," he remarked.

"Should I worry about it?" she countered good-humoredly as she threw another losing seven.

"Oh, I don't know. It depends on the stakes, I suppose." His eyes grew warm before he looked away and threw a winning point. "Maybe we should gamble for something. That might catch your interest."

"I have no money," she pointed out.

"Shall we gamble for our clothes?" he suggested, laughing.

Susanna was lying on the floor propped on one elbow. She laughed back at him, tossing her hair away from her face. "I only have two pieces of clothing on. Why bother to gamble for them?" She gave him a level stare as hot as his own. "If you want to take them off, you know well enough how to do it."

Court dropped the dice, taking her into his arms and rolling her under him. "I do," he replied.

Susanna thought dizzily, before she stopped thinking at all, that her cooperation did not seem to be dulling his interest, nor even making him careless. He had hardly been out of arm's reach of her since he had left briefly while she was asleep early in the morning to get what little was left of her clothing, and most of the time he had been a good deal closer than that.

74

On the morning of their fourth day in the cabin, Court announced a hunting trip. "You'll have to leave me untied,'' said Susanna. ''I can't go through that again.'' This is it, she thought, her heart speeding up. I'll leave as soon as he does.

''But I'm taking you with me,'' he replied, smiling. ''You delight me too much to leave you behind, love.'' He cupped long fingers behind her head and kissed her lightly on the lips and then at the base of her throat.

Susanna's heart lurched, then slowed to an even pace, and her arms curved compulsively around his waist. She had to admit to herself that what she was feeling was relief because she did not have to leave yet.

''Sweetheart, I'm not liable to forget how frightened you were. Did you really think I'd do that to you again?''

''Well,'' said Susanna jauntily, ''do you have a rifle for me? I'm a crack shot, you know.''

Court grinned and handed her an old rifle, taking the better one for himself, and they set out on foot with Susanna asking eagerly what game they could expect to encounter.

''Nothing,'' he replied, ''if you keep talking. Animals have sharp ears, and they get out of the way when they hear noisy humans in the vicinity.''

''That's all very well, Aaron, but I need to know what to look for. I have no idea of what kind of animals to expect or even what kind to shoot at. You don't want me wasting bullets on animals that don't taste good or—''

''Well, Susanna, if you see a porcupine, don't shoot it. No one eats porcupine, and they resent being shot at; they shoot back.'' She looked quite astonished. ''Quills,'' he explained. ''And if you see a mountain lion, you might as well know that no one eats them, although I've heard they sometimes eat people. And don't bother a coyote. I never eat coyote. And don't shoot at any frogs."

"Frogs?"

"I realize that frog legs are tasty, but if you hit the frog, there's not much left, and if you miss, he hops off, so it's a waste of time and ammunition shooting at frogs."

"Oh, you're teasing me."

"Not at all. Everything I've said is good advice. Now, I know you think we ought to shoot a bear, so if you see one, you'll have to suit yourself, but I don't like bear meat, and I won't help you carry it home. Deer and mountain sheep are better, but it's not likely you could track a sheep, and although I like venison, I'm not crazy about the idea of carrying home a deer on my back."

"Isn't there anything small we could carry home?"

"If you see a rabbit, you'll have my full cooperation; rabbit's tasty and easy to carry. Squirrel's passable. And if you see a beaver, you can shoot it just for spite."

"Why don't you like beaver?"

"In a hat, there's nothing better than a beaver," Court admitted, "but you let a beaver loose around a nice stream and pretty soon you've got a lot of good trees chewed down and a pond you don't want and a lot of sloppy marsh. You'll see what I mean about beavers later. They play hell with irrigation projects around here too. There's a story about a rancher who was trying to irrigate a meadow to grow winter feed, and the beavers kept interfering, so he put out a scarecrow to frighten them off, and the next morning he found they'd gnawed down his scarecrow and built it into their dam."

Susanna was laughing at the end of this recital. "Is that true?" she demanded.

"No telling," he replied. "Now, what I kind of had my mind set on shooting, if we can get some, is duck. There should be some up at this beaver pond we're heading for."

"Ducks? Lilith used to take me to feed the ducks in the park when I was little."

"Not likely these'll be the same ducks, so you don't have to get sentimental about them."

"Oh, Aaron, I didn't mean that. I just meant I'll know a duck when I see one."

"Well, don't hold your breath. The pond is over an hour from here, maybe two, and we may have luck with something else before then."

They covered the ground at an easy pace, doing less climbing than the day before and stopping more often, but eventually, having seen nothing else to hunt because of their conversation, they came out upon an open alpine meadow carpeted with columbines both on the flat and on the hillsides. Susanna breathed out a soft sound of wonder and knelt to pick and examine the first flower that came to hand.

"Look," she cried, holding it out to him. "The bottom petals are deep, deep purple and then it fades to such a lovely blue. Isn't it wonderful?" She threw her arms around his neck, laughing and exclaiming, "Oh, what a beautiful place this is, Aaron."

"Worth the walk?" he asked her.

"Of course."

"Wait till you've tried to walk here," he warned. "You'll see what I mean about beavers." He led her carefully toward a pond on the far side of the meadow, cautioning her to keep quiet and explaining in a whisper how she was to shoot ducks when they rose from the water—if, of course, there were any. Then they lay in high grass near the pond and waited so long that Susanna dozed and was awakened by the sound of Aaron's rifle firing shots in rapid succession. By the time Susanna had picked her rifle up, the ducks had come and gone. "Damn," said Aaron, rising.

"You didn't get any?"

"Of course I got some—three. It's just that you can always count on a duck to fall anywhere but on dry ground. Two of the damn things went into the water and one into the marsh."

"What will we do?" asked Susanna.

"You head out that way—straight toward the tree that's lightning-struck. See it?" Susanna nodded. "The bird fell about three hundred yards from here. Take off your moccasins and step easy."

"Do you mean I could be sucked under? Is it quicksand?"

"Of course not, Susanna. It's just messy. You rather swim for the other two?"

"I don't know how to swim."

"Straight that way." He turned her in the right direction. When she looked hesitatingly over her shoulder, he was stripping off his clothes, and she turned her head away quickly. When she glanced back again, he had waded out into the pond and begun to swim with strong strokes. Susanna was running into mud and water ankle-deep and beginning to lose interest in ducks for dinner. By the time she found the duck, she had fallen twice and was well spattered with mud. Then to have to carry the poor, limp, bloody thing back with her over the same slimy route was bad enough, but to have

Aaron returning, looking clean and cool with his two ducks and then laughing uproariously at the sight of her was really too much. Susanna was about to throw her duck at him when he caught her wrist.

"Temper, temper, little squaw. The mud will wash off."

"Yes, and I'm going to wash me and the clothes at the same time," she replied with determination.

"I'll enjoy it much more if you wash them separately," he said, grinning.

"Who cares about you?" she snapped, dropped the duck, and splashed angrily into the water. "Good heavens," she cried. "It's even muddy here in the pond."

"It's the beavers," said Court who, having tied the three ducks together and hung them from a tree, was coming back in after her. "Blame it on the beavers."

"At least they had the good manners not to laugh at me," she retorted, and hit her hand sharply on the water and sent a sheet of it splashing into his face. While he was laughing and shaking the water out of his eyes, she reached down, scooped up a handful of mud, and hurled that at him. It hit with a splat in the middle of his chest and oozed down his belly. Court dove low into the water and began to swim toward her, and Susanna, in trying to back away from him, was soon out of her depth and in trouble. However, he lifted her out of the water and then ducked her as soon as she stopped sputtering.

"Since you can't swim, I think you've started something you can't finish," he whispered, chuckling.

"You're wrong," she whispered back breathlessly. "You're not going to drown me."

"Maybe a little," Court replied.

"Not even a little." Susanna was clinging to his neck and began to kiss him, darting her tongue between his lips. She had not done that before, and his arms tightened around her painfully. "You see," she said. "You're holding me tighter already."

"You're a little devil," he replied, "and this would be a lot more fun if you hadn't insisted on wearing your clothes in."

"But then I wouldn't get my clothes clean, would I? And after all, cleanliness is next to Godliness, and making love probably doesn't come into that scheme of things at all. And now if you'll see that I don't drown, I want to wash my hair."

"Watch out," Court warned. "Some beaver will probably think it would add just the right touch to his dam."

Susanna giggled and ducked her head repeatedly under water, still clinging to his arm. Finally he took her back to shore and put on his clothes while she wrung what water she could from her hair and skirt and then put her moccasins back on. He hasn't made love to me today, she thought. Maybe he is losing interest. Maybe all I need to do is take the initiative a few more times, and he'll let me go. Susanna straightened from lacing the Indian boots and walked, trailing water, over to where he sat on a rock, pulling his buckskin shirt over his head. When Court stood up, she twined her arms around him and nuzzled his chest, rubbing her tongue against his skin.

Court could feel her body becoming hot against him, and his hands tightened on her. "Jesus," he muttered under his breath, but he set her back from him. "We've got about two hours of daylight left,

Susanna. If we want to make it home before dark, we'll have to save this until later."

Susanna, her suspicions confirmed, shrugged and turned obediently to the trail, walking ahead of him with her clothes clinging tantalizingly to her body. Court was tempted to snap her back against him and—he shut those ideas away and pulled ahead of her, setting a hard pace that punished them both and kept their minds on the next step along the trail rather than other distractions.

75

Susanna built up the fire under Court's direction while he prepared two of the ducks for the spit. Then he advised her to take off the clinging tatters of the wet skirt so it would dry faster. She hesitated but reminded herself that cooperation was working, causing a slackening in his interest, and she took off the skirt, reflecting wryly that she was back to early days with only his silk shirt to wear—unless she preferred the scratchy Roman-style blanket, and the blanket was not available unless she wanted to take it off the floor where he had spread it in front of the fire.

"Come on," he invited. "I'll comb your hair out for you." Obediently Susanna sat down on the blanket facing the fire, her knees drawn up to her chin, and Aaron began the slow process of untangling the damp strands of her hair. Once he said, "You like this, don't you?"

"M-m-m," she murmured. Her eyes were half closed, and she was bemused by the sensation of the comb in her hair, by the flickering patterns of the fire, and by the explosive pops of grease dripping

from the ducks and igniting in tiny bursts of color,
fire within fire.

"I like to comb it," Court mused. "It's strange
the ordinary things that give people pleasure." He
fell silent, and for the most part neither of them
spoke after that. Their silence was easy, sleepy,
companionable. To Susanna it seemed a sort of
peaceful ending to a long tempestuous interlude.
She began, when he had put the comb down, to
braid her hair, but he pulled her fingers away.
"Leave it," he ordered. "I like it loose." Susanna's
lips compressed, but he distracted her by suggesting
that they make bread.

"We have no oven," said Susanna. "You
obviously don't know how to make bread."

"And you don't know how to make cow camp
bread." He rose and she watched him make the
dough with a casual disregard for measurement or
any of the other niceties she had been taught. "The
best thing about cow camp bread," he explained,
"is that you don't need an oven or even a pan—just
a couple of sticks and a fire, and when you've got it,
it's a plate for your food that you don't have to
wash; you just eat your plate." He wrapped the
finished dough around sticks which he made
Susanna hold while he checked and turned the
browning ducks and stirred the beans he had put on
that morning before they left. Then he took two of
the sticks from her, leaving her with two, and showed
her how to hold them over the fire. When the bread
was golden, they uncurled it and piled beans on it,
and they tore the duck meat off the bones with their
fingers and teeth.

"Good?" asked Court, grinning.

"M-m-m," she agreed, trying to eat bread and

beans without dumping them on his newly washed
shirt and to wipe grease from her chin with her
hand, which was greasier, if anything, than her chin.
"But messy," she added.

"Wipe your chin with your other piece of bread,"
he suggested. "You can lick your hands off when
you're through."

"I don't see why we can't use the plates and
utensils."

"We're roughing it," he replied. "It does people
good to get back to the old ways from time to time."

"The old ways for me," declared Susanna, "were
freshly laundered tablecloths, china and silver—not
a greasy duck leg in one hand and a dripping lump
of bread and beans in the other."

"Not my fault you had an unfortunate
childhood," he retorted. "Anyway, I'm tired. I
don't feel like cleaning up dishes."

Susanna sighed. "That's a reason I can agree
with." She did as he had suggested, used the last of
her bread to wipe off her face, then licked her
fingers before she stretched out on her stomach
before the fire with her head pillowed on one arm.

"More coffee?" he asked, stepping over her to
pour himself another cup.

"No."

Court went back to the bench to finish his second
cup and to study her. She made a lovely picture—
waist-length hair pushed carelessly back and glowing
blue-black in the firelight; face slightly flushed with
the warmth from the hearth, her lashes almost
resting on her cheek; the long line of her back and
gentle swelling of her buttocks covered only with his
white shirt; then her thighs uncovered to the knee,
slightly golden from the days in the sun, and finally

the closely laced Indian moccasins outlining her
calves and feet. No woman at the Fallen Angel,
expensively and revealingly turned out in velvets and
laces, looked more seductive than Susanna did in her
makeshift clothing, he reflected, his mouth turning
up in a wry smile.

He put down his cup and went to sit beside her,
resting his hand lightly on the silk that covered her
soft bottom. He felt her tense ever so slightly at his
touch. "Shall I join you?" he asked idly. Not
knowing what he had in mind, Susanna did not
reply, and Court stretched out on his back,
pillowing his head where his hand had been. She
found the weight of his head pressing against her,
pressing her pelvis and hips to the floor, an erotic
stimulant, and she had to force herself to relax and
turn her thoughts elsewhere.

"How did you learn to make cow camp bread?"
she asked curiously. "Were you ever a cowboy?"

He answered only after an interval so long that
she thought he was choosing to ignore her question.
"Not in the sense you probably mean," he finally
replied. "My pa owned a ranch southwest of here
for a time. We came up from Texas when the
Jicarilla Apache Reservation was opened up in '76.
Before that he ranched in Texas—not too success-
fully, but we had some cattle left after we lost our
land to the bank for debt, and he'd heard it was
good cattle country up here."

"Was it?"

"Good cattle country? Was then—tall grass up to
your stirrups. We couldn't believe our luck. No one
could in those days. Lots of folks came up from
Texas, and later Easterners bought into big ranches,
but now between the blizzards winter-killing the

stock and the overgrazing, the cattle business isn't what folks thought it would be then."

"And you brought your stock all the way from Texas?"

"All the way from Texas. Lotta men came up with the herds first, but Pa brought us all. We had a covered wagon and a year's food we bought with the last of our money, a few household things, seeds, some chickens. My ma drove the wagon; my pa, my brother, and I herded along with an old man who came with us."

"What fun it must have been for you," said Susanna wistfully.

"It was pure hell most of the time; had to tie logs on the wagon to brake it down the mountains; had to freight across the rivers on rafts. My brother was washed away and drowned before we ever took up land, so just three of us ever saw the new place. The other children had died of diphtheria in Texas years earlier."

"Aaron, I'm so sorry." She was beginning to regret ever having questioned him.

"Why? You can't be sorry for what can't be helped," he answered matter-of-factly. "So if I was a cowboy, it was for my pa. I rode herd when I wasn't in school. Before we got to Colorado my mother had taught me, taught all of us; she was an educated woman. Here in Colorado kids had to attend school, which my dad, who couldn't even read, didn't like at all. It cost him twenty cents a month to send me, and he had to have a man to replace me for herding during school time. He probably wouldn't have let me go if there hadn't been a five-dollar fine for not sending me and if my mother hadn't kept after him about it."

"Are your parents still on the ranch?"

"My parents were both dead before we'd been here five years. My mother was shot down by rustlers in her own doorway when she was handing them lunch. She probably never knew it was coming. Men stopped by ranch houses and demanded food, never dismounted, and people gave it to them to avoid trouble. But these men belonged to a gang that had been rustling my pa's stock, and he'd shot one of them. They were paying him back, and she was by herself. Not that it would have helped if Pa or I'd been there. When a stranger knocked, the women always answered. Man answered in those days, he was liable to get shot. But not too many men would shoot a woman. Ma was just unlucky that day. Pa went after them, and they killed him. Bank took the land and stock for his debts."

"Aaron, what did you do? How old were you?"

"I was sixteen. I went prospecting. Panned for gold for a couple of years, and when I got enough, I went to Denver and looked out the best lawyer in town and talked him into letting me read law with him."

"How did you happen to choose law?"

Court laughed. "Must have been my last name."

"Then what happened?" Susanna prompted because he had fallen silent.

"Oh well, I read law and I did some investing. I'd meant to use the gold to last me through, but I was never much for letting money lie. Banks have a way of failing and taking your money with them. So I put it into one thing and another, and I had a lot more by the time I was ready to start out on my own. Came to Amnonville because of the gold strikes and because it looked like it was going to keep growing once the railroad came in."

"Has the town met your expectations?" she asked curiously.

Court smiled to himself at her way of phrasing the question. "Don't you know by now that my expectations are mixed at best? Yes, Amnonville has met my expectations. I've made a lot of money and I have a good law practice because I'm good at making money and practicing law, and I've also lost a lot because life is full of bad luck—even for the luckiest of us. Amnonville has a way of burning down from time to time. I've lost most everything once and a hell of a lot the night I first met you. And how have you found your life, Susanna? All happiness?"

"Not really," Susanna replied. "I was very happy before Lilith left home, but I was a little girl then. After that my parents never let me go anywhere or see anyone. I didn't even go to school; I had tutors at home. And they picked my books and my clothes and my activities, and they never seemed to be very happy with me, even when they completely controlled my life. Then they died and I came here."

"Sounds like a hell of a childhood," he remarked and fell silent. Susanna closed her eyes against sadness—and memories. "You look at your life and you look at mine," he resumed after a time, "or anyone's, for that matter, and it seems like people get more bad hands dealt them than good, and most of the time there's not a thing we could have done to prevent the bad ones. I've always figured that it doesn't pay to regret the past, any more than it pays to worry about the future since there's nothing to be done about either. The only thing we can do is take our happiness when we're lucky enough to find some. And you and I, love, are on a lucky streak. We may never be any happier than we've been this week." He turned, sliding his hand under her hips and beginning ·to kiss the smooth, soft flesh on which his head had been resting. Susanna tensed in surprise. "Sh-sh," he whispered. "Lie still, love, and let me pleasure you." The hand beneath her curved into the soft down between her legs to touch her intimately. With his other hand, he parted her thighs and slid gentle, searching fingers inside her while he continued to press small kisses and flicks of the tongue against her buttocks until she was weak with tremors of excitement.

When he turned her on her back, she was acquiescent, eager, expecting that he would come into her, and so she was caught by surprise when instead he brought his mouth down on her. Shocked and panic-stricken, she attempted to writhe away, but his hands at her thighs were suddenly firm and purposeful, and with his mouth and tongue he ravished her, sending waves of fire over her, bringing her from pleasant tremors to a thrashing, burning earthquake of climax that left her flushed with embarrassment when she came to herself.

He gave her only a few minutes respite before, moving upward, he poised to enter her. Susanna pushed weakly against his arms, unwilling to let him entice her further into unknown and unimagined realms of abandon, but Court ignored her hesitation and, pushing her knees apart with his, took her gently so that each second of interior movement, penetration or withdrawal, caused her anguished sensation that seemed to go on and on unbearably until she gave up all separateness of self and wrapped her legs around him and closed rings of hungry muscles on him, seeking deeper penetration, contact so close that they melted into each other, final consummation and peace, all of which they

found together as he released into her the warm
flood of his desire, and her body absorbed him and
was fulfilled.

For a while she floated, her body still locked to
his, her mind cut loose from any reality but the
physical peace he brought her. Then he himself
summoned her back by shifting her to lie sprawled
on top of him and telling her that she pleased and
excited him more than any woman he had ever
known. Lilith flashed into her mind. He had known
Lilith. Had Lilith rested like this on him after wild
and shameless bouts of loving, helpless and sated
like some animal?

"I love the contrasts in you, Susanna," he
whispered. "One moment you're a laughing child,
hurling mud at me; another you're an innocent girl
unchanged from the night I first saw you in that
damned virginal nightgown, and still another—"
His arms tightened as he sat up and lifted her to
carry her to the bunk. "And still another time
you're wild with desire, flushed and hot under my
hands, my wanton witch." He captured her lips as
he laid her on the bed and lowered himself beside
her.

"No more," she whispered.

"No more," he agreed. He drew her in tight
against him and slept almost immediately. Susanna
did not.

She lay awake in his arms, thinking of how she
had fooled herself. She had given herself freely to
him, and he was not bored, and he never let her out
of his sight. There would be no escape, and the
result of her plan had been that she was becoming
more deeply enthralled, that the thought of leaving
him was harder, that the things he taught her body
to accept, to want, were more—shameful. And how

long would it be before she found herself with child? How many times did it take? Tonight it seemed he had claimed her very soul. If she stayed, there would be nothing left he did not own, no part of her that belonged to herself. And in return all she had were his words spoken a day earlier in a surge of remorse because she had branded herself a whore. He had declared himself *bewitched*. He had said that he *burned* for her. But that was lust, not love. He had never, ever mentioned marriage. Lilith had said he would never take a wife, although Susanna did not know why and couldn't ask him. So all he offered her were lovemaking and words. He had called her his *beloved, wanton witch*. What did wanton mean? Nothing good, she guessed. And *beloved*? Tenderness for the moment but nothing for tomorrow. Aaron did not believe in tomorrows, only todays; he had said so often enough.

She had to get away, and his anger and remorse that afternoon had been the key. He had been furious with her suggestion that he thought her a whore, that she was like her sister. Susanna shivered. She knew how to escape from him. Tomorrow she would demand payment. She would tell him that since he had made her a whore, he must pay for her services. He would be furious again, and his anger would destroy whatever strange value he put on their relationship. In anger he would set her free.

Tomorrow, she told herself. Tomorrow I must destroy this spell before it is too late. Tomorrow I will demand payment, but dear heaven, what will I have sold that I can never reclaim?

76

Eyes leaden with exhaustion, heart heavy with unhappiness and fear, Susanna awoke to find Aaron smiling at her with a tenderness that made her close her eyes again to hide her own pain. "Do you know what we're going to do today?" he asked.

"No," she whispered—not wanting to hear his plans or his voice, light with happiness.

"Nothing—We're not going to do a thing. We'll feast off the fruits of our labors and be lazy. We'll lie in the sun by the stream and kiss and watch fish—whatever pleases you."

It sounded enchanting to Susanna, enchanting and heartbreaking because she knew now where she was going to be when she declared herself a whore and demanded payment for her services, past and future—if he wanted any future services. She doubted that he would.

"Out of bed, woman," he commanded, laughing and dragging her up with him. "I'm going to stuff that little belly of yours with flapjacks and bacon and then drag you off naked to some place where I can kiss it in the sunshine. Are you blushing, Susanna?" He planted a lighthearted kiss on the tip of her nose and pushed her into the rocking chair. "It delights me to think that you still blush when I threaten to kiss your pretty stomach," he said as he knelt and moved his lips in light kisses to her navel, which he caressed deeply with his tongue. Susanna felt the flush on her cheeks cover her whole body. "M-m-m. You like that. I can feel your skin turning warm. What else do you like, Susanna? Shall we postpone breakfast?"

"No," she said, turning her head aside. "You're embarrassing me."

"All right, sweetheart, we'll wait till later to find out what else you like." His voice held a warm promise that made her shiver like someone in the throes of fever, and before he released her and rose, he flicked his tongue across one vulnerable pink nipple and further rent the tatters of her self-control.

When she seemed to have no appetite for breakfast, he teased her and fed her himself—lovingly, as if she were his cherished child. His spirits were so buoyant, his behavior so endearing that she was almost in tears by the time he brought her to the stream, but once there, he coaxed her into laughter and made her forget for a time what she meant to do. He insisted that they make a skirt of wildflowers to replace hers, which he called a disgrace, and he even made a start on the construction before she convinced him that they should not denude the area of flowers. They had pinecone-throwing contests, and made up silly stories, and explored the stream looking for a mythical Indian named Fat Feather. They gave pompous names to birds and bugs that crossed their paths, and waded in the stream, and tried to catch fish in the icy water with their fingers. They rolled in the grass and hid from one another, and stuffed themselves with berries instead of eating lunch, and generally conducted themselves like the children they had never been. And finally when the sun was high and hot, they lay under the trees with their arms around each other and the leaves forming shifting patterns of coolness on their faces, and they dozed.

When they woke, Susanna knew that she had to do it—while she still could—and she willed an icy unconcern to fill her mind, as if she were only a spectator about to witness a painful scene in which she had no part, a scene involving characters for whom she had no empathy.

She turned on her side so that her head rested on her elbow, although his arm was still beneath her. "Won't you have to get back to town soon?" she asked idly.

"There's no hurry," he replied. He was on his back, completely relaxed, and he did not turn.

"But it will be expensive, won't it—keeping me here," she persisted, "especially when you're letting your business affairs in town go?"

Then he did turn, and he frowned slightly, not taking her meaning. "How much are you paying me?" she asked, as if it were a matter of curiosity.

"Paying you?"

She watched confusion come into his eyes, and it almost thrust her from the cold place where she had isolated herself. But then the confusion was gone, if it had ever been there, and a shutter, gray and cold, seemed to close and lock away all the warmth and laughter of the morning. Susanna swallowed hard, willing herself to continue. "I have no idea what the going rate is," she admitted lightly. "Am I worth as much as Lilith?"

"You want me to pay you for this week?" he asked carefully.

"Didn't you plan to? Lilith said I was a fool before—to give myself away."

Mondragon's words rang in Aaron's head. "You're like a poor man who can't afford the price and so must do without." But it seemed that Carlos had been wrong; both of them had been wrong about Susanna. Court had not thought she had a price and he had been wrong, but if her price was money, he had it, so Carlos too had been wrong. "You asked me if you're worth as much as your sister. The answer is yes," he replied. "You've been worth more to me than Lilith ever was."

"Thank you." Susanna managed a taut smile. She wanted to run, but she knew there was no getting away until he let her go. She had to continue, to make the whole thing into a nightmare so that he would want to let her go, couldn't wait to see the last of her. "Am I paid by the night?" she asked. "But that wouldn't be fair because we did it in the daytime too." She wasn't going to say "made love," not ever again. "Maybe it should be a certain amount for each time. I'll have to trust to your sense of—"

"Have you been counting?" he interrupted, rage beginning to creep into his eyes.

Susanna saw it, hoped it would put an end to this horror. "Oh, yes. I'm sure I can remember accurately. Do you want the numbers?"

"Not yet." His voice grated with fury, and fear suddenly swept her, washing away the feeling of dull sickness and regret. "Not yet, Susanna. We'll wait for a final accounting. Right now I've a mind to avail myself of your increasingly expert services. You can put it on my tab. Do you know what that means?"

"No," she faltered, and he gained a certain grim satisfaction as he saw that damnable, cool assurance fading from her eyes. "I want to go home now," she whispered.

"You'll go home when I say you can go home, when I'm through with you." He was sick with disgust, with her and with himself. She sounded like Lilith. God, had he done that to her?

"I don't want you to touch me anymore,"
Susanna cried.

"Whores get touched by anyone who can pay.
Are you sure you haven't chosen the wrong profession?"

"I didn't choose," Susanna cried desperately. "I
was injured and drugged the first time you took me,
and after that you deliberately pursued me when I
couldn't remember what happened."

His face turned white. "Get back to the cabin."

She had risen on her knees, her hair in wild tangles
on her shoulders. "I didn't ask you to bring me
here," she screamed at him. "And I've never been
with anyone but you. This is your fault, your
fault—"

Her voice was rising in hysteria, and Court
couldn't listen to any more. He fastened his hands
on her shoulders and cut her off. "Shut up,
Susanna. If you know what's good for you, you'll
be quiet. You've never been that unwilling," he
added bitterly. "Now get back to the cabin, unless
you want me to drag you there." He pulled her
roughly to her feet and followed behind her to see
that she obeyed him. The sound of his footsteps was
the sound of fear and despair to her. However, she
had no reason to be afraid. Court no longer wanted
her.

When they reached the cabin, he did not go in; in
fact, he did not return until long after moonrise,
after she had cried herself into exhausted sleep.
Wearily he slid in beside her, pushing her without
force to the far side of the bunk so he would not
have to feel her body against his, would not have to
touch her—although he could not escape the sound
when she wept in her sleep and struggled desperately

against the grip of her nightmares. He was finally driven outside again to seethe in the cauldron of his own resentment.

When she awakened, he was standing beside the bunk as he had been the first morning, and for a moment she was not sure why she had such a terrible feeling of sorrow and loss. "You should have accepted what we had, Susanna," he said quietly. "It was too good to be thrown away so callously for some ugly notion of barter you heard from your sister."

At the mention of Lilith, Susanna blinked back tears. Lilith had lost him, and now Susanna would lose him too, but for her it would be more than the loss of a customer; it would be the loss of her heart, of her longing to love and be loved. How would she ever live the rest of her life with Aaron hating her, and he did. She had no doubt of it.

"You don't have to be afraid," he continued, mistaking the anguish in her eyes for fear. "I'm going to take you back today, this morning. I'll pay you whatever you ask—more, I imagine, than you ever dreamed of charging, for I too can remember all our times together, and I've put a high value on you. I just hadn't thought of it in terms of money. But before we go, Susanna, I'm going to make love to you one last time."

"No."

"Yes," he disagreed gently. "This is so you'll remember how it was with us before you destroyed it. I want you to have regrets, as I shall. How many times have I told you that people should cherish the present? You never believed me, so I'm going to give you a memory to carry with you into the future."

He pulled the covers out of her fingers gently and

stripped them away from her. He stilled her protests with kisses and her struggles with caresses. He soothed away her tears and her pain and her fear with a gentleness so sensitive to every quiver of her nerve ends that she was helpless under his attack. And then he carried her with him beyond anything either of them had ever known, into a sensuality and satisfaction so complete that neither of them could be free, in body or in mind, of the other—ever again. And then he made her get up, and dress in his shirt and the soft moccasins he had given her and the ragged skirt, all of which he had to put on her himself because she was too stunned to obey, and he put her behind him on the horse, because he could not stand to see her face, and he took her back to town—over long miles of trail, past the cabin where he had brought her from the fire and it had all begun, onto Copper Street, where she asked timidly if they could not take another route and was refused, all the way through town to the front door of the Fallen Angel.

There were few patrons at the bar when they entered, probably none who recognized Susanna in her ragged condition with her hair tangled around her face and down her back. Lilith, however, was there, talking to a liquor salesman, and turned to stare at them unbelievingly, not sure of what she was seeing.

Court had to take Susanna down the length of the bar to her. "Lilith," he said quietly, his face expressionless, "I'm returning Susanna to you. You'll have a draft on my bank by the end of the afternoon which I'm sure you'll find generous, whatever your arrangement with her is. It's in payment for the week we've spent together. I trust there'll be no quarreling about what I owe her. Susanna.'' He bowed with courteous formality to the dazed, ragged girl, and he left.

VI
The Jail

77

Hardly able to believe that the dusty, ragged, half-naked gypsy in front of her was her sister, Lilith rushed Susanna up the stairs before anyone could recognize her. The girl exuded a compelling aura of despair and dazed sensuality that might well have created a riot to equal the one she had precipitated just before her departure.

"Why the devil aren't you safe in Denver?" Lilith demanded when they were in her office with the door locked behind them. "You'd better explain to me double quick what you've been up to."

Susanna dropped wearily into a chair and rested her head on her hand, the mass of tangled black hair falling forward to obscure her face. "It's as he said, Lilith," she replied in a voice dragging with weariness. "I've been with him in his cabin all week—and he's going to pay me for my time."

"Your time? What does that mean?"

"Just what you think. Just exactly what you think."

"By God, Susanna, this is really too much. After that mess with Penvennon. After I found you in that cave with Court, naked and—and—"

"Compromised?" suggested Susanna indifferently.

"You even smell like a—a—"

"Tramp? Lady of ill repute, as Mr. Penvennon would say? I am. Or I will be when I get the money. That's all it takes, isn't it—being paid? I thought you'd be proud of me. This time I didn't let him make a fool of me. I demanded to be paid. Maybe I won't offend you anymore when I've had a bath. There was only a stream there—no gold-footed bath tubs and soft towels like you have here at the Fallen Angel, and after yesterday—and today—he wouldn't let me—he—" Her voice trailed off into tears.

"Oh God, Susanna. Why did you go with him?"

"I don't know."

"You said you were going to Denver. What happened?"

"I don't know what happened, Lilith. I was sitting in the dining car looking at the menu, and suddenly he was there—ordering breakfast and telling me train stories and pouring coffee, and then I was sick, and the next thing I knew I was in that cabin with no memory of how I got there."

"Sick? What do you mean you were sick?" Lilith snapped up the pertinent fact in the story.

"Sick. Sick to my stomach and dizzy and faint—fainting—"

"He drugged you."

Susanna shook her head. "I don't know. He said he carried me off the train at the next town and checked my bag at the station and took me away to the cabin."

"The bastard drugged you."

Susanna was wiping her hand across her eyes and did not comment.

"What happened then?"

"He kept me there. He said I belonged with him.

He—oh, I don't want to talk about it. I just want to go home. I paid dearly enough to get here."

"What does that mean?"

Susanna wondered if she could make her sister understand just how much it had cost her to give up the remaining time she might have had with Court, to drive him away for good. "I can't talk about it," said Susanna despairingly.

"What did he do to you?" Lilith demanded.

"It doesn't matter now, Lilith. When I insisted that he pay me, he was furious and brought me home. It worked."

She began to weep again, and Lilith, kneeling beside her, said, "I'm sorry I yelled at you, honey." She put her hand tentatively on Susanna's shoulder, and Susanna leaned against her, crying out her heartbreak. "No matter how bad it was, Susanna, you did the right thing," Lilith assured her. "You were smart, and you got away."

"Yes, I got away, but I'll never be able to forget this morning. He said I wouldn't."

Susanna shuddered with grief, and Lilith assumed on the basis of her own experience that Susanna was weeping over remembered cruelty, not remembered tenderness. She held her sister and hoped that the girl would not confess any of the details. "What I can't understand is how you ever got mixed up with him in the beginning," she said, almost to herself.

"It was the opium, I guess," Susanna replied. "I couldn't remember for a long time what happened after the fire, and then when I did and he knew I remembered, it—it happened again, and after that I couldn't seem to help doing what he wanted. I wanted to too, I guess."

"The opium?" Lilith's eyes narrowed. "After the

fire was the first time?"

"Yes." Susanna nodded. "After the fire."

"When you were hurt and drugged?"

"It was like a dream—one at the edge of your consciousness when you first wake up, but you can't quite remember it."

"Yes, I know what you mean," her sister replied absently.

"I have to go home, Lilith. I can't talk anymore or—or anything."

"Of course, Susanna. I'll get a carriage."

"Why bother? Everyone must have seen me riding into town like this."

"No one would have recognized you, Susanna. I hardly did myself. Don't worry about this—not about any of it. Don't even think about it. I'm going to take care of things."

"I don't want the money, Lilith. I don't want to know how much it was or even to hear about it. Give it to a church or an orphanage or something. But don't—"

"I'll take care of it. Everything." She went to the door and hissed to the first person she saw in the hall, "Get Quincy."

78

Quincy had taken Susanna, bundled into a concealing cape, down the back stairs of the Fallen Angel and into a closed carriage for the ride home, never having been told by anyone why the girl looked as she did or what had happened to her. Clara, more confused than Quincy, had bathed her and put her into a clean nightgown and a clean bed. Then finally Lilith, having personally supervised all this, had time to think about what had happened, and her anger grew. He had drugged Susanna—Susanna! A sweeter, more innocent child had never existed, and he had drugged her—not once but twice—the first time seducing her when she was injured and helpless, the second time kidnapping her and holding her for a week, doing God knows what to her. The draft on his bank came in the late afternoon, and the amount astonished Lilith. He must have kept Susanna on her back for—Lilith closed her eyes. None of the infuriating things she had imagined about that relationship came anywhere near the reality as Susanna had revealed it that afternoon. It was—it was—the world she had chosen for herself offered no words to adequately express the revulsion she felt toward Court as a result of his treatment of Susanna. Only blind, wordless, consuming anger was an adequate response to the man. "He's a—a scoundrel," she said aloud, trying the word for effect. It sounded foolish beside the reality. But revenge would satisfy. Oh, revenge would be sweet if it hurt enough, if it did enough damage, if it lasted long enough.

When the night crowd was beginning to fill the rooms downstairs, when men were drifting upstairs with the girls, Lilith was indifferent. She sat in her office with a glass of brandy in her hands, and she planned, she plotted, she spun webs of hate in her mind from her heart's gall, and then she moved to fling them out. She called in Carlos and Quincy and told them in the bluntest terms what had happened, described in the most vivid words the condition in which Susanna had been returned to her. Carlos remained impassive, but Quincy, who loved the girl in his fashion, turned white, and his mouth pulled down in hard lines.

"There's nothing fer it," he said softly. "I'll have

to kill him. Shoulda done it when we found em in that cave, but I knew we might not a got her out but fer him.''

"That's not what I want," said Lilith. "It's too late for killing."

"No, it ain't. First place, it'll be a fair fight, so I'll never have to swear in court as to what it was about. I'll see her name don't come into it at all. No need fer anyone to know what happened but the five of us, an he ain't gonna be alive to tell it.''

"It's too quick," said Lilith, her eyes shining with a baleful light.

Carlos, knowing her well, was not surprised at this reaction. "What would you have?" he asked softly.

"Maybe I'll ruin him first," she mused. "Run him into the mud until he's a miserable pauper. Then—"

"That ain't enough," snapped Quincy. "That ain't nuthin.''

"I'm not sure you have enough money to do that, querida," said Mondragon. "You shouldn't underestimate him."

Her eyes were narrowed, staring into some private vision. "No matter," she muttered. "First, I want to get my hands on him." She turned, smiling, to Quincy as if she had reached a decision. "I want you to bring him here. Can you do that, Quincy? Can you get him for me?"

"I reckon. What happens when he gits here?" Quincy asked uneasily.

"That's not your concern. Just you bring him. I'll take care of the rest."

79

Susanna moved with a numb preoccupation through her house. She noticed with surprise that the furniture which she had gone to Denver to check on had arrived in her absence, but Susanna was no longer interested in it, telling Clara to put it wherever she thought best. She started the canning she had planned before she left, but it usually terminated with Susanna standing in the kitchen staring into space and the fruit burning in the pan; Clara was left to salvage what could be salvaged and to clean up the rest.

When Susanna had been back four days, she dressed in the red and black dress that had roused Aaron's anger and went to the Fallen Angel. Lilith protested, but she need not have worried. Susanna stared through customers who tried to get her attention and referred the ardent ones to Quincy without even a flicker of emotion. She wandered from room to room there as she had at home. She never saw Aaron. It had not occurred to her that she might. She did not look for him.

Quincy did look, however, and without success. By making discreet inquiries, he found out that Court had stayed in town transacting business during the afternoon and evening after he had returned Susanna. Then he had disappeared, and no one seemed to know where he had gone—or possibly those who knew were not saying. Either way, Quincy could not find Court, although he had hit upon a simple plan to get the man to the Fallen Angel if he could be found. Having reached a dead end for the time being in his search, he had to wait, wondering if Court could have left for good. It seemed unlikely, since Court was not a man to apologize for his actions or to back away from the results of them, any more than he was liable to leave so many business interests and clients unattended. Quincy was a patient man; he knew that in less than two weeks time the judge would arrive to conduct trials and that Court would be in town then if ever. He could wait.

Lilith was less patient. Her anger burned. She saw her sister wandering like a ghost through the saloon and the dance hall and the gambling rooms, and she wanted to settle the score with Aaron Court. She did not know what to do for Susanna, what to say to her, but now she did know what she wanted to do to Court, and somehow she felt that would help, that once revenge had been exacted, Susanna would recover. If Lilith had dared, she would have asked Susanna to go home where the girl could not dampen the nightly high spirits at the Fallen Angel, but Lilith was afraid to say the wrong thing, almost to say anything. In desperation she sat Susanna down in her office one night and handed her the books, the bills, the gambling receipts, every piece of paper that pertained to the financial records of the business. Three hours later she returned to find her sister still at work. The next day Susanna came at noon instead of at seven. She never came in again at night. She found the figures soothing, impersonal. They reminded her of nothing she was afraid to think of, nothing that would hurt. She worked at the books every day and felt content and safe—as safe as a person sleeping at the edge of a black pit could feel.

80

A week before the circuit-riding judge was to arrive, Court returned to his cabin outside of town as quietly as he had left. Days earlier he had conducted what business had to be seen to and then simply walked away into the mountains, taking only a knife and his rifle. He lived off the land as he had done in the years after he lost his family when he was traveling from camp to camp, panning for gold. Having lost Susanna, he found that the solitude and the rigorous life again eased his bitterness and regret. When Court had to return to Amnonville, he did. His anger had burned away, and he was able to settle into his house and his business routine.

Quincy, who had people watching, heard of it and went out to the cabin south of town. He found Court leaner and harder than he had seen him in years. It was difficult to believe that anything could ever have sprung up between Susanna and this man. The plan Quincy had worked out seemed less feasible to him now that he had seen Court and assessed his mood. Still, he had to try.

"What do you want, Quincy?" Court asked inhospitably, leaning against the door in such a way as to make obvious his disinclination to invite his visitor in.

"Susanna wants to see you."

"Why?" Court certainly did not want to see her—or anyone who reminded him of her.

"She just does. I'd say you owe her that much," Quincy added.

"Owe her? What an unfortunate choice of words. I would have thought that Susanna had been well paid," said Court grimly. "In the coin she wanted.

We're quits." He gritted his teeth against the anguish he still felt when he remembered that their relationship was over.

Quincy controlled his anger with difficulty. "She'll be in Lilith's office tomorrow at nine in the morning. Will you be there, or shall I tell her you ain't got the guts to face her?" He let the contempt he felt for Court color his voice openly.

"Has she decided to make me another business proposition?" Court asked, his own bitterness rising like gall in his throat, making him welcome the prospect of the fight that was brewing between himself and Quincy. He wanted to strike out at someone. Quincy would do very well.

Quincy too would have been glad to oblige, but he had promised Lilith. Perhaps later he could settle the score with Court. For now he spat at the man's feet and left.

The last gesture, more than anything he had said, ensured that Court would walk into the trap that awaited him in Lilith's office.

Although Court had suggested that Susanna's reason for wanting to see him again might be to renew a profitable arrangement, he did not believe that. His reaction to Quincy's unconcealed contempt had triggered the remark. What had the man expected of him—that he marry Susanna? That would have been a disaster. All marriages were—for the wives, for the unfortunate children they bore. And Susanna had never indicated that she wanted to marry him, only that she wanted to be paid for her time. In truth he had no idea what she could want with him. He would have thought they had each said all there was to say and that she would never want to see him again—any more than he wanted to see her again.

For the first time he entertained the notion, if only briefly, that she might be pregnant, but he dismissed it without consideration, irrationally sure that had she been carrying his child, he would have known it. The thought stirred him in a way that he did not want to dwell on, and so he dismissed it out of hand. All of which left him with no ideas at all on what she might have in mind. The request for a meeting seemed inexplicable, and anything that could not be explained rationally made him uneasy. But then he had never been able to understand Susanna's behavior.

When he walked into Lilith's office, however, the explanation was simple enough. Susanna was not involved at all. Only Carlos and Quincy were there—and Lilith with a look in her eyes that sent Court's hand sweeping without thought toward his holster. He checked the motion in time. She, startled by his action and holding a small derringer on him, was not so quick of reflex. She fired and hit him in the shoulder. Court's face paled, and he leaned slowly back for support against the door he had just entered, his hand going up to cover the slow welling of blood from the wound. "Is that what I'm here for, Lilith? So you can kill me? I should have stifled my natural reluctance to shoot a—lady."

"Whatever I decide to do to you, you deserve," she snapped viciously. "Drop your gun belt to the floor."

"Get it yourself," he retorted.

"Do you want me to kill you?"

"I reckon—if you'd meant to—you would have—done it already." Court's speech was interrupted by short, labored breaths.

Quincy was cursing as he approached the wounded man with caution and removed the weapons, although when he got close, it appeared to be safe enough. Even Court's ability to remain upright seemed tenuous, and his right hand hung limply at his side, the blood making a long stain down the white sleeve of his shirt and falling in occasional drops from his fingertips. The left hand was still applying pressure to the wound to stem the flow of blood.

"This doesn't seem like—your style, Quincy," Court remarked, his voice low and grating with effort. "Lies—or was Susanna—really in on this?"

"No."

"I thought not. Not your style—or hers—"

"You want him to bleed to death?" Quincy asked Lilith.

"No," she replied. "Tie him up and see to the wound." She had not meant to shoot him, not initially at least, and because her plans had gone awry, she was even angrier than before.

"Maybe you'd like—to tell me now—what this is—all about, Lilith," said Court as Quincy tied his hands and then wadded a scarf and pressed it against the wound, binding it in place with a veil from Lilith's hat, which he had found tossed carelessly on the desk.

"Bullet went all the way through," Quincy remarked to no one in particular. "Ain't too bad."

Court walked with slow care to Lilith's desk and sat down in her chair, saying sardonically, "With your—permission," even as he leaned back. "And the—reason for my visit?"

"You know damned well why you're here."

"Weren't you satisfied with the—amount of the draft? I was much more generous with Susanna— than I ever was with you, Lilith, but then—she was a more—satisfying partner—on all counts." He leaned his head back wearily. "Younger—more beautiful—much more—enthusiastic—" And more lovable, he added to himself, realizing abruptly that he did love Susanna.

"You unmitigated bastard!"

"There's no reason—to feel slighted—Lilith," Court assured her sarcastically. "It's all a matter of—personal preference—after all. I'm sure the town is—full of men who—would prefer you if they had the chance—to exercise an—option."

Her eyes were blazing with fury. "Do you really think this whole thing is a joke?" she demanded.

"Obviously not—since I've just been—shot over it." The situation seemed even less tolerable because he realized that he would never have a chance to do anything about Susanna, whom he now knew he wanted under any circumstances, even marriage, if she would have him.

"I'm going to have you thrown in jail for kidnapping and rape."

"No," said Quincy sharply.

"Kidnapping and rape," Lilith repeated. "Are you still laughing? You'll hang."

Court realized with a pain greater than that radiating from the gunshot wound what such a scandal would do to Susanna, and he knew he had to deflect Lilith if he could. "Hang?" he echoed as coolly as possible. "Perhaps, but it will be—a most embarrassing trial—for both you and your sister— since I shall certainly testify that—there was never any question—of rape." His eyes narrowed. "In fact—I can provide—as many intimate details—as the judge cares to allow." Let Lilith think about that prospect. With difficulty, he gave her a sardonic smile. "It should be—the most scandalous —trial—that Colorado—" His breath was coming shorter as he continued to speak.

Lilith, beside herself with fury, cried, "Do you think a jury would believe anything you say once they find out you drugged her and took her when she was a virgin—even worse, that when she refused to see you again, you kidnapped her and forced her to—"

"All events—are subject—to varying—interpretations—Lilith," he replied, thinking he had also loved Susanna through it all, wishing he had known how much before it was too late.

Infuriated, Lilith snatched up a riding whip that lay on the desk and slashed his face, leaving a thin line from temple to chin.

For the first time Carlos intervened. He closed a restraining hand over hers and said quietly, "Any more of that would be a mistake, querida. The gunshot wound can be explained, but a beating would be awkward to account for with the sheriff."

Lilith was trembling with rage and jerked her hand away. "I'm going to flay the skin off him. I want to see him cry as many tears as she's cried."

Her voice seemed to come to Court from a long distance. Why had Susanna been crying, he wondered dazedly, when she had got what she wanted? Or had he misinterpreted her demand for payment because it had hurt him so badly? In a last effort at consciousness he turned to Lilith. "I'm afraid the whipping you—plan to give me—may not be as satisfying—as you—antici—" His voice was trailing away. Why had Susanna been crying? "Hate to dis—appoint a lady—even a—" He passed out before he could finish.

"You can't charge him," Quincy said angrily.

"It is her prerogative," Carlos replied, casually

resting his hand on his gun. "Do not let past friendship influence you."

"It ain't a matter of past friendship. The scandal
would kill Susanna."

"She won't appear in court," said Lilith, her face
set. Carlos knew that Lilith would not be moved
from her revenge, would not be satisfied until
Court's neck was in the noose. And if the scandal
forced Susanna to leave Amnonville for good, he
assumed that that outcome to the whole affair
would please Lilith as well.

81

Court's unconscious body had been delivered to the
sheriff and his blood mopped up in Lilith's office
long before Susanna arrived at noon to begin work
on the books. That afternoon she was preoccupied
with her sister's investment in the MacFadden
Hotel; Susanna wanted to see the McFadden books
so that she could find out why the hotel was not
making more money than it was. Rather than risk
having Susanna hear gossip at the hotel about
Court's arrest, Lilith had the books brought to her.
At the Fallen Angel those who were aware of the
arrest had been warned to say nothing to Susanna.
Quincy thought she should be told, but Lilith, after
an acrimonious debate, had ordered him to remain
silent.

Consequently Susanna returned home at five
under Quincy's protection with no idea that her
name was becoming the source of the town's most
virulent scandal. People stared at her with avid
curiosity on the street—some sympathetic, even
horrified at what they had heard had happened to

her; some cynical, disbelieving the charges and
asserting that she was no better than she should be,
that sister of Lilith Moran's, and a liar if she said a
man of Aaron Court's prominence had taken advantage of her. Whatever their beliefs, there was
hardly a person in town who did not have an opinion
by nightfall, and the townsfolk talked of nothing
else. Susanna, making the trip from her sister's
office in her usual state of numb apathy, noticed
nothing. She was told nothing by Clara, who had
had her orders. She went to bed in ignorance. She
rose in ignorance to sit crocheting antimacassars
that she would forget about before she finished
them. She went to Lilith's office again in ignorance.
Respectable women talked of her endlessly, and she
talked to her sister of unnecessarily high linen bills
and possible waste in the restaurant kitchen and
damages in the maids' quarters where wild parties
were reputed to take place after hours—all probable
causes of low profits at the hotel.

"I think I should spend a few days observing the
whole operation, Lilith," said Susanna.

"I'll just sell my interest," replied her sister
hastily.

Susanna shrugged. "You might put the money
into several Chinese laundries. The town needs
them, and their overhead is so low that they make
money. If we had a monopoly, we could raise the
prices and the profits. Did you know that Chinese
laundrymen sprinkle the linen they iron by blowing
water from their mouths? I think that's disgusting. I
informed mine that he would have to stop that
practice. Think of sleeping on sheets that a
Chinaman has spit on."

Lilith found it rather unreal to hear her sister discussing Chinese laundrymen and their ironing

practices while a scandal was boiling around her the likes of which the town had never seen. Lilith herself, in her drive for revenge, had not anticipated the proportions that the case against Aaron Court was assuming. She had thought she could hush it up, but now she was unsure that she could even keep the matter from her sister. For one thing, the sheriff was demanding to talk to Susanna. Lilith had pleaded her sister's state of horror and shock, but she could hardly maintain that excuse if Susanna roused herself enough to go around town buying into Chinese laundries. Lilith sent her home in a carriage that afternoon lest some citizen or some reporter from one of the two local newspapers get hold of her as she walked home with Quincy. Clara was given orders to let no one into the house.

82

Quincy had been strongly against having Court arrested—not because he felt that Aaron was innocent of the charges, but because he did not want to see Susanna exposed to more contempt and gossip in the town than she already had to endure because of her sister's business. He had been overruled. Once Court had been thrown in jail, Quincy had felt that Susanna should be told before she heard from some other source. Again he had been overruled. Now as her notoriety grew, he was appalled to think what a terrible shock the whole unsavory situation would be to her when she finally found out, as he had no doubt she would. How could she not?

Her unemotional conversation about her Chinese laundry plan, as they rode home in Lilith's carriage, struck him as a terrible irony. First, while humiliating troubles lay in wait for her, she talked inconsequentially about the price of bulk starch. Second, she addressed those ideas to a man who had no interest in mercantile adventures. Had she been telling Aaron Court, she would probably have had an instant offer of partnership in the venture; Court, who was always ready to invest, always on the moneymaking end of every deal in town, would undoubtedly have offered not only money but himself or some hireling to pressure every Chinese laundryman in town into a laundry cartel. What a fool Court was, Quincy reflected; he should have married the girl and spent the rest of his life making money and babies with her. Instead he sat in jail waiting to hang, as he well deserved, and Susanna sat with blank eyes, talking of profits.

By noon the next day Quincy had decided that, no matter what Lilith wanted, Susanna had to be told. He delivered the girl to the office and was relieved to see that Lilith was not there. "How are you fixed for money, Miss Susanna?" he asked.

"Oh, this venture will not put me in a precarious financial position," Susanna assured him. "Besides, I don't doubt that Lilith will decide to join me. Because of her interest in the hotel and because of the amount of linen she uses here, it would be to her advantage—even beyond the general profits we can expect to make."

"I wasn't thinkin of that. You're gonna have to let me git you out of town." Susanna looked up from her figures. "I thought maybe Denver, but I don't figger that's far enough. Reckon we better go to Frisco."

"Has Lilith put you up to this, Mr. Quincy?"

"This is purely my idea, Miss Susanna. I got to

tell you somethin she don't want you to know—somethin you ain't gonna want to hear, but—well, you gotta. Better you hear it from me than someone else, someone who ain't a friend."

"I have never questioned your friendship, Mr. Quincy, but I do have a lot of work to do this afternoon. What is it you seem so hesitant about telling me?"

"It's about Aaron Court."

"I do not want to hear anything about Mr. Court." Her face had flushed and then gone dead white.

"He's in jail, ma'am."

"Please do not mention his name to me again."

"Charged by your sister with kidnappin an rape."

Susanna's eyes closed and she looked sick. After a minute, she opened them again and stared at Quincy. "Am I to understand that my sister made these charges on my behalf?"

"That's just about it, Miss Susanna. She's—well, she's madder than you can imagine. I reckon it's partly my fault for gittin him up here. I never figgered she'd shoot him—"

"Lilith shot Aaron? How badly was he hurt?"

"Not bad—just a shoulder wound. An Carlos, he stopped her when she hit Court with a whip—not that the bastard doesn't deserve whatever he gits—still, she's just not thinkin. She thinks you won't have to testify against him, but the prosecutor will call you, sure as shootin, Miss Susanna. I just don't want you facin that."

"What will happen to Mr. Court if he is found guilty?" she asked.

"Oh, he'll hang. No jury—not in the West—is gonna let him git by with kidnappin you an using drugs on you—an—an—all the rest. "But he'll hang even if you ain't here to testify. The conductor an the hotel clerk in the town where he carried you off—they can testify. He said you was his sister. An the posse we took into Packard Valley—they can testify, if need be. It ain't as if they need yer testimony to hang him, but if you're here—well, you'll be called, an—an I won't have you humiliated. I—"

"Thank you for telling me all this, Mr. Quincy. My sister should certainly have done it herself. I shall consider the matter. And now, if you don't mind, I have work to do." Susanna picked up her pen and began to write figures in a ledger, making it clear that Quincy was dismissed. He did not want to leave, mistrusting that cool response, but he left as she had asked and stayed all afternoon at the bar watching the stairs for signs that she had given way to her emotions.

And Susanna had begun to feel again—for the first time in days. But not the fear of public shame; she did not look that far ahead. She could think only that because of her, Aaron had been shot, had been beaten with a whip, had been, was even now in a filthy jail, a prisoner, and would be hanged. She remembered the hanging of Elias Packard all too well; Aaron had taken her into his arms to block the sight of that horror. She could still feel the texture of his coat beneath her cheek and the hard muscles of his arms around her back. How many times had he held her? And could she let him die like that, dropping from a tree limb with a rope around his neck, and his horse kicked out from under him, because he had wanted her—when, God knows, she had wanted him too?

Susanna sat in front of her ledger all afternoon,
making inconsequential financial remarks when
Lilith put her head in from time to time, and never
once thinking of the figures in front of her. She
thought only of Aaron—of all the times good and
bad—the ecstasy and the fear, the pain and the
pleasure. And blame. It seemed to her that they were
all to blame—Aaron and all the things that had
happened to make him believe what he believed
about life and how it should be lived; Quincy, who
had let things happen, for whatever reasons of his
own, when he should have offered her the
protection he was hired to give; Lilith, whose
motives seemed suspect, composed of volatile
mixtures of love and hate; and Susanna herself, kept
ignorant by harsh parents and then exposed to
temptations and confusions and desires she was too
weak and foolish to handle.

She sent word downstairs at five o'clock that she
was not yet ready to leave, that she had more work
to do. Quincy waited, sure that ultimately he would
be taking her to San Francisco. She had guts, but no
woman would want to face a public trial of the sort
that Court would undergo. Had he told her enough?
Quincy asked himself. Should he have quoted
Aaron to make the point that she could not allow
herself to be hauled into that courtroom? She would
be as much on trial as Aaron.

But Susanna, upstairs with her ledgers in front of
her, was on trial in her own mind. She had long since
stopped caring about the opinion of others. After
Court had paraded her through town and left
her—ragged and filthy—in the Fallen Angel, she
had really ceased to care about what the town
thought of her. She had reached a true isolation in

which she cared only for her own self-respect, and
she came that afternoon to believe that she was as
guilty as anyone in the matter of Aaron Court and
Susanna Moran. It was dusk turning to night and
the sounds of night business were beginning to drift
up the stairs when she made her decision and helped
herself to a cloak that Lilith had left hanging on a
coat tree. The cloak was too long, but she did not
notice, letting it trail down the back stairs behind her
and into the dust as she entered the alley and then
the main street, heading north on Copper into the
after-dark bustle of the town. She walked quickly,
ignoring, not in fact hearing, the cowboys and
miners and drunks who spoke to her as she passed.
She carried a wall around her that held others away
from her—from her mind and her body.

When Susanna reached the jail, the prisoners had
been fed and the sheriff, by himself in the office,
was having his own dinner. He half rose from his
chair, his mouth full of mashed potatoes and red-eye
gravy, a pork chop in his right hand, and mumbled,
"Evenin, ma'am."

"Good evening, sheriff," she replied. She
recognized him from the visit she had paid him when
Aaron was trapped by the Packards in his cabin, and
so she needed to waste no time on identification. "I
understand you have Aaron Court imprisoned here
for—for kidnapping and rape."

"That's correct, ma'am, but we ain't lettin folks
in to stare at him. Had to put him in the back room
to discourage the curious, an I don't allow no
visitors less he wants to see em, so it's no use yer
askin lessen yer a friend."

"I am not here to visit," said Susanna, who fervently hoped to complete her mission without seeing

Court at all, then or ever. "My name is Susanna Moran."

Sheriff Maxie dropped his pork chop. He had not recognized her. "Glad to see you've recovered, ma'am. Been needin to take yer testimony."

"I have not come to give testimony, sheriff."

"Now see here, ma'am. I told yer sister an I'm tellin you, I have to git a statement from you. I ain't gonna ask you no embarrassin questions lessen I kin hep it, but this here is a hangin offense an—"

"I have come to withdraw the charges."

The sheriff swallowed a piece of unchewed pork in his surprise and felt a sharp pain in his throat which prevented him from speaking for several seconds. "Why?" he asked when he was able to. The girl looked exceedingly prim and ladylike now that he saw her again, wearing a pale gray dress with touches of eyelet at the throat and wrists and her hair pulled properly back in a bun. She might have passed for a young schoolteacher come West to take on a one-room school until such time as she could find herself a respectable husband. She certainly did not look like a woman who had caused a riot at the Fallen Angel, a riot at which he had arrived too late to see Susanna in her low-cut gown. Nor did she look like a woman who would willingly spend a week alone with a man to whom she was not married. "How come yer withdrawin the charges?" His assumption was that she would rather see Court go free than be questioned in public or anywhere else.

"The charges are false, sheriff," she replied. She had given thought to the wording she would use so that she would have to tell the fewest lies in order to obtain Court's release. "I was—I willingly stayed with Mr. Court in his cabin.''

"Did you now? You sure?''

"Quite sure," Susanna replied, pretending desperately that she was someone else, somewhere else so that she would not further disgrace herself, after that admission, by trembling or weeping. If she could remain calm a few more minutes, she would have accomplished her purpose and could go home.

"You was up there for a week with him of your own free will? Went there willin, stayed there willin—''

The sheriff's wording gave her little choice but to lie, and she drew breath to do so but was interrupted by an excited man who burst into the office announcing a gunfight at a gambling parlor—three people had already been shot and more injuries or deaths were threatened.

Strapping on his gun belt, the sheriff said to Susanna, "That it, ma'am?" Susanna nodded. "Well, there's no tellin when I'll be back, but if Aaron's innocent, I reckon you won't want him held any longer than necessary." The sheriff picked up a ring of keys and tossed them to her. "He's in the first cell in back.''

"Oh, but I—''

"He might want to ask you just how he come to be in jail," the sheriff added, "that is, if he's innocent like you say.''

Susanna did not want to see Aaron or talk to him, and she stared at the sheriff aghast. It had never occurred to her that such a casual approach could be taken to the release of prisoners. The sheriff, for his part, did not think for a moment that Susanna would free Court. He clapped his hat on his head, ready to leave, and made his last statement on the matter. "If, as you say, ma'am, he's innocent, just let him loose an put the keys back on the nail, if you'll be so kind," and he left her alone in the jail with only a drunk sleeping in the cell that fronted the office and, presumably, Aaron to be faced in the back.

Susanna shivered. Aaron probably thought she was the one who had made the charges—oh well, what did it matter? She would unlock the door, tell him he was free, and leave. She had no obligation to talk to him, and he, more guilty than anyone else in this hopeless situation, deserved no explanations.

She took up the key ring and opened the door the sheriff had indicated. It led to a corridor with three sets of barred doors. The whole area was hardly lighted at all, and Susanna could see only the outline of a man's body as he sat on a cot with his back against the far wall of the cell. The tip of his cigar glowed red in the shadows, and she could make out the white bandage on his shoulder. Otherwise it was almost impossible to identify him as she glanced nervously into the dark cell and fumbled with the key, which didn't seem to fit the padlock. Still, it had to be Aaron.

"Sheriff?" he asked.

She recognized his voice but said nothing.

"Who is it?"

"Susanna," she replied reluctantly.

He was up off the cot and across the room in one swift movement, clamping the cigar between his teeth and her wrist between the fingers of his good hand.

"What are you doing here, Susanna?"

The pressure of his fingers were neither harsh nor restricting, but she could not have pulled her wrist away. She concentrated desperately on getting the key to turn in the lock, and it did, grating and then releasing the door. "You're free," she replied in answer to his question.

To her distress, Court did not leave his cell; he drew her inside. His mind had sorted through various possibilities with lightning cynicism and come up with the idea that she was facilitating his escape from jail so that he could be killed here or elsewhere by law officers or a posse, thus freeing her from the humiliating necessity of facing him in court. And who could blame her? Lilith had probably told her of the testimony he had threatened to give? "Why am I free?" he demanded.

"I withdrew the charges."

He could feel her trembling in his hands, and he drew her to the window so he could see her face in the light from the street. "You withdrew the charges? Why? Kidnapping and rape—that's what you've accused me of, isn't it?"

"No."

"What do you mean—no?"

"Lilith brought the charges."

"Still, you must have—"

"I didn't know about any of this until today."

Court frowned, his whole perception of the situation beginning to change. "Nevertheless, you said repeatedly while we were up at the cabin that I'd kidnapped you."

"You did," said Susanna, "but—"

"All right, I suppose that technically speaking I did, and maybe you've even managed to convince yourself that I raped you—that last time before we came back, for instance."

"That wasn't rape," she said, her voice almost inaudible.

Court drew in a sharp breath, feeling just a ray of hope for the first time in days. "All right, that leaves us with kidnapping," he persisted. "If you said I didn't kidnap you when you really believe that I did, then you were lying. Why would you lie for me?"

"It wasn't all a lie," she whispered. "Part of me always wanted to be with you—and to stay with you."

Court flung the cigar into the corner and narrowed his gaze, trying to ascertain the truth of what she was saying. He believed that she had wanted to be with him, but to stay with him? She'd denied that at the cabin. And none of it explained any willingness on her part to withdraw charges, to declare herself a liar to the whole town. In fact, if Susanna had really wanted to remain with him at the cabin, that meant he'd been a greater fool in his dealings with her than he'd realized.

Susanna knew he was waiting, that she had to say more. "And—and I withdrew the charges because I couldn't see you hurt—or killed."

"Why?" Again he was unsatisfied with the simplicity of the answer. She might have said that of anyone—that she didn't want to see them killed. "Lilith wants revenge. Why should you care what happens to me?"

She felt then as if she were surrendering to him more completely than she ever had when she was in his arms. "Because—" She had turned her face away, and her voice was the barest wisp of sound. "Because I love you."

"What did you say?" There was surprise, disbelief in his voice as he forced her to look at him again.

"I can't let them kill you because I love you." Her voice was clear enough then and her eyes steady. What did it matter if he knew the truth? she thought. This was the end of it.

"You love me?" Court was filled with elation.

"Yes," she said sadly. He slipped his arm around her waist and leaned against the wall, pulling her with him. He said nothing, and Susanna did not know what to do. He probably felt sorry for her. "I know it's hopeless," she whispered, "and I don't expect to see you again, but I still couldn't let them—"

"You're going to see me every day for the rest of your life," he contradicted her firmly. "You're going to marry me."

Susanna was struck dumb, wondering if this was some cruel trick. "Why would you suggest that?" she asked, bewildered. "You don't want to marry. Everyone knows that. And especially me—my name is so smeared in this town—"

"That's nothing to me," he interrupted impatiently. "I'm not marrying the town." She'd said she loved him, so, by God, she could damn well marry him, he decided. He wanted a legal claim to her. And he did not want any arguments—just her agreement and an immediate ceremony before she changed her mind about loving him. "You weren't lying when you said you loved me, were you?"

"No, but—"

"Good." He believed her. She had shown her love in his arms repeatedly if reluctantly in the past, and he wanted to be sure that she never ran away from him again. In fact, it was unconscionable of her to attempt to evade his offer of marriage.

"Did you have something better in mind?" Court

asked sharply. "What are you going to do with your life, Susanna? You'll surely never make a whore. Your experience with Penvennon should have shown you that. You haven't been with anyone but me, and when you tried to convince me that you were doing it for the money, you forgot to cash the bank draft."

"I didn't forget," said Susanna indignantly. "I didn't want your disgusting money."

"There, you see. You'd make a terrible whore."

Susanna muttered angrily, but Court plowed right on. Now that he had made up his mind to marry her and she had admitted she loved him, he was desperate to talk her into it. "Maybe you're thinking you're a good shot with a rifle, but I'll tell you, love, female gunwomen aren't in much demand out here." He grinned at her. "The thing you do best is belong to me."

"I'm a good bookkeeper," she said defensively.

"Fine. You can keep my books. I've got twice as many as your sister. Marrying me is damn well your only sensible option, Susanna."

She glared at him. He was talking as if marriage were a business arrangement. Keep his books? That wasn't what a woman in love wanted to be offered. "You can hire a bookkeeper," she snapped, "if that's the best reason you can think of for marrying me. Why *did* you ask me?"

"To keep you, Susanna. Everything I've ever done was to keep you with me." His arms tightened, and his mouth covered hers with all the dizzying arrogance of demand that he had made on her so many times in the past. "We'll settle it before the hour is out."

"What do you mean?" She was finding it hard to hold on to her indignation when he kissed her like that.

"I mean the judge is over at the hotel—got in this noon and came straight over here to tell me what he thought of officers of the court who get themselves thrown in jail on unsavory charges. You can tell him I didn't rape you, and then he can marry us. If I have anything to say about it, we'll be in bed before moonrise."

Susanna stared wistfully over his shoulder at the bars on the cell window. She wanted to marry Aaron. She'd never wanted to do anything more, but if he didn't love her, if he was just doing it to please some judge—

"Well?" he prompted impatiently.

"I've always wanted to marry someone who loved me," she said sadly.

"I love you." He looked astonished. "Of course, I love you. Why would I be proposing to do something as foolish as getting married if I didn't—"

"You never said so. Never," she pointed out suspiciously.

"I'm doing this poorly, aren't I? Well, I've never asked anyone to marry me before, never expected to, but look, Susanna, I put my life on the line when the Packards kidnapped you. I risked going to jail when I carried you off that train. Hell, I *am* in jail. If I didn't love you, I'd have jumped at the chance when you asked for money. I could have paid up and forgotten the whole thing. But I didn't want to let you go. And I didn't want you to—to care so little."

"But Aaron—"

"What you're really asking is why, if I love you, I never asked you to marry me before this."

"Yes."

"My father loved my mother, Susanna, and she

loved him, and out of that marriage came five deaths—all of them but me—dead.'' His mouth was set in a grim line. ''I guess I've always thought marrying was like spitting in the face of fate—asking for bad luck. In fact, I thought even loving someone was taking the same risk. Which is why I was so slow to admit to myself how I felt about you.''

''Then why are you asking me now?'' Susanna suspected that his sudden change of heart had more to do with the charges her sister had brought than with any newly discovered feelings for her. Anxiously she waited for his answer, knowing that no matter what he said, she would want to be his wife. Still, she hoped with all her heart that he expected to be happy with her.

''Susanna, I've finally got it through my thick skull that, no matter what happens in the future, there'll be no happiness for either one of us unless we're together. Are you brave enough to take that kind of chance with me?''

In answer she pressed against him and whispered, ''I'm not afraid, Aaron—not if you love me. I think our future will be wonderful.''

His arms tightened fiercely around her, and he murmured into her hair, ''Beloved little witch. It won't be all passion and laughter, you know.''

Susanna smiled. ''It won't be all tears either,'' she promised him.

Epilogue

Having just returned from a tedious afternoon at his law office, Court lounged in the doorway and relished the sight of his wife. Susanna had to be the only woman in the world who looked enticing with ink stains on her fingers, eyeglasses sliding down her nose, a ledger on the table in front of her, and her second child beginning to distend her slender waist-line.

She looked up and her blue eyes danced with pleasure. "We've doubled our money on the Chinese laundries in just two years," she announced triumphantly. "And the McFadden's a huge success. Isn't it lucky we bought it from Lilith?"

"Um-m-m," said Court, wishing she would put young Aaron, Jr., down for his nap. The child was playing at her feet, a game that involved tugging hard at her skirt, then rolling over and giggling when she peered down at him with a look of exaggerated outrage. The two of them seemed to enjoy the play-acting immensely.

"It's a gold mine—the McFadden—especially since I stopped the drummers from getting the waitresses and maids tipsy and then following them up to the top floor for immoral purposes."

"That's been going on for years," said Court solemnly. "Why, I myself—"

"You did not," interrupted Susanna indignantly.

"I was going to say that I myself know many respectable Coloradans with fond memories of those parties on the top floor at the McFadden."

"Too bad," said Susanna. "I've moved the girls out to a boarding house with a proper woman to look after them, and I'm renting the rooms up there to the very customers who used to behave so scandalously." She grinned smugly.

Court chuckled, but he was glad that his wife's fetish for propriety hadn't extended to their own relationship.

"Oh, and Mrs. Penvennon came to call this afternoon."

He stiffened, frowning, for he still suspected the respectable ladies in town of a desire to snub Susanna, although their husbands knew it would be a dangerous mistake.

"The Ladies' Mission Guild at the church wants me to be the new treasurer. I think it's because I'm a choir member, don't you?"

"Possibly," he agreed. He even attended church himself now and then, but only when Susanna was the soloist. "More likely it's because they figure you'll double their money." She had the most amazing head for business. He'd never have dreamed a woman could be so canny or such a wonderful commercial partner.

Laughing, Susanna exclaimed, "We don't invest mission money. We spend it on the heathens. Stop that, Pippin!" She scooped their son up off the carpet.

"Isn't it time for him to take his nap?" Court asked.

Susanna giggled. "Why, did you want to take one too?"

"Could be."

"With Pippin?"

"No, love, with you."

"But we've already done our Christian duty that way." She patted her slightly rounded stomach and gave him a mischievous smile.

"True," said Court gravely, "but we might want to stay in practice, just in case we like the second baby as much as we liked the first. Of course, the new one may be a holy terror, in which case naturally we'll have to move into separate bedrooms and espouse chastity."

"Never," said Susanna, laughing as she rose with the child. "Time for bed, Pippin."

The baby gurgled and waved his arms at his father, crying "Da da da da da" as he was carried away.

"Are you coming?" Susanna called over her shoulder. Aaron was.

THE BEST IN HISTORICAL ROMANCE

from LEISURE BOOKS

LOVE'S LEGACY by Rosemary Jordan. Irish lovers flee England's tyranny for a chance at happiness in America.
_____2422-5 $3.95US/$4.95CAN

UNTAMED DESIRE by Kim Hansen. An Eastern woman and a man as rugged as the West find passion and pleasure on the prairie.
_____2442-X $3.95US/$4.95CAN

EMBERS OF DESIRE by Patricia Pellicane. An innocent young lady and her Indian captor discover love in the turbulent times of the Revolutionary War.
_____2446-2 $3.95US/$4.95CAN

LOVE'S SAVAGE EMBRACE by Melissa Bowersock. A beautiful halfbreed's heart is torn between two worlds—and two lovers.
_____2151-X $3.75US/$4.50CAN

SWORD OF THE HEART by Maureen Kurr. Lovely Alix Beaucamp risks her sacred honor to win the heart of a mysterious dark knight.
_____2467-5 $3.95US/$4.95CAN

Breathtaking Historical Romance
Robin Lee Hatcher

"Lively, tempestuous romance!"
— *Romance Readers Magazine*

HEART STORM. From the New York theatre to the London stage, Niki O'Hara followed her dream to become an actress —and tried unsuccessfully to deny her feelings for the handsome, arrogant Adam Bellman.

_____2318-0 $3.95 US/$4.95 CAN

PASSION'S GAMBLE. After her first passionate embrace with Colter Stephens, Alexis Ashmore knew she could never love another. But the gamble she was forced to take to win his love would jeopardize their future if she lost.

_____2412-8 $3.95 US/$4.95 CAN

STORMY SURRENDER. Young Taylor Bellman was forced to marry a wealthy older man to save her family plantation. But it would take a gallant Yankee visitor to awaken her sleeping heart.

_____2585-X $3.95 US/$4.95 CAN

_____2595-7   HEART'S LANDING $3.95 US/$4.95 CAN

_____2487-X   PIRATE'S LADY.   An Autographed Bookmark Edition. $3.95 US/$4.95 CAN

_____2638-4   GEMFIRE. Special refraction engraving on cover. $4.50 US/$5.50 CAN